Don't Forget to Remember Me

The Remembrance Trilogy—Book 2

by

Kahlen Aymes

TELEMACHUS PRESS

Don't Forget to Remember Me

Published by Telemachus Press, LLC
http://www.telemachuspress.com

Visit the author blog site:
http://www.kahlen-aymes.blogspot.com

ISBN#: 978-1-938701-05-4 (eBook)
ISBN# 978-1-938701-06-1 (paperback)

Version 2012.08.20

Printed in the United States of America

10 9 8 7 6 5 4 3 2 1

In loving memory of my friend, taken far too soon…

Gisela M. Gagliardi

We won't forget to remember you…

Acknowledgments

Sincerest appreciation, as always,
to Kathryn Voskuil, Elizabeth Desmond, Sally Hopkinson,
Ali Halbmaier, Jena Gomez & Samantha Fisher
for all of your help and continued support.
Without you, the blogs and novels would not happen.
Words can not express my gratitude.

Thank you to the team at Telemachus Press.
Your professionalism is appreciated.

And Olivia...
for putting up with me and my ever-present laptop.
I love you.

Don’t Forget to Remember Me

The Remembrance Trilogy—Book 2

~1~

Ryan~

I WAS SITTING in my own personal hell. I was weeks away from becoming a doctor myself, yet my hands were tied as Julia lay on a gurney in the next room. She was my whole world and she could be dying while I was helpless of the outcome, unable to do a Goddamn thing.

My mind was racing with questions. Were they ordering blood gases? Was she in shock? How much blood had she lost and did she need a transfusion? Could she breathe on her own? When the hell were they going to do the scans that would determine the extent of her internal and head injuries? I thought my head would explode along with my lungs.

"What was she even doing in Boston?" I didn't even realize I'd said the words aloud.

"What *the fuck* is happening in there?!" I yelled, as panic seized my voice and made it unrecognizable.

Min, my friend and fellow med student, shook her head sadly. "We don't know yet. Dr. Brighton is heading up the team. I know how much you respect him, so just let him do his job. You can't work on her, Ryan. You can't be impartial about someone you love this much. This is what's best for Julia."

Aaron put his arm around me to urge me toward the waiting room, but I shrugged him off impatiently. I felt claustrophobic; beginning to hyperventilate.

"Can you just tell me *something*? Go find out? They need to get her to radiology. When the hell are they going to order those tests?" I asked, turning back to Min. I was still trying to figure out how I was going to get in there. If I were a resident, I'd have just walked in, but not as a student. Even one who was graduating with Cum Laude honors in just a few weeks.

She nodded and placed her hand on my shoulder before disappearing through the doors of one of the trauma rooms.

I tried to look in, but all I could see were a bunch of doctors and nurses scrambling around the room at a frantic pace. My heart stopped when I saw Julia's arm hanging off the edge of the table. Still as stone. Someone was intubating her and someone else was cutting off her clothes. Jenna was hanging up an IV bag near one end of the table and then inserting some medication into a port with a syringe, while Dr. Brighton conducted an examination. My whole body felt like it would explode into a million pieces, my skin crawling so much I wanted to rip it off.

"Let's go to the waiting room," my brother said softly. "You know they can't take her anywhere until she's stabilized. Can I get you some coffee?"

I shook my head and went to gaze out the window, into the night and the lights of downtown. "I can't, Aaron. I can't sit around in there and do nothing! My God, what am I going to do?" My voice cracked and I cleared my throat. "I have to *do* something! Tell me what you know about the accident, and don't bullshit me."

"Uh, the cops who came in with the paramedics said that the cab driver was trying to get on Storrow Drive from Leverett Circle and it was plowed broadside on the rear passenger's side.

The driver is here too, but he's only got minor injuries. The guy driving the other car was killed, dead at the scene. The police said they found empty booze containers in his car and he was traveling at least 50 miles per hour. We're lucky Julia wasn't thrown from the car at that rate."

I closed my eyes and put my hand up to rub the back of my neck. I didn't know what I was feeling. I wanted to scream and cry at the unfairness of it all, yet I was numb, frozen. My knees were weak and I fell into a chair in the small waiting room. I dealt with this shit on a daily basis and it didn't faze me in the slightest. But this was my baby and I couldn't handle it.

There was a woman playing in the corner with a small child and I watched them build something with Legos. I stared at them, wanting something, anything, to focus on. My vision blurred and I felt a sob rise up in my chest, but struggled to keep it from bursting forth. I clasped my hands in front of me and hung my head in defeat. Aaron was sitting next to me and placed a comforting hand on my back.

What was she doing here? I pulled her engagement ring off of my finger and rolled it around in my hand with the bracelet. *Please, God. I'll do anything. Anything!*

I drew in a shaky breath and leaned back in the chair. "Aaron, I can't just sit here."

There was a commotion and the doors opened. I jumped up and rushed toward them. Several doctors and nurses were pushing the gurney out of the room along with an IV stand, a ventilator, oxygen and EKG. I saw Dr. Brighton and Jenna with them as I strained to get a look at Julia.

"Uhhh…" A groan ripped from my chest at the site. "Dr. Brighton…please. Can I see her? Is she conscious?"

He turned sad brown eyes on me and shook his head. "Ryan, I don't have time to talk right now. We need to do a chest

X-ray, probably a CT scan of her head and torso. I'm fairly sure she has a bad fracture on the left side of her skull. The blood is from a superficial laceration on her hairline which we've got under control, but we don't know if there is internal bleeding yet. I can't waste time talking now, son. I'm doing my best for her, I promise, Ryan, but she is critical."

I started shaking again as I looked on and they wheeled her away from me. Her clothes had been cut off of her and a white blanket placed over her, leaving bare skin visible below its edge. Her hair was matted with blood and she had so many machines connected to her and over her face I couldn't recognize her. "I want to see her." I knew it would be impossible. To save her life, time was imperative.

"As soon as we get these tests and know more, Ryan. There is no time to waste now." Jenna came forward and put her arms around my waist to give me a quick hug.

"Here is what I know," she said as she stepped back and looked up into my face. "We intubated, but she is still struggling to breathe. We think she has a pneumothorax on the left side, maybe some fractured ribs. Her left shoulder is dislocated; she has lacerations and contusions to her face and scalp and the left side of her body. She probably has a head injury and some internal bleeding and, as you know, that is what the scans should tell us. I have to go with her, but, I'll let you know when I know more details. I'm…so sorry, Ryan," she said before she turned and hurried down the hall after Julia and the rest of the team, disappearing behind the double doors leading to radiology.

Aaron's arms came around me, under my arms to catch me as my knees started to buckle. *This couldn't be happening.* The dislocated shoulder and broken ribs weren't life threatening, but if she had a head injury or internal bleeding, time was of the essence. Even the collapsed lung could be dealt with, but all of it together…I could lose her. I fell into Aaron's arms and began gasping for breath and clutching at his shoulders.

"Aaron," I cried brokenly. "This isn't happening. Tell me this isn't happening. Jesus…I love her so much. I can't lose her." It was closer to a prayer than anything I'd ever said.

"We have some of the best doctors in the world here. Just have faith, Ryan. We have to believe she'll be okay." His arms tightened around me and lifted me enough to get my feet under me. "She'll be okay. We all love Julia. We *all* love her, man." His voice broke on the last sentence as he hugged me. If Aaron was crying, then he didn't believe she'd be okay. He *never* fucking cried. In all the years I'd known him, I'd never seen him shed a single tear.

I pushed away from him and pulled out my phone. I dialed the familiar number, pacing back and forth in the room that Julia and the medical staff had just vacated.

"Hello?" my father answered the phone and I felt a new wave of emotion overcome me.

"Dad…"

"Ryan? Is that you? Did something happen?" His voice was anxious and I could hear my mother's distressed voice in the background as well.

"I need you to get to Boston right away. Julia's been in a car accident. Her cab was broadsided and it looks like she has a serious head injury. Please. If she needs neurosurgery, I don't want anyone else touching her. I'm going out of my mind. Just…*please come.*"

"My God, Ryan. Yes, we'll come, but if she does have a head injury, you have to let them treat her. Don't wait for me, do you understand? You know as well as I do, that treatment must be immediate. Waiting could kill her or leave her with serious brain damage. The first hour or two are critical, you know that! Ryan!" Dad yelled when I didn't respond.

My eyes were burning and I couldn't get the words out so I just nodded. Aaron ripped the phone from my shaking hand.

"Hey, Dad. Yes, okay. Call me with your flight details and I'll pick you up at the airport." Aaron turned his back to me and kept talking into the phone. "No, he's not handling it well. Not at all. I've never seen him so out of it. Are you sure? Okay. Yes, I called, but her mother didn't answer. Yes, I'll call again. Love you guys. Bye."

I slid down the wall until I was sitting on the floor and rested my arms on my bent knees. Aaron closed the door and sat down on the one chair in the now empty room. The symbolism of it shook me to the core. Stark, empty space where Julia used to be…cold and sterile.

I put my head in my arms and let the emotions I couldn't contain wash over me. My shoulders shook in silent sobs until I finally had to gasp for breath and Aaron touched my shoulder.

"Mom and Dad are on their way. Ryan, I'm so sorry. She's going to be okay."

"She has to be, Aaron. She has to, or I won't survive," I whispered brokenly.

"You need to try to pull it together, Ryan. You have to be strong for Julia. She wouldn't want to see you like this."

"Hmmph," I let out my breath heavily. "*Julia* would want me to be honest about my feelings. And I feel like I'm falling apart…helpless. Like I'm dying myself. I want to be in there and take this all away from her. I'd take her place if I could," I choked out and I fisted my hands over both eyes.

Aaron was right. Unless I wanted her parents and Ellie to freak out, I needed to get control of my emotions. Even more importantly, when they let me see Julia, I had to be calm and reassuring. *If she was conscious.*

We sat there for what seemed like an eternity. Aaron left a couple of times to get coffee, but I didn't move, praying that she would be okay and reliving so many of the wonderful times we'd shared. The day we met, the first time I kissed her or when we made love, when I put the engagement ring on her finger, the many Sunday coffee dates we were forced to spend on the phone, the move to New York. In all of my memories she was beautiful and smiling…whole. Not broken and bleeding. "Oh, my God," I ground out brokenly. "No, *please.*"

I ran my hand through my hair and stood up to answer my phone immediately as it started to ring. It was Julia's dad.

"Hello, Paul."

"Oh, thank God. Ryan, what do you know?" His voice was frantic, the catch in his voice giving away the level of his emotion.

"Not a lot right now. They took her to radiology for some scans. She probably has a skull fracture, but we don't know the extent until after these films. She has a pneumothorax and a dislocated shoulder, contusions on her head, face and torso and probably some broken ribs." My voice had taken on a clinical tone, on autopilot, as I rattled off the list.

"What's a pneumothorax?"

"Oh, sorry. Um, a collapsed lung." He gasped on the other end of the phone and my strong façade fell by the wayside when my voice thickened. I put my hand over my eyes and took a deep breath. "Paul, I'm really scared. All I want to do is get in there and help take care of her, but they won't let me. They…won't let me. I feel…so incredibly helpless."

"Jesus." Paul sighed. "Ryan, I'm sure you're doing all you can. I'm glad you're with her. I'll get there as soon as I can. I've changed planes in Chicago and I'm already onboard. Ellie called and said she was going to meet me at the hospital and Marin is on her way, too."

He was trying to comfort me when his baby girl was fighting for her life. I wished I could be that strong, but then, I'd seen her. I'd seen the blood and the machines and despite the fact I was around it all the time, because it was Julia, it wrecked me.

"Yeah. My parents are on their way as well. If her head injury looks bad, I want my father here to consult or…God forbid, operate, if it's necessary."

"I hope it isn't that serious, but I'm thankful that Gabriel is coming. I've made my bargains with God already. I'll see you in a couple of hours. Julia is lucky to have you, Ryan."

It's that serious. I closed my eyes in silent prayer.

"I'm the lucky one. She means everything to me, Paul." I could feel my chest constrict again as I hung up the phone.

"Ryan?"

I turned to a shaken Jenna re-entering the room. "They've taken her to ICU. She has a fracture to the left side of her skull. We were able to re-inflate the lung, tape up her ribs and pop her shoulder back in. There is some slight swelling to her brain but radiology didn't see any bleeding on the CT scan."

"Is she breathing on her own?" I asked, fearing the answer with everything I had. "Did you need a chest tube or did the lung re-inflate on its own?"

Jen came forward and hugged me. "We were able to suck the air out with a big syringe so we didn't need to tube her. She's on a vent and hasn't regained consciousness," she said quietly.

I hugged her back. "No doubt due to the edema. All we can do is watch her now and make sure we catch any bleeds or fluids. We're not out of the woods until she wakes up. Have they got her on blood thinners? Is the coma induced or not?" I asked wearily. I was exhausted and started rubbing the back of my neck. The next three or four days would tell the story. If she didn't wake up before that, the chances were, she never would.

"Ryan, stop trying to be a doctor. You've got enough to deal with," Aaron began, but his words upset me. My jaw tightened and I bit back the words I wanted to retort.

"I want to know what is happening," I said instead.

"She's on several meds. She didn't wake up on her own, but Dr. Brighton ordered barbiturates to keep her asleep so her brain can heal and to help reduce the swelling. I don't need to tell you the particulars," Jenna said. She looked as exhausted as I felt and her eyes were red and swollen.

She moved back from the embrace and took my hands. "Thank you, Jen. I appreciate all you've done. Can I see her now? Is Dr. Brighton still with her?" The array of questions fell from my lips like rain.

"I'm sure they're watching for hemorrhage. It's common with traumatic brain injury," Aaron interjected quietly and more contrite than before.

I shook my head and started walking out of the room, my intention to go straight up to ICU, but Jenna put a hand on my arm to stop me.

Her voice shook and she cupped my face with her palm. "Ryan," she said hesitantly her blue eyes full of sadness. "Julia had some vaginal bleeding. It was quite excessive."

"She had internal bleeding?" I asked in panic. My heart started racing again but Jenna shook her head.

"Ryan, um…" She raised her tear-filled eyes to mine and brushed my hair back from my face.

"Jen, what is it?" I choked out. "What is it that you're not saying?" Fear, even more prevalent than before, engulfed me.

"Did you know that Julia was pregnant?"

Until that very moment, I thought it couldn't get any worse. I was wrong. I felt the blood drain from my face and I clenched my fists hard enough for the nails to draw blood.

Hearing that Julia was expecting my child should have made me the happiest man on earth, and instead it left me aching and empty. My Julia, lying broken and still, in a bed seven stories above me. I whirled away from Jenna to lean a hand on the wall to steady myself. "Oh, my God," I gasped for breath. "Jesus, no!"

The tears I thought had run dry began to squeeze out of my tightly closed eyes. My stomach ached and my head throbbed. My chest wouldn't let me breathe and my throat constricted with the sobs that wanted to break out of my chest. "Why the hell is this happening? To someone as good as Julia?" the words ripped out of my chest.

"We still have Julia, Ryan," Aaron pointed out. "That is the most important thing right now. Try to focus on that."

I nodded and put a hand over my aching heart. I didn't need to ask if she'd lost the baby. I already knew.

Jenna was openly crying now. She nodded and grabbed a tissue from the box on the counter to wipe at her eyes and nose. My hand started tugging on the shirt over my heart in silent hope that it could remove the pain that was manifesting there. I felt like a black hole had just opened up and swallowed me alive and there was nothing I could do to claw out of it.

"How far along was she?" Aaron asked.

"A few weeks, maybe," Jenna answered softly. "We managed to get the bleeding stopped fairly easily and she won't need a D and C."

I moved away from both of them, not wanting anyone touching me. I could hear them talking but it was like I was hearing their voices from underwater. "*Five* weeks since we were last together, but technically they'd measure it as seven," I said more to myself than to either of them. The night she told me about Paris, the night I put the ring on her finger…the night we conceived our child.

Jesus, is there anything else you can do to me? To her?

"Weren't you guys using protection, Ryan?"

"Aaron. Stop being an insensitive ass," Jenna shot at him. "Now isn't the time for that."

I tried to swallow the lump in my throat, nodding. "Um…yeah. Julia was on the pill, but she'd had a sinus infection and was on an antibiotic course shortly before we were together. I'm such an idiot! I should have realized…This is my fault. I should have protected her."

"Julia wouldn't think that way, Ryan. I'm sure she was happy about the baby. She loves you so much," Jen answered.

The gravity of what this meant rushed over me in waves. Yes, she would have been so happy.

My child…with Julia. I'd imagined what it would be like to see her swell with the evidence of the mad love we felt for each other. Nothing would have made me happier. Now, I felt cheated at the unfairness of it. And Julia…she'd be the most wonderful, giving mother. I saw it in the way she took care of everyone around her. I was angry because now she lay near death, and when she woke up…*if* she woke up, I had to tell her she'd lost our child. *Our* baby.

"That's why she came to Boston." My heart constricted to the point of pain. "She wouldn't tell me something like that over the phone."

"Ryan, I'm so sorry. You'll be able to have more children," Jenna's voice was trembling and she wiped at her eyes. Aaron gathered her close to his side.

"If she survives, you mean?" I asked hopelessly.

"Ryan, I should beat you senseless! Stop thinking like that. Julia needs you to be strong right now. She needs you like she's never needed you, so get your head out of your ass and start being more positive! We're all here and we're going to get her through this." Aaron's voice was loud and his tone hard. It should have shaken me out of my heartbroken haze, but it didn't.

"When Paul and Marin get here, don't tell them about this. They have enough grief to deal with because of Julia. They don't need more to contend with."

I shook my head silently, then turned and rushed from the room. I had to get out of there, had to be alone to deal with the agony before I could go up and be with Julia. I had to run, scream or both or I'd explode. I ran as fast as I could, the cool night air rushing over my face and through my hair. I ran so fast that the tears were pushed back across my temples by the wind. Finally, when I reached the footpath that ran through the park near the hospital, I slowed my pace and sank down on my haunches. It was the middle of the night and no one was around. No sounds except the crickets, a few birds and some distant traffic.

Why? My heart screamed. Why?! Why?! *Fucking Why*?!

My shoulders started to shake violently and I wrapped my arms around myself. Pretty soon my anguished voice was crying out my thoughts. "Why, in God's name? Jesus, *why*?? Ahhhhhhhhhh!!! Why did this happen??!!" I screamed into the silent night. I wasn't sure how long I remained where I was, crying for long minutes. "She didn't deserve this. She's so good," I cried brokenly, but more softly now.

I furiously brushed the tears from my face before starting my walk back to the hospital. *What was I doing? I had to get to her as soon as I possibly could.*

My face was surely swollen and red and I couldn't speak without the telltale signs of my tears lacing my voice, but I didn't care. I had a new resolve. Julia was going to be fine. She was going to live and I would be right beside her for the rest of my life. This was a detour, a little bump in the road. I would expect a full recovery, to move to New York as planned and then our wedding.

My vision blurred again.

And, we'll have more babies, Julia. Gorgeous babies with your amazing eyes.

I'd felt such joy at the knowledge that she was carrying my child, however fleeting it was before it had been replaced with horrible devastation at the loss. Sharing that with her was something I wanted. Desperately.

The elevator doors opened into ICU and I stopped to use the hand sanitizer that was located in the hall before the double doors and then pushed my way through. Jenna, who was off of her shift in ER, was waiting with Aaron and she motioned toward a room to her right. I preceded them in, bracing myself for the sight I was about to face.

Julia was lying in a mire of wires and machines; beeping and wheezing noises violating the silence. There were cold packs around her head, her face swollen and bruised. The vent tube was coming out of her mouth and there were IV's in both arms. Everywhere I looked there were tubes. Her arms lay above the covers, pale even up against the white blanket. I dropped to my knees beside her bed, fresh tears beginning again.

"Julia, I'm so sorry, baby. I'm here, my love." My voice aching as I bent to kiss her cheek softly, my hand closing around her still one. "Please…come back to me."

Of course she didn't move and maybe she couldn't hear me considering her drug induced coma, but I had to say the words.

My forehead rested on the hand I held as I willed her to feel my presence beside her.

Aaron pulled a chair close to Julia's bedside and offered it to me. "Ryan, I'm going to take Jen home. I'll be back."

"Uh," I turned and stood to embrace them both. "Aaron, you don't have to come back tonight. It's so late. I'll wait for the others. They will be here soon."

"Mom and Dad called while you were outside. They landed at Logan and are catching a cab. Dad's coming straight here, but sending Mom to get a hotel room and drop off their bags," Aaron said as I let him go and sat down in the chair.

"Okay. Thank you both for being here. Especially you, Jenna. I can't tell you how much it helped having you in there when I couldn't be." I hugged her again and she wiped her eyes as I released her.

After they left, I moved closer so that I could hold Julia's hand and my thumb rubbed back and forth over the top of her fingers. The nurses came in to monitor her vital signs, although I was watching them myself, and to change the cold packs around her bandaged head. Her breathing was shallow, even with the vent, but her pulse was strong. I was told that Dr. Brighton would be in at 6 am to check on her.

I couldn't take my eyes off her or the damn machines that kept reminding me of the gravity of the situation with their sounds. Every second felt like a year. My eyes were burning and dry. I pressed the heels of my hands to both of them and rubbed. I brushed her right hand with my lips and then settled in, looking away from her face, unrecognizable with swelling and angry bruises, only to check on her vitals.

Paul arrived first, still in a suit, but rumpled…looking as rough as I felt. I stood to embrace him. We both held onto each other for dear life. "I'm so sorry, Paul. I'd give anything if I could take this away."

He didn't say anything, but moved to the edge of the bed and looked down at Julia. He gasped in shock as he took it all in. "It doesn't even look like her." His voice broke on the last word. "Julia?"

I put my hand on his shoulder and squeezed.

"Can you fill me in?" he asked quietly.

I took a deep breath, preparing myself for the reality check I was about to give us both.

"She has a pretty serious head injury." I couldn't believe how clinical my voice sounded as I ran through it, trying to keep the medical terminology to a minimum. "She's on barbiturates to reduce the metabolic rate of her brain tissue. That's important because it will reduce blood flow and hopefully curtail swelling, one of the worst things that could happen after head trauma. We're also watching for any increase in pressure from fluids." I sucked in all the air my lungs could hold and walked to the window. Her father sat in the chair next to the bed while I continued. "She had a laceration on her forehead and some bruises over a good portion of her body. Her left shoulder was dislocated and she has three fractured ribs. Her left lung collapsed and had to be re-inflated." I swallowed the pain rising up in my throat. "The drugs will keep her in a coma so that her brain can heal. They'll gradually reduce them if there are no complications, and hopefully...she'll wake up and be...Julia."

"My God. Do you think she'll have brain damage, Ryan? What effect would swelling have?" Part of me wished I didn't know the answers.

My throat tightened up even more. So much; I wasn't sure I could even get the words out. "Um...the confines of the skull don't allow room for the tissue expansion caused when the brain swells. The only place it has any room to expand is down, and it, uh…" I put my hand on my hips and blinked my eyes several times to try to stop the tears, but my voice was shaking, "puts pressure on the brain stem which controls involuntary body functions, like heart and lung activity." I closed my eyes, not wanting to face the possibility of that happening to Julia. "Everything possible is being done to keep that from happening. My father is on his way. If she needs a shunt or bolt, he'll be here to do it. I don't trust anyone else to *fucking* touch her!" I whispered brokenly and turned back toward the bed. I sat down on my haunches near her face so I could look at her. Her head was wrapped in a white bandage, some of her dark hair was plastered to her face, still caked with blood, and her face was swollen with black circles under both eyes.

"A shunt or bolt?"

"Uhnggg…" I tried to clear the tears from my voice and I ghosted my fingers across the velvet softness of Julia's cheek. "They are ways of draining fluid, and would need to be placed surgically. The amount of fluid and where it originates would determine which of those procedures are used. Right now that's not an issue, so I'm praying it won't become one. If her brain swells further, it could be, though. The next 48 hours are critical."

"Could she die?" I could tell he was crying, even though he was trying to hide it. Paul was a man's man, old school and wouldn't want to openly show emotion. Even over his only child. Part of me envied his control because I felt like I was falling apart.

"No!" I replied sharply. "Please don't even say that! I can't even think about that happening." I lowered my voice, more conscious of the tone I was using. "I'm sorry, Paul. It's just…I can't even contemplate losing her. I don't know what I'd do."

Paul drew in a deep breath and nodded. "I'm so thankful for you, Ryan. I know she'll get the best care because you know what the hell is happening. It makes me feel safer, somehow."

"Thank you, Paul. That means a lot to me, but I feel more helpless right now than I ever have in my entire life." I let my head fall to my hands.

Minutes later, my father arrived and thankfully, I didn't have to explain anything. He could tell just by looking at her charts, which I assumed he'd already done before entering the room. Dr. Brighton left instructions with the nurses to give him access and the resident on duty knew as well.

I lost it again as my father's arms closed around me. "Oh, my God, Dad!"

"Ryan, we'll do all we can. I'll stay as long as Julia needs me, son." He embraced me tightly and placed a hand on the back of my head. "Your mother will be here soon. She's very worried. You know how much she adores Julia."

When he released me, he turned and offered Paul his hand. "Hello, Paul. It's good to see you again, but I wish it was under better circumstances."

"Yes. I was expecting a wedding pretty soon," he murmured and my heart broke all over again. I went out into the hallway and asked the nurses if we could get a few more chairs.

And so the vigil began; all of us sitting in silence, watching Julia. My father, Aaron and I conferred with the doctors and monitored the equipment. When Julia's mother, Marin, arrived she was hysterical and Paul took her out of the room. I understood it and wanted to comfort her, but I couldn't leave Julia.

I never left her side. When my mother came, she just sat beside me, rubbing my back or bringing me coffee and sandwiches that I didn't touch.

It must have been a new day because the nurses changed shifts and the other's clothes changed. Jen and Aaron came and went, Aaron doing his rotations and Jenna working downstairs in ER.

Ellie and Harris finally arrived the following morning.

Ellie looked terrible, her eyes bloodshot and red-rimmed, and clutching Harris's hand for dear life until she ran to me. My arms closed around her as she sobbed into my shoulder. "Ryan, I'm so sorry. How is she doing?"

"She hasn't gotten any worse, so that's something, but it's...not good, Ellie. Her injuries are extensive." Hearing my words, Marin started crying again and my mother tried to comfort her.

Ellie pulled back, her expression pained, apparent that she knew about the baby. I pleaded with her silently not to say anything and prayed that she would read it in my expression.

"I'm sorry I wasn't here sooner. I um...I was in New York visiting Julia, helping her pack and then when she...came to Boston; I got a plane to L.A. I wasn't even home when Aaron called me to let me know about her accident. Harris met me at the airport and we turned right around."

I nodded. "I *know*, Ellie," were the only words I could get out but she understood what I was trying to say.

"I'm so sorry, Ryan. *So* sorry." Her grey eyes were wide, her chin trembling. "Julia...was so happy about it. She decided not to go to Paris."

I closed my eyes against the burning ache that consumed me. "Thanks, Ellie. It would mean the world to Julia that you guys are here, as it does to me."

I returned to my place beside Julia's bedside until I felt a hand on my shoulder.

"Ryan, you need to go home and get some rest. You're going to make yourself ill." My father's voice was firm. "You'll be no good to her if you kill yourself."

"Dad…I'm not going anywhere. If you guys want to leave, go ahead," I said woodenly, still watching for any signs of consciousness from Julia. "Take Marin to dinner." I glanced across the bed at the woman who was brushing the hair off of Julia's forehead again and again. I tried to smile at her. "You should get out of here for a while."

"What about you? Will you come with us?" Marin was a slight woman and I could see a little of Julia around her eyes, but that was where the similarities ended. Julia had Paul's coloring and his attitude.

I let my breath out in a huff, and shook my head. "I'm not going anywhere. My place is here."

"Ellie is here now. She can stay with Julia as can Elyse or I. Go get something to eat and sleep. Even Paul's gone back to the hotel to get some rest. You should, too," my father insisted.

I shook my head again but didn't say a word. The truth was, I was scared shitless and I didn't want to leave for even a second in case something happened. Maybe she'd wake up and God, what if I lost her? I'd never forgive myself if I missed even one second with her. I'd blown off my classes and clinical. I didn't even know if any of my professors were aware of my situation. I didn't know what day it was. Graduating mattered little to me at this point. If something happened to Julia, if she didn't wake up, or if she woke up damaged, my life would be over anyway.

Everyone cleared out except my mother and me. I was thankful for the silence. Mom was sitting on the window sill, her sad eyes watching me. I sat and held Julia's right hand, as I'd been doing since I'd walked into this room the night she was admitted. I was thankful that I could let the façade fall away and allow the emotions that I'd been struggling to hide, come to the surface. Sobs rose in my throat. My mother came to kneel next to me and put her head on my knee.

"Ryan…Julia wouldn't want you to hurt yourself. It's been three days and you should go home. Eat, shower and sleep."

"I *can't leave*! What if…something happens?" My voice broke and tears formed in my eyes. I wiped at them impatiently. She moved and put her arms around me and I melted into her, sobbing into her shoulder, but still rubbing my thumb over Julia's wrist. "I love her so much, Mom. Jesus, she has to be okay."

"You have to have faith, Ryan. Julia is strong and she has so much to live for. She has *you*."

"It's been too long," I answered. "If she doesn't come out of it soon, it's less likely she'll survive." I pulled my mom's arms from around my shoulders and stood, putting a hand to my eyes as I moved away to stand at the foot of Julia's bed. "They've reduced the medications that keep her asleep, but she still isn't waking up. She gives me everything and I can do nothing here. *Nothing*!" the words ripped from my chest, dripping with agony.

"Oh, Ryan, God won't take Julia away from you," she said softly. "I promise."

"Mom…you can't make promises for God." I looked at the ceiling in an effort to get control of myself. "Can you let me have some time? I haven't been alone with her since that first night. I need to talk to her. Please?"

Her arms encircled my waist from behind and she kissed the back of my shoulder. "Of course, baby. I'll close the door and then you open it when you want us to come back in, okay? Don't you dare say goodbye to her. Understand? If you want her to fight, you mustn't give up, darling."

I rubbed her arm and nodded. "Okay."

When the door closed, the sounds seemed to grow louder. Beeping of the heart monitor, dripping of the IV, air whooshing through the vent; sterile hospital sounds, not the beautiful voice or the lilting laughter that I longed for. I wanted to scream at the injustice of it all. My gorgeous, vibrant Julia was lying here still, silent, unmoving; at the mercy of these *fucking machines*.

Every breath hurt. My gaze fell to Julia's chest, rising and falling in time with the ventilator. Dr. Brighton talked about weaning her off to see if she could breathe on her own, but I was adamant that we wait until after the medication had ebbed a little. If she wasn't waking up, she wouldn't be able to breathe without assistance and I wasn't willing to take that risk. Paul had agreed with me, trusting my judgment. Thank God.

Another CT scan showed there wasn't significant swelling in her brain, which was a blessing. It was something positive, but until she opened her eyes, I would have no relief.

I fell to my knees next to her and laid my head on her stomach. Her left arm and her ribs were injured, but I wouldn't hurt her by laying my head below her navel. My hand wrapped around hers and I closed my eyes as a tear squeezed from each one.

"Julia…you have to wake up." My right arm around her hips tightened. "God, I'm so lost. Please, don't leave me, baby." I took a shaky breath and fought back the sobs threatening to break free from my chest. I'd denied the possibility of losing her to Paul and to everyone else, but my education and my reasoning told me it was possible. "It's like we're one person…I can't live without you. I love you so much."

I lifted my head and looked into her face. It was still swollen and purple bruises were all over the left side. My heart ached at the site and I stared at her, willing her to wake up. I spoke softly to Julia and then to God. "Dear God, please let her be okay. I'd give my life gladly if you would only spare hers."

I stayed on my knees next to her, holding her. I talked to her, repeating the words over and over, feeling her body move with each breath. At times, tears ran unabashed down my face and I didn't even bother wiping them away, the blanket on the bed absorbing them as they fell. "Please, God. *Please*."

It could have been minutes or hours, but finally her hand stirred under mine. My head instantly snapped up to find her green eyes open and staring back at me. I could see the panic and pain behind them but in that moment, I thought she was the most beautiful sight I'd ever seen. It meant that she was aware of her surroundings, so chances of brain damage were minimal.

Thank you, Jesus.

~2~

Ryan~

JULIA BEGAN STRUGGLING against the tube invading her throat but her injuries kept her movements to a minimum. She grimaced as pain shot through her, looking at me with wary eyes. Her brow furrowed as she took in her surroundings. The ventilator tube was strange and frightening and her right hand lifted toward her mouth. She tried to speak, but the vent tube prevented anything but a raspy whisper.

I jumped up and sat on the edge of the bed, still in shock myself as I restrained her good hand from pulling at the tubes. "Honey, stop. You're in the hospital and this has been helping you breathe. We'll get it out, but you have to stop fighting right now. I know it feels weird, and you won't be able to talk. Just please relax."

My heart leapt within my chest. Julia's eyes were wide and frightened and confusion clouded her features. The green irises were glassy as she shook her head, frantically trying to talk but I stopped her with a shake of my head.

I was capable of removing the tube, but wasn't allowed to without a physician's permission. I put my hand on her thigh so she'd meet my eyes. "It's okay, baby. I'll have that out very soon." I reached up and pressed the call button on the side of her bed.

"Yes?" the voice on the intercom answered.

"Can you please come in here? Julia's awake and the vent is scaring her. Is Dr. Brighton around or my father? We need one of them, stat."

I lowered my voice again. "Honey, I was so worried…going out of my mind." I held my breath, trying to make sure she didn't have any brain damage as I watched for her reactions to anything and everything. I placed my hand at the side of her face and ran my thumb along her cheekbone. Once again, Julia tried to pull at the tube, her eyes connecting with mine. "Just concentrate on my eyes, and breathe through your nose. It will keep you from gagging. If you can understand me, will you blink for me?" She blinked once and nodded slightly.

I dropped my head as tears flooded my eyes. This was the miracle I'd prayed for. She was going to be okay. I'd been so scared and now the relief was equally intense. She resumed struggling, trying to speak. The effort made her gag and choke.

"No, sweetheart. They're coming to take out that tube. You've been in an accident, but you're going to be fine," I said reassuringly, hoping that the calm tone of my voice would soothe her. I relaxed when the room flooded with people. That damn tube would be out in a matter of seconds. My father and three nurses, one of whom quickly turned off the vent and started to gently remove the tape holding it in place on Julia's jaw.

"Julia, we are going to ask you to cough. Do you think you can do that?" Kari, the day nurse asked.

She nodded, but still looked frantically from one to the other, her good arm going up to pull at the tube. I grabbed her wrist and gently brought it down to the bed again. "Stop struggling, please."

"Okay, when I say three, cough and I'll pull out the tube," Kari said. "It will feel strange and you'll have a little bit of a sore throat afterward. Are you ready?" Julia looked into her face and nodded once. "One, two, three," she said as she pulled out the tube. Julia coughed several times and pulled her hand from underneath mine to go up to cover her mouth.

I poured some water from the pitcher on the bed stand and offered it to her, but her hands moved up to the bandage on her head and she tried to move her injured arm. A sling restricted her movements so her shoulder could heal properly.

Another nurse inserted a syringe into an IV port and Julia's eyes got heavy instantly and her movements slowed. I put the glass to her lips and she took a small sip.

"We're sedating her because she can re-fracture her ribs if she moves around too much," Dad murmured as I returned the glass to the tray.

"I *know* that, Dad." I brushed the back of my fingers across her forehead as her eyes fluttered closed. She was trying to fight the sedative, but it was impossible. I leaned down and kissed her gently, nuzzling my nose against her temple and sighed deeply.

I backed up and ran both hands through my hair as the gravity of what had just happened hit me. My legs felt weak and I leaned up against the wall for support trying to focus on my father. He blurred before my eyes as they started to burn, but the strong hand on my shoulder was reassuring. "She's going to be okay, son."

"It's a miracle." I nodded, wiping at the wetness in my eyes with the back of my hand.

Soon the room was clear and Julia was resting peacefully. I was sitting beside her, holding her hand again. She was very sleepy, but I wanted to talk to her. I rubbed my thumb back and forth over the top of her hand.

"Julia? I'm here with you, babe. Everyone is here. Your parents, Ellie and Harris, Aaron and Jen. Everyone who loves you is here. I love you so much," I whispered and used my other hand to brush her hair back. She tried to lift her eyelids slightly but the medicine had her on the verge of sleep. I brought her hand up and brushed my lips across her knuckles, unable to tear my eyes away. I grimaced at the bruises that were beginning to turn green around the edges. Her left eye was blackened and her face was swollen. It hurt to think of what she must have felt during the accident. *What did she suffer?*

"What happened when she woke up?" my dad asked. He was standing behind me and I had to shake myself out of my thoughts. "Did she give any indication that she knew what was happening?"

I laughed incredulously. "She blinked and nodded when I asked her if she understood. I'm so *relieved*, Dad!" I stood and his arms closed around me in a comforting embrace.

"That's excellent, son. We'll see how she does in the next couple of days, but I want to order more tests to make sure there isn't any permanent brain damage. She may have difficulty with muscle coordination due to the location of the injury." He patted my back and then clutched at it. "I'll go find Marin and Paul. They went to the cafeteria to get lunch. You should call the others and then go clean up before Julia wakes up. You look a mess, Ryan. Shave, for God's sake. You probably scared the shit out of the girl."

"She's seen me worse," I laughed and my chest physically hurt as my lungs pulled in the air. Was this the first time I'd breathed in four days? I bent to kiss her on her forehead and then rested my head lightly on hers, relishing the feeling of her breath on my face, proof that she was alive and would recover.

Thank you. I'll never ask for another thing as long as I live, I silently prayed as I moved away. I couldn't tear my eyes away from her sleeping face. The cut along her hairline held 6 stitches and looked angry and sore.

"Ryan...Ellie, Aaron and Jen?" Dad reminded.

I pulled out my phone to do his bidding. Jenna was working and Aaron was on his way to pick up Ellie and Harris at their hotel.

Soon everyone was back at the hospital and I was being ushered out the door. I was exhausted, but I wouldn't stay home long enough to sleep, only to shower and change into clean scrubs so I could do my rotations after I went to check on Julia.

Dr. Brighton had contacted my professors, and the chief resident, so they would allow me to make up my coursework and schedule replacements for my hospital shifts over the past three days.

The longest three days of my entire life.

I had ten messages from Tanner on my cell phone as well as two from Liza and one from Min. Min was checking on Julia, Tanner was asking what the hell happened and Liza was pestering me with another of her barely concealed ploys to help her with research. She knew I was engaged to be married, but she never stopped trying to get me to screw her. She had no self-respect which turned my stomach.

After my shower, I felt much better and rushed back to Mass General as fast as I could. My hair was still damp when I walked into Julia's room. Everyone was gathered around the bed blocking my view, but I heard her talking softly to her parents and I closed my eyes at the sound. Once again, relief surged through me. In the darkest moments of the last few days, I thought I might never hear that sweet voice again.

Six sets of eyes turned and my father immediately came forward, his open hands in front of him, gesturing for me to stop.

"Ryan, I need to talk to you in the hallway."

"Okay, in a minute," I said impatiently. "I want to see Jules."

"Ryan, we need to talk first," he said sternly. His tone was very low, like he was trying to keep anyone else from hearing what he was about to say.

"Now? Dad, please…I…" I began but he grabbed my shoulders and turned me toward the hall.

"Yeah, *now*."

The manhandling pissed me off. "What the hell?" I questioned in agitation. Why was he keeping me from Julia? She'd wonder why I wasn't with her immediately.

"Julia seems to have some memory loss and trouble with coordination on her left side. She can't move her toes, but she feels a pin prick. Motor function manifests near where she hit her head, so it's common with injuries like this. I'm sure it will get better with time, but she may need some help with walking at first."

Memory loss? I nodded and waited for more of an explanation, but he just looked at me. "Okay. What sort of memory loss? Short-term, long-term, *what*?"

"It's strange. It seems to be selective. She remembers her childhood. Paul, Marin and Ellie, but has no memory of me. We mentioned you, Ryan, and she doesn't appear to remember you either."

"*What?*" I asked in disbelief. My heart dropped into the pit of my stomach. *How can she not remember me? We can't breathe without each other, for God's sake.*

"She's very confused. I needed to warn you before you go in. I know it's a shock, but we don't want to overwhelm her. You have to keep your emotions in check." He placed a hand on my shoulder in an attempt to comfort me. I was still trying to wrap my head around it and was slightly reeling. "This will most likely pass, son."

"Did she ask about the baby?" I asked with serious hesitation. This memory loss wasn't good, but I was thankful that she was recovering.

"Not a word. She hasn't said much to anyone other than her parents. I know you didn't want to upset them, but don't you think we should tell Marin and Paul about the baby, Ryan? In case Julia does ask, we don't need any emotional outbursts from them when she is so fragile. Her vitals look good and I've ordered some broth for her. Dr. Brighton and I agree that we should monitor her memory loss and coordination issues and get her back on solid food before she's discharged. Her ribs will be sore, but we'll get her up and walking today."

My mother moved behind me and slid her arms around my waist. I put an arm around her shoulder as her eyes reflected her sorrow that Julia didn't remember me.

My mind was racing. "Okay, yeah. Can you take them out and tell them while I get a chance to talk to Julia alone?"

"Don't tell her too much, Ryan. I know you're anxious and can't wait to get in there, but remember, she doesn't know you."

I rubbed my hand over my face and my mother's arms tightened around me. "My God, Dad," I murmured as the implications sank in.

"Let's just be gentle and supportive and see how she progresses. She'll be able to cope with losing the baby better if she remembers everything on her own. Right now, let's concentrate on getting her physically well. We'll do some tests to try to figure out what's causing this."

I left my mother in the hall and followed Dad back into the room. My heart was racing, palms sweating. How in the hell would I handle it when my beautiful girl didn't know me? I steeled myself for what I would face in the next seconds.

"Would everyone like to join me for coffee in the cafeteria?" My father invited the others to leave. Some of them nodded, others gathered their things and moved away from Julia. Her bed was elevated to a sitting position. When her eyes met mine, I searched for some sign of recognition. She watched me walk in, but didn't speak.

"See you in a bit, Jules. Love you." Paul placed a kiss on Julia's forehead. Thankfulness, like I'd never known, rushed through me when she smiled up at him and spoke.

"Love you too, Daddy." Her voice was soft and a little raspy, a remnant from the breathing tube.

On his way out, Paul came toward me and threw his arms around me. "Ryan, I'm so relieved."

I patted him firmly on the back. "Yeah. There hasn't been a second since she woke up that I haven't been thanking God," I said so only he could hear. "There are no words to tell you how much I love her, Paul."

"You don't have to, son. We know," he said as he waited for Marin to join him.

The thick bandage on Julia's head had been replaced with a smaller one and most of the blood had been cleaned out of the hair at her left temple, but the most amazing thing was that her eyes were clear and alert. My hand went to my heart as I walked slowly toward her. My instinct was to run and gather her close, but that would frighten her.

"Bye, honey. We'll be back soon." Marin squeezed her hand before preceding Paul, Ellie and Harris out. Ellie's eyes met mine briefly as she passed. She looked worried, squeezing my arm before she walked around me and out of the room, shutting it behind her.

Finally, we were alone.

"Hey. You gave us quite a scare," I said gently when her soft eyes fell on mine. I saw a lot of questions there and wondered if she had any recollection of me at all. The situation would have me freaking out if I didn't think she'd eventually get all of it back, but right now I was just damn happy that she was alive and awake. That was all that mattered.

"Hello." Julia's voice was timid and her eyes wide as I sat on the edge of bed.

"How are you feeling?" I asked in a low tone, trying to keep my voice steady. Emotions flooded through me at record speed and I was struggling with each and every one. I was aching to touch her, to hold her close, but I couldn't behave like we were lovers. No matter how much I was dying to.

"I'm pretty sore. My side really hurt and my head is throbbing." She was hesitant and uncertain in her response.

I longed to touch her face, but moved slowly and took her hand instead, my fingers going to the inside of her wrist to check her pulse. It was steady and strong, and I glanced at the dry board where the nurses kept track of her other vitals. Her blood pressure was perfect and most of the beeping machines had been disconnected.

"I'll tell the nurses to get you some medication to manage the pain." I checked the charts and saw that Dr. Brighton had prescribed Vicodin. "We want to get you up for a short walk soon and will need the medicine to kick in before that. It might make you a little sleepy, but that will be better than the pain you'd feel without it. We have to get the circulation in your legs going. The sooner you get up and about, the sooner you'll get out of here." I tried to reassure her in calming tones but felt like I was babbling. I needed to let her lead any personal conversation.

Her eyes followed my every move. She didn't look scared, but Julia searched my face for something I couldn't quite comprehend. It was difficult because I knew her so well and it was usually easy to read her emotions.

"Are you...my doctor?" Her eyes moved over my scrubs and the stethoscope hanging around my neck, then back up to my face.

I tried to lift my lips in a small smile, but my heart squeezed in pain. *She doesn't remember me at all.*

"Hmmph," I let my breath out in barely veiled frustration as I pulled up a chair and sat down next to her bed. "No, Julia. I mean, I'm a fourth year med student and I will be a doctor in a few months, but I'm your..." I stopped and considered what to say. "I'm..." I didn't want to lie but didn't want to cause harm or to overwhelm her. "We've been friends a long time. Don't you remember me at all?"

Her eyes widened again as I said the words but she shook her head. She looked apologetic, like she felt bad for me. "Ellie mentioned you. You must be Ryan."

It wasn't a question. I nodded and tried to swallow the lump in my throat, looking down at my lap briefly, not wanting her to see the pain behind my eyes. My throat was aching when I tried to speak.

"It's normal that you might forget a few things for a while. You had a nasty head injury. You will remember everything in time, okay, honey? I'm just so glad you're going to recover." I couldn't help myself, I finally reached out then and moved my fingers along her jaw as she nodded but did not recoil from my touch. "So many people love you and are here to help you. Jen and Aaron, Ellie and Harris, your parents and mine."

"I don't remember all of them either. I do remember Ellie from college. And my mom and dad."

"Do you remember Elyse, Aaron, Jenna or Gabriel?" She shook her head slightly and sadness washed her face. As horrible as I felt, it had to be more confusing and frightening for her. Every instinct told me to pull her to me and comfort her, to soothe her fears with soft caresses and kisses. I clenched my teeth against the urge and just focused on her words.

"No. Gabriel has a very good bedside manner, though. He seems like a very good doctor." She looked up from under her lids. Her right arm moved across her stomach and was rubbing on her left wrist under the edge of the sling.

"Gabriel is my father and is the most renowned neurosurgeon in Chicago." An astonished expression flashed across her face and I smiled at her, taking her hand in mine. "See? We spared no expense to get you better. He and my mother, Elyse, flew in immediately. Aaron is my brother and Jenna, his girlfriend. Aaron is at Harvard with me and Jen is a nurse here. She was part of the trauma team that worked on you when you came in on Wednesday night."

"Is Chicago where you grew up?" I nodded shortly, agonizing internally because I had to tell her things she already knew. Julia knew everything; knew me better than I knew myself and it hurt that she didn't remember all we'd shared. I sucked in my breath and she continued, still watching me closely. "You and Gabe look alike. I can see it in the eyes, but you have your mother's coloring."

"You're very observant. That's an excellent sign," I said tightly.

"What's causing this?"

"At this point, we're not sure. We'll do another MRI this morning to make sure that there isn't any problem with fluids. Most likely, it's just due to the blunt trauma you suffered or just the shock of the whole ordeal. I don't want you to stress over it. I'm sure it's only temporary and you're going to be just fine."

She still looked worried but nodded. "Yeah. Okay."

"Hey. You might not want to remember everything. We fight a lot and Aaron teases you constantly." The corners of my mouth lifted in the start of a grin.

She smiled and cocked her head to one side. "Why would we fight?"

"Because…you're so damn stubborn, of course. You tell me I'm a moody ass." I laughed and her smile widened. "Truthfully, we don't fight that much, but when we do, watch out! It's usually a blow out."

"Hmmm…Do I win?" Her mood was lightening. She bit her lip and looked at me through veiled eyes.

"Yes. But, only because I *let* you." We both burst out laughing and for the first time in days, my heart relaxed, the tightness in my chest subsiding. She grimaced against the pain laughing caused her broken ribs.

"Oh, I'm sorry, honey. I shouldn't have made you laugh."

"No. That's okay. It's good. I mean, yeah, it hurt, but…it was worth it."

Her hand worried back and forth on her wrist with increasing urgency and I stopped her movements with my own. "Are you having pain in your wrist, Julia?" I asked in concern. She had several IV's and one of the veins could have collapsed. My fingers skirted over the skin as I turned her hand over and examined where the needle was inserted. There wasn't any evidence of a problem.

"No…it's weird; I just feel…" she glanced down and then back up at my face, "Something's wrong with my wrist. It doesn't hurt, but it feels like something is wrong. I know it's strange." She rolled her eyes and tried to shrug but grimaced in pain instead. "I'm sure it's nothing."

My heart leapt at her words. Yeah, it was nothing alright, except the bracelet that was now in my top dresser drawer with her engagement ring. She was missing it. Hope surged and I smiled broadly, causing her to smile back at me.

"What?" she asked softly through her smile.

I shook my head. "Nothing. Try not to move too much for a few days. Your shoulder will feel better soon, but your ribs will take a month or two before you're completely without pain. All we can do for them is tape you up and limit your movements." I stood up and pressed the button for the nurse's station. "Can you please bring the pain meds Dr. Brighton ordered for Miss Abbott?"

"Sure, Ryan," the voice on the intercom answered.

"Julia, I'm supposed to go to work, but I'll come back to check on you several times today, okay?" Her face fell a little. "Sweetie, if you don't want me to go, I won't. You're my favorite patient, you know."

She bit her lip again, uncertainty in her eyes.

"No…That's okay. I wouldn't want you to do that. This is part of school, right?" When I nodded, she continued. "I don't want to mess up your classes and have you fall behind because of me. I'm…I'll be fine."

"Are you sure?" Truthfully, I didn't want to leave, but I knew that once her memory returned, Julia would kick my ass if I screwed up graduating after we'd both sacrificed so much. Especially now that she was going to recover and so many others were with her, she'd want me to take care of my obligations.

"Yes. You don't have to come back for my walk either. Dad can help me."

"Julia," I admonished her. "I *want* to help you, okay?"

She smirked. "Okay. Is this you being a moody ass?" she quipped.

"Uh...yeah," I acknowledged. "And, no more arguments from your *stubborn* ass." We both were laughing lightly.

"Okay."

"You *will* have them page me when it's time for your walk, right?" I cupped her face in my hand and bent down to kiss her forehead, closing my eyes as I felt her warm skin beneath my lips.

"Okay. Take your time. *Obviously*, I'm not going anywhere." There was fear behind her eyes, even as she tried to joke around.

I took her hand and looked at her seriously. "Julia, I know this is a little scary, but it will pass, okay? Do you trust me?"

"Yes. I mean, I don't even know you, but...I feel like I can trust you."

I smiled and held her hand. "That's because you *do* know me, honey. I'll never let anything hurt you, I promise." It was the truth, but I felt like I was lying to her by not telling her what we really meant to each other. She swallowed and her eyes burned into mine, holding my gaze. I felt as if I were drowning and the only way to save myself was to kiss her mouth and share her breath.

"Later, when you come back, will you tell me about us? About the time I've lost? I'd like to remember." Her eyes were soft and searching and she was slightly trembling.

"You will. I promise, okay? You just need time. Until then, we're all here for you." I brushed my thumb along her jaw line in a whisper soft touch and bent to kiss her forehead. "I'm so happy you're okay. Shit, I was scared. I don't know what I would have done," I said against her skin and breathed in her scent. Her little hand wrapped around my wrist and as I pulled back from her I squeezed her hand.

"We must be really good friends. You make me feel…very safe and happy. It was nice to meet you."

My heart squeezed painfully again. "You mean it was nice to *see* me. And yes, we're very close."

She smiled and nodded. "Okay, yeah."

"Get some rest and do your best not to move too suddenly, okay sweetheart?"

"Doctor's orders?" she asked softly and looked up at me with her large green eyes.

"Nope. *Ryan's* orders. I'll be back later," I said as I forced myself toward the door. The nurse with the pain medication walked in as I left to go find the others.

In the hallway I was greeted with another doctor that I didn't recognize. He didn't work in trauma, so I'd never seen him before. He was a few inches shorter than me with dark hair and broad shoulders, maybe in his early thirties.

"Ryan Matthews?" he asked.

"Yeah?" I put my hands on my hips as I stopped in front of him. "And you are?"

"Dr. Spencer Moore. Tom Brighton asked me to consult on the Abbott case."

"Nice to meet you, Dr. Moore." I extended a hand and he shook it warmly. "Consult in what capacity?"

"I'm a psychologist and psychotherapist. He explained to me that Miss Abbott had a bad accident involving a head injury, and also lost a child, is that correct?"

I'd managed to push that misery to the back of my mind, but now the pain came back in a rush. I pinched the bridge of my nose as my eyes closed. I quickly opened them and focused on his face. "Yes. She has several injuries."

"And memory loss?" I nodded and he continued, "Well, after the MRI we'll know more, but Tom feels, based on the previous two, there is probably no physical reason and so it may be psychological. Probably the loss of the child. I'm just here to counsel her and help her talk through any feelings of confusion she might have. Basically, to help her cope to the point that she regains her memory."

I didn't say anything for a moment and the silence was getting uncomfortable. I rubbed the back of my neck. "Ryan, I'm told the young lady is your fiancée, so am I correct in assuming that the child was yours?"

I dropped my eyes and nodded once. "Yes, it was mine."

"I'm so sorry for you both. If you need to talk, please feel free to call me. It's important to let her remember on her own and since you can't talk with Julia about this, you may need an outlet." He handed me his card with his office numbers.

"Thank you. My family is here, and I'm really just trying to concentrate on Julia right now, but maybe. I appreciate the offer."

"Julia…" he said her name and raised an eyebrow. "A beautiful name."

"She's beautiful in every way. She's perfect."

"She's lucky to have someone so devoted. This could be a tough road and she'll need all the support she can get. I'm going to go introduce myself to her now. I'll keep you in the loop."

"Thanks. I have to get to my rotation. I'll check in several times today. Nice to meet you."

We shook hands and I turned to leave at the same time my mother and Ellie returned from down the hall.

"How did it go?" Elyse asked gently. The concern on her face very apparent and I tried to reassure her.

"Pretty well, I think. She's alert and her eyes are clear. She's going to be fine, Mom." I ran a hand over my face as my eyes blurred. "She'll be fine," I said again, more to myself than to her.

"Are *you* okay?" Her worried eyes were skeptical.

I nodded. "The most important thing is that Julia is alive. I have faith that her memory will come back, so it's a waiting game. Dad and the other doctors don't want us to tell her too much. It's best to just let her remember at her own pace."

Ellie grabbed my hand. I knew what was coming next. "Ryan…" she began hesitantly but I didn't want to get into this conversation right now. I had to do my rounds and didn't need to fall apart.

"It's okay. I know what you're going to say," I said tightly as my jaw clenched and she squeezed my hand again.

"I've never seen anyone as in love as Julia is with you, sweetie. There is no way she's going to forget all you've meant to each other. I *know* she'll remember." Her voice was cracking but her eyes never left my face.

"Thank you, Ellie. I know. That's what I'm holding onto right now."

"She wanted that baby so much. She was so happy; Ryan. All thoughts of leaving you and going to Paris were gone. All she wanted was to see you. She was bursting to tell you…couldn't wait to get to Boston…" her voice dropped off.

The tightness in my throat threatened to choke me and I blinked at the burning tears that wanted to invade my eyes. I nodded and put my hand over my eyes, using my thumb to wipe away a tear before it could fall. I felt Ellie's arms slide around my waist and my mother's hand rested between my shoulder blades. "Uhngggg…" I tried to clear the tears from my voice and I swallowed hard. "I'm so pissed! It's not fucking fair, is it?"

Her arms tightened and she pressed her face into my chest and shook her head. "You'll have more babies with Julia, Ryan. And, they'll be perfect."

If I didn't untangle from her and get to work, I was going to lose it. My hands closed on her shoulders and moved her out of my embrace before I angrily brushed another errant tear from my face. "Look, Ellie, I have to stop being such a pussy and get to work. I told Julia I'd be back for her walk, so I really need to get going."

A look of understanding spread across Ellie's face. "Okay. We can help if you don't get back."

"Thank you, but I want to be there for her. See you later." I turned and walked away. There was no way I wouldn't be back in time. I wanted Julia to know she could count on me. Paul and Marin were walking back, and I could see they had both been crying. Dad was behind them and he nodded at me, silently communicating that he had told them about the loss of our baby. I could tell by the way they were looking at me that they wanted to talk to me about it, to offer comfort, but I couldn't handle it.

"I'm sorry. I just…I can't talk about it right now." I ran a hand down Marin's arm and she brought her other hand to her mouth, closing her eyes in pain. I thought it was best to give them the basics and get down to ER so I didn't have a meltdown.

"Julia is talking to a psychologist that Dr. Brighton called in, but can you guys get it together before you go in there? I don't want her to see us all crying because it will just make her ask questions and she might not be ready for the answers." I waited for them to answer. Paul just looked at me and new tears trickled down Marin's face. I needed to bail. "Look, I gotta go. I love you all."

I took one deep breath after another as I made my way down to the ER and when I walked in I had my emotions under control. Min, Liza and Tanner were there, too. They all had questions in their eyes; their expressions were full of sympathy. Even superficial Liza had sadness written all over her face, but I ignored them and went to find the chief resident so I could get right to work. It was busy, with lots of patients and I was thankful for the workload. The rooms were full and there were a few in the area with curtained partitions. None of the others should have been standing around gawking at me.

I turned and held out my hands, shooting them a dirty look. "Hello? Don't any of these patients need attending to?" If they were pissed at me, they would be less likely to make small talk. Liza's face hardened, she threw down a clipboard and huffed off.

My lips twitched in the start of a smile. *Excellent.* Min pursed her lips upon seeing my smirk and Tanner just shook his head. It had the desired effect, however; and they scattered, each one helping a different doctor.

Dr. Clark was the attending resident and, with a skeptical gaze, he handed me the chart of a kid who had fallen out of a tree house. He was a short man with very dull brown hair and sharp blue eyes, whom I respected.

"Dr. Brighton told us about Julia, Ryan," he began. "We all get it if you don't want to be here."

I shook my head. "No, she's awake and alert. I'm okay. I need to work. At least for a little while. Graduation won't wait for me and Julia wouldn't want me to blow it when I'm so close. She'd hand me my ass on a platter." I knew that for a damn fact.

Dr. Clark chuckled in response. "She sounds like exactly what you need; someone as hard on you as you are on yourself, Matthews."

"She can be hard on me, yeah, but oh so soft, too...depends on the situation." I smiled and pushed back the curtain to face the screaming child and his parents.

Julia ~

My head and shoulder ached. Every time I moved pain shot through my torso like nothing I'd ever felt before. The scratching in my throat left the urge to cough, but I fought against it. The few times that I couldn't help it, it hurt so damn bad I felt like screaming.

I looked around at the room. Typical hospital setting. A dry-erase board on the wall, opposite the bed; the nurses' names written on it with the vital statistics which were updated hourly. The television on the bracket near the ceiling was too high to watch comfortably. To my right, two IV bags dripped silently. My left arm was in a sling and the tight bandages around my ribs constricted my breathing. Thankfully, the bed was elevated to prevent me from sliding down and there were pillows propped under my arms. I relaxed and my mind wandered. *Where was everyone? Where were my parents and Ellie? Where was...he?* My eyes filled with tears.

The whole situation was confusing and frightening; waking up with something gagging me, in pain, unable to move and not knowing where I was. It was all very unnerving.

There had been the angel face and that amazing voice crooning to me in low tones. He'd been holding me and begging me to wake up...dragging me out of the darkness. There were tears in his incredible blue eyes when he looked up at me. Deep blue with aquamarine circles around the pupils, fringed with lots of dark eyelashes. I couldn't tear my own away as he told me to stop struggling and that I would be fine. Something in those eyes calmed me. I trusted those eyes.

I didn't remember much after that; people bustling around, coughing and getting sleepy. When I woke, I was surrounded by my parents, Ellie and three others that I didn't recognize, but no sign of the gorgeous man from before. My eyes searched the room. My mother reached for my hand and Ellie offered her a chair.

"Hello, Julia," she said. "Are you looking for Ryan?"

"Who?" I asked. Ellie shot a glance at the attractive blonde man to her right and then at my parents.

"Ryan, honey," Dad said.

"I sent him home to clean up." The other man stepped forward and I could see the same kindness in his face and eyes...they were the same as the man who must be Ryan.

My mother looked at me with a big question in her eyes. "Do you remember Ryan, Julia?" Her voice was hesitant and quiet.

My mind had reeled and I shook my head. "Not unless he was the one who was with me when I woke up."

"Yes," the man who looked like him nodded and smiled.

"He's quite handsome, isn't he?" I asked timidly with a soft smile. I felt silly for saying it, it was so obvious.

Ellie laughed and cocked her head. "Yes. Quite. The nurses are constantly whispering and staring at him." The devilish gleam in her eyes sparkled and the blonde man nudged her in the shoulder making her look his way.

Everyone got quiet and stared at me expectantly. I looked from one to another, hoping someone would tell me something.

"Who is he then? Are we friends?"

She glanced at the one they called Gabriel, and he shook his head ever so slightly.

"Yes. We're all friends. We met in school," Ellie explained as the door opened and the object of our discussion walked in, even more handsome than before, if that was possible. His hair was damp and his face clean-shaven; he came and took my hand when everyone had been ushered out. He was dressed in hospital

scrubs with a stethoscope around his neck. So, he was a doctor, this Ryan, who Ellie said was my friend...

I closed my eyes, now alone in my room after my talk with Ryan, struggling to fill the missing holes of him. Surely, if he'd cried over me, I should know him. Gabriel and Dr. Brighton said that it'd probably all come back, but sitting here, without being able to remember, left me feeling lost.

I remembered Ellie and the first half of my freshman year at college, but then it was pretty much a blank. My dad left a newspaper on the tray over my bed and I could see that it was almost eight years later. He had some grey hair and my mother looked more tired than I remembered her. I wondered how I had changed as well. Ellie's hair was longer, but she looked pretty much unchanged. *Would I look old?* I would be 26 now. And, then there were all of these people that I couldn't remember at all. Tears slipped from my eyes in mourning over the loss. How could so much disappear just like that?

And Ryan...Ellie seemed hesitant to talk about him except to tell me we met at college. My heart was still thumping at his breathtaking good looks and I could still feel where his lips had burned into my forehead. I felt strangely drawn to him. His gentle teasing and the velvet softness in his tone when he spoke put me at ease.

Bringing my thoughts to the present, I looked down at the bed linens until a noise at the door startled me. Another new person walked into my room.

Okay, so is this a doctor or someone from the past? I didn't feel anything special coming off of him. None of the familiarity or magnetism that I'd felt with Ryan. He walked closer and smiled.

"Hello, Julia." His voice was deep and clinical. "I'm Dr. Moore."

I sighed in relief. Not another forgotten person from the past. "Hi. Are you here for another test? I'm sort of tired right now." The pain pill was starting to make me sleepy.

"No. Dr. Brighton and Dr. Matthews asked me to check in on you. I wanted to introduce myself since we may be spending time together."

"Are you a physical therapist?" I wished he would just cut to the chase already. His methodical prodding wasn't my style. "I'm having some difficulty moving my toes, but I can feel my feet. I'm supposed to be getting up for a walk, so it makes sense that you'd be…" He shook his head and so I stopped talking.

"I'm a psychologist."

My deep intake of breath caused a sharp pain to shoot through the left side of my chest. "Why? Do they think I'm crazy?" I asked, wincing.

Dr. Moore shook his head. "Not at all, but, if there is no physical problem, they just thought talking a little might help you remember."

I snorted unconsciously. I'm sure he found it insulting because his face tightened slightly. "Well, thank you, but I hit my head. Surely, that's the reason I can't remember, right? I have more than enough people to talk to. There are nine of them, at last count."

"No one is insinuating that there is anything remotely wrong with you, Julia, but I've dealt with cases like this before. I'm only here to help."

I regretted my snarkiness but, I was skeptical. "I'm sorry. I don't mean to be rude, but it's all a little overwhelming."

"Well, that's why I'm here. You might feel more at ease talking to someone impartial. Your family and friends might be more emotional and you don't need to take that on right now.

You need to concentrate on what you need to do to heal, okay? Focus on yourself."

"I'll try."

"So, Dr. Brighton will call after your MRI this afternoon and let me know the results, alright? I'll stop in tomorrow and we'll see how you're doing."

"Dr. Moore, on your other cases, how long did it take for them to remember?"

"I've only had two others like this. It took one about a month and the other one…well; he never did get his memory back completely." My eyes widened and my mouth dropped open in surprise. "But, he's built a new life and he's perfectly happy now. He has new memories."

His eyes dropped to my left wrist that I had closed my right one around. I couldn't seem to stop touching it and rubbed back and forth. My damned eyes welled again and threatened to spill over. I didn't want to lose eight years of my life.

"Why are you doing that? Are you in pain?" Dr. Moore asked.

I stopped immediately and pulled my good hand away. "No. It doesn't hurt. I guess I'm nervous or something. I'm sad that I can't remember, and losing all that time, and *people*, hurts. I feel isolated."

His eyes narrowed slightly but he smiled gently. "Is there anyone or anything in particular that makes you sad?"

I licked my lips nervously, not really sure how much I trusted this new doctor. "Uh…yes, I guess. I mean Ryan, Aaron and Jenna, mainly. Supposedly, we were all very close friends, so not knowing them is upsetting."

Especially Ryan. I wanted to know everything about him and exactly what our relationship was.

"Well, you'll probably remember them all in time, but it may not come back all at once. Do you remember your job or where you were living?"

I shook my head.

"Well, don't fret so much, okay? So, I'll see you tomorrow. Try to rest as much as you can."

He left me alone and I closed my eyes. The medicine was making me sleepy. *So* sleepy. The nurse came in to take my blood pressure, but when she closed the blinds and left, I drifted off to sleep in the quiet room.

*****

The room was darker. The sun had changed position and was casting long shadows from the window. That meant I'd slept for hours and probably missed my walk with Ryan. I wasn't really sure why he intrigued me, other than how gorgeous he was. Even though I had no memory of him, I found myself looking forward to seeing him. My heart sped up at the thought. I yawned and brought my right hand to my mouth as I glanced around the room.

There wasn't much furniture in the room, save the bed, one recliner and another small chair. I turned my head and stopped. Ryan was asleep in the big chair, his head lolled to one side and one hand was tucked under his chin, a thick lock of hair falling over his forehead.

An unknown number of moments ticked by as I lay watching him sleep just listening to the steady rhythm of his breathing. I didn't want to wake him. He'd looked so tired before and from what I could see, he needed rest.

The door began to open slowly, Ellie and Harris walking in. I put a finger to my lips to shush them then pointed to Ryan's sleeping form. They came quietly to the edge of my bed and Harris bent to kiss my cheek.

"What time is it?" I whispered.

Harris was quite good-looking and it was apparent in the way he was always touching Ellie that they were lovers. She deserved to have someone love her like that.

"Four thirty," Ellie answered softly.

"Looks like Ryan is finally getting some rest. He needs it," Harris murmured.

"Yes, he looked tired earlier."

"He hasn't slept in…" Ellie stopped and glanced at Harris. "Well, he's been concerned for you."

I nodded. It was evident in his actions, his tone of voice and his very presence. "We must be good friends. I wish I could remember…" my throat constricted slightly.

Ellie put her hand on mine. "Oh, honey, you will. We were all great friends. Have you seen Aaron and Jen?"

"Yeah, they stopped in earlier. It was somewhat awkward, but they seem very nice. Aaron is funny. Jen smacked him when he made me laugh." I smiled.

"Sounds like them, yeah," Harris answered and then nodded at Ryan. "How long has he been out?"

"I don't know. I was asleep for a while, too. He was there when I woke up."

A knock at the door signaled Jenna and another nurse coming in. "Hey," she said. She used her foot to do something to the bottom of the bed. "Time for the MRI, babes."

The other nurse, Kari, smiled at me. "Let's get your vitals before we scoot you out of here." She placed a blood pressure cuff around my right arm and shoved a paper thermometer in my mouth.

"You guys gonna let sleeping beauty over there sleep?" Jenna asked Ellie and Harris.

"Well, he hasn't slept in days, so probably." Ellie nodded.

"He'll be furious if he isn't told what's going on with Julia. Wake his ass up."

Kari finished the blood pressure reading and took the thermometer out of my mouth, just as Ryan stirred in the chair.

"Yeah. Wake my ass up." The nurse blocked most of my view, but I could tell he was running his hands through his hair and rubbing his face sleepily. "Jen, Aaron said you finished at four, so are you just here for the scenery?"

"Nice, dickhead. I'm here to keep Julia company during her test. See, Ryan? *I* get to go with her and you can't."

"Pretty soon you'll start chanting *Na Na Nuh Boo Boo*, right?" he said sarcastically.

"Hey, whatever it takes to get a rise out of you," she shot back and started to move the bed, pulling the foot of it toward the door, while Kari hooked the IV bags on the side railing and took her place to push at the head.

"Uh, pretty sure getting a rise out of me isn't your responsibility," Ryan teased.

Jen rolled her eyes and I blushed. "See what an obnoxious jerk he can be? I don't know how you put up with him."

Ryan was on his feet and came to the side of the bed, holding up his hand for Jenna to stop. "Hey, did you sleep okay?" His blue eyes were sparkling and he flashed a big smile.

"Not as well as you did, apparently." I smiled back.

"Well, it's a relief. I can sleep now that you're better. Our parents are around somewhere. I'll find them so they'll be here when you come back."

I was struck by his eyes and I nodded slightly. “Okay.” My eyes locked on his imploringly, hoping he could read the question lurking there. *What about you?*

“I’ll be here, too. Maybe we can get in that walk after all?” he said softly.

“I’d like that.”

“Back off, Casanova. We have business to attend to,” Jenna said shortly.

Ryan shot her a dirty look before she pulled me out into the hallway and winked at me. “He’s always getting his panties in a bunch, that one.”

“Yeah, he told me I always called him a—”

“Moody ass,” we both said in unison and she nodded.

“Understatement of the century!”

*****

Later that night as I picked at my dinner of grilled chicken and mashed potatoes, my parents and Ryan’s, along with Ellie, Harris and Ryan, were all there, sitting around me. Ryan was hovering around at the foot of the bed, and my mother was sitting on the edge.

“Eat up, honey. You need to regain your strength.”

“Uh, have you tasted this, Mom? You eat it,” I said in disgust and shoved the tray at her. “I’m not dying; I don’t have a heart condition, so why do I have to eat this crap?”

“I’m sure it isn’t that bad,” Marin said as she took my fork and took a bite. Her face crumpled and she grabbed a napkin and spit out the food into it. “Ugh.”

My head cocked to one side. “Exactly.”

Ryan smiled and took out his cell phone, punching something in to it. I watched him, wondering what he was doing. He didn't put the phone to his ear, but shoved it back into his pocket. I raised my eyebrow but he only smirked.

"Julia, we need to talk about what's going to happen now," Gabriel said in a serious tone. "Dr. Brighton feels if we can get you walking and eating, you should be able to go home in a day or two. We've been talking and wondered what you would like to do?"

I looked at the many expectant faces turned toward me and wasn't sure what to say. "I guess…I don't know what the options are."

"Well, you can come home with me to San Francisco, or go with your mother to Kansas City, as soon as you're well enough to travel. Ellie has offered to take you back to New York and stay with you for a while." Dad was concerned and my mother's face echoed his expression.

"Why are we doing this?" Ryan interrupted. "Julia *is not* going to go to New York right now." He sounded angry and looked agitated. "There shouldn't even be any discussion about this. Her doctors are here in Boston and *I'm…*" he stopped. "Well, there are three of us here with medical training. Who could take better care of her? We can toggle our shifts so that someone is always with her. I've already discussed this with Aaron and Jen, so can we move on, please?"

My mouth dropped open. It sounded like he already had it planned.

"Ryan," Gabriel admonished. He looked at his son and then back to me. "Julia, I know you don't remember them, so would you feel comfortable doing that? We understand, if not."

"Uh…" Ryan began. "Julia, I really think this is the best solution."

"Ryan. *Enough*," Gabriel said sternly. "Julia?"

I looked from my parents, to Ryan then Gabriel.

Ellie stepped forward and took my hand. "We'll support you with whatever you want to do."

"Fuck!" Ryan muttered and shoved his hands in his pockets before leaning up against the wall and staring at me.

Why is he so upset?

Elyse went to her son and put her hand on his arm. "Ryan, calm down. This is just a discussion."

"I thought you'd be on my side," he said under his breath, never taking his eyes off of me.

I opened my mouth to speak but struggled with what to say; overwhelmed with everything and amazed at the level of devotion being shown on my behalf. The blue fire in Ryan's eyes kept my attention. His jaw set, the muscle in it working overtime.

"I hadn't thought about it, but I appreciate your willingness to help me."

"Julia, we all love you," Elyse said softly.

I looked at my parents, wondering if they would be upset if I chose to stay in Boston. Truthfully, I knew that Ryan would take care of me and I should be with him. I didn't understand why I felt that way; I just knew it was so. Maybe it was the gravity of his response or his conviction, but whatever it was, it was real.

"I'd like to stay by the doctors. Dr. Moore said he can help me remember." I looked down at my lap and fought back the pain and emptiness that overwhelmed me. "I can't tell you how sad I feel not remembering you." My eyes flitted over Ryan and then to Harris. "And, Aaron and Jen. How can I go back to a life and job that I know nothing about? I think it's in my best interest to try to figure this out, so if it's okay, I think I'll stay here."

"*With me*? Julia, we'll move you in with us so that we can take care of you." Ryan's voice was filled with panic and I realized that I hadn't said where I'd stay. He thought I meant in Boston, but maybe somewhere else.

I nodded ever so slightly and he drew in his breath in a deep sigh. "Okay." He looked pointedly at his father. "Good."

The room seemed tense, everyone quiet until the door burst open, not so gently.

"Room service!" Aaron came in with a brown paper bag and a Styrofoam cup with a straw sticking out of it. "One Yuppie burger and Coke for our little Jules." His huge body and bright grin filled the small room. My mouth dropped open in surprise as Ellie took the bag and began removing the food to spread it out in front of me. My stomach audibly growled at the wonderful smells.

"Did you get the rings?" Ryan asked. Onion rings were my favorite.

"Dude. It's *me*. What do you think? You said rings, you got rings."

It was surprising how huge the burger was. "I'll never be able to eat all of this," I said as I started to reach for one of the rings.

"Don't expect you to, Jules. Ryan will help with that. Standard operating procedure."

My mother opened five or six of the ketchup packets and emptied them onto the paper wrapper of the burger. I dipped the ring into it and took a bite. "Wow. This is good."

Everyone laughed as I tried to lift the burger with one hand. It had Swiss cheese, mushrooms and bacon. Again, my favorite. "Aaron, how did you know my dinner wasn't fit for dogs?"

"Seriously? Ryan texted and asked me to go to Uburger and set you up. I gotta run though, 'cause Jenna is waiting."

"Thanks for bringing this, Aaron. I owe you one," I said with my mouth full.

He laughed. "Two words, Jules. *Blueberry muffins*," Aaron said as he walked toward the door. "Blueberry muffins. Jen has lots of assets, but she can't cook like you."

I remembered cooking more than my mother when I was growing up. "No problem. When I can move, okay?"

Ellie, Harris, Elyse and Gabriel left shortly after Aaron, leaving me in the room with my parents and Ryan. He was sitting on the edge of my bed and I shoved some of the food in his direction. He smiled and picked up an onion ring and ate it.

"I guess I'll take your mother out for dinner, Julia." My dad ran a hand down the back of my head. "We're so thankful you're okay, baby."

I wanted some time alone with Ryan so I hoped he wouldn't leave too soon. He'd had a long day, and probably had homework to do.

"Um, okay. Mom…" I looked up at her and smiled, trying to reassure her. "Let Dad take you out. I'm going to be okay now that I have real food," I joked and held up my cup before bringing the straw to my lips. "I love you."

When they left, Ryan remained on the bed with me. "Do you want the television on?"

I put the drink down and shook my head. "Uh huh. What's texted?"

"What?"

"Aaron said you *texted* him about the food. Is that some sort of code for something?" I took another bite of the burger.

"Oh." He chuckled. "It's typing on your phone. It works like a call, but you don't talk, you type. The words come across on the screen of the person you call…or text, as the case may be."

"Sounds weird."

"You're the queen of texting. We do it constantly."

"Really? Hmmm…" Ryan smiled and nodded. I shoved the remaining two thirds of my burger at him. "Want this?"

He smiled and picked it up. "Like you needed to ask." He took a big bite and I grabbed another onion ring. It felt easy being with him even though I barely knew him. He picked up the soda and took a pull on the straw. "Don't worry, I don't have cooties."

I laughed. "Something tells me I would have your cooties by now if you did."

His lips parted in a big grin. "Definitely."

"So…are you going to tell me about us?" I asked hesitantly. He sat back a little and met my eyes. Ryan didn't seem in a rush to answer, like he was considering what to say.

"We've known each other since our freshman year in undergrad."

"Ellie told me that much. But we share food and *cooties*, so…what else?"

He smiled and took another bite, and shrugged. "Like I said, we've known each other a long time. We don't think we should tell you too much. It will be safer for you to remember everything on your own. Can't you just trust me?" His comments were light and offhanded.

"That's just it." I rubbed my wrist and his eyes followed my movements. "I do trust you, even though I know nothing about you, but I'm *curious*. You can't know how frustrating it is not to know about your own life."

"I told you today, we're close. You've been my best friend since the minute we met, okay?" He plopped the last little bit of the hamburger down on the wrapper and went to the sink to wash his hands.

"How did we meet?" I asked. He was telling me some of it so I decided to keep on until he put a stop to it.

"In Psych 101. Waste of academic effort. You couldn't stand that class."

"Really?"

"Yeah. I didn't like it either, except we used to write notes on each other's notebooks. I can't tell you too much or you'll laugh and hurt yourself."

I couldn't help but smile at the expression on his face, but then he turned serious and looked intently into my eyes. I had a strong urge to touch him and wished that he would come closer so that I could.

"Hmmm…so best friends, huh?"

He licked his lips and looked away. "Yep."

"Like how?" I kept pushing, watching the emotions flit across his face. He had a very strong brow and jaw line, a perfectly straight nose. My heart sped up as my eyes fell to the full lips.

"Are you feeling okay? Does your head still hurt, honey?" Ryan asked.

"No, it doesn't. Why won't you answer me?" I persisted with a frown.

"Julia. Let's just concentrate on getting you better, hmm?" He scooted closer and brushed his thumb along my chin, electricity shot through me like a rocket. "There is plenty of time for finding out about the past."

Ugh! "Why won't you tell me? Were we pals? Friends with benefits?" His eyes widened and he drew back slightly. "Distant acquaintances?"

"No, no and *no*." He stood up. "Ready for that walk?"

"Tell me. Then I'll walk."

"Julia, you're going to be the death of me. What part of *we don't want to influence your memory* don't you understand?" His voice was coaxing and gentle, melting around me like honey.

"What's the big deal? Was it so bad?"

"No. Not bad at all." He sighed and sat down again, taking my hand in his. "Like I said, *we're close*. Can't you leave it at that, please? You'll remember soon and then it won't be such a mystery."

I looked down at the hand holding mine. Ryan rubbed his thumb across the top of my fingers.

"Hey," he said softly and squeezed harder when I wouldn't look at him. We sat like that for a few seconds until he sighed and finally spoke. "When I left for medical school, you told me that I was the most important person in your life. It was the same for me, and that hasn't changed, okay?"

My heart clenched inside my chest. I knew he was important. I'd felt it since I first laid eyes on him. I nodded but still wouldn't meet his eyes. He bent and brushed his mouth on my temple. "We take care of each other and I will always be here for you, Julia."

I turned my head slightly so my nose rested against his cheek. He smelled of soap and cologne. Absolutely delicious and strangely familiar. His hand came up to the side of my neck and cupped the back of my head. "Okay," I answered softly.

"Now…how about that walk?"

~3~

Ryan~

THE LAST FEW days had been joyous, painful, amazing and freaking *long*. Julia was progressively improving and I was spending as much time with her as I could. They'd taken out the IV's and the catheter and she was eating pretty well considering her aversion to hospital food. She still stumbled at times when she did her walking, but they'd moved her out of ICU the morning after she woke up.

Her memory hadn't improved, but I kept telling myself it would over time. We'd talked and joked around and it was bittersweet when she asked questions that she already knew the answers to. It felt like it had when we first met, instantly connected but not voicing or showing the real feelings.

I took a deep breath and tried to convince myself; *she will remember.* When she did, would she remember losing the baby, too? It scared the shit out of me. Julia was so strong, but this was more than she'd ever dealt with. Dr. Moore, Dr. Brighton and my father all agreed that the loss of the pregnancy was most likely the thing triggering the memory loss. The consensus was still not to push her memories. There was no physical reason. Her brain tissue looked completely normal and all of her other cognitive skills were perfectly intact. I was thankful for that, at least. It could have been so much worse.

The past week felt like a year and I was literally exhausted. I hardly went home and my bed had become a stranger because I spent every night at the hospital with Julia. While it was awkward at first, she soon came to accept it. When Marin or Ellie offered to stay, I only left to shower, get food or work.

In the evenings, when everyone else had left, I brought my laptop and studied from the chair in her room. Julia would spend the time reading or drawing, and once in awhile, ask me questions about what I was doing. Sometimes, we'd talk; play cards or a reverse type of twenty questions. She asked me things about my past *and* hers. It was fun and we laughed a lot, but I struggled not to tell her more than I should. Just as always, she was genuinely interested in everything I had to say. The bright side of the situation became spending lots of time with Julia and that Liza wasn't stalking me when I was in Julia's room.

I rushed around to pick up the apartment before bringing Julia back later that afternoon. Jen wasn't much of a housekeeper and Aaron was a complete slob. The sink was filled with dirty dishes and the bathrooms were gross. I cringed. My mother was here working to help get the place in order, and she would not be happy with the state of things. She went into my room to get my laundry, leaving me to wish I'd beaten her to it.

"My God, Ryan! You boys live like pigs! Is this how it always was when Julia came to visit?" she asked in disgust.

"It's worse now because I haven't been around. Jen cleans up some, but mostly I do it and I've been with Julia every minute, Mom! Can you cut me some slack?"

"Considering you're graduating with honors and you've been so good to Julia, I'll let you off with a warning," she smiled as she came out with her arms laden with clothes. "Aaron and Jenna's room is worse than yours."

Ellie called awhile earlier and she and Harris were on their way over to help clean. The apartments she'd shared with Julia were always spotless. Aaron and I still lived like we did back at Stanford.

"Yeah, and Ellie will have my ass over this mess," I said as I filled the sink with water. Our apartment was old and didn't have a dishwasher. It was in a brownstone, with radiant heat and extremely tiny closets. Jen was constantly complaining about the closets. She and Aaron planned to move into a house after graduation. Aaron was concentrating on internal medicine and could go into private practice after he finished his residency. I was hoping that we would all end up close enough to see each other on a regular basis. Julia wanted to be near Ellie too, but her career was really going to dictate her choice.

I plunged my hands into the water and continued to wash the dishes, lost in my thoughts. I stopped.

What if Julia doesn't remember? In three months, I would graduate and had planned to go to New York to be with her. *Will she still want me?*

My heart dropped. She'd been receptive to my presence, even to the point of letting me sleep in the big chair in her room overnight. Marin and I struggled over who would stay, but she acquiesced after one night she stayed with Julia and I slept in the waiting room down the hall anyway.

"Ellie will understand, Ryan. We all know where you've been this week." She put her arms around my waist from behind as I worked. "No one expected anything else."

She backed up and scratched my back through my scrubs. "Julia's getting her very own doctor and housekeeper in one. Lucky, lucky girl."

I rinsed off a fry pan and stacked it in the metal dish drain next to the sink as Mom went to sort the clothes. I shrugged but didn't speak.

"Ryan, I know you haven't mentioned it, but do you need to talk? About the baby? I'm worried about you, honey." My mother paused, her voice thickening slightly.

For a split second, I stopped too; but then reached for the next pan that needed washing and plunged it in the water.

"Mom, I appreciate the offer, but I'm just…I guess I've been concentrating on getting Julia better. Nothing would've been worse than losing her, so I haven't really dealt with…" my voice wavered and I sucked in my breath, "the baby yet. After that first twenty-four hours, it's been sort of surreal. It's Julia I've been worried about, compounded by our lost past. That's all I can take right now."

"I understand, honey. Just know that your father and I are here for you. We love you both so much."

"I know, Mom. I'm grateful for all you've done. Having Dad here has been my saving grace." I continued to wash the dishes and she put a load of laundry in the washer just as Harris and Ellie burst through the door.

"Hey!" Ellie said happily and came to hug me. "How are you holding up?"

Harris followed her in. "Hello, Ryan, Elyse. Gabe asked me to let you know he's got the bags from the hotel and he booked you on a 5:30 flight."

"You guys are leaving?" I turned toward my mom. "So soon?"

Ellie patted me on the stomach before starting her search for cleaning supplies, pulling out a bucket and some floor cleaner from under the sink. She threw a duster at Harris.

"Slave driver," he muttered but threw off his coat and went in the living room to start working.

My mother came into the kitchen and pulled out a chair. "Dad has to get back to his patients and you've got everything under control now."

I nodded, drying the dishes I'd just washed, putting them away as I went. I couldn't meet her eyes. I worried what it would be like when Julia was here with three people she barely knew. "Yeah, I know. It's just that Paul and Marin are leaving too, and even though Julia said she'll be fine with us, I don't want her to feel alone here."

"Ryan, Julia could never feel alone when she has you, okay?" Ellie smiled then wrinkled her nose in disgust. "Good God! This place is horrible!"

"I hope you're right, Ellie," I murmured and went to the furnace closet to get the mop and rags we'd need to finish the job.

"Ryan, Jules loves you; even if she can't remember. Relax!" Harris called from the other room. The apartment was so small that every word any of us said could be easily heard.

"When are you gonna make an honest woman of Ellie?" I asked, in an attempt to change the subject.

"I've tried. She's putting it on hold."

"What? *Why*?" I asked incredulously.

"Ask *her*," he said and seemed a little bit pissed off, but kept to his task of dusting the television and entertainment center.

Ellie filled the bucket with hot water from the sink and added some cleaning solution before she answered. "Harris, come *on*! You just signed that record deal. Married rock stars don't sell records!" she said in exasperation. "You know I love you."

"I'm hardly a rock star, El," he mumbled.

She stiffened. "Maybe you would be if you started thinking like one."

"Maybe you're not sure you can handle his new life style before you commit to it? Eh, Ellie?" I asked as she set the sudsy bucket in front of me.

"How about if you shut your yap?" She hissed and frowned at me.

Wow. Direct hit.

"When are you gonna give Julia her engagement ring back? And the bracelet? She is constantly messing with her wrist, and it's all I can do not to reach out and stop her, for God's sake."

I'd thought of it many times in the last days. She only had the ring a few weeks before the accident and most of that time we'd been apart. I longed to see it sparkling on her finger, and I missed the bracelet on her wrist. My heart squeezed at her words.

"Not yet. You know what the doctors said."

"She *will remember*," Elyse added almost inaudibly. "I have faith. Ryan, go strip your sheets for me, please."

I went to do my mother's bidding and she followed, closing the door behind us. I pulled the pillows off, started removing the cases and wondered why she'd need to get me alone.

"Ryan, do you want me to stay for a while? I can let Gabe go home without me. If you need me…" I realized how extremely lucky I was to have such wonderful, supportive parents.

"Oh, no, that's alright, Mom." I bent and pulled the sheets off the bed and threw them on the pile with the pillow cases. "I'm just a little nervous about bringing Julia here. She has to be feeling a little apprehensive under the circumstances." I sat on the bed and ran my hand over my jaw. "It hasn't been easy for me to see those questioning looks on her face, the blankness when something she can't remember is mentioned. It…hurts," I said in a flat tone but my heart constricted just a little. It had to show on my face.

"Ryan, I can see that she trusts you. Her face lights up when you walk into the room. She knows that there is something between the two of you." She sat down next to me. "It will all work out, baby. Will you give her back her jewelry?"

"I'm not sure if it's time yet. Dr. Moore, and even Dad, thinks that we should be careful about rushing things. I tend to agree. When she does remember, you know it's going to hurt like hell. Because…"

"Of the baby, I know." She ran her hand through the hair at my temple. "But you'll get her through it, Ryan. We can all feel how much you love her and she will, too. You've been so strong and brave, honey, but it's okay to grieve," she said sadly.

"I'll live," I said shortly, trying to dismiss the pain evoked by her words. I wasn't strong. I was weaker than I'd ever been in my life. She wasn't there the first night and didn't see how I completely fell apart. "Mom, really, I'll be okay. Julia is my focus now."

"Don't you mean *always*? Nothing's changed, sweetheart." She smiled sadly. "She's always been your first thought. Just don't try to overprotect her from the truth, Ryan. You might be cutting your nose off to spite your face, and more importantly, Julia might not thank you for it."

"Yeah, I've thought about that, too. We always tell each other everything; it's been exceptionally hard not to talk to her."

She glanced at the photo above my desk that Julia had given me for Christmas four years ago. "Wow, that's a beautiful picture. Amazing, actually. She could be a model."

I smiled and bent down to gather up the linens. "I know. Lucky bastard, aren't I?" I laughed. "I'm in love with that picture."

"Why haven't I seen it before?"

"It's very personal…it's just mine. I don't really share it with anyone."

Her gentle laughter joined mine. "I understand, but if you don't want to push her memories, you probably should take it down for now. Julia will be in here, right?"

"Yes, I'm giving her my room and taking the couch. There are a lot of things I need to hide, I suppose: our music, her phone with our messages, the pictures." I swallowed, trying to push down the sadness welling up inside my chest. "I feel so lost. Shit, I don't even know if I can keep it all from her, even if I try. I don't feel right about it."

"Just take down the picture, Ryan. Put it in a drawer and don't worry about all of it too much. Let what happens, happen. I understand you don't want to nudge, but maybe you shouldn't hide either."

I nodded. She made sense. "I'll play it by ear and see how she does. I'm scared, Mom. What if she never remembers me? I don't know what I'll do, if…"

She enfolded me in her arms. Mine were full, so I couldn't hug her back, but her hand came to the back of my head and she kissed me on the cheek. "She will, honey. You're unforgettable."

"Oh, yeah? Who told you that?" I asked softly, trying to blink back the tears that suddenly burned my eyes.

"*Julia*." I dropped the sheets and hugged her tight.

*****

Ellie took charge and we had the place cleaned up in record time. She and Harris were leaving in the morning. Later, I was planning on ordering some food if Julia was up for it. Again, it was a risk, because it would be like the last few months at Stanford after Ellie started seeing Harris. It could cause her memory to flash, but Mom was right. I couldn't control everything and wanted Julia to feel as normal as possible, even if I was unable to be myself. I couldn't act like her lover, which would take concentration on my part. Everything about her called to me. She was so fragile, which pulled hard on my need to protect her.

The parents were all leaving on early evening flights. Marin and Paul were anxious about leaving Julia, but trusted me to take care of her. Marin was more of a wreck than Paul, but then, he knew me a lot better and had seen us together more.

We were meeting at the hospital; Aaron was taking them to Logan International and I was bringing Julia home.

When I arrived with my mother, Dad and Paul were waiting in the hallway outside Julia's room. I felt nervous and giddy at the same time, which seemed insane after everything we'd been through.

"Hey," I said. "What's going on?"

"Dr. Brighton just finished examining Julia and she's been cleared for discharge." I nodded. Dr. Brighton called me with an update, so I already knew. "Marin is helping her change into street clothes."

"Paul, thank you for being here; I know it meant a lot to Julia."

Sadness filled his expression. "Thank you, Ryan. I was about to say the same to you."

I looked him straight in the eye. "I promise to take good care of her."

He reached out and patted my arm. "I know that, son."

I turned toward my father. "Dad…" I began and felt my throat tighten up slightly, the gratitude I felt having him here to oversee Julia's case rushed through every cell of my body. The constant rush of emotions was beginning to make me feel like a pussy, but there was no stopping it. "Thank you."

He put his arms around me and I hugged him back. "Of course, Ryan. We all love Julia so much. Where else would we be when you needed us like this?"

"Are you sure you don't want to move your practice to New York?" I laughed lightly as we drew apart.

"Ha! Your mother wouldn't leave Chicago, even if I wanted to. Maybe someday you and Julia can move home."

Paul laughed. "No way she'll leave New York. Even though I'd love to see her closer to home, too, she'll never leave her job! She loves that glamorous shit." He hesitated before continuing. "Ryan, are you still planning on going to New York for your residency?"

"Um…yes, unless she objects. I can't bear to be apart from her anymore, especially after this." I hadn't considered that she might feel it an intrusion now. "I guess I need to talk to her about it." Dread washed over me as I drew in a deep breath.

"Ryan, stop. Julia will want you with her. Three months is a long time. Her memory will be back by then," Paul reassured me. I tried to smile, but a cold sweat was breaking out on my forehead. I rubbed the back of my neck in agitation. "Ellie told me she talked to Julia's boss. What was her name? Meredith?"

"Yes, Meredith," I answered. "I asked Ellie to call since I was too much of a mess to deal with it at the time. She's been great. It's been a blessing. Julia can concentrate on getting better now and not worry about work."

The door opened and one of the nurses came out, carrying a hospital gown. "All set! Dr. Brighton has released Julia. I'll be back with a wheelchair," she said, smiling as she passed.

I peered in and Julia was sitting on the bed in a pair of black yoga pants and a blue button down blouse. Her coat was lying near her, but she couldn't wear it over the sling. She'd have to drape it over her shoulders.

The two women were deep in conversation. My stomach clenched, wondering if something had been mentioned about the baby. Two sets of tear-filled eyes turned to watch us all enter the room. Julia's full lips trembled at the corners in a hint of sad smile.

"Ryan, you're here." Her eyes lit up and my heart leapt.

"Of course, I'm here. You're stuck with me." I smiled and glanced at her mother. "Hello Marin. How are you doing?"

"Oh, I'm just being a sap; sad about leaving my baby." She used both hands to wipe away her tears.

"Mom, please," Julia said under her breath and glanced up at me through cautious eyes, wiping at her tears with the back of her right hand. "I'm hardly a baby."

"I agree," I nudged her chin with my thumb. "Hardly." I was rewarded with the rush of blood to her cheeks as they bloomed in response. *Beautiful.*

"So…what are you kids planning tonight?" Marin asked.

My mother moved around the room, gathering up Julia's things and putting them in her overnight bag.

"Um…" I wrinkled my brow and shrugged. "Nothing strenuous. We'll get Julia settled and then Ellie and Harris are coming for dinner."

Julia's eyebrows went up in speculation as she teased me. "Oh? Are you cooking, Matthews?" I was standing close to where she was sitting and she nudged me with her good shoulder. My heart stopped. It was our nudge and she used my last name. I'd felt that nudge hundreds of times and I smiled wide in elation at the familiar gesture. Subconsciously at least, she was still my Julia.

"Pfft! Never. If you were up to it, I'd make you do it, but as it is, we'll order in." Everyone burst out laughing.

The nurse showed up with the wheelchair and I stood back as Paul helped Julia into it. Every instinct told me to go to her, but he wanted and needed to help her as much as possible before he left Boston.

I wrapped my arm around my mother's waist as we all followed them out. Marin walked beside Julia, holding her hand as I watched the nurse push her down the hall. I couldn't take my eyes off her, and was thankful for all of these people who loved her so much.

Mom's hand came up my back and her fingers closed around my nape, motherly adoration shining from her eyes. "You make me so proud, Ryan. Aaron, too. I couldn't ask for better sons."

"Mom, don't get all mushy on me, now," I teased. "I'm a mess as it is."

"Give her a break, Ryan. It's her prerogative to get mushy over her brilliant sons. Mine too," Dad said with mock sternness.

We exited the revolving door as the nurse brought Julia out of the wheelchair entrance. Aaron was lounging against my car parked at the curb, a goofy grin plastered on his face.

"There she is!" Aaron boomed as he tossed me the keys and walked toward Julia. "How are you, itty bit? You look good. That shiner makes you look tough," he teased. Her bruises were getting yellow and lightening, with only slight hints of the purplish blue showing through her translucent skin. Before long, the only tangible reminder would be her fractured ribs.

And the memory loss.

She smiled brightly. “I’m really good, Aaron. Thank you for letting me stay at the apartment.”

“I’d kick Ryan’s ass to the curb before I’d say no to having you, babe,” Aaron said enthusiastically and laughed. She smiled up at him, shook her head and glanced at me. I shot her a wink. “Hold onto me, Jules,” he said and lifted her easily out of the chair. She winced a little as he stood her gently on her feet. It was difficult for me to do nothing, but I didn’t want to overwhelm her. She needed space to say goodbye to her parents and to mine.

I watched as her parents hugged her goodbye. Marin sobbed until Paul pulled her away and she melted into his arms. My heart ached for Julia as silent tears slid down her face. My mother took her in her arms, crying along with the others.

I swallowed hard and looked at Aaron. He was looking at the ground, clearly moved as well. Dad brushed his fingers on Julia’s cheek softly. “You let me know if these boys give you any trouble, okay? I’ll kick them in the ass,” he teased. Julia burst out laughing through her tears, which made her wrap her good arm around her torso to minimize the pain. “I’m sorry, Julia,” my father said as he kissed her temple.

“No, it’s okay. Thank you; for everything.”

I moved up and opened the passenger door to my CRV. “Are you ready?” I asked quietly.

“Yeah,” her eyes were crystal clear and sparkling, the remnants of her tears still on her lashes.

I slid my arms around her to support her weight as she lowered herself into the car. “Thank you. I love you all,” she said as the car door closed.

Marin sobbed into my shoulder as we said goodbye. “I thank God for you, Ryan. Thank you for being here for Julia.”

"I wouldn't be anywhere else. She's my whole world. You know that," I said quietly, so only she would hear. I shook Paul's hand and hugged each one of my parents. "I hope to see you all in May for graduation, okay?" I couldn't contain my anxiousness to slide into the car beside Julia and called out to Aaron. "Harris and Ellie are coming over at six. When will Jen be finished?"

"I think five, so we'll be there. Enjoy the day, bro'. You've earned it," he patted me on my back as I walked past him in front of my car.

"Thanks. Have safe flights and call us to let us know you're home, please. I love you…all."

Julia's delicious scent surrounded me and I paused to take a deep breath. She looked at me expectantly and then turned to wave at the others on the curb.

My hands gripped the steering wheel tightly as I started to pull away. I could feel her gaze like a physical touch. "What?" I asked.

Her eyes roamed over me, taking everything in, but she shook her head. "Are you okay? Are you sure you want to do this."

"Julia, enough. Why would you ask that?"

"I'm a mess," she complained.

"You can have a shower back at my place. You'll just have to be careful of your injuries. If you want to wait, Jen will be home soon and can help you wash your hair."

Julia frowned and looked away. "I feel like a damn invalid."

"It's only until your shoulder heals. You'll be able to move more when the sling goes away."

"Yeah, but these ribs. They hurt like hell."

Frustration at being dependent flashed over her features. There was a time, just two weeks earlier, when she would've been fine leaning on me and letting me help her with the most personal tasks, but now, I needed Jen's help. She and Aaron had been very gracious. We'd worked it out so Julia would never be alone, and the hospital had been accommodating in rearranging our shifts. It didn't hurt that my advisor was Julia's attending and chief of staff.

My phone rang and I pulled it out. *Liza. Shit.* I turned the phone off and shoved it back in my pocket as I drove.

"Ryan, you don't have to stop your life just because I'm here. Take your calls. I'll plug my ears." Her soft smile lit up my life and I rolled my eyes at her.

"It's just Liza. You know how she is."

I stopped and glanced in her direction. She bit her lip and shook her head. "Nope. I don't."

"Uh, she's just some chick that stalks me to help her study," I said dismissively.

"Ah…" she murmured. I could sense her hesitation but knew her. The wheels were turning. I struggled with what to say and decided it was better not to say anything. "She wants to be more than a study partner?"

Shit. "I guess, yeah, but I have no interest at all. I never have. She's been shamelessly chasing me since Gross Anatomy back in year one."

Julia cocked her head and considered this for a moment. "That must really suck for you." She was biting her lip to hold back a smile, but the dimples in her cheeks deepened. "I mean, having women chasing after you all the time. How utterly exhausting!" she teased. "You *poor* baby."

"As a matter of fact, yes it *does*. It's annoying as hell and her insipid excuses get more ridiculous all the time."

"Why don't you just say *no*?"

"Hmmph! I have! More times than I can count."

"Surely there is something attractive about her. She must be smart if she's at Harvard."

How in the hell did this conversation land on that twit anyway? "Julia, she's constantly professing her stupidity or lack of study skills to get me and probably ten other guys to help her. Honestly, I think she's more lazy than horny. She doesn't want to do the work and it's easier to get someone else to do it for her."

Her eyes widened and then she laughed. "Hmmm…you underestimate your pull, Matthews."

I grinned. "Oh? Do tell."

"Nope." She popped her 'P' when she said it and looked out the window.

"Julia, come on. I broke my back sleeping in that fucking chair for a week for you; the least you can do is stroke my ego a little."

"Like it *needs* stroking," she scoffed. "The nurses were drooling over you constantly. I think they would have let me die, except then you wouldn't be coming around anymore." She rolled her beautiful eyes again. "Where's Ryan? When's Ryan coming in next?" she imitated them in a sing-song voice. "That's all I heard all damn week!"

I burst out laughing. If I didn't know better, she sounded jealous and I was fucking ecstatic. Even if she didn't remember, she still wanted me.

"And? What did you tell them?" I asked, raising my eyebrows when we stopped at the light near my apartment.

"That I wasn't in charge of your social calendar, but that their best bet of catching you was between one and four am," she smirked mischievously.

I reached over and grabbed her hand in mine. "Sounds about right…"

She smirked as the light changed. "Ryan, you must have a girlfriend, don't you?"

"Why do you think that? I've been very busy with school and my…friends."

"Because. I just know you have one. You're too good-looking not to."

I huffed. Good. She still thinks I'm attractive, but how in the hell was I going to hide that *she* was my girlfriend? "Do you think you have a boyfriend?"

"No. If I did he would have been with me at the hospital."

"Yes, probably every minute." I chewed the inside of my cheek to keep from smiling.

We pulled in and I parked in the back. After I helped her out of the car, she stopped me by putting her right hand on my chest and met my eyes, her expression serious. I left my arms around her.

"Don't you think, as someone who shares food and cooties with you, you should tell me about your girlfriends? You said we were close, Ryan," she admonished ruefully.

"Julia, there is no one to tell you about!" *Shit, that was about the closest I could get to telling her the truth.* "Can we move on from this subject now? It's boring the shit out of me."

She looked hurt and I immediately regretted the shortness of my tone.

"I just thought…well, if it were me, I'd want to know if a strange woman was staying with you."

I released her and pulled her bag out of the backseat, along with her purse, flinging both over one shoulder and wrapping the other arm around her waist to offer support as we walked slowly up the stairs and into the building.

"If it were you, we wouldn't be having this ridiculous conversation. And you're not some strange woman!" I said in exasperation. "Look, I only have time for school, work and you right now, so can we leave it at that? I promise not to bug the shit out of you about your boyfriends either."

I opened the door and waited for her to go in. "That's because you already know everything about me, Ryan. I'm trying to find out about you. I want to know you better."

"If you knew me any better, we'd be the same damn person."

She sucked in her breath. "Maybe that was true before, but that isn't how it feels right now." I opened the door to the apartment and pushed it open for her. She leaned up against the doorjam and looked at me until I used my arm to gesture her in.

I removed the coat from her shoulders as she walked past me, hanging it up in the entryway. She moved around the small apartment, taking in the large leather sofas that dominated the living room and the small kitchen with the wooden table, the archway that separated the living room from the kitchen and the brick fireplace.

"This is nice."

"You and Ellie decorated everything. It's as nice as it can possibly get. Jenna doesn't have a head for that sort of thing. She's more interested in football and rock music."

"I like her. She's very witty and smart. I like football and rock music, too."

Yes, I know.

She was more distant after my last remark and I hated it. I walked up behind her and put both hands on her shoulders but careful of her injuries.

"Do you need anything? Are you hungry or thirsty?"

"*You* tell *me*. I mean, since we're the same *damn person*," she quipped over her shoulder and moved away toward the living room, leaving my hands to drop to my sides.

I joined her as she eased herself on the couch and ignored the underlying sarcasm in her tone. "You need a Vicodin for the pain?"

"No. It's not bad and Ellie's bringing wine later. I can't have any if I take those damn drugs."

I grabbed the remote to the television and sat down, turning toward her without turning on the television. "Look, Julia, I'm sorry. I was only playing around before. I used to say smartass shit all the time and it was funny. I didn't mean to upset you."

"I'm not upset," but she looked down until I nudged her chin up with my thumb. "I'm sorry, too. I should be more grateful. After all you're doing for me."

I sighed heavily. Gratitude was not the emotion I was looking for. Of course, I was taking care of her…that's what you do when you love someone more than life.

Ugh! "I don't have a girlfriend!" *I have a fiancée' that, right now, is driving me insane!* I searched her eyes, hoping she would relax and not worry. "Of course, I'd tell you if I did. We tell each other everything. That isn't going to change, okay? You *will* find everything out about me, but not in one afternoon. You need to rest." She nodded slightly and I slid my hand from her chin to cup the side of her face. Her hand closed around my wrist. I wanted her mouth so bad that I let my thumb rub across her lower lip. I knew it was dangerous, but I couldn't help myself. I bent to kiss her temple instead and then released her gently.

I flipped on the TV and searched for something to watch. Julia liked the Food Network, so I turned it on and Rachael Ray was making her thirty minute meal thingy. Julia eased back against the pillows and lifted her legs after I motioned with my hand for her to put them on my lap. I tossed the remote on the end table and unlaced her shoes, dropping them one by one on the floor with a thud, my hand closing around her feet to begin massaging through her socks. I wanted any excuse to touch her.

"I never understood why you watched this crap. You can cook much better than her."

"But *you* can't," she smiled slightly, her lips twitching up at the corners.

"What? I know I can't. That's why I have you. What's your point?" I watched the screen as Rachael ladled a bunch of stock into a pan with toasted spaghetti. I wrinkled my nose in disgust. "What is that shit, anyway?"

She chuckled softly. "My point is that maybe I was hoping *you'd* pick up some skills."

My head snapped quickly toward her. "Julia? Did you remember something?"

"No." She shook her head and gently shoved my arm with her foot. "But it stands to reason, doesn't it? Maybe I won't be around forever."

"I guess it does make sense that you'd want me to be able to feed myself, but don't go getting any ideas about not being around forever. That shit isn't happening." I squeezed her foot again and my heart swelled at the smile that spread across her face. "So, what is that crap she's making?"

"Uh…it looks like a play on risotto, but with pasta instead of rice. I bet it's good."

"Nah. Give me your Pad Thai any day."

"Is that something I make a lot?" I nodded slowly, not sure if I should have mentioned it. "Okay, I'll make it as soon as I get rid of this sling. When will that be?"

"Mmmm…probably another week or two. It's the ribs that will take longer to heal. We'll need to keep you taped up, and if you move around too much when the sling goes away, it comes back," I warned.

"Are you going to be such a hard ass with all of your patients, *Dr*. Matthews?"

"No," I said simply and continued to watch the show and rub her feet.

"No?" her eyebrow went up and her mouth lifted on one side.

"That's what I said, Abbott." I tried to keep it light. "If you need a hearing aid, I can arrange that, too." I couldn't help it, I burst out laughing.

"Fuck you," she giggled right along with me.

"Not tonight, honey," I shot back. She tried to stop laughing and keep a straight face, but she couldn't quite get the job done.

"Baby, I think you've got me confused with that stalker girl. What's her name again? Lucky? Linda? Lucy?" Her voice was laced with amusement.

I laughed again loudly, my shoulders shaking with the effort.

"Might as well be, for all I care. Sure, *Lucy*! That's it." I was still laughing and she crumpled into another fit of giggles. The lilting sound of her laughter made my heart sing.

"Ow! Stop making me laugh!" she kicked at me again.

"Oh, sweetie, I'm sorry! Stop kicking me, Julia!" I grabbed her foot. "Stop moving, I don't want you hurting your ribs, honey, but I absolutely feel like I must tickle you now." I whipped her sock off and started raking my fingers down the bottom of her foot. She was ticklish as shit and I knew exactly where to get the most reaction out of her. She screamed in protest. I tried to hold her leg still with the opposite hand so she couldn't move. This was for fun, but I didn't want her hurting herself. I ran my fingers under her arch just once or twice to show her I meant business, the muscles of my arm working hard to hold her still.

She was squealing for me to stop when Aaron and Jenna came in to find us laughing on the couch in front of the TV. They looked shocked.

"Are you gonna be nice?" I laughed.

"Yes! *Stop*! Ryan!"

"Ryan! You're gonna hurt her!" Aaron yelled at me from across the room. Jen walked past toward the bedroom they shared, casting a dirty look my way.

"Does she look like she's hurt, A? We're playing, for God's sake! I barely touched her."

My hand still on her leg, I looked into her face after Aaron nodded sternly in her direction. Julia's eyes were tearing and I panicked, sitting up quickly.

"Julia, did I hurt you, honey?" I moved to her side instantly, kneeling on the floor in front of the couch.

She shook her head. "Um…only a little from laughing. I'm okay." I sighed in relief and ran a hand through my hair.

"Shit, Ryan! You stupid asshole!" Aaron yelled. "I ought to knock you on your ass!"

I ignored him. "I'm sorry. That was stupid of me, Julia. Aaron is right. I should have been more careful."

She glanced at Aaron over my shoulder and then back into my eyes. "No, I'm fine. You guys are so protective; like you're my big brothers or something."

"Or *something*," Aaron quipped. I wondered if Julia caught his tone.

My face felt hot as my skin flushed. Julia saw it, too. Her hand came out to touch my shoulder. "Ryan, I'm fine. You didn't hurt me."

I frowned. It had to have hurt her a little and I was pissed at myself for letting myself get caught up in the moment and forget how badly she was injured. "I know it had to hurt, Julia, and I'm really sorry. It won't happen again."

"Hey, we were having fun. I'm not a porcelain doll. I can take a little jostling."

"Not yet. In a month or two, maybe." She reached out and touched the side of my jaw.

"I'm *okay*," she said softly.

"Okay." I took her hand from my face and kissed the inside of her wrist as I got up and turned toward Aaron. He was walking away into the kitchen and opening the refrigerator.

"Did the folks get off okay?"

"Yeah. Dad said to call him at least every couple of days to keep him in the loop about how Jules is doing." He took two beers out and offered one to me. I walked into the kitchen and took it.

"What do you know about this other doctor? Moore, right?" Aaron asked as he opened his beer and then took a long swig.

"Not much. He's a shrink that Brighton asked to consult. I barely spoke to him." We were keeping our voices low and I glanced over my shoulder. Jenna was sitting with Julia on the couch and they were talking. Julia nodded her head before I turned my attention back to Aaron.

"The fact is we already know why she's forgotten."

I set the beer down and leaned on the counter, turning so I could see into the living room. "Yeah. They think that if she talks to someone else, the memories may come back gradually. It'd be a huge shock to have everything come rushing back all at once."

Aaron stared for a long moment without speaking.

"*What*?" I asked.

He shrugged. "Nothing, bro'. Just…how are *you*?"

Why was everyone asking that?

"Fine. It's hard. I have to keep reminding myself she doesn't know me anymore."

"She'll remember you, dude. You two are sickening. There is no way she's not going to remember, Ryan." He took another drink of the beer. "But I meant, how are you dealing with the loss...?"

I cut him off. "Aaron, can we just focus on Julia? That's all I can think about. That, and getting to graduation."

"I'm thinking about proposing to Jenna, but I'm worried about the effect on Jules," Aaron said quietly.

"Julia wouldn't want you to put it on hold. She loves both of you and she's been saying for years that you should have a ring on Jenna's hand. After all, you've been with her longer than we've been together. It's way overdue, man. You're lucky she hasn't kicked your ass to the curb by now." I smirked at him.

"It's all that good sexin' I give her," he joked.

"Spare me the raunchy details!" I'd heard them humping and bumping in the room next to mine too many times to count and it wasn't an experience that I enjoyed. "Try a little tenderness. She might appreciate it."

"Okay, I hear a sappy song in there somewhere. Pretty soon the angels will drop down from heaven playing their harps and violins! I won't believe that you two don't get down and dirty sometimes, little brother."

"Shut the hell up," I replied and we both laughed.

"What are you making me for dinner, honey?" Aaron said loudly and knocked me in the shoulder before he went to sit in the big arm chair at one end of the couch.

"Yeah, what are you making for dinner?" Julia raised her eyebrows at me as I followed him in. She was so cute when she teased me and my heart sped up. I loved spending time with all of our friends, but if I had my way, I'd have spent the entire evening alone with her.

"Ah Jules…too bad you're not up to it. I could really use some home cooking!" Aaron said. Jen moved onto his lap and she shoved him in the ribs. "Hey!" He protested and reached up to pull her down for a kiss. "Your talents in other areas make up for it, babe."

Jenna laughed and Aaron wound his hand in the back of her hair.

"I would if I had the use of both of my arms, Aaron. What did I used to make?" Julia's eyes followed the loving gestures between the two and I wondered what she was thinking.

"Everything," I answered for him.

There was a knock at the door. It would be Ellie and Harris.

"Looks like the gang's all here," Jenna said from behind me. "Now we can decide on the food. What do you feel like, Julia?"

"Um, I'm not that hungry, so whatever you all want is fine by me."

"Julia!" Ellie called from the doorway. Harris smirked as he passed, obviously mocking his girlfriend's over-enthusiasm.

"Good to see you, Harris."

"We wouldn't miss this, Ryan. Thanks."

The girls gathered around Julia in the living room and Aaron, Harris and I sat at the kitchen table.

We ordered Chinese from a local dive that delivered, and sat around the living room with plates on our laps and three open bottles of wine. I watched Julia closely as she laughed and talked with everyone, carefully listening to the interaction for any signs of her memory. She asked Jenna a bunch of questions about how she met Aaron; and Ellie prattled on about Harris, her job in Los Angeles and things we all did in college.

When everyone was finished, I gathered up the plates and took them to the kitchen while Ellie followed with the empty cartons.

"Hey, how are you holding up?" she asked quietly.

"Good. I'm good." I rinsed the plates and stacked them in one side of the sink as we talked.

"Julia seems to be doing fine. She's curious about things. Especially you."

I stopped what I was doing and turned to face her. "What did she say?"

"She wants to know about your relationship with her. She senses that you're not just friends, kiddo."

"I told her we were close friends. Close, Ellie. As in best friends."

"I know all that, but she keeps coming back to it. Jen is having a hard time not telling her about you. Everything about Aaron is connected to you."

"Not everything. Jen and Aaron were together before I met Julia."

"I know that, but you get what I mean. How does she act around you when you're alone?"

"Sometimes relaxed, sometimes nervous, always curious. I know she feels there's something more between us. I'm not great at acting indifferent where she's concerned, and it's a tangible force that pulls us together."

"Are you sure that pretending is the right thing to do? Maybe you should just tell her, help her deal with the pain of losing the baby and then get on with things. It could hurt her if you pull away."

I took a deep breath. It was nothing that I hadn't considered. "She'll remember when she's ready. It's not about me, it's about her. She just needs time without pressure. I'm not pulling away necessarily. I'm just not forcing anything."

"Hey! What are you guys whispering about in there?" Jen called.

"Nothing! We're just cleaning up!" Ellie answered and we walked back to the living room.

Julia had her legs curled under her on the couch, looking sleepy with her head leaning on her right arm. Aaron had Jenna back on his lap in the chair and Ellie went to join Harris in front of the fireplace. There was plenty of room on the couch next to Julia, but I chose, instead, to sit on the floor in front of her and lean my back against the couch.

"So? Let's play a game or something," Aaron ventured. "Quarters, Pictionary or Trivial Pursuit?"

"No quarters for Julia, Aaron. Sorry."

"Yeah and she'd kick our ass on Pictionary," Harris laughed at the obvious.

I felt Julia lean toward me slightly. Her warm breath rushed over the skin at the back of my neck, causing goose bumps to rush over the rest of my body.

"Truth or dare?" she asked softly.

I turned to look at her, searching for some sort of recognition before I spoke. That was our love game and we hardly ever played the vanilla version with the others. It was so intimate, so personal. *Just ours*. Even if I wanted to try, it wasn't a good idea, and I seriously didn't want to crack that open in front of the others. "I don't think so. Not tonight," I shook my head as I answered quietly.

The others watched our interaction in silence, even though they couldn't hear what we were saying. She leaned back and sighed. "Why not?" she insisted.

"Julia, I know what you're trying to do. Quit it."

It was like everyone else disappeared from the room as her eyes burned into mine. "What am I trying to do?"

"Get me…all of us, to tell you things that you want to find out about your past. Things you can't remember." *And I can't play that game with you without getting aroused.* She looked down but didn't speak, so I continued. "If you could remember, then you'd know that I only take truth about ten percent of the time anyway, so it isn't likely that you'll find out anything."

"You're not the only one here, Ryan. Some of the others will take truth as their option."

"No," I said firmly. "End of discussion."

"You know, you're not my father," she said sharply.

"No, thank God. But, I'm looking out for what's best for you. Please trust me, Julia." I reached out and wrapped my hand around hers. "Just give yourself time, babe."

"Babe?" she questioned as her right eyebrow shot up. She called me on the endearment and I couldn't take it back. I dropped my forehead to rest on the top of her hand that I held in mine and let out my breath before returning my gaze slowly to hers.

"Aaron called you babe at the hospital and you thought nothing of it. Why is it different with me?" My voice low and taking on a deeper tone against my will.

She bit her lip and swallowed. "It just *is*."

I ripped my eyes away from her face.

"So…it looks like its Trivial Pursuit! Get the damn thing set up, Aaron. Ellie, is there anymore wine?"

~4~

Julia ~

"JULIA?" RYAN CALLED from the other room. My heart thumped at the sound of his voice calling my name. The past week had been scary, wondrous, unfamiliar, yet...*familiar*. It was weird. I was with three people I barely knew, but I felt so comfortable, at home, taken care of, and loved. Ryan insisted I take his room and I felt incredibly guilty, though it was eerily comforting to have his scent around me at night. When Dr. Brighton said I could lose the sling and start moving around a little more, I'd insist on taking the couch.

Sighing deeply, I glanced around the room for the 20th time in a week, trying to learn whatever I could from what I found there. Material things didn't seem to matter to Ryan. His wardrobe consisted of jeans and t-shirts, scrubs and sneakers. He had a few nice dress shirts and three pair of dress pants hanging in the closet. Two pair of dress shoes rested on the floor. Ryan's keyboard was expensive, but I sensed it was more about function than status. That, and the guitar resting against the wall in the corner, suggested to me that he was a serious musician. I longed to hear him play, to watch his long fingers stroke the keys. Something told me he was brilliant.

Other than his desk, the medical reference books and laptop, there wasn't much else. It was conspicuously lacking photos or other art adorning the walls. I could only guess that he was so focused on school that he didn't have time to care one way or the other about aesthetics. From what I'd seen, he spent most of his time studying. So dedicated. So real.

There was an intensity that went beyond friendship and I was strangely amazed and excited by it. He was so beautiful, he stole my breath away and his gentle teasing made him more and more endearing as the days passed. We bantered with an easy camaraderie but with a sizzling undercurrent that never went away. I felt like I'd known him forever, but was always so excited to see him. I looked forward to every moment that we spent together and missed him when he wasn't home. Our talks had come to be the best part of my days, but I found myself wanting more…just *wanting*. It left me uneasy; feeling slightly vulnerable and on edge. I thought about him constantly and yearned to know the truth about our past. I was sitting on his bed, lost in my thoughts, when he knocked on the doorframe and poked his head around the edge.

"Honey, are you okay? Ready to go?" His voice held the concern that was mirrored on his face. Ryan came into the room and hesitated in front of me. I glanced up, taking in his casual dress of jeans and a long sleeved t-shirt with a monotone graphic design down the left side and sleeve. Totally hot; a soft sheen of stubble on his face only made him sexier. How much testosterone must he have to grow that beard in only a few hours? The thought made my body quicken and I blushed.

"I'm fine." I lifted an eyebrow at him in question and smiled. "No hospital today?"

He shrugged and grinned at me. "Well, I can work if I want, but I thought we'd hang out after your appointments." He bent down and slid an arm around me to lift me to my feet.

"Ryan, I can stand up on my own." He had the grace to flush, letting me go and instantly I regretted my rash words.

"Yes, but I know it still hurts getting up and down."

"Does it?" I asked. He just looked at me, his eyes narrowing. He didn't like it when I tried to hide my discomfort, so I decided to change the subject. "Won't you be bored waiting around?"

"Nah." He shook his head slightly. "I'm taking my laptop. I have some research to do," he dismissed my objection easily. I should have known that he'd find some way to work at least part of the day.

Ryan's fingers spread out gently on my back as he led me down the hall and into the living room. He grabbed my long black wool coat and helped me put it on my right arm and draped it over my left shoulder. "You'll get rid of this damn sling today, don't worry."

"It can't be soon enough. I promised Aaron blueberry muffins and he reminds me daily." Ryan grinned as he put on his own coat. I reached out to run my hand along the front of the soft leather. The scent and supple softness under my fingers darted through my head. His hand closed warmly over mine and my eyes flew up to his.

"Julia? What is it?" he asked; an unspoken knowledge in his eyes. *Are you remembering?* I struggled for the elusive flash of something that would connect me to our past, but it was fleeting. It was gone before it could solidify in my mind. *Damn it!* I closed my eyes for a split second.

I shook my head slightly. "Um, nothing, I guess. What did you have in mind for later?"

"We'll play it by ear, okay? Let's see how tired you get."

"Yeah, sure. That's fine." He was so damn overprotective but I really wanted to get out of the apartment for awhile. "I think I'll be okay. It will feel good to do something."

We were going to see Dr. Brighton for a checkup and then I had another appointment with Dr. Moore. *Dr. Moore.* I wasn't sure what to make of him. He asked questions designed to get me thinking, but mostly all we'd discussed were things I *did* remember. I didn't understand how that was going to solve my current problem. We talked about my childhood, my parents and my friends growing up. I didn't get it, but maybe there was a method to his madness. It was too early to tell. To give him credit, he'd only asked me how everything made me feel twice, a typical shrink thing to do...*how did it make me feel that I forgot most of my college experience, my career and my best friend? Okay, seriously?*

I huffed and Ryan caught it. He opened the door for me and waited, his eyes skirting over my face. "What?"

"I'll tell you on the way."

Aaron was sprawled on the couch watching TV. "Bye, Aaron," I called over my shoulder.

"Have fun," he threw back. "Hey, Ryan! Can we hit the gym later? Do you have time?"

"Not sure. I'll call you."

Surely the two men spent a lot of time working out. Aaron was bigger, but Ryan was leaner with more clearly defined muscles in his arms, legs and ass. I let my imagination run wild beneath his clothes. I could see the outline of his pecs through the t-shirt he was wearing and his broad shoulders and lean hips provided plenty of food for thought. Obviously his abs would be clearly defined as well. I swallowed and hoped he didn't catch me staring. He didn't seem to notice, thankfully. Heat infused my cheeks and I pressed the back of my hand to my face while Ryan closed the car door after me, walking around the front of the car to slide into the driver's seat beside me.

He shoved the key into the ignition and glanced toward me before putting the car into gear. "Well?" he asked expectantly.

"What?" It was chilly outside and I shivered. Ryan reached forward to turn on the heater. Always so in tune with what I needed.

"What were you thinking about inside? You said you'd tell me in the car."

I smiled, taking in the seriousness of his expression. He looked worried. "Oh, I was just thinking about my last session with Dr. Moore."

He pulled onto the expressway, quickly accelerating and looking over his shoulder to merge into traffic. "Yes, *and*?" He was impatient.

"Nothing, really. It just seems sort of useless talking about things I remember. I thought the point was to help me remember what I forgot, not take a trip down memory lane."

"Well…he probably wants to ease you into it. Just give it a little time, okay?"

I sighed. "Ryan, there really isn't anything wrong with me. I mean, I'm not freaking out, I'm not crazy…do I really need a shrink?"

His brows dropped over his eyes as he considered my question. "Julia, I understand your frustration, but I don't think he's trying to be patronizing. Tell him you want to concentrate on the other stuff."

"Why can't you just *tell me*, Ryan? I feel…ugh!" I sighed and threw myself against the seat.

"You need to remember on your own."

"In the entryway when I touched your coat, I had a flash. I remembered how it felt and smelled. I saw it in my head for a second but then it vanished before I could get the whole picture."

"At least you're getting something. I believe that it will come back, sweetheart."

I was frustrated and angry. I couldn't remember even something as simple as a leather jacket. "What happened that you don't want me to know about? Are you a serial killer or something? Was I?"

He burst out laughing which only pissed me off even more. "Hardly!" When I looked out the passenger window and didn't answer, Ryan sobered. "It's only been two weeks since the accident. Give yourself time to heal. You're expecting too much, too soon," he said gently.

I didn't speak to him for the remainder of the drive and when we pulled into the hospital parking lot, he helped me out of the car, pulling me into his arms and kissed my temple. I closed my eyes and breathed him in. He smelled like cologne and soap, fresh and musky. I relished the feel of his warm lips on my forehead. His mouth was soft as it moved when he spoke.

"I'm sorry that I laughed. That was insensitive of me. You've been going through a lot and this whole thing is confusing and frustrating…but it's going to be okay, babe." His hand rubbed up and down on my back and I longed to wrap my arm around him and lay my head on his chest. "It's going to be okay. We'll go have some fun after all this necessary bullshit, I promise."

My heart was doing somersaults at his nearness, my body reacting in all sorts of delicious ways. I honestly didn't understand how I could've been this close to him and just been his friend. He was too amazing in so many ways and he really cared about how I felt, which was a lethal combination.

Fucking irresistible.

He kissed my forehead again then moved his mouth down to my cheek. His breath washed over me in a wave of heat and I finally let myself lean into him. I had an overwhelming urge to lift my chin so I could feel those pliant lips on mine. My right hand curled around the fabric of his shirt underneath his open coat. Ryan pulled back and brushed his fingers along my jaw. "We'll be late. We have to go."

I swallowed and nodded. "Okay."

He took my right hand and we walked into the hospital and to Dr. Brighton's office without speaking. I trusted Ryan implicitly, feeling safe and protected whenever he was with me. I saw his perfect profile out of the corner of my eye and realized I wanted him to be more than my best friend. *Much more.*

*****

Two hours later I was sitting in Dr. Moore's office waiting to start our session, and Ryan was in the waiting room working on one of his cases. I rubbed my right arm with my left, thankful that the sling that kept me confined was finally gone. My shoulder was stiff but the only pain I had left was my still-healing ribs. It would still be several weeks until they were completely healed but the tape had been replaced with an elastic girdle that fastened with Velcro. It was tight and I felt like it added ten pounds underneath my knit shirt. Worst of all, I'd still need help getting it on and off.

Poor Jenna. She'd become my nursemaid, helping me with bathing and dressing and always being so gracious. She was funny, very kind and witty. I liked her a lot, but felt helpless and ridiculous that I needed her so much. I never realized how much

I took simple things for granted. Not being able to take care of myself was completely humiliating.

Dr. Moore looked at me apologetically and shrugged. I used the time he was on the phone to take in his dark hair and business suit. He looked polished and professional, handsome in a stiff sort of way. He had a pleasant face and easygoing demeanor that probably worked well in his profession. I found myself comparing his slicked back hair with a wild shock of golden brown. He was shorter than Ryan by several inches and stockier, his neck thicker and his skin ruddier. His features weren't as classically beautiful, and his eyes deeper set. I flushed when I realized what I was doing.

"Listen, Dave, I have a patient. I'll talk to you later. Goodbye." He hung up the phone and then folded his hands on his desk as he leaned forward on his elbows. "I'm so sorry, Julia. That was rude."

"No, that's okay."

"How are you feeling?"

I cleared my throat. "Still sore, but so much better."

"That's excellent, but I meant emotionally. How are you handling things and how is it staying with your friends?" He smiled warmly, listening attentively.

"It's good. Ryan is very protective and Aaron is always sweet. Jenna has been so helpful, but I feel bad for her; I'm such a burden. I do get uptight at times and feel guilty about intruding and I hate that I can't remember. I want to know them, you know what I mean?" I was rambling.

"Sure. That's understandable. It must be disorienting."

"Um…I'd classify it more as frustrating. It's worse because no one will tell me anything. Conversations get stilted. It's not fair that they have to watch everything they say and do. It makes them uncomfortable and I hate it. Why is it necessary?"

"We all feel it's in your best interest. You'll remember, if and when you're ready. No one wants to force or prod."

"How would you feel if you had a huge hole in your life and no one would give you anything to go on? I mean *eight* years? It…hurts to have lost so much."

"I can only imagine. I'm sorry that you're going through that, but I do believe that you'll get at least part of it back over time. Try not to put so much pressure on yourself." His eyes narrowed slightly as he leaned back in his chair and tented his hands in front of him. "Is there anything in particular that you want to talk about today, Julia? Anything you feel I can help you with?"

I sighed. "Can you get Ryan to tell me what the hell is going on? I am constantly racking my brain, willing myself to remember. It feels like there's more between us."

"What makes you say that?"

"Just…everything. It's a feeling. The way he looks at me and takes care of me. The tone in his voice changes when he talks to me. How he makes me feel."

"How is that?" he asked.

I hesitated. My feelings for Ryan were personal. There were many complicated layers, so instead of trying to articulate them all, I picked the most obvious and unobtrusive one. "Hot," I blurted out, embarrassed.

Dr. Moore smiled slightly. "What do you think that means?"

I started to feel like we were going in circles and it left me feeling tense. *Shit. Didn't I just say it?* "I find him extremely attractive."

"Have you told him how you feel?" he asked, tangibly hesitant.

"No." I struggled for the words to explain. "I mean…if he really does only see me as a friend, I'd be humiliated. Can you please tell me and save all this angst?"

He completely ignored my prodding.

"Don't you think it's possible that the new living situation, the close proximity and how much you rely on him could cause those feelings? You're both very attractive people and I don't think Ryan is oblivious to that either, Julia. It's natural in this situation, him being one of your caretakers; you both might feel that way."

Ugh! Ryan my caretaker? Was I in a fucking nursing home, now?

"Of course. I'm not retarded, for God's sake, but I just feel that with Ryan, it's more than responsibility or even friendship. More than sexual attraction. I don't see him as a nursemaid. Far from it; and he'd be pissed if I did." His eyes widened at my presumption of Ryan's feelings. "Do we really have to do this? Why do I have to explain? Telling you that I find Ryan attractive isn't going to make me remember. And, it feels like it's something that I should only share with him…when I'm ready."

"Are you comfortable enough to talk to him about it?"

I shrugged. Honestly, the prospect freaked me out, like I was baring my soul. What if we really *were* only friends? I'd make a huge fool of myself and it would hurt me more than I was willing to face. "Er…I'm still working that out."

The doctor nodded. I tried to read something on his face, to figure out what he knew. Of course, he talked to Ryan and Gabriel. They were both doctors on my case. At least, Ryan might as well have been, considering he was almost out of med school. "Well, he's so accomplished and I feel very proud of him," I hedged tentatively. "Like I have a personal stake in him. It fills me up in ways I don't understand."

"He has done very well. Don't you think, as his friend, that you'd feel that way, too?"

Ugh! Always more open-ended questions and never any damn answers. "Of course," I said in defeat. This wasn't going anywhere. "But not so intensely."

"And what vibes are you getting off of him, Julia?" he asked cautiously.

"He's protective and attentive. He takes care of everything I need. He touches me and it's like an electric current runs between us. I think he feels it too. At first I was stunned, but now…I want it. He seems…cautious about getting closer to me, and he refuses to tell me about our past."

"Well, he's very intelligent, Julia. We've discussed this and Ryan doesn't want to do anything that might cause the memory loss to become permanent. He's practically a doctor himself and he agrees." I rolled my eyes involuntarily, and Dr. Moore smirked. "What do you think will help you remember?"

Not more psycho-babble bullshit, that's for sure.

"I don't know. If I did, don't you think I'd *do* it? No offense, but I don't think therapy is going to be a fucking miracle cure."

"Julia, there is no need to get belligerent. I know you're upset and frustrated. I'm here to help you." He stood and moved around his desk to sit on the edge in front of me, one leg hitched up and hanging over the corner. It felt like he was intruding, too close and, suddenly, I was remembering a line from that movie with Patrick Swayze. *This is my dance space; this is your dance space. You don't come into mine, and I don't go into yours.* I cocked my head at the thought, and picked at the fabric of my jeans so he wouldn't see the amusement dancing on my face. He seemed harmless enough. Very nice, but so damn patronizing.

When I didn't answer, he continued. "You're probably right, you don't need to be analyzed, but I'll be available if you need to talk. We won't need to meet in the office anymore. You can just call me if you need to talk and we can do so as friends. I don't want you to feel pressured from anyone, including me."

Okay, what? "Uh…sure, I suppose that would be okay."

He smiled. "Good. So call me Spence."

"Spence…?" I tried it out. It sounded so damn goofy, I wanted to laugh out loud. Old men in plaid pants were named Spence.

"That wasn't so hard, was it?" he asked easily and smiled.

"Totally," I said flatly, and he grinned at my honesty.

"Before we end today, I wanted to ask if you've had any memories of your job?"

I shook my head. "Not really. Ellie told me that I worked for Vogue, which seems surreal. That is amazing in and of itself; but I don't remember anything about the work. Which, considering I don't remember my education, is probably a good thing," I said sardonically. "Hmmph!" I let out my breath.

"Just take it one day at a time. I'll let Dr. Brighton know that you won't need any more formal sessions, but please do call me, Julia. If it's okay, I'll call to check on you once in a while."

"Sure, I suppose."

"Have you talked with your parents or Dr. Matthews?"

"Just about daily. Gabe talks to Ryan about me too, so he gets a double dose. Poor thing."

He smiled and nodded knowingly.

"Yes. Do you have a ride home?"

The corners of my mouth lifted. "Ryan is waiting."

"Of course."

I stood and picked up my coat, but Dr. Moore stood and took it from me, holding it up so that I could slip my arms inside.

"Thank you. I appreciate your help." I offered him my hand and he used it to pull me into a loose hug.

"It's been my pleasure. It's been nice getting to know you."

"You, too...*Spence*." I forced the word out.

"Have a good afternoon." He put a hand on my shoulder sliding it over my back and patted me gently.

I offered my thanks again and proceeded to the waiting room. Just as I had pictured, Ryan was bent over the laptop with a legal pad on the table to his right, writing notes down at the same time.

He looked up as I approached. "Oh, hey! How'd it go?"

"Well...I'm not crazy." I grinned. He smiled back, powering down his computer and gathering up his things to put them neatly away in his bag.

He laughed softly. "No shit. We didn't need to pay some jackass a hundred and fifty dollars an hour to tell us that."

He made me smile. "Yeah, he's not that big of a jackass. He's nice, but it felt like the Spanish Inquisition." Ryan stood up and threw on his coat and hoisted his laptop bag over his shoulder.

"I'm sure. Ready? You can tell me about it over lunch. I thought we'd go to Downtown Crossing, maybe get lunch at Goodlife. Sound okay?"

I nodded since I had no idea about either place. Obviously, from what he said, we'd been there together before. My eyes stung and I blinked rapidly in rebellion to the possibility of tears. *Another thing I can't remember.*

It was a beautiful early April day, but the air was still brisk and the breeze made it even colder, despite the brilliant sunlight. I dug into my purse and pulled out my sunglasses to slip them on. "Yeah. Sounds good."

"I don't want to over-do it."

"Can you please stop worrying? I'm feeling so much better, Ryan. Really."

"No. I can't stop; so get used to it," he teased lightly.

I nudged his shoulder. "No moody ass today? I like it." I was smiling so big my face hurt. I was seriously looking forward to time alone with Ryan. Maybe he'd be less guarded and I'd have a better opportunity to find out more about my past and our relationship.

His arm slipped around my waist to pull me close as we walked.

"No moody ass today." He laughed again and I loved the sound. It made my heart thud and I slipped my now sling-free left arm around him in return. It felt…perfect. "I'm feeling pretty happy today. And *very* thankful." His arm around me tightened and I never wanted him to let me go.

The mood was light, but I sensed an undercurrent of deeper meaning in his statement. I was enjoying Ryan's happy mood and was looking forward to the afternoon, so I didn't push.

At the restaurant, he chose a booth along one side of the bar. There were partitions of cherry wood which would make it easier to talk. It was fairly busy and bustling, with soft rock music playing in the background. My eyes searched for something familiar. Ryan slid my coat off and hung it up on the hook on the outside of the partition and did the same with his.

I winched slightly as I moved in the booth and Ryan's eyes narrowed as he watched.

"Stop," I admonished. "I'm fine."

He leaned back against the booth and studied me with intent blue eyes. "I didn't say anything."

"I know what you're thinking. Quit it."

He leaned forward and reached across the table toward me. Without thinking, I automatically placed my hand in his and his fingers closed around mine. "What exactly am I thinking?" His tone was teasing and one eyebrow shot up. His mouth twitched as he tried to hide a smile.

"I can handle a little pain."

"Hmmm," was all he said.

The waiter came, gave us menus and took our drink orders before leaving us alone to peruse the offerings. I decided it was time to start the conversation.

"Ryan, have we been here before?"

"Yeah, a few times," he said quietly, not glancing up from the menu. My heart fell because I couldn't remember. The look on his face told me he was processing the same realization. "Mostly at night. Jen likes the DJ. The food is good, too."

His disappointment was obvious, but he quickly hid it, glancing up at me as he continued talking. "What do you feel like?"

"Maybe the hummus wrap. It sounds good."

"Yeah, it is." He closed his menu and reached for his water glass.

"Can we come some evening? I mean, it might be more familiar then," I said hopefully. He studied me carefully, his features softened and he nodded.

"Sure. So tell me about your session with Dr. Moore." His eyes darted to mine. "If you want," he added.

"It was nothing really. More questions. We came to the conclusion that I don't need a therapist."

Both of Ryan's eyebrows lifted in surprise. "Really? I figured he'd have you coming in for a while."

"Nope. He's taking a new tack. Less formal, I suppose."

"In what way?" Ryan tensed slightly. "Um, uh…what did you guys talk about?"

I bristled. If I wanted Ryan to be honest with me, I'd need to be honest with him, too. Just as I was about to speak, the waiter came and took our order. Ryan ordered my wrap and BBQ steak tips for himself. His illustrated practice at it suggested the closeness that I felt between us. He picked up his beer and waited for me to continue.

"Well, I told him how frustrated I am about what's been lost. Especially the stuff with you," I said hesitantly, watching for a flicker of something that would confirm my suspicions. My heart tightened as I watched his reaction. He brought his eyes to meet mine and again reached for my hand. "I told him that his questions did little to help me remember and I wished someone would tell me something."

"And…his response?" His words were carefully placed, guarded.

"That it was for my own good. Basically the same thing you've said. But I'm so tired of hearing that, Ryan!"

His thumb rubbed the top of my hand over and over. "I know. I'd tell you if I thought it was what you needed, but I won't do anything that could hurt you. You believe that, don't you?"

I knew it was true, but that didn't make it any easier. "Yes," I sighed. "I can deal with not knowing about some of it, but with you…Ryan, I want to know about *us*."

He looked away and out into the restaurant. "Like what? Things we do when we hang out? I'll tell you anything you want about me, Julia. We hung out a lot in college, we went to concerts and parties…took some trips together. Sometimes the others came with us. All of us…we're pretty close."

He wasn't going to do more than give me a rundown of events and try to bury anything real in layers and layers of superficial facts. He was trying to distract me by confusing the issue, trying to take the focus off of anything remotely personal.

"What kind of trips?"

"Ski trips or camping. Spring break in Tahoe or Cancun. Stuff like that. Sporting events, concerts. Lots of things." The list came out flat, uncomfortable and hesitant.

"Yes. I guess with all the history there would be quite a bit," I said quietly. Finally, he turned back to face me, the muscle in his jaw working as he clenched his teeth. It appeared this was as difficult for him as it was for me. I sensed sadness behind his eyes that went beyond the frustration I felt.

"What about your music? Did you play for me?"

"Yeah. Often."

I sensed the answer before he even said it.

"You have a beautiful singing voice, Julia. I love listening to you sing as much as you like hearing me play. Music was something we shared. I haven't played in weeks."

My throat tightened at his admission. It was something.

"What about after you came to Boston? Were we still in touch? Did we still see each other?"

"Julia..." He stopped and ran a hand through his hair. It seemed a nervous habit when he was agitated. "Sure. Not as much, but we're still friends, aren't we? Doesn't that tell you we kept in touch?"

"Is that what we are really?" I asked a little too sharply even to my own ears, the impatience I felt seeping through my words. "Friends?"

"Always," he answered seriously. "I thought that was already established."

I nodded, but I was disappointed. I wanted to hear something deeper and I figured it showed in my expression and could be heard in the shortness of my tone. I instantly regretted it. I wanted today to be special.

"Then what's with this doubt? Can we just have fun today, please?" His words echoed my thoughts and I nodded in response. Ryan visibly relaxed. "You didn't tell me the rest of what happened with Dr. Moore."

Okay, so he moved the subject away from where I wanted to go with it. "He wants to be my friend, too."

Ryan didn't speak for a moment, his cobalt eyes contemplative, like he wasn't sure what to say.

"What? Like how?" he asked almost against his will. It made my heart swell but I decided not to press him for more and instead let myself bask in his obvious concern. I wanted to feel closer, to get him to share more, not build walls that would cause him to back away.

I cocked my head to one side and shrugged. "Hell if I know. Maybe he can join us on camping trips and shit," I said with false sarcasm that wasn't lost on Ryan. He knew I was baiting him, and I fought not to laugh at his incredulous expression. I bit my lip and looked up through half-closed eyes. Deep down, I was certain there was more than what he was telling me. I wanted to test him, if ever so slightly.

"Pfft," he joined in the teasing, a beautiful smile spreading across his face. My heart soared and I laughed. "Not if you expect me to be there." He rolled his eyes.

"Would you let me go without you, Matthews?"

"Not a snowball's chance in hell." I let the laughter bubbling in my chest, out in full force. That would have to be good enough for now. It was very telling when he grinned in response.

"Wow. You must really be a *good friend,* Ryan."

"Hmmph," he snorted and I laughed out loud again.

I leaned back as the waiter came and set our food down in front of us. My stomach rumbled as I picked up my fork.

"Put it this way…I'll do what is necessary to keep your cute little ass out of trouble."

"Spence called you my *caretaker*, if you can believe that."

"Is that so? Hope you set him straight."

"As a matter of fact, yeah," I said as I sliced off a piece of the wrap, wondering if Ryan picked up my use of Spence's first name. "Do you really think my ass is cute?"

"So it's Spence now, is it?"

I shrugged and swallowed the first bite. "Like I said, friends, but don't worry. I only have room for one over bearing ass of a best friend and it appears the position's been filled." My jaw jutted out and I struggled not to smile.

"Good answer." His eyes sparkled with amusement as he finally dove into his lunch.

Ryan~

Julia was watching TV with Jen, Aaron was at the gym and I was stuck in front of the damn computer yet again. I'd called my brother earlier to tell him that I couldn't join him despite really needing the exercise.

Julia and I spent the afternoon roaming through the shops downtown. We had a really nice time, but being near her was taking a toll on my control. I found myself starting to touch her several times and caught myself. It was harder than hell not to pull her close, press her body to mine and kiss her like I'd done a million times before. Her laughter sucked me in and I was losing my resolve to keep my distance. The cool air brought a blush to her cheeks and the wind whipped the hair off of her beautiful face, now almost completely void of bruises. My hands itched to wind in those silken strands more and more as the day progressed, a mixture of heaven and hell.

Sequestered in my room on the pretense of studying, I tried to get my bearings. If I joined the girls now, I'd pull Julia onto my lap and wrap her in my arms. I missed her as much as I did when she and I had been separated, but maybe it was worse having her this close and not being able to make love to her or show her my feelings. I was in agony.

I glanced at the clock. Just past ten PM. I pushed my laptop back on the desk, put my head down in my hands and closed my eyes. They were burning from looking at the computer and I was tired. Julia must be, too. I wasn't sure how long I stayed like that, not moving when a soft knock on the door lifted my head.

"Yes?"

The door cracked open slightly. "Ryan? Are you hungry?" Julia's soft voice preceded her into the darkened room. She had changed into flannel pajama pants and a small white t-shirt. Her hair was in a knot at the top of her head. She looked so warm and inviting. I couldn't help remembering the nights I'd peeled those very clothes off of her luscious body and made passionate love to her for hours on end.

"Uh, sure. I could eat, but don't put yourself out on my account, honey."

"Aaron called and hinted that he wanted me to cook." She chuckled gently. "He knows I got my straight-jacket off today," she said, a smile still curving her full lips. My eyes stared as she licked them once. "So…any requests?"

I turned in my chair as she lurked in the doorway. "Didn't Aaron tell you what he wanted?"

"Uh uh. Jen said he'd eat anything."

I ran a hand through my hair. "Yes. That's a fact." She looked so alluring, all I wanted was to gather her close and bury my face in her hair. "Um, well then…can you make Pad Thai?"

She smiled. "Okay. You look tired, sweetie." That sweet voice melted around me like honey, and my heart thumped rapidly inside my body at the endearment. *Maybe she does remember me.*

"I am. Aren't you? We had a big day."

"A little. I'll bring yours in when it's ready."

"I can come out there."

"I think you should have your room back, Ryan. I'll take the couch from now on."

"No," I dismissed without a second's hesitation.

"Do you always have to argue? I can fit better and I'm feeling much better now."

"No," I said again. "Julia…" But this time it was her turn to dismiss me.

"We'll discuss it in a few minutes. I have to see what you've got in the kitchen."

I smiled and rubbed the back of my neck tiredly. I'd given Jenna a grocery list so that Julia would have what she needed, in anticipation of an occasion such as this.

"What?" She caught my smile and hesitated on her turn from the room.

"Nothing. You'll probably find everything that you're looking for in there. Just a hunch."

Her face split into a beautiful smile. "You think? I must have a guardian angel," she scoffed.

"No, I do. Jenna."

"Oh. That was sweet of her."

The outside apartment door burst open loudly from the other room. "Juuulllllliiiiaaaaa!" Aaron called. "I hear you're healed, honey, and I'm hungry!"

Julia burst out laughing, but stopped short, gathering her arms around her ribs in a grimace. I moved toward her and reached for her, feeling the elastic bands of the brace around her middle, tucked up against the lower edge of her bra. "Pretty sexy, eh?" she said and rolled her eyes.

"Yes." I looked down into her deep green eyes, overwhelmed by the need to take her mouth with mine. She had no clue how she affected me. If she were wearing a burlap sack, I'd think she was the sexiest woman alive. Touching her caused my body to spring into action uncomfortably. I tried to hide it and returned to the desk, shutting the computer down and plunging the room in darkness, giving myself time to get it under control.

"Do you want to help? Or, just hang out with me while I cook?" Her hopeful voice came through the dark. I realized that it had been more than three hours that I'd been locked away in my bedroom.

"Lead the way," I said and followed her into the kitchen. Aaron came forward to hug her. "Aaron, easy, she still has some pain."

"Dude, please." His arms enfolded her small form gently. "Did you have a good day today? Jen said you went out after your appointments."

"Yes, it was a nice day." Her eyes met mine as I leaned on the breakfast bar. "Fun." She moved to the refrigerator and took out some chicken, eggs, scallions, garlic, tamarind paste and cilantro. "Ryan? Are the noodles up here?" She pointed to a cabinet above the sink where she'd arranged all of the pasta, rice and canned goods when we'd first moved in the summer before med school. I nodded and got them down so she wouldn't hurt herself.

Julia gathered some other items, placing them on the counter, then filled a cup with water and put it in the microwave to boil. When it was finished heating, she dropped some of the tamarind paste into it. I'd seen her make Pad Thai so many times; I probably could have made it myself.

Jenna and Aaron perched on the stools at the counter while Julia started chopping the scallions and I filled a glass bowl that I'd retrieved from beneath the counter with hot water. I opened the rice noodles and plunged them into the water to soak.

Julia threw a glance at me and smiled as she worked. "Hmmm. If I didn't know better, I'd say we'd been here before. Jenna, thank you for the finely stocked kitchen."

"Are you kidding? These two made the list and I was happy to do it as long I don't have to cook." She tossed her blonde hair over her shoulder and Aaron patted her on her rear.

"Hmmm…anyone want tofu?" Julia glanced up from her chopping to ask.

I took out a cereal bowl and a fork and placed them next to the eggs. "Not necessary for me. You guys?" I asked the others.

After it was agreed that we didn't need tofu and I'd pulled the wok out of the drawer underneath the oven, I took two beers from the refrigerator and handed one to Aaron. Jenna shot me a look. I smiled and took the hint, handing her the one I'd just opened, turned and grabbed another. Julia would probably take a pain pill before bed, so I found a bottle of Perrier and poured it into a glass. I reached into the refrigerator for a lime and placed it on the cutting board.

Julia sank down on her haunches to rummage through one of the cabinets at the same time as I cut a wedge from the lime and squeezed it into her glass. The rest would go into the meal. "Don't hurt yourself, Julia. I can get everything out."

"I'm fine, Ryan. Except…no peanut oil."

"Oh, hell. Does that mean you can't make it?" I was seriously disappointed and immediately decided to send Aaron to the store.

"I think I can improvise. Do you have peanut butter?" She opened the cabinet where it was kept and removed it along with the vegetable oil. "The only other thing I need is red pepper flakes." The spices were arranged in one of the drawers near the stove and she automatically went to it and pulled out what she needed. My eyes shot to Aaron, who nodded and smiled knowingly…Julia was remembering where everything was. Jenna winked at me and smiled as well. Elation rushed through me and I sucked in a deep breath of relief. Julia didn't even realize that she remembered.

Aaron leaned in and whispered, "One small step for man…"

"No shit," I agreed as my face split into a huge-ass grin. Julia was working over the wok, throwing the cut up chicken into the heated oil and Jen came over and ruffled my hair, kissing me on the cheek before tugging Aaron by the hand.

"Hey, dipshit," she said to him and nodded into the living room. Alone in the kitchen with Julia, I sat on one of the stools, nursing the beer while I watched her work.

She was so efficient and went about it as always…practiced and methodical. She knew exactly what she was doing and quickly drained the noodles in a strainer, tossing them to get all the water off before dumping them into the wok. She walked over and placed the bowl and two eggs in front of me without a word.

"Fork?" I asked.

She handed it to me and went back to the stove. I scrambled them with the fork before handing them back over to her.

"Thanks." Julia pushed the noodles to the side and poured the liquid eggs into the pan, quickly scrambling them before mixing it all together.

Taking it from the heat, she took the lime and squeezed it over the noodles, causing a big sizzle and then used her hands to scoop up the fresh herbs and toss them on top of everything. It smelled wonderful and after she had the meal on the plates, she placed one in front of me and turned off the stove.

She used the back of her hand to push the hair off of her face, picked up two more plates and delivered them to Aaron and Jenna on the couch. "Julia! You're my dream come true," Aaron laughed. "Thank you! It smells incredible."

"My pleasure." Her tinkling laughter was music to my ears and she came in and picked up her plate and sat down next to me. I couldn't take my eyes off of her as she raised her glass to me. "To a great day," she said, nudging my shoulder gently with her own.

I smiled, nudged her back and touched the neck of my bottle to the top of her glass. "Yes it was," I agreed.

"I really had a nice time today, Ryan. Thank you for taking time off to be with me."

"You don't have to thank me. I enjoy being with you." I filled my fork and then my mouth with the delicious meal. The flavors of the peanut, cilantro, hot peppers, garlic and chicken burst on my tongue. "Mmmm…So good, Julia."

"You work too hard." I was sitting to her right and she ran her hand up my back to squeeze my right shoulder. Her innocent touch left me wanting more.

"It's only for a little while longer," I said, trying to concentrate on what I was saying and the food in front of me, rather than how she was making me feel.

"Mmmmm. But, then you'll have residency, right?" I nodded, knowing without a doubt the next question that was going to leave her lips. I was surprised we hadn't gotten around to talking about it in the past week.

"Well, have you decided where you're going?" she asked pensively and took another sip from her glass. "And…what about Aaron?"

"He's staying in Boston; Mass General." I purposely left off particulars about my destination and left out that they would be getting married in the not too distant future. She and I were closer to it than they were, and I was afraid mention of it would be too much for her to handle.

"Yeah, and? What about you?" she asked. Her persistence certainly hadn't changed with the loss of her memory.

I took another bite to stall and by the time I had swallowed, I knew what to say. "Um…well, I've got several offers from various hospitals." *That part at least is true.* "So, I'm not sure yet." *That part isn't.*

"Oh, I see." Did she really? Did she get that I'd follow her to the end of the world and back again? All I wanted was to be with her every day for the rest of my life. Nothing else mattered anymore.

We looked at each other in serious silence and shared something unspoken. The connection was undeniable.

"This is really excellent, Julia!" Jenna called from the other room, effectively breaking the spell. "Thank you."

We continued to eat for a few minutes and she pushed her plate away with almost half of the food still on it. It was clear to me; her mind was working through what just passed between us, grasping to remember something. I felt sad for both of us. I wanted to comfort her but wasn't really sure how to do it, considering the state of the circumstances. Instead, I tried to lighten the mood.

I pulled her plate in front of me when I was finished with mine and she smirked at me. "What? It's too good to waste," I said and proceeded to finish her food using her fork. Once again, so typical of how we behaved. These were little hints that I could give her without laying it all on the line.

She yawned and I realized how late it was. "Julia, why don't you go into my room and sleep, honey? I'll clean up the kitchen."

She shook her head. "No. You work so hard and all I do is lie around. I'll clean up. I told you, I'm taking the couch from now on."

"No. You're still healing. I won't have it."

"Please Ryan," she pleaded. "You need to sleep in your own bed. I'll be fine on the couch."

"I still have to finish that research report, so I can't yet. You might as well take the bed. If the light from the computer won't bother you, I can use the desk in there. Otherwise, I'll move out here to the table." I was holding my breath, hoping that she'd take me up on the offer. I wanted to be near her as long as possible, even if I couldn't touch her as I wanted. Hearing her breathe as she slept would be enough.

I took both of our plates to the sink. "Please, Julia. I want you to be comfortable. Do you need a Vicodin?"

"Maybe, but I hate taking those damn things. They make me so tired, and I'd like to stay up with you for a while." She moved up behind me and reached around to set the dirty wok in the empty side of the sink.

I turned and brushed my fingers along her cheek because I couldn't help myself. "You shouldn't be in pain. Did Jenna help you with that brace? Is it tight enough?"

"Yes to both questions. You don't need to worry about me so much, Ryan. Honestly," she said quietly.

"I don't mean to be over the top, but I *will* worry about you, Julia. I can't help it. Come on. Leave this until tomorrow." I took her hand and led her toward my room. Jen was already asleep, her head resting on Aaron's chest as he flipped through the channels.

"See? The couch is occupied anyway," I teased. "Night, brother."

"Night. Thanks again, Jules."

She nodded at Aaron and padded softly down the hall behind me. I closed the door and went to turn the computer on. She waited by the door until the soft light illuminated the outline of the bed. I met her there, pulled the covers back, waiting for Julia to climb in. "Do you need help getting down? Does it hurt?"

"I'm fine. It's getting a little better," she said bravely but her face showed the pain as she eased herself down on the bed. I pulled the covers up and went to get some water so she could take her medicine. Afterward, I turned to move away. "Good-night, honey." The room was cast in a soft blue glow that made her hair and eyes appear almost black, an even sharper contrast to her alabaster skin.

Julia grabbed my hand. "Hey, can you sit here for a minute? I wanted to talk if you have time." She patted the bed next to her and I sank down as if I had no will to resist.

"What is it?" I searched her shadowed features. Her eyes sparkled in the low light, but I wondered what she was thinking. "Are you okay?"

"I'm fine. I want to go to New York to get some of my things and see my place. I called Ellie and she agrees that it might help me remember."

I stiffened in protest. "Julia, I don't think so, sweetie. Not yet. You're still healing and this weekend I have to work both days. I'll have to check my schedule but I don't think I can go for at least two weeks. Can we just wait and see how you are?"

One hand was still holding mine and she ran the other down my opposite arm, stopping when she got to my forearm, her little fingers closing around it. "Well, you don't need to come."

"Oh, yes, I do," I said adamantly. There was no way in hell I would let her go alone.

"Ryan," she sighed. "I'm not a child and I'm not going to hurt myself by taking the train to New York." Her voice was insistent. "I also spoke to my dad. He thinks I'll be fine and you know how protective he is. If you expect me to believe that we are only friends, then you'll have to let me go."

I was silent for a minute and reached out to brush her hair back. "I know this is hard for you and you feel like I'm dictating and that isn't my intention. Try to understand my point of view. I almost lost you and I will not take risks with you now. We'll go, but it can't be right away, okay?"

"Jen and I talked earlier. Aaron is working this weekend too, but she isn't. I knew you wouldn't want me going alone, so I asked her to go and she agreed. It will give me some time to get to know her better, too. We'll have a girl's weekend."

"Are you planning on having Ellie meet you as well?"

"Maybe. Please trust me. We'll only be gone for three days. That is all the time Jenna has off."

"Babe, it has nothing to do with trusting you." I wanted to be mad at her for even suggesting it, but couldn't. I fully understood her need to take care of herself. Part of me was terrified that she'd stay in New York and not come back to Boston, but I knew I needed to let her find some independence. My chest felt like steel bands were constricting my breath and making my heart hurt. Panic welled. She sensed it because her little hand found my jaw and grasped my chin, forcing me to look at her. I struggled to push the emotions down.

"Hey. I'll be fine." Her thumb moved over my chin and across my lower lip. I felt a groan rise up as desire fused with the protectiveness I was feeling. "Ryan."

"Uh…let's talk about this tomorrow, sweetheart." She was tired; the Vicodin would make her more so in minutes and if I didn't get some distance I wouldn't be able to stop myself from kissing her or spilling my guts about exactly how much she meant to me. My mouth was already dry and my pulse increased, pushing blood in places I didn't need her to notice. "I need to get this paper finished and you need to rest."

"*You* need to rest," she almost whispered. Her voice was so soft and gentle, filled with concern. "You're not the only one who worries, you know."

"I will. Very soon." I leaned down and bushed my lips against her forehead, inhaling the sweet scent of her skin and shampoo. I allowed myself to open my lips and press another kiss on her temple.

"I'll share the bed with you." The words were barely audible and I wondered if it was my imagination. "It's big enough. We can have a slumber party."

"Mmmm…we'll see." I wanted to agree immediately, but I wasn't strong enough to resist her being so close. If nothing else, my feelings would pour out in waves. If I did give in to that guilty pleasure, she'd need to be fast asleep first so the temptation wouldn't be so agonizing. "Goodnight…" *my love,* my mind screamed.

Fuck, I thought as I sat down in front of the computer. I seriously needed to work, but I was so damn distracted. I fisted my hands in my hair. I knew she needed to get her independence back, but I was so damned scared of letting her leave. It would be three days of hell. I glanced over my shoulder at her, lying in the bed. Julia lowered her arm toward me, beseeching me to come to her. It was all I could do not to run back to that damn bed and gather her close.

I sat there in the dark listening to her deep breaths until I was sure that she was asleep. I'd never felt so damn protective. I wanted to feel her heart beating next to mine, needed to feel her breath rush over my face and touch her soft skin with my eager fingertips.

I tried to focus on the article in front of me. The screen blurred before my eyes and I realized how exhausted I really was. I didn't want to leave, to collapse on the couch in the other room. It took all my strength, but finally, that's exactly what I did.

~5~

Julia~

THE LIGHT WAS shining through my closed eyelids so I rolled onto my side and threw my arm over my face. Pain shot through my body. I moaned in protest and opened my eyes. Despite my arguments, I was in Ryan's room, in his bed…*alone*. He didn't take me up on my slumber party offer and must have gone into the living room when he finished studying.

I was filled with disappointment. As confusing as this whole thing had been, he was the one point of light, my stability in what could have been a nightmare. I knew I could count on him unconditionally. I also knew we were more than friends. I felt it in my heart, felt it in my body…in my very soul. My eyes blurred with emotion. Why couldn't I find Ryan in my mind, when he was obviously the most important person in my life? It hurt me and, worse, it hurt *him*. The pain on his face whenever he asked me if I remembered and I had to tell him *no, crushed me.* I pushed myself into a sitting position. More pain throbbed through my ribcage, even though I tried to use only my arm and not the muscles in my stomach or back, but somehow, it didn't hurt as bad as my heart. I brushed two single tears off my face and stood up slowly. I wanted to see Ryan and more, *feel* him.

I opened the door to the bedroom and the apartment was quiet. No one was up and as I walked into the living room, my eyes were drawn to the couch. The comforter and pillow Ryan used were folded and stacked neatly on the cushions. My heart fell. He must've gone to the hospital early even though he made no mention of it the night before. *He works so hard. He's so dedicated and caring. So gorgeous and giving.* I started to run my hands through my hair, but lifting my arms above shoulder level was excruciating and I stopped with a grimace.

I went into the kitchen and the dishes from the night before were washed, dried and put away. I flushed. *Ryan.* I busied myself making coffee and pulling out the things I needed to make the blueberry muffins I'd promised Aaron. It made me feel useful to do something for them. I opened the refrigerator and found the eggs, milk and blueberries. There were lemons in the drawer with the berries and I pulled three of them out as well. Muffins were easy and I decided to make lemon poppy seed, too. Provided, of course, there were poppy seeds in the spice drawer. I opened it and ran my fingers over the labels until I found them. My fingers hesitated as something flashed through my mind. I stopped. I knew exactly where to find everything. A smiled brightly as the knowledge settled over me. I was still grinning when Jenna came down the hall. I was mixing the batter, and turned to preheat the oven.

"What are you smiling about, girl?" Jenna asked as she took down two cups and filled them with the freshly brewed coffee. She sat one next to me and took hers to the breakfast bar, plopping down on one of the stools. She looked ruffled, but her skin held a healthy pink hue and her eyes sparkled with amusement.

"Um…I realized I know where everything is. It's great, isn't it? I mean…I've cooked here before and remembered, right?"

Jenna smiled with a nod. "That *and* you arranged this kitchen; when we first moved in, you drove out here with Ryan and stayed with us for a week." She took a drink of her coffee as I dumped the blueberries into the batter and folded them in. "Shit, I probably shouldn't have said anything. Ryan will have my ass but he noticed last night. You should have seen his face."

"He won't really tell me anything."

"I know. He thinks he's doing the right thing."

"And, you don't?" I filled the muffin tins as we talked.

"I don't know, Julia. I guess it isn't for me to say. We all want the best for you."

"Well, he's very evasive when I ask him direct questions."

"Did you mention your decision to go to New York?" she asked.

"Last night."

"And?"

"And…he doesn't want me to go without him. Has he always been like this or is it just because of my accident?"

She snorted. "He's, uh…well, I suppose he's always been protective of you, but the accident has made him more so, naturally."

I put the muffins in the oven, set the timer and then washed the bowl so I could re-use it to make the next batch.

"Julia, that's enough muffins. Aaron doesn't need more than two dozen."

"Oh, I'm making a different kind. I thought since you and I were going away for the weekend that I'd leave the boys with some food. I'm going to make lasagna, too."

"You're too good and I'll never be able to live up to it. Aaron isn't used to being so spoiled."

Something shot through my mind. A feeling of wanting to make Ryan happy, to take care of him and it stunned me. The spoon fell from my fingers to the floor, splattering the batter everywhere. The breath left my chest in a rush.

"Are you alright?" Jenna asked, full of concern.

I nodded and tried to bend down to get the discarded spoon but grimaced at the effort. Jenna got up and picked it up, putting it in the sink, then began wiping up the batter that was now spattered on the floor and cupboard.

"I was just wondering if Ryan was used to being spoiled, that's all. Was he?" I was cautious and my eyes darted to hers.

Her mouth opened and then closed. She threw the rag back in the sink. "Oh,yeah. At least, more than Aaron." She smiled and raised her eyebrows suggestively. "I try to make up for my lack of cooking skills and spoil him in other ways."

"Ah." I didn't pry but I got her point. They were cute together, balancing each other out. Aaron was playful and silly, very intelligent, but that part of him wasn't overtly on the surface. Jen was sarcastic and grounded but very sweet deep down. "Anyone can cook, Jen."

She shook her head. "Not like you. I'm a good nurse and I have a solid head on my shoulders, but you…you're talented in several ways. *Very* artistic."

Ryan brought me some drawing pads and pencils while I was in the hospital, but I felt weird with it. There wasn't anything that I really wanted to draw except Ryan, but that seemed intrusive and personal. I drew a couple of the nurses and made drawings from pictures of some of their children, but I wasn't able to do a great job while one of my arms was incapacitated and I couldn't anchor the page properly. I grimaced at how horrible they'd turned out.

"From what I've seen, my talent isn't that impressive." I rolled my eyes.

"Julia, you're too hard on yourself. Your arm's been in a sling, for God's sake."

I grated some lemon zest into the batter after I'd made sure the milk and eggs were all mixed in. I didn't want the juice or the zest to curdle the milk. Not that it would have made that much difference. The oven timer beeped and Jenna removed the muffins. I had a dish towel laid out on the counter and she dumped the tin over to empty it.

"Should I wash this?" she asked.

"If you don't mind." I flipped the fresh muffins over and then dumped a good portion of poppy seeds into the lemon batter.

After a couple of minutes, I was refilling the pan with the new batter and topping it off with the crumb topping I'd made. "Why lemon, Julia?" Jenna was seated and eating a hot blueberry muffin. "I mean, why not banana or apple?"

I opened the oven and pushed the tins in. "Um…just a feeling. Why?"

"No reason," she said, but something in her face made me probe.

"Jen, what is it?"

"Nothing."

I nodded in acknowledgment of her question. "Oh…I see. They're Ryan's favorite, aren't they?" My heart already knew the answer.

She popped the last bite of her muffin into her mouth and nodded. Happiness burst at this little bit of knowledge.

"This is an excellent sign. You always make both when you're here. You'll make your boy very happy when he sees those."

"*My* boy?" I asked cautiously.

She chuckled. "Duh, Julia."

*****

I made arrangements to take the 4:15 train to New York. Depending on how I felt once we got there, we could stay just tonight or the entire weekend. I'd finished packing a bag and was coming out of the bathroom when I heard Ryan's angry expletive.

"What are you doing? Jen, you know this isn't a good idea!" His voice was loud but then suddenly quieted. I hesitated in the hallway, longing to hear what he was saying. "Goddamn it! I don't want her going without me!"

"Ryan, it will be fine. I won't let anything happen."

"Jenna! It isn't about that. What if she remembers? I have to be with her when that happens. I *have* to," he said tightly with something like desperation underlying the words. I couldn't see his face, but already I could picture the pain.

"Even if Julia stays here, you might not be with her when she remembers. Be realistic. You could be at the hospital or on campus. There are no guarantees, Ryan. At least you're using the word *when* instead of *if* now."

"You don't have to tempt fate, do you?"

"It isn't up to me. Or you. She's made up her mind." Jenna's voice was resigned and flat. "If I don't go along, it won't stop her and you know it."

He sighed deeply and I could hear shuffling around the kitchen. "Shit, I know," he said so softly I could barely hear it. "I just worry so fucking much."

"It will be okay."

I moved toward them, walking harder than necessary so they would hear me coming into the room. Ryan was leaning up against the bar, dressed in his ever-present scrubs. Jenna was in jeans, a red t-shirt and brown knee-high boots…clearly ready to leave. Her overnight bag was resting near the door and I set mine down beside it.

Ryan pushed himself away from the counter and walked to me as I hovered by the door. "Hey. How are you feeling?" He pushed my hair off of the left side of my face gently. I ached to press into his hand.

I smiled at him warmly. "I'm good. Ready to get going."

His eyes softened slightly. "Please wait until I can take you." His left hand took mine and squeezed it as he looked at me imploringly. "*Please*."

I tipped my head to one side. "We've already discussed this. It's not a big deal, Ryan, okay? I even made some food so I don't have to worry about you and Aaron starving while I'm gone."

He looked up at the ceiling. "You're worried about *me*?" he said under his breath, more to himself than to me.

I put a hand on his arm and Jenna left the room discretely. I looked into his dark blue eyes and recognized the deep level of panic even though he was trying to hide it from me. "I'll be fine. I'm more worried about you guys. Do you think you can turn the oven on to three hundred and fifty degrees and remember to take the lasagna out in an hour?" I said in a teasing tone.

He looked down at our hands and rubbed mine between both of his. "Julia, please understand that I can't have anything happen to you. I don't like how I'm feeling at the prospect of not being with you in case something happens. What if you need me?"

I removed my hands from his and put my arms around him, pressing my head to his chest. His arms enfolded me instantly and he inhaled deeply, his chin came to rest on the top of my head.

We stood holding each other for a minute until finally I found my shaking voice. "I *do* need you. I know that. But not to take me to New York." My arms tightened and I felt his hands moving up and down on my back. I wanted him to understand that I felt the deep connection between us, and even not remembering, he'd come to mean so much to me. "It'll be fine. Please don't worry."

"Of course I'm going to worry. Like crazy," he said reluctantly, pressing his lips to the top of my head. "Will you call me tonight when you get there?"

I moved back and looked up into his face. "Okay. I promise." My fingers found the front of his shirt and tugged on the fabric. His hands still lingered on my arms when Jen came back and walked to the door.

"Ready, Julia? We don't want to be late."

"Is Ellie meeting you?" Ryan asked, never taking his eyes off of mine.

"I wish she could, but it's a lot of cash for the flight for just two nights."

"Do you need a ride to the station? I can take you." His words were slow and measured; the muscle in his jaw working overtime. I wanted to soothe him, but the holes in our relationship left me wondering how.

Emotions I didn't recognize welled up in my chest and caused my eyes to burn. I blinked at the unexpected tears and struggled to clear my throat. "Uhmmm…nope. Jen called a cab."

"Yeah, and it's already here," she said and pulled open the door. "Tell Aaron I'll talk to him later, will you, Ryan?"

He didn't answer her, still focused totally on me. "Do you need some money?" he asked softly, his fingers lingering on my shoulders and then sliding down my arms.

I reached up, touching the edge of his jaw, and shook my head. "I'm fine." I stood on my tiptoes and placed a kiss where my fingers had been, letting my lips linger and my eyes close. He trembled slightly and suddenly there was nothing I wanted but to stay right there with him. "See you soon," I forced out tightly.

He nodded without a word and then glanced over my head at Jenna.

"Be careful. Call me if anything happens."

She rolled her eyes and held the door for me. "We'll be fine. Don't be such a worrywart. Go work out with Aaron or something. He misses you in the gym. Eat the fabulous meal Julia made for you and just take it easy. Come on, Julia. Let's get the hell out of Dodge."

I felt nervous on the way to the station and Jen chattered endlessly about all the shopping she wanted to do the following day. The look on Ryan's face as we left made me very sad. He was being silly and overprotective, but somehow I understood the sadness. I felt it too, and it was familiar. Like leaving him was something that I did a lot.

I had many questions and maybe on the ride down to New York, Jenna would be more willing to share. My phone vibrated in my purse and as I reached inside to get it, Jenna huffed. "Can't he even wait until we're on the damn train?"

She was right; it was a text from Ryan. Texting was something that he'd showed me when he brought me home from the hospital. It was a fun way to keep in touch.

Please be careful and call me later. I'll miss you. –R

I rubbed my thumb across the words on the screen.

"What?" Jen asked sarcastically. "Did he burn himself on the stove?"

I smiled and shook my head and then burst out laughing. Jenna had such a dry sense of humor, and it was impossible to remain sullen. "Uh, no. At least, not yet. He said he'll miss me."

"No shit. Nothing like stating the obvious. Men are such fucking babies. Ever notice that? They act all tough but really they're a big pile of fluff and feathers. Sometimes with big gooey centers."

A warm rush of heat flooded my cheeks. “Ryan seems…very strong. So accomplished and hardworking. Both he and Aaron are like that.”

“Yes. They’re both remarkable. Ryan is the more sensitive of the two. He’s always so in tune with the needs of others. Even people he can’t stand, he helps.”

Ah yes, Liza. I knew what she was hinting so I decided to take the bait. “I’m sure he’ll make a good doctor. He told me about that fellow student he helps, if that’s what you mean.”

“Stalker bitch. It’s pathetic the way she tries to wrap it up in paltry attempts to get him to help her.”

“I’m surprised he fell for it.”

“Oh, he didn’t. He knows what she’s after, but he feels a responsibility to the patients. To make sure she knows what she’s doing.”

“Well…that isn’t his responsibility.”

“Ryan makes everything his responsibility. Haven’t you figured that out yet?”

“Hmmm…maybe that’s why he feels so responsible for me. For my recovery.”

“Are you kidding me? Hardly, Julia. You’re something else all together.”

I looked down at the message again and started to type a reply. My heart swelled with hope at her words.

I already miss you, too. Thank you for understanding. I’ll be okay. Promise.

“Jen,” I began as I replaced my phone inside my purse, “Do you think…what if I never remember? Do you think Ryan and I will still stay the way we are?”

She pursed her lips and considered for a moment.

“I…I mean, he told me we were close. Do you think we can be again?” I stammered.

Her hand came out to rest on mine. "You two will always be close. In observation, nothing seems to have changed much. You see the way he is with you."

"Yes, but I can see his pain. I don't want to hurt him. I can't explain it, but when he hurts, I hurt, too."

Her hand squeezed mine. "Yeah. I understand." She wasn't saying much and I wanted to scream in frustration. I bit my lip in consternation as the cab pulled up to the station, hoping that this weekend would help. I desperately wanted to find some connection to Ryan, something that would shed some light on the real status of our relationship. Feeling as I did about him after only this short time, how could I have known him for eight years and only been his friend? *And why the hell aren't they telling me anything?*

Ryan~

"Ryan, get your ass in here and eat some of this, man. If you don't, I'm going to have it all gone and Julia will beat my ass!"

I stood, with my hands on my hips, staring out at the window and the tire tracks left by the cab that took Julia and Jenna away. The tightness in my chest kept me from feeling hungry, even though it smelled delicious. "Just save some of it, piglet. I'll eat later."

"Okay, but you don't know what you're missing. She has fresh bread sticks and salad too. Brownies and the muffins. Man, I swear to God, if you don't marry that girl soon, I'm going to marry her myself."

My heart fell. Yeah, that was the plan and every day I prayed that I would wake up and see recognition on her beautiful features, her green eyes glistening with the memories that meant the world to us both.

"At least have a beer," Aaron called.

"I thought you wanted to go work out. You shouldn't drink first. Drink after, jackass." I moved in and pulled out a chair, leaned back and sprawled my legs out in front of me.

Aaron's face sobered but he still kept forking food into his mouth. It did smell really good.

"Okay, so no beer. What about a muffin?"

"What? Are you my mother?" I muttered irritably. It wasn't fair to take it out on him and really what would make me feel better was finding an outlet for all of the pent up aggression. "I don't feel like a blueberry muffin, Aaron. She made those for you anyway."

"I guess she did." He nodded and swallowed. He reached out and flipped the dishtowel covering the muffins on the table. "But, who in the hell did she make these for, huh?"

My eyes glanced up and I saw a plate full of lemon muffins, just like she always made with extra crumb topping. I took a deep breath, and reached for one, bringing it up to inhale the aroma.

"So, if she isn't remembering, then how in the hell did she know to leave that crumb stuff off of my muffins and load yours up?" He smiled and shoved me in the shoulder.

I shrugged. "She's only remembering subconsciously, little things like this. I need her to remember everything, Aaron. The loneliness is killing me." I felt the ache thread through my voice. "Being near her and not having her…I'm in hell."

"Why? She's *here*."

I frowned at him. "Never mind. You don't understand and I'm not in the mood to explain it. Let's go to the gym when you're finished eating. I feel the need to beat the shit out of something, so will you spot me on the bag?"

"Yeah, but I want to lift, too, okay?"

"Sure."

The rumblings in my stomach finally got the better of me and I ate the muffin in my hand and went to change into my gym clothes. As I was tying my shoelaces, my phone vibrated and I pulled it out of the pants I'd just left on the floor. There was a message from Julia but before I could read it, the phone rang.

"Hi, Ellie," I answered. "I wish you were going to New York. Jen and Julia left about an hour ago."

"I wish I could. I wanted to call and check on you. How are you holding up?"

I leaned back on the bed until I was lying looking up at the ceiling, my legs bent at the knees over the edge. "I'm fine, I guess. I miss us and I want her back. I need to know she loves me. It's torture. I'm such a pussy."

"Oh, Ryan," she said quietly. "She trusts you completely. I can tell when I talk to her. She's worried about you. She knows you're suffering which tells her that there is more between you."

"I guess I'm not doing a great job of hiding it," I said in disgust.

"You know that she loves you, Ryan. She's hoping that she'll remember in New York."

"Yeah? Well, I'm afraid she'll remember losing the baby and I won't be there to take care of her. She can't go through that without me, Ellie. I couldn't bear it."

"Oh shit, Ryan! I should have thought about this before!" Her voice was filled with anxiety.

"What is it?"

"Right before Julia left to come to Boston, she took a pregnancy test. We both left so fast, I'm sure it's still in the bathroom…"

"Fuuucck!" I sat straight up as I said it, my pulse starting to pound. I could hear the blood rushing in my ears like a freight train. "If she sees that, it's sure to hit her like a ton of bricks." I ran a hand through my hair and looked at my watch. Their train wouldn't get into New York until 8:45.

"Uh, call Jen. See if she can beat Julia into the bathroom and get rid of it. Make sure you tell her to remove the box from the trash as well."

"Yeah. Okay." I sucked in a breath so big my lungs threatened to burst. "That could work. I'll text her. Julia would ask about a call."

I could hear Ellie sigh too. "I wish I could be there with her this weekend, but with Harris playing and the short notice, I just couldn't get away."

"It's okay. I'm glad Jenna was free. Ellie, what else could she find?"

"Hopefully, she'll just get some clothes. She may get a glimpse of her job offer in Paris. She was in the middle of packing, but otherwise, a few pictures, Ryan. She has pictures of the two of you together scattered around. Some of the six of us. More of Elyse, Gabriel and her parents."

"I shouldn't have let her go."

"She's gonna remember sometime, Ryan. Maybe sooner is better than later."

"I hope she does, but I'm torn. I know it will kill her. She'll be so hurt. I'd give anything to keep her from that."

"Anything? Even the last eight years?" I lost my breath. "You two will have more babies. She'll get over it if she still has you." I didn't say anything which prompted Ellie to continue. "How are you dealing with it?"

My eyes blurred as pain surged inside. "I'm…not."

"You're not what?"

"I'm not…dealing. I've sort of pushed it down. I can't bear to think about it. I didn't know how badly I wanted her to have my baby until it was lost." The tears ran down my face in silence and my voice broke. "I want *everything* with her. Words can't…A child would have been…an amazing gift. I love her so much." Angrily, I brushed the tears off of my face and cleared my throat. "Listen, I have to text Jen and Aaron is waiting for me."

"Ryan. I'm so sorry." The sympathy in her voice dripped off her words. She was crying, too.

"Yeah. Thank you. I'll call you if something happens, okay?" I wiped my face with the back of my free hand and rose from the bed.

"Okay. If you need to talk, call anytime. I love you both."

"Love you, too. Thanks."

After I hung up, I went into the bathroom and splashed some cold water on my face briefly before firing off a text to Jenna.

Pregnancy test in bathroom. Get in there first and get rid of it. Box too. Counting on you to save my life.

My heart was pounding a hundred miles an hour until her answer came five minutes later.

Holy shit. Okay. I'll let you know when it's done.

Thx.

When I went back into the other room, I breathed a small sigh of relief. Aaron was changed and waiting impatiently. "What took you so long, gorgeous?"

"Don't start with me. Like I said, I'm ready to beat the hell out of something and I'm in no mood for inane chatter."

"What the fuck is your problem? It's all that pent-up sexual tension that's eating you," he said as he followed me out the door. "Don't take that shit out on me. Do something about it."

We drove to the gym in silence and when we got there we both hopped on a treadmill for a twenty minute warm-up. We had a routine that we varied based on what our needs were. Today, I had a lot of frustration to get out, so it would be boxing and kickboxing. Aaron let me go first, bracing the bag against his body. He spread his legs to get a good foothold and then motioned to me with his hands that I could begin.

As I hit the bag over and over, varying my punches in strength and angle, one thing was occupying my mind. *Julia.* How much I missed her, how much I wanted her, how it was driving me crazy not to be able to touch her and what she might remember in New York. I felt helpless, angry, frustrated, hurt and downright horny. I was getting hard just by being near her, feeling the heat radiating between us, and her scent. I was hungry for her like I'd never been; missing the connection even more than the sex. I needed what only she could give me, had aches in places only she could assuage.

The university gym was in the student center and always busy no matter the time of day. It wasn't unusual to see someone that we knew. Out of the corner of my eye, I noticed Liza and Claire lingering in the doorway to the weight room where Aaron and I were working the bag. Sweat was starting to run down my body in rivets as I attacked the bag without mercy.

"Looks like you've got a fan club," Aaron murmured and nodded over his shoulder toward them.

"Stupid bitches," I grunted between punches. "After four years, you'd think they'd get a damn clue."

"They *are* hot," Aaron said. I stopped to wipe the sweat out of my eyes with the towel around my neck. It was awkward with the gloves on, but they were starting to burn.

"Hadn't noticed," I said and went back to my workout.

"Ryan, come on. Julia's been away all this time and I love her dearly, but you're a guy. Guys have needs. It doesn't have to mean anything and they're certainly willing."

I didn't say anything, just hit the bag harder. He was jolted and readjusted his stance. I couldn't believe he would even make that suggestion. He hadn't said anything like that since before we graduated Stanford. Not since Julia and I were friends and I was frustrated as hell. *Don't even fucking go there, Aaron.*

"And now…you seem so miserable. Maybe you need to cut loose a little."

"That's what I'm doing," I said through clenched teeth while I kept pounding the bag with all my strength.

"You know what I mean."

"Don't." I never thought my brother would say this shit to me and I didn't want to hear it.

"You're leaving here in a couple of months. God knows you need it. You're ready to blow, brother. Julia doesn't remember. She wouldn't have to know."

"Aaron, I said that's *enough*!" I yelled angrily. I was so pissed I felt like my body would fly apart.

"Ryan…" he began, but I shoved the bag with such force that he stumbled back and nearly fell.

"*Shut up*! Just shut the fuck up, Aaron!" I felt the rage and pain well to overflowing. How could he even suggest such a thing? "I'll smash your Goddamn face in if you say one more word, do you hear me?!"

"I'm just looking out for you! I see you suffering, you asshole! You're killing yourself! You better think twice before you threaten me little man, because I'll take your. Ass. *Out*!" He came at me and shoved me in the chest. Without thinking, I pulled back my right arm and let it fly with all the force I could muster, hitting him in his face at the temple.

He sprawled backwards onto the mats as tears welled in my eyes.

"Noooo!" I screamed at him. "Maybe it's in you to fuck around on Jenna, but I will never do that to Julia!" Others were watching but I didn't give a flying fuck. Liza and Claire moved in closer to see what was going on, their eyes wide and mouths agape in silent supplication. "It is *impossible* for me to even think about anyone else! You know that, so just shut the hell up! It would kill us both, for God's sake! I'm in *love, damn you*!! So much I can't even fucking breath. She's all I want! She means everything and I just want her back like we *were*!" I was yelling, my chest was heaving. I took three stumbling steps back and began to turn from him, still on the floor, staring up at me with a stunned look on his face. "*She's all I want*," I said more softly, defeat and heartbreak lacing my tone.

I moved toward the locker room, ripping at the laces on the gloves with my teeth. I couldn't breathe and was horrified by the stunned faces of those watching, but mostly that I'd just hit my brother.

"Ryan!" I heard Liza's insipid little voice mewling behind me. It sickened me that she would chase me after what she'd just witnessed. For God's sake. I'm sure she heard the entire confrontation and she was chasing after me like some bitch in heat after she'd heard me say I was in love with someone else. Even Claire looked disgusted by Liza's display. *Fucking incredible.* "Ryan, wait," she called again.

I held my hand in the air after I'd shoved the glove that I'd just removed under my arm. I walked faster until I was able to escape to the sanctity of the men's locker room where she could not follow.

I pulled off the other glove and threw them both on the floor next to my locker, kicked off my shoes and shed all of my clothes in a pile. I grabbed a towel and went into the shower. The whole time my mind raced and my heart ached. *I just punched my brother*. I punched my brother over suggesting what Tanner and any normal red-blooded guy would suggest when one of their friends was in my situation. Except my situation wasn't what they would consider typical. I leaned a hand on the wall to support my weight as the hot water rushed over me and stood there unmoving for several minutes.

My head was bowed and my eyes were closed, so I didn't hear Aaron follow me. When he spoke I was startled and my head shot up.

"I'm sorry, Ryan," Aaron began, "I know how much stress you're under and I know how much you love Julia. It's just that no one likes to see you suffering. I just thought if you could take the edge off, then you'd feel better. I've never seen you this fucked up and I was grasping at straws. I wasn't suggesting that you leave her; just that you close your eyes and be selfish for twenty minutes. It was stupid."

"Julia is all that matters. Nothing can make me feel better except her," I said softly, reaching for the soap. "And when I *close my eyes*, she is all I fucking see, so what you are suggesting is completely impossible. Sometimes, I feel like no one can understand how much I love her. No one gets it. Not even you." I lathered up my body quickly, longing to get home and call her. "Julia was the only one who knew and now I'm just so terrified that she won't remember how much we meant to each other. It's killing me. I've lost those eight years as much as she has," I admitted honestly.

"She still gets it; even if she doesn't know it yet. She made you lemon muffins, dude."

I closed my eyes and swallowed the lump in my throat and nodded. "I'm sorry I hit you, Aaron. There's no excuse for my behavior. I was a little wound up before we got here. Ellie called and told me that the positive pregnancy test was still sitting on the counter of Julia's bathroom and I freaked out a little bit." My voice was wooden, but I couldn't help it. If I let myself soften, I'd probably completely lose it. I was exhausted and emotionally spent.

"Holy shit. I sometimes get so focused on Julia's recovery that I forget about the baby. I'm sorry for being such an insensitive ass. I'm sincerely sorry, Ryan."

I turned off the water and stepped out, wrapping the towel around my waist at the same time. He was still dressed and would most likely go back and lift weights for another hour.

"I'm going home. Can you get Tanner or someone to bring you when you're done?" I dried my hair with another towel and ran a comb through it roughly.

"Yeah. No sweat." He patted me on the shoulder after I threw on my clothes and then walked out of the locker room. We wouldn't speak about this again.

Julia ~

"Hey, Julia! It's good to see you! Where have you been?" The nameless bellman called after me as Jenna and I passed through the marble lobby on the way to the elevators in the high rise building that I apparently lived in.

"I guess I do live here," I said under my breath. "Hi!" I called and waved to the bellman.

"Were you in Boston with Ryan all this time?"

Okay, so he knew Ryan. Of course he did. "Uh, yep." I smiled wide and nodded happily.

"Well, it's nice to have you back. We missed your pretty face. Who's your friend?"

"Oh, this is Jenna. She's a friend from college."

Jenna extended her hand to the man and he took it willingly. He gazed at her and she smiled. "And you are?" she asked.

"Adam, ma'am."

"Nice to meet you, Adam."

It was a good thing that Jenna took over the conversation because I was a little out of it, looking around the building and trying to pull things out of my memory. The tall glass windows, the high ceilings and the brass fixtures reflected off the black marble floors.

I was shaking slightly as we rode the elevator up and walked down the hall, again trying to remember something and chagrined because I didn't. The floral smell was familiar though. That was something, at least.

"I really need to use the bathroom, Julia. Would you mind if I use it first?" Jenna mentioned as I pushed open the heavy wooden door and walked into the apartment.

"Yeah, sure," I said offhandedly. She took off down the hall while I glanced around. There were pictures of my parents and the six of us scattered in small frames around the living room, some of just Ryan and me…more of only Ryan. The furniture was large and plush and the plants were dead. I walked over to one of them, and messed with the dried leaves.

There were candles in several places, all of them somewhat burned. The scent of vanilla lingered and there was contemporary art on the walls and a large mirror over the fireplace. An art table sat beside the window with a large lamp above it. The colors were some of my favorites, dark greens, taupe and browns. The kitchen was small with marble countertops and stainless steel appliances. Surely this place was expensive and I wondered more about my job at Vogue.

I dropped my bag on the couch and wandered to the bedroom. The door was open and I could see the queen size bed from the hall. It had lots of white bedding and fluffy pillows, but was strewn with clothes and open suitcases. *Did I make this mess getting ready to go to Boston?* I couldn't believe I would have left it like this and I started to replace the outfits still on hangers back in the closet.

Jen walked in and sat down. "Anything?" she asked.

"Um, the smells are familiar but I don't recognize the photos…or the apartment really. It feels familiar, but I have no actual memory of it." I looked around the room. More burned candles on the bedside table and a large upholstered chair by the window and small table with a decorative lamp with a moss green shade. "Was I always this messy? It doesn't seem like me."

"No, I don't think so, Julia," she said, but didn't elaborate.

"I thought I'd walk in here and everything would flood back," I said sadly. "Wishful thinking, I guess."

I fell into the chair and brought my legs up, curling them under me and leaned my head on my fisted hand.

"I'm sorry, sweets. Maybe with more time here, you'll remember something." She moved a pile of folded sweaters over so she could sit on the bed without messing them up.

"Yeah." My phone rang in my purse in the other room and I jumped up to get it before it went to voicemail. I chastised myself as pain shot through me and I walked more carefully toward the sound. Of course, it was Ryan.

"Hey."

"Are you there safe and sound?" His voice sounded tired.

"Yeah. Fine. How has your night been?"

"Don't ask."

"You sound exhausted. At least while I'm here, you get your bed back, hmm?" I teased gently.

"I guess."

"Ryan, what's wrong?"

"Nothing, honey. I'm fine. I'm just waiting for you to tell me." I knew what he meant. He wanted to know if I'd flashed.

"Oh, well, no, I haven't remembered much. Some of the scents are familiar, but nothing concrete really."

His heavy sigh flooded the phone. I wasn't sure if he was upset or relieved. "Well, you'll remember when you're ready. Don't worry about it. I'm just glad you're there safe. You're not going out tonight are you?"

"I don't really feel up to it. My ribs hurt. I might have Jen help me into the bath. That is, if I have a bathtub. I haven't been in the bathroom yet." I laughed softly but he didn't join in.

"You have a bathtub, honey."

"Have you been in it?" I prodded.

"Yes. Take a bath, a pain pill and go to bed. Jen should sleep on the couch. I don't want anything bumping into you and hurting you."

I sank down in the chair by my art table and noticed the black portfolio sitting on its side next to it. I leaned down and traced the fingers of my free hand over its edge. "Ryan, stop. I can't have her sleeping on the couch when she was so nice to come with me."

"Julia, don't argue. Can you just do what I ask for once?" he said in irritation. I flushed uncomfortably at the tightness in his tone.

"Why are you mad at me?"

"I'm not. I just want you to take care of yourself. I tell you this stuff for your own good, not just to hear myself talk."

"Okay then what's bugging you?" I persisted. "Something is up. Tell me what it is."

"Julia…Just let it go. I'm fine," he answered flatly. The silence hung like a lead balloon over the conversation. He was withdrawing from me and I didn't like how it made me feel.

"Why are you lying to me? I'm worried about you."

"Don't worry, I'm just worn out. I worked out really hard and now I'm going to eat and go to bed. I'm glad you're safe, baby." His voice softened and warmed slightly.

"Okay. Maybe you should take a bath, too. Are you sore?"

"Not yet. Probably will be tomorrow. I'm gonna go get some of the lasagna. It smelled really good when Aaron was eating earlier. Thanks for the lemon muffins, honey. Did you know I loved them?"

"I figured it out because something just told me to make them."

"I'm glad you did. I miss you. So much." My heart squeezed as the words ripped out of him involuntarily.

"Me, too." The truth of it was profound. A familiar ache constricted my chest. "It feels like I've missed you like this before. It hurts, not like the normal way people miss each other. Like it's so much more."

"Yeah, it hurts."

"Ryan, tell me. Just *tell me*."

"Julia, I'll call you in the morning. Do what I said and rest. Please?"

He was so friggin' exasperating when he clammed up like this, and always when I was getting closer.

"Okay. Goodnight, then."

"Night."

When the phone went dead, I threw it back on the couch. I bent over and pulled up my portfolio, intending to take it back into the bedroom and look through it with Jenna, but it was open and several drawings fell out and scattered all around the floor.

Ryan, Ryan, Ryan. They were all of Ryan. My eyes welled with tears and I sank slowly to my knees, carefully gathering them up so they wouldn't be damaged. I picked one up and examined it closely. I brushed at the tear that had slipped onto my right cheek with the back of my hand, worried that my tears would fall on the drawings and ruin them. Most were in pencil, but there were some in charcoal and a few in watercolors.

A sob caught in my throat as I looked at them, so lovingly created, so detailed and perfect. It was hard to believe they were mine. My fingers ran over the signature. I knew, for sure, that these were done by my hand, and the lack of memories hurt.

Jenna must have heard because she came out of the bedroom. "Julia, what's wro…ong?" She stopped when she saw me on the floor with my drawings all around. "Oh my God," she breathed.

I looked up at her as more tears slid down my face. "Look at all of these…just *look at them*."

"Yes. I know. Are you okay?"

I wasn't sure if I was or not. "When did I draw these?"

She sank to the floor next to me, careful not to hurt the drawings and put her arm around my shoulders. There were tears in her eyes. "All along. You started in college."

I put a hand over my mouth to stifle the sobs. "Did I love him and he didn't love me back?"

"No Julia, the man is over the moon for you. You already know that, don't you?" she asked softly. When I didn't answer she got up and left the room. "I'll be right back," she called over her shoulder. She came back in seconds, carrying a picture frame. She was standing above me where I was on the floor and she sank down onto the couch. She held it out to me, and I took it carefully in both hands.

"Uhhh…" I gasped as I looked down on it. It was a poem or letter and it began, *I love you because…*I sat shaking in silence as I read the words he'd handwritten, the tears falling uninhibited from my eyes like rain. Jen didn't say a word, just waited as I read it. At the end, the words shot straight to my heart and my mind flashed to candles and firelight, to warm arms around me and my hands wound in dark golden hair.

You breathe your life into mine.
You're all my dreams come true.
You are *my* Julia. Only *mine*, forever…
Because of all of this and so much more…
I need you. I want you. I adore you.
I love you…more than my own life.
Ryan

My hand hovered over the glass, over his words as I sat there stunned, my heart racing so fast it felt like it would burst. "My God," I finally managed to breathe and looked up at Jenna. Her brow was creased and she was wringing her hands. "I'm…overwhelmed. Do you know when he wrote this?"

She moved to the floor next to me. "I think around the time you moved to New York. Julia, did you remember something?"

"Just a little. Nothing I can really articulate. I…love him. *That's* what I remember. I can't place specifics, but…he's…*everything*."

Jenna's eyes filled with tears and her hand reached out to rest on my shoulder. "Oh Julia, I'm so glad you realize that. He's been so lost."

"This..." my hand skirted over the glass again, "and the drawings have helped. It means so much to me that you came here with me and helped me like this." I placed my hand over the one on my shoulder and squeezed. I set the frame back on the couch and then picked up two of the drawings. "I sense...sadness around some of these pictures. Not all, but some of them hurt me. I was in pain over him."

She nodded. "He'll be so mad at me, but I won't let you suffer this and not tell you."

I wiped at the tears on my face and tried to smile. "Thank you."

"You and Ryan were friends. You both dated a few other people, but you and he were always together. Sometimes, when he went out with someone else, you'd stay in and draw. You were sad, but we never knew how upset you were. Ellie and I asked you to go out, but you'd stay in alone when he...well when he..."

I nodded. I didn't need her to say the words. The pain washed through me and I could remember feeling it then; being left behind while he went out and made love to someone else. It felt so real; it was like it was happening right in that moment, fresh and raw. My face crumpled and I covered it with both of my hands.

"Ryan loves you, Julia. As you can tell now...he loves you *so* much."

"I know." The truth of the words burst through my barely controlled sobs. "Maybe I can't remember all of it, but I *feel* it. I get flashes and in those moments, he just fills me up. Why didn't we date? Why would he date others? Didn't he love me then?"

"The rest of us saw what was between you and we tried to get through to you, but you and Ryan are so similar. Neither of you were willing to risk your friendship on a love affair that might end badly. After Aaron and Ryan got accepted to Harvard, the prospect of not having each other nearby forced you both to admit that you were in love with each other."

I started crying again. The floodgates burst and my shoulders shook. "Oh, God! He must be suffering so much now."

"You're alive, Julia. He's so thankful. Thank God he isn't too great at hiding his love. You sense it."

I nodded and tried to sniff back the tears. "I do. I need him to tell me, to let me love him now."

"He will in time. The first time you spent together as a couple, you drew him and he brought that picture with him back to Boston. That was the first time Aaron or I found out about your sketches. You told Ryan about the ones you did on those evenings alone and he shared it with us. You amazed him and he was so proud of you. I've never seen a man so in love, Julia. So, dry those tears. It's all going to be okay. He's been in love with you since the moment you met."

She hugged me as tight as my injury allowed and I wrapped my arms around her. "Thank you, Jen. I needed to hear this."

We spent several minutes looking through the drawings. "It's almost a sin for someone to be that gorgeous. You've certainly captured him perfectly, Julia. It's like looking at a series of black and white photographs. Was that Ryan on the phone?"

"Yes. He wants me to take a bath and go to bed. It actually sounds pretty good right now. I'm wiped." I wanted to be alone with my thoughts of Ryan, to search my mind for memories.

"Okay, do you need help?"

"I think I'll be okay, but thanks."

"I can help you get in the bath if you'd like. Ryan will kill me if you slip and re-fracture your ribs."

"I just need a little time alone. Do you mind?"

"Not at all. I understand. I'm just going to find a blanket and pillow for the couch."

"You can share the bed."

"Hmmph! No I can't." She smiled and turned her phone toward me.

Please let Julia have the bed. I don't want her to re-injure herself by sharing. I'll make it up to you. Love you and thanks for taking care of her. –R

I nodded and left the room. After I pulled some clean clothes from the dresser, I made my way into the bathroom. More candles and fluffy towels adorned the all-white room. I looked in the drawer of the vanity, found the lighter and lit the candle closest to the bathtub and turned on the water, adding bubble bath. I turned off the vanity light, leaving the room glowing in the candlelight. I stripped off my clothes slowly to avoid any unnecessary movements and I thought about hanging them on the back of the door, but lifting my arms would surely hurt. I discovered a dark blue button down hanging there. It was too large to belong to me. I dropped my clothes on the floor and gathered it to me, bringing it to my face to inhale the scent. It was faint, but it was Ryan. I breathed in deeply, relishing in his essence. He was hanging on the back of my bathroom door, filling my portfolio, filling my heart. I wanted him to fill my life. *In every single way.*

As I lowered myself slowly into the bath and leaned back in the warmth of the water, I knew what I'd be wearing to bed that night.

~6~

Ryan~

DAMN, IT WAS a long day! My rotations started at 5 am and afterward, I had class until 2 pm. I'd just come from spending 2 hours at the library, working on a diagnosis assignment. The research involved in that shit was endless and if I tried to do it at home, forget it. It was almost ten and I just wanted to shower and fall into bed. My grumbling stomach reminded me that I hadn't eaten since eleven that morning. I climbed the stairs thinking that maybe, just maybe, I could coax Julia into making me something simple. Maybe an omelet and toast. Whatever she came up with had to be delicious.

Since she and Jen had returned from New York the prior weekend, things had been falling into a routine. We still argued over sleeping on the couch and sometimes I let her win, mostly because it meant I could lie where she'd been, surrounded by her scent. I mused at my weakness. Aaron hadn't mentioned the episode in the gym but I knew he felt terrible. He was left in no doubt of my perspective. Sex isn't love, but after Julia, it was impossible to separate the two.

She was constantly inside my head.

I was working a lot and our time together was scarce. Outside of a walk in the park last Thursday afternoon and a few hours watching television together last night, we'd hardly seen each other. I worried when Jenna told me she'd found the poem I'd written the same Christmas that I'd given her the bracelet. I was pissed I hadn't remembered to have her take it down so Julia wouldn't see it. Jenna admonished me. *"And how was I supposed to do that? Wait here Julia, while I remove all evidence of your former life? You're just damn lucky I was able to get to that pregnancy test in time."*

Jen said they hadn't talked much about it, so I had no idea what went through her mind or what she remembered. Maybe they did talk and Jen wasn't telling. Seeing it, Julia had to know how much I loved her, though we didn't talk about it. I didn't ask and she didn't volunteer anything, but something changed between us. The tone in her voice, the way she found reasons to touch me more and more, all indicated that she *knew*. It was driving me fucking crazy.

The workload was a blessing in disguise. While I missed her terribly, it helped me focus and get my shit together. I still ached for her. The nights killed me, knowing she was soft and warm and only a few feet down the hall. I found myself staying at the library or at the hospital later just to make it bearable. It confused the hell out of Julia, but it was one more thing we didn't talk about. I regretted it, wanting to wrap myself around her, ease her fears and confusion, but was terrified that I wouldn't be able to control the overwhelming love and *want* that I felt. She had to see how hungry I was and I didn't want to burden her with anything more than she already had to deal with.

I came into the apartment and set my laptop case and backpack by the door, sighing in exhaustion. The lights were low, Aaron sitting on the couch, watching something on ESPN. My eyes scanned the apartment.

Aaron heard me come in. "Get your ass ready. We're going out," he said shortly.

"No way. I'm starving and all I want is to shower and go to bed." It amazed me how Aaron's ass never seemed to be dragging like mine, but then his internal medicine program didn't require nearly as many hospital hours that my trauma specialty did. "Where are the girls and why are you so dressed up?" My eyes took in his dark jeans and burgundy button down.

"Jen is getting dressed and uh…well…Julia is out with Moore." He cringed when he said it. I felt like I'd been kicked in the chest. Every muscle in my body tensed as I froze in place and turned to look at him. I'd never considered she'd actually take him up on his offer.

"*What* did you say?" I asked quietly.

"Um…she went out."

"What the fuck?! On a date?" I exploded.

"Don't know if I'd call it a date, dude. She was on her way out, to meet him, when I got home and uh…she did look amazing, Ryan."

My heart started racing as I paced around the room, not quite sure what to do with myself. I felt panic, pain and anger course through every cell of my body. "How?"

"What do you mean, how? She walked out the fucking door and got in a cab."

"Hell, Aaron! I mean, how does she have a date with one of her Goddamned doctors?" I was furious, heat rising up under my skin. I wanted to claw that shit right off of my body.

"Said she was bored, always being stuck in the apartment. It probably doesn't mean a damn thing. Calm down and go change your clothes."

Both hands threaded together on the top of my head. "You said she looked good though. So why, if it wasn't a date? How could you let her *go, Aaron*?! Why the hell didn't you call me?"

"They were meeting at the Four Seasons, so she had to look nice. She's an adult. I *couldn't* stop her, Ryan! So..." He shrugged. "Let's go crash his party."

Four fucking Seasons?!

I was already on my way down the hall, ripping off the shirt to my scrubs. My face hadn't been shaved in the past 18 hours, but what the hell, I didn't give a shit. The Four Seasons was a classy hotel with a restaurant and music, but it was still a Goddamn *hotel.*

He better not lay one finger on her or I will beat his fucking face in!

Jenna came out of their bedroom as I passed.

"So, I guess Aaron told you," she said flatly and smirked at me with one raised one eyebrow.

I didn't answer, just breezed past and slammed the door to my room. I pulled some black dress slacks and a white button-down out of my closet, throwing them on as fast as I could. I didn't wear a tie, but donned the blazer that went with the pants and ran some water through my hair. That was all the time I was going to spend getting presentable. I hurriedly put on some black socks and pushed my feet into black dress shoes and threaded a matching leather belt through the loops at the waist of the slacks. I opened the door to my bedroom, checking my wallet for cash on my way back to the living room.

"Okay...let's go." Both of them stood staring at me like I was an alien from outer space. "I said, *let's go*!"

Jenna chuckled and it only served to piss me off even further. "I've never seen you get ready so fast, pretty boy. Shit, what was that? Like thirty seconds?"

"You drive, Aaron. I'll bring Julia back in a cab." My heart was racing, my breathing shallow. I was so upset that my hands were shaking.

We all piled into Aaron's Suburban. Jenna slid into the center and I got in beside her, adjusting the collar of my shirt once I settled in the seat.

"Calm down, Ryan. She just wanted a night out." I didn't answer, running a hand over my face. "What are you planning to do?" Jenna asked pointedly. It was apparent by her cross expression that she didn't like my choices of the past weeks and thought that I was likely getting what I deserved.

"I don't know what the fuck I'm planning, Jen! If she wanted a night out, she should have told me."

"When Ryan? You're not home lately. Julia thinks you're avoiding her so why would she tell you?" she asked. The hard edge to her voice was loaded with disapproval. "And tell you what? 'Hey, *best friend*, Ryan, I'm bored, lonely and *horny as hell*?' I mean, you'd think she has the plague the way you've been avoiding her. Can't take it when she got a little taste of the truth in New York?"

"Jenna," Aaron admonished. "I don't think you're helping the situation."

"He should know what she goes through, Aaron. What did she tell you about our trip, anyway?"

"Not much," I muttered, keeping my eyes plastered to the road in front of us, mentally calculating how long it would take to get to the hotel.

"Mmmm, well, maybe you should ask her. You know she saw the letter."

My heart fell. "Look, I appreciate that you care about Julia. I do. But what the *hell* do you know about what *I've* been going through? I'm in *agony*. Being near her and not being able to touch her or tell her how I feel is killing me. So don't tell me to calm the fuck down when she goes out and finds someone to replace me." I glared at her.

"But you *can* touch her and tell her how you feel, if you weren't so damn stubborn! She doesn't want to replace you, you dumb ass. That's what I'm trying to tell you! Keep your head buried in the sand if that's what you want. Fine by me."

She crossed her arms and didn't say another word. We were close to the hotel and I stopped to consider what I wanted to do.

"Aaron, can you drop me off and meet me inside? Jen, get Julia away from the table for a bit, please. I've got a few things to say to that prick."

"Ryan, don't make a scene," Aaron warned.

"That's not my intention, but he will be clear on what the fuck is going on. He's known all along that we're together. I mean, who the hell does he think he is?"

Aaron pulled up to the curb and I opened the door. "Ryan, take a deep breath. Think about Julia. She only wanted to get out of the apartment," he said.

I hoped that was all she wanted, but Jenna's words were swirling around in my brain. I'd kept my distance and maybe she was thinking I didn't care about her. Shit, I never told her that we were together like that, but it felt like she knew. After New York, she had to.

I sucked in my breath so hard I thought my lungs would explode. "See you inside." I pulled on my jacket collar and the cuffs of my shirt in a last ditch effort to calm myself. *Lost cause.*

I walked into the hotel and straight to the Bristol Lounge and told the hostess that I was meeting someone already there. "We didn't think we could make it, but their party of two will turn into a party of five. Can you accommodate us?" I tried to calm my nerves but my hands were still shaking. Nervous agitation made me run my right hand through my hair a couple of times while I waited for the answer.

"Yes, sir." She indicated into the dining room. "Can you see them? Maybe they are already at a table that will be appropriate? If not, we can move them." My eyes scanned the room and soon found Julia and Moore at a table near the window. The place was elegant, with white linen tablecloths and soft music coming from the band near the dance floor at the front of the room. It was a mixture of Latin rhythms and soft rock with lots of acoustic guitar. Something Julia would particularly love. My heart sank to my stomach and my skin felt like it was on fire. I could feel the heat seep over my chest and up my neck to my face. My jaw set in determination.

"I see them, and I do think the table is large enough. Can you just bring one more chair please?" I asked politely, trying to mask how furious I was. I walked toward them and I took in the scene. Julia was sitting with her back to me; her beautiful tresses flowing down over the top of her strapless black dress in luxurious waves to the middle of her back, and the creamy skin of her shoulders and arms were there for the world to see. A haze of red flooded my vision, I clenched my teeth and my nails dug into the palms of both of my fisted hands.

Moore was talking softly with a smug smile on his thin lips, his eyes raking over her. The thoughts running through his head were clear in his expression. I wanted to beat his fucking face in. I was barely in control when I finally reached the table.

He caught sight of me first, stiffened and paused mid-sentence. I stopped a few feet behind Julia and waited. When he stopped talking altogether and stared, she finally turned to look over her shoulder.

Her mouth fell open and a look of shock crossed her delicate features. "Ryan," she gasped as her eyes met mine. What did she expect me to do under these circumstances?

"Good evening, Julia. Dr. Moore." I pulled out the chair next to her. "May I join you for a few minutes?" I sat down without waiting for an answer.

The other man opened his mouth and promptly shut it.

"Of course," Julia murmured, still stunned as her eyes shifted over my jacket and white shirt, then back up to my face. She frowned and shook her head slightly. "Wha…What are you doing here?"

"Aaron and Jen were going out and I was starving. I haven't eaten since late morning." I spoke to her but my eyes narrowed on the other man. "Aaron suggested this place. What a coincidence to find you here."

"Yes. Isn't it?" Moore pushed his chair back a little and threw his napkin on the table.

"We've only just ordered, so why don't you all join us for dinner?" Julia looked anxiously into my face. She knew damned well this was no coincidence.

My eyes were trained on Moore's face and the corners of my mouth lifted slightly at her invitation. *What did you think? That she was going to tell me to leave you two alone? Fucking hardly.*

"That would be nice, thank you. You look gorgeous, baby," I said, my voice purposely caressing. "Spencer, do you mind?" My eyes dared him to say *no*. I settled into the chair next to Julia, my lips still twitching at his pissed-off expression. The waiter brought another chair and set it on the other side of the table.

"No, not at all," he smiled tightly. "Julia and I were just talking."

"Oh? Did I interrupt a therapy session? And, at the Four Seasons, no less." Sarcasm dripped off of each word.

Julia shot me a look that said I was pushing a boundary. Thankfully, Aaron and Jenna walked up to the table.

"Julia, fancy finding you here," Aaron said jovially. She shifted in her seat uncomfortably.

"Hi, Julia. It's nice to see you. Dr. Moore," Jenna said politely as she took the seat between the two other men. "Have you already ordered?"

Julia leaned toward me when the waiter brought us menus. "I thought you wouldn't be home until late."

"Uh huh. I guess *ten* is late when you start at *five fucking AM*," I said shortly under my breath, so only she could hear me. She stiffened and moved back to her original position. I instantly regretted the words that made her withdraw.

Shit.

The meaningless conversation continued until we ordered and then I sat back and glared at Moore. It made Julia uncomfortable, but I could barely contain myself from flying across the table and strangling the little bastard. I knew what he was up to, even if Julia was oblivious.

Right on cue, Jenna went into action.

"Julia, will you come with me to the bathroom? My zipper is broken and I need your help to pin up the back." The corners of my mouth lifted as Julia nodded and they both rose from the table.

"Oh, of course. Please excuse us," Julia said as they left and we all stood with them as they moved away. My eyes took in the rest of her dress, how it hugged her perfect curves and left her long legs visible from six inches above the knee, to the stiletto heels that I loved on her.

Normally I'd be completely aroused, but I was livid that she would dress that way for another man.

"Well, well, well," Aaron began and started to rub his hands together as we took our seats. "This should be fun. I haven't seen my little bro' this worked-up in years." I held up a hand to silently ask him to let me speak.

"What do you think you're doing, *Dr.* Moore? This is seriously close to crossing the line of professional ethics," I said coldly.

He shifted in his seat, smoothing down the front of his shirt with his left hand. "Julia is no longer my patient. We're friends, so it's nothing of the sort," he replied, his tone flat. My chest tightened. "Ryan, this is evidence of how Julia has changed. Surely, she would have told you if you were as close as you believe?"

I was getting more and more furious with every syllable he uttered. "You know nothing of our relationship or the feelings between us. She's mine and you'd do well to remember it. If you think I'd let some little prick move in on her, then, you're seriously mistaken. I'll tell her everything, even at the risk of hurting her, before I'll lose her."

Aaron sat back, glancing between the two of us, rubbing his jaw and sporting a silly grin.

"That will accomplish exactly what you fear. Julia may feel differently now. She tells me you two are friends. You may have to accept that's all she wants now."

"Hmmph." I snorted. "Not fucking likely. She doesn't tell you everything. I should never have listened to you."

He shrugged. "Clearly, she is not telling *you* everything either, Ryan. The fact remains that she isn't ready to remember the miscarriage. It's not in her best interest to tell her or to consummate your relationship, which could be the catalyst. I've come to care for her as I know you do. I'm simply trying to offer her friendship and guidance."

"By bringing her to a *hotel*? You're crazy if you think I don't know what you're up to. I ought to beat the shit out of you right here and now. You'll never touch her while I have a breath left to prevent it," I growled. I wanted to kill the bastard. My breathing increased and my heart felt like it would fly from my chest. "Never doubt that our relationship has been consummated a thousand times over. She *knows* she belongs with me even if she doesn't remember. She lost *my* child. *Mine*." My throat thickened and my vision blurred.

"Calm down, Ryan. You're overreacting. I understand that your emotions are out of control, but you're completely misreading my intentions. This is a nice place, and she deserves an evening out. From what Julia tells me, the only thing she *knows* is that you're never around and are pushing her away. She's confused by the mixed signals. She needs to spend time with someone more…emotionally available."

"You bastard," I spat at him. "Julia is aware of my obligations right now. You know nothing of her needs." I was ready to tell him that I knew her better than anyone else, but the girls came back to the table. Julia looked at my face and her brow dropped in concern. She swallowed and then glanced over at Moore. Rage filled me that she would give a Goddamn what his reaction was.

The waiter brought our salads and I ordered a bottle of white wine that I knew was one of Julia's favorites. Jenna struggled to carry the conversation and Julia and Moore made small talk, but overall, I spent the meal brooding. Suddenly my ravenous appetite was non-existent.

I drank three glasses of wine, but didn't eat more than five bites.

"Ryan, I thought you were starving," Julia leaned into me and her perfume became more pronounced. I'd given her that perfume for her birthday the year we met and she'd worn it ever since. My eyes glanced over the translucent skin of her shoulders, her bare arms and then to the creamy curve of her breasts visible over the top of the dress.

"I've lost my appetite," I said shortly. "You look…amazing."

She smiled softly. The compliment pleased her very much. "Thank you."

"You know how gorgeous you are and don't think that looking beautiful will keep me from being pissed off."

"Why are you upset?" She grinned and then bit her lip in an attempt not to laugh. Her eyes were sparkling in the candlelight and my heart stood still.

"Stop baiting me, Julia. What in the hell are you doing here with him?"

She started to respond, but the waiter came by to remove our plates. I used my hand to motion him to me, "Do you have a piece of paper and a pen, please?" Moore's eyes landed on me many times during the meal and then his gaze always settled back on Julia. I decided to show him that she did remember on many levels and she belonged to me by her own free will.

I wrote down the title that had become *our song* ever since the Christmas Eve night in Estes Park, Colorado when I gave her the bracelet four years ago; ever since the first time we made love to it. *God, would she remember the lyrics, would she remember the reason her wrist felt empty?* I handed over the note and asked him in quiet tones to give it to the band.

"What are you doing?" Julia questioned.

"Nothing," I said. I knew she felt like I dismissed her, but I wanted her true reaction when the song began.

"Well, should we call it a night?" Moore asked stiffly. "Julia, I can take you home."

I chuckled menacingly. "I don't think so. She lives with me, so obviously she'll leave with me. Don't strain yourself." The wine relaxed me to a degree, but I was still on edge. Julia's tight expression said the confrontation was getting to her, but I needed to remain where we were until the song played. "Besides, I'm enjoying the music and I'm sure Julia would like to stay out for awhile, wouldn't you, babe?"

Her eyes lit up and she nodded.

"Sure. Spence…wanna stay?" she asked.

I hoped he would. If he left, he wouldn't get to witness what I knew was about to happen.

"Hell, let's *all* stay!" I flashed a smile that didn't reach my eyes.

"Oh boy," Aaron muttered.

"No shit," Jen added. "This oughta be good."

"Okay, I'll stay," Spence replied.

I helped Julia with her chair and placed a hand on the back of her waist. We found a new table closer to the dance floor. I needed some liquid courage, so I went to the bar and ordered a round of Julia's favorite shots.

I set the lemon drops down in front of everyone, lifted my glass and waited for Julia to pick hers up.

"Do I like these?" she asked with a soft laugh.

"Yeah. Ellie hates them, though." We both downed the drinks and she wrinkled her nose a little.

"I wasn't expecting it to be so sour, but it's good."

The music was soft and when Moore got up and moved to Julia, I tensed. He really was living on the edge. My jaw clenched as he held his hand out to her. All I could think about was that his hands were about to be on Julia's body.

"Julia, shall we dance?"

"Uh…" She bit her lip. I could feel her gaze but I didn't meet her eyes. "Okay."

I watched him lead her to the dance floor, sighing deeply.

"Ryan, it's just a damn dance," Jenna cautioned.

"I know," I nodded, my eyes still on Julia. "But, he wants her."

"She's a beautiful woman. Men are going to want her, and…women want you, too. Just look at those two at the bar. They're eye-fucking you right now." I hadn't even noticed. "Maybe you should ask one of them to dance. Give her a taste of what she's dishing out," she suggested.

"Jen, this isn't a damned game," Aaron shot at her. Apparently, our little altercation in the gym had clarified his thinking.

"Yeah, that would only confuse things more," I agreed, never taking my eyes off the couple on the dance floor. He held her hand in his, while the other rested lightly on her waist. Anything more and I'd be out of my chair in a flash. "Anyway, I'm not interested."

Aaron got up. "Okay, well, we'll keep an eye on him, then." He took Jenna to dance, leaving me alone at the table. I reached for Jen's half-full glass, downing the rest of it in a quick gulp. I ordered another round as the song ended and everyone came back to the table. Julia sat down and I pulled her chair closer to mine.

"Did you have a good time?"

"It was fine," she said shortly. Moore took the chair on her left so she was effectively sandwiched between us, but the table was round so he and I were almost facing each other.

"Mmmm…" I answered as I threw some money at the waitress who brought the drinks.

"Cheers, Spencer." I lifted my glass and waited for him to lift his. His name felt like acid on my tongue.

"Thank you, Ryan."

"No problem." We both drank at the same time.

"Is it your intention to get drunk?" Julia asked, irritation lacing each word.

"No. It's my *intention* to get *numb* so watching some bastard put his hands all over you won't bother me so much." We stared at each other unflinchingly, our eyes locked together. The skin of her cheeks flushed until finally she broke away and joined in the others' conversation.

As the strains of our song began, I sat back and waited as the lyrics began. The acoustic guitar and bongo drums filled the room in the slow, sultry strains.

Her eyes snapped up to mine, desire rising up within me like a tangible thing, my body reacting at the intensity as her lips parted and her hand reached for mine.

It spurred me to action. My fingers closed around hers and I rose from the chair, slowly pulling her up with me, my eyes never leaving hers.

We didn't speak, just held hands as we moved onto the dance floor. I took her in my arms, pulling her close and turning my face into her hair. My hands pressed her to me, the swell of her breasts pressed against my chest. Her hands slid under my jacket to fist in the back of my shirt. I felt like if I didn't kiss her, I would die right there. My eyes dropped to her mouth and she lifted her face in silent permission as her eyes slowly closed.

I let it happen. I wanted it. Needed it like I needed air to breathe. Our bodies swayed together as our mouths fed on each other over and over again. The words to the song communicating what I needed her to know…as my mouth went back for more. Kiss after kiss, we couldn't get enough, our lips ghosting and finally tasting, sucking on each other like we were starving.

I pressed my hardness into the softness of her stomach because I couldn't help myself and she moaned into my mouth.

"Ung…" I slid a hand up to the back of her head and into her hair, our mouths slanting across each other so we could get closer, our tongues sliding into each other's mouths like they had a million times before. So familiar. So absolutely delicious.

"Julia…" I dragged my mouth across her jaw and up to her temple as the music ended. It was so hot between us that I was sure everyone in the room must be burning, but all I could do was rest my forehead on hers and look deeply into her eyes. My fingers brushed her cheek as I pulled back slightly. "God, babe…"

"Mmmm, huh."

"Let's get out of here," I whispered as my mouth hovered over hers. She nodded very slightly and the movement succeeded in pressing her lips back to mine.

I placed one more soft kiss on her open mouth, before releasing her, then lacing my fingers through hers to lead her back to the table. I paused briefly to speak to the others as Julia picked up her clutch from the tabletop. Aaron and Jen were smiling. I didn't need to ask Julia if she was okay with leaving, I could feel it in the way she was clinging to my hand, her other hand curled around my bicep.

"We're leaving. See you guys at home." I glanced down at Moore, who looked embarrassed and contrite. I smirked almost against my will. "Goodnight."

"Bye," Julia said as we started to move away, my hand still threaded through hers possessively.

I led her outside and asked the valet to get us a cab. The breeze had come up and she shivered. I handed the attendant a ten dollar bill and then shrugged out of my suit jacket and placed it around her shoulders; then wrapped my arm around her.

She didn't speak but melted into me, resting her head on my shoulder after we climbed into the cab.

I inhaled deeply. This was my baby in my arms. Finally in my arms; like before. She turned her face into my neck and I tightened my hold.

"I know that song," she whispered.

"I knew you recognized it when you grabbed my hand under the table. The look in your eyes spoke volumes."

"It makes me feel…" she stopped and I waited anxiously. "Like I need to be closer to you."

"Me, too. Those kisses were amazing, baby," I whispered against her hair. Her hand tightened on my arm and she nodded.

When the cab driver pulled up outside the apartment, I reluctantly let her go to pay him. I offered her my hand and she took it, stepping out beside me.

Once we were inside, I slid the jacket from her shoulders and placed it over the back of a chair in the kitchen. She walked into the living room and sat on the couch in the dark.

I wasn't sure what she remembered or what she was feeling, but I wanted to be close to her. I sat next to her, slowly reaching for her hand again. "Julia…do you want to talk?" My body was aching and all I wanted was to press her back into the cushions and kiss her again and again.

"I don't know." Her eyes searched my face in the darkness. "I'm afraid if we talk about what just happened back there…it will disappear."

"No, it won't, babe," I barely got the words out.

She reached out and took the hand I offered. My thumb rubbed over the top of it again and again. I was certain, if I tried to speak, my voice would betray my emotions. Maybe I'd scared her and maybe she needed some space, but the silence was like a huge fucking exclamation point on the make-out session on the dance floor.

I craved her body and her mouth. I wanted to feel her hands on my body, to sink into her softness, to lose myself in our incredible love…yet, we just sat in the darkness. I didn't know what to say to make things right. The air vibrated around us in silent anticipation, but neither one of us moved.

I couldn't take it. I had to get away because if I didn't, I was going to make love to her right here on the couch. My body was throbbing, my heart aching, both to the point of physical pain. "Julia, honey, I think I need to…uh, be alone for a little while."

Even though she fought it, I could see the pain behind her eyes. She bit her lip and ran her hand through her hair. "Are you leaving?" she said, the throb in her voice landed my heart in my stomach like a stone. "Are you mad at me? I didn't mean…"

I considered what to say. Mad wasn't the right word. Hurt, devastated, broken maybe, but any anger I had wasn't directed at her. I cleared my throat, trying to get the emotions under control.

"No, I'm not mad, sweetheart." I bent to kiss her forehead and then spoke against it. "I just…I'm gonna play the piano for a little bit. After that shit with Moore and then the dancing, I'm wound up pretty tight." I brushed the back of my knuckles along her jaw and moved away to look in her eyes. She was so beautiful, literally breathtaking. It hurt to look at her. The sorrow, the pain…the *want,* all there for me to see.

She swallowed so hard I could see her throat constrict, but she nodded. "I'm sorry."

I stopped in my attempt to turn from her. "Hey." I nudged her chin up with my index finger. "Living so close like this, it's bound to get tough. You're incredibly beautiful and I'm only human. That's why I haven't been around as much. I thought it would make it easier. I'm sorry. I should have known you needed me."

And...I'm so in love with you I am barely able to breathe. I want you so damn much I feel like I'm going to combust.

Her green eyes melted as she looked at me, leaning into me slightly. The warmth of her body seeping into mine made my desire even more pronounced. I wanted nothing more than to take her in my arms and make love to her until she was breathless and spent. My cock was so engorged, that I thought it would pop the zipper on my pants. Throbbing, I yearned for the release that only Julia could give me. It felt like years since I'd held her naked body and buried myself deep within her soft heat.

"Should I leave? Go back to New York? Would it make it easier for you?"

I didn't hesitate. "Julia, no. It's just hard being this close to you, feeling like I do. Like I said…I'm only human."

"So *be* human, then," she almost moaned and my breath caught in my throat. I didn't think I'd be able to speak without my emotions pouring out of me like rain, but couldn't stay this close to her either. I was losing my grip on my closely guarded control. I brushed my knuckles against her cheek again.

"Baby, you know we can't do this right now. I'm sorry." I turned and walked down the hall to my room, shutting the door quietly behind me. I knew she was confused. *Fuck, I was confused* and it was rotten to leave her after what happened on the dance floor. I leaned up against the door, straining to hear what she was doing. There wasn't a single sound.

I pushed away from the door, my body still burning from the events of the evening. My mind was, too. Filled with her taste, her smell, the feel of her softness pressed so intimately against me and those soul-shaking kisses.

Everything told me to just treat her like she was mine, like we were us, like it was fucking meant to be. She remembered the song, and maybe I hadn't played fair, but Goddamn it! I wasn't letting that little cocksucker try to move in on what was mine. I sucked in my breath, turning the knob slowly and then pulled it open a crack. I needed to know she was okay. The apartment was dark and so quiet.

Did she leave? I panicked, but then I heard the sound of her crying softly from the living room. I couldn't stay away and quickly went down the hall. Julia was still in her dress, curled up on the couch and hugging a pillow tightly to her chest. I ached to comfort her, but what would I say? I wasn't sure, but I had to say something. I sat on the floor next to the couch, turning toward her, needing to see her beautiful face.

"Go away," she mumbled into the pillow and turned further so her back was to me. "Just…leave me alone, Ryan, *please*."

I reached out a tentative hand toward her and started to rub her back. She tensed, but I kept up the massage with gentle fingers until finally she started to relax.

"Julia, there is nothing in the world I want less than to hurt you. I…" I wanted to tell her I loved her so damn bad. "I adore you. You know that, don't you?"

"Then why are you doing this? Why won't you tell me anything? It feels like you want me to know. It felt like you wanted me when we were dancing." Her voice was trembling and my heart hurt for both of us.

I sighed heavily and hung my head. Leaning my elbow on the couch, I held my head with my hand, scooting closer.

"Will you turn around?" I asked very softly. "Julia, please." Finally, she shifted slightly toward me and lowered the pillow. She had mascara tracks trailing down her cheeks and her eyes were still glassy. I reached out to brush her tears away with both of my thumbs, rubbing them across her skin again and again in slow strokes. "*Yes*. I wish I could tell you. And, I do want you. You felt how much." I paused. "After tonight, it's apparent to me that Moore has ulterior motives, so I don't want to trust him, but he...obviously cares about you. I do think he believes that you need to remember on your own. On that at least, I trust him."

"What could happen if you told me? What are you all afraid of?"

I looked into her eyes and brushed a tear-dampened tendril away from her face.

"If we try to trigger it, it could be too much and you'll either never get your memory back or maybe you won't forgive me. I couldn't bear to lose you."

"Forgive you for what?" She got the little crinkle above her nose as she frowned and shook her head. "I don't understand."

My brow dropped as I considered what to say. I looked down for a minute before answering, wondering how much I should tell her, but she deserved something. She was hurting and I couldn't stand to see her tears. I swallowed and made myself meet her eyes. "For making you remember something that you want to forget." I ran my hand over her shoulder and down her back. "Can you trust me? Believe me, there is nothing I want more on this earth than for you to remember, but we have to take things slowly. I will not hurt you in *any* way."

"I *know* we loved each other, Ryan. Can't you at least give me that much? Why does everyone insist that we're only good friends? I feel that we're so much more."

"We were friends first, but yes...there was a lot more." Her gaze was intense and sparkled in the moonlight coming through the window. "Please don't push for more tonight, babe. I know this is hard, but it will all work out, my love." Her eyes widened and she gasped. I reached out and ran a single finger along the side of her face, eyes dropping to her mouth. My thoughts went back to the kissing on the dance floor earlier. I wanted more so badly that my mouth went dry. "Yes. My *love*, okay?" She nodded so slightly I barely saw it, but her eyes filled with unshed tears that tugged at my weakened heart. "*Always*. Uhnggg," I cleared my throat. "I need to go take a shower. Do you want to sleep in my room tonight?"

"With you? I want to be close to you."

I stiffened and she sensed it. I wanted nothing more than to wrap myself around her, but it would be torture to stop there.

"Uhnnn, Julia," I groaned. "I don't think that's wise, baby."

She nodded with certain sadness to her expression. "Okay. I thought you were going to play the piano?"

"After my shower." I wanted to hold her, to make love to her, to kiss her for hours. I was starving to touch her; the loneliness between us was like a raging storm. Just looking at her, I knew she felt it, too.

"Would it be okay if I listen for awhile?" she whispered and ran her fingers lightly along my jaw. I pressed my cheek into her hand, wanting to feel more of her touch.

So much for my needed time alone, but I need you more.

"Yes, *please*." I smiled faintly and leaned in to kiss the side of her face, breathing in her scent as my eyes closed. Perfume, freesias and Julia. "I'll be out of the shower in a couple of minutes. If you want to take a bath when I'm done, I'll wait for you to finish before I start playing. Yes?"

She nodded and ran a hand down my arm as I got to my feet, her fingers closing around mine as I moved away.

God, I love her. Being close to her like this was what I wanted, yet it was so painful. I went into the bathroom and stripped out of my clothes, hanging my shirt on the back of the door and letting my slacks and boxer briefs fall on the floor. I turned on the water.

My dick was still aching. I thought about trying to masturbate to take care of it, but it wasn't just sexual tension. Yes, being near her, knowing how amazing we were together in bed and not being able to take her was torture, but more than that, I *missed* her. There was a deep sadness behind the wanting and trying to get myself off wouldn't fulfill me. I doubted I'd even be able to come that way anyway. I needed Julia and only her. *Wanted* only her.

I stepped under the cold spray and gasped at the shock. I was tired and emotionally spent. As my erection relaxed, I turned the water warmer to ease the ache in the muscles of my back and neck. The stress of the long hours at the hospital, school obligations and this constant worry were slowly driving me insane. Normally, I'd lose myself in her softness, her velvet touch, her soothing words and her kisses. I missed those kisses almost more than anything else. Tonight on the dance floor practically had me undone.

"Jesus Christ!" I swore under my breath as I cranked the water back to ice cold and let it hit me straight in the face. I stood under the spray until I started to shiver.

Throwing open the shower door, I quickly grabbed a towel and immediately put it over my head and started rubbing vigorously. Thankfully, my body was back under control and I breathed a sigh of relief as I wrapped the towel around my waist and started the bath for Julia. I added some of the bath salts she loved, a remnant of the times she'd visited. My heart thumped at the memory of our many candlelit baths together. I rushed to put on some sweatpants and a t-shirt, and then opened the door to my room, calling to her softly.

"Julia, I have the water running for you, honey."

She hadn't moved from the couch, but now she sat up and padded down the hall in her stocking feet. "Thank you." She let her hand run across my midsection as she passed and even through the shirt, her touch burned. My stomach muscles tightened in reaction as she disappeared into the bathroom.

I ran my hands through my wet hair and sat down at my keyboard, contemplating what to play. It was obvious that music triggered her memory. I was trained in classical piano, but so much of the time, we'd picked contemporary tunes and sometimes she'd sing along. That was what I loved best. She had a wonderful singing voice that was mostly wasted in the confines of her bathroom. The corners of my mouth lifted slightly as I ran my hands over the keys in a series of chords just to warm up. I sat there in silence for minutes, listening to the sounds in the bathroom. The water sloshing had me aching to burst through the door and look upon her naked body, to touch her…to *have* her. My body quickened in desire.

I shook my head to clear it. *Damn, Ryan. The music, remember?*

This was a chance to hint without telling her facts of her life. I looked at the ceiling as I searched my brain for the right song. *I knew*. I began to play the soft, slow melody of one that she was very familiar with. In fact, it was one that she'd bought me the sheet music for because she wanted to hear me play. It was a simple tune, but the lyrics were powerful.

I should have known I couldn't play this song without choking up. I closed my eyes, and let my fingers find the melody, losing myself in my memories. My throat tightened; my heart beating heavily inside my chest. The bathroom door opened quietly, startling me from my thoughts and my hands paused over the keys. Julia came in wearing only the shirt I'd left on the back of the bathroom door. I was stunned by her simple beauty with her hair piled on top of her head, and the top buttons left open to just below her breasts, leaving the curves bare to my view. My fingers ached to reach out and touch her, to draw her to me, but I forced myself to resume playing as she moved toward the bed behind me, out of my eye line.

She didn't speak, only sat listening. My mind raced, wondering if she recognized the song. I didn't hear her come up behind me, but her fingers wound through my hair and her other hand rested on my shoulder. It was all I could do not to lean back into her softness and feel her soft curves against me. I drew in a shaky breath as her mouth opened on the skin at my nape, her tongue licking my skin as she drew away.

"Will you play it again, Ryan? It's so haunting and beautiful…" she said softly, her lips ghosting over me. I could feel her breath rush over my neck and ear.

I was helpless under her touch. What could I do but bend to her will? I nodded and began the song again as she moved carefully to my side and straddled the bench facing me, the white shirt tails pooling between her firm thighs. I glanced toward her as the music began. Julia leaned her forehead on my shoulder, one hand resting on my bicep. My head snapped to the side when she began to sing the lyrics, her other hand rubbed up and down my back.

I was dying. The words were so powerful and her voice caressing; feeling her so close and having her hands on me was like a religious experience. It was all I could do to keep my shaking hands on the keys.

When the last notes faded, we remained on the bench, her head still resting against me. I kissed her hair and then she moved her forehead slowly back and forth against the muscle of my shoulder.

"Do you remember anything about that song? Other than the lyrics?" I asked in a husky whisper, my lips still up against the top of her head. She smelled so enticing and my body stirred anew, but her nearness was something I had to have.

"Yes. I gave you that sheet music, right?"

My heart leapt. "Uh huh. We've done this before. I play, you sing." I brought my arm up and around her, pulling her closer. "Are you okay?"

"No," she began. "I don't think I am." Her voice was weak and shaking. I wasn't sure if it was from sadness or desire.

"Julia, what can I do to make this easier?"

She shrugged but didn't raise her head and her hand reached out to slide down my thigh to the inside of my knee.

"Tonight, dancing…it felt so right to be in your arms, Ryan. I want more."

I closed my eyes. *I want more too, but I don't know if I can stop there.*

My hand slid up her back, to the back of her head and I laced my fingers through her hair. "Julia…" I breathed.

She drew in a shaky breath, and her voice trembled. My body betrayed me and I started to shake, even though I struggled to hold it in.

"Ryan, I want you to touch me. You make me…" She stopped, and squeezed my thigh, bringing her head up to meet my eyes. "I want…I mean, when I'm near you I'm just…" Her lids dropped halfway down and her mouth parted. I could see the same desire in her face that I'd seen a thousand times. I knew exactly what she was trying to say even though she was struggling with the words. "I'm just…"

"Fucking *vibrating*?" I asked with a groan.

"Yes," she answered without hesitation. "Will you touch me?" She took my hand and lifted it to her breast and tried to arch into it. The movement still caused her pain. Her eyes closed and she bit her lip. I let my hand slide across the side curve of the soft flesh, over the fabric of my shirt and she let out a small mewling moan. My body surged in response.

I turned and slid my arms around her fully, under her legs, turning her so she was straddling my lap, facing me, but careful not to hurt her. My muscles flexed but she was so small, I took her weight easily.

"You're so strong," she whispered, her nose nuzzling mine and her little hands moving up my chest over my shoulders. Her lips were parted and her sweet breath rushed hotly across my face. My body swelled even more and tented my sweatpants. There was no hiding my desire and I didn't want to. She needed to know how much I wanted her. I stared into her deep green eyes and then rested my forehead on hers.

"You don't know what you're asking," I breathed and pushed the loose tendrils off of the left side of her face. I bent to kiss where her head injury had been, dragging my lips across her cheekbone and down to her jaw. "Julia," I whispered against her silken skin. "God, I don't know if I'm strong enough for this. You smell so good."

Her head fell back and she moaned. "Uhhhhh…"

My left hand raked down her back toward her rear and even though I knew I'd find nothing underneath, I was still gasping as my hand wrapped around her bare butt cheek. I pulled her closer, as I placed wet, open-mouth kisses along the curve of her neck. When her hands slid into my hair, her fingers grasping and tugging, I was lost. My lips found hers in a hungry kiss, my tongue never hesitating to bury itself in the warm recesses of her mouth.

Oh my God. She kissed me back with everything she had, our mouths feasting and sucking on each other like we would never stop. Both of my arms pulled her closer and I could feel the heat coming off of her core and seeping through my sweats.

"Uhnnnn, God, Julia," I moaned when she winced slightly. "Baby, we can't. You're body isn't healed enough yet." My mouth hovered over hers, not wanting to lose the contact. "I don't want to hurt you."

"It's worth the pain, Ryan. Please. I'm...*dying*." My breath left me in a rush as her lips reached for mine again. I kissed her back, more softly this time. There was nothing that would make me hurt her. No matter how my body was aching or how much I wanted her.

Something that sounded like a sob erupted and her hands slid down my chest, massaging the muscles. "I've wanted to touch you like this, Ryan. You're so beautiful."

"Julia...you don't know what you do to me," I groaned as one of her hands closed around my cock through my sweats. My head dropped to her shoulder as she squeezed and pulled a few times up and down the shaft, moving her thumb across the head when she got to the top. "Stop, I can't take it," I begged, but she only repeated the motion. "Ugh..."

My hands went to the back of her thighs and I lifted her with me as I stood up, stepping over the bench. I released her legs letting her feet touch the floor, but still supported her weight with my arms around her back.

"Ryan, no..." she pleaded. Her hand came up to cup my cheek. "No...please." She shook her head frantically.

"Julia, you're ribs will hurt if we make love. You won't be able to take the thrusts without pain." I buried my face in her neck as I spoke. "Dear God," I groaned.

I sank back down on the bench in front of her and ran my hands up the sides of her body under my shirt. I didn't unbutton it further because the site of her nakedness would drive me insane. My thumbs brushed against both of her taut nipples and she gasped. I kissed her breastbone and dragged my mouth toward her right breast and nipped at the nipple through the fabric.

"Ryan, God…It's torture."

I turned her gently so her back was to me and let my hands continue to roam her body, drifting down over her concave stomach, and the soft curls at the top of her sex. My body was so hard it hurt, the skin covering my dick so taut, I thought it would split open. I groaned and let my head fall forward until it rested on her back, just under her shoulder. It was a blissful, aching torture that I never wanted to end.

My hands closed around her hipbones and I urged her backward. "Babe, sit on my lap." As she did as I asked, my arms wrapped around her and I turned my face into her neck. "I'm going to touch you but try not to move too much…I want this to be all about pleasure. Please be still."

My hands slid down her thighs to her knees and I pressed them open, bringing my hands back up on the insides, over the velvet skin. I could feel her trembling and I almost died. "Oh, baby…I've missed touching you like this." The words ripped from my chest in a guttural groan, but I couldn't stop them. I moved my legs apart and with hers draped over mine, it spread her open for me. She leaned back against my chest and dropped her head to the curve of my neck in anticipation.

Her breath hitched as my hands resumed their roaming, over her torso, one hand moving up to her breast to tug and tease the hard little nipple and the other sliding down over her stomach and further still.

The moist heat between her legs was telling and I groaned against her, kissing her neck with my open mouth, sucking on her skin while I let my fingers part her sensitive flesh. She gasped as I dipped my middle finger inside her to bring some of the slickness up to the place aching for my touch, and started a slow pulsing rhythm.

"Uhhhh..." she breathed. Her back arched and I felt her wince.

"Julia, I'll pleasure you...I'll make you come, but be still or I'll stop. I won't let this hurt you." I hardly recognized my own voice. It was low and animalistic. Telling the woman I loved more than life that I was going to make her come did amazing things to me.

She turned her face toward mine as my fingers worked on her, slowly; her breathing deepened and her hands clutched at her sides. I never wanted to stop touching her. I wanted this to go on forever and I could feel how sensitive she was, gasping each time my finger moved. I slowed my pace, wanting to build slowly, to make it amazing when I finally allowed her over the edge.

I closed my eyes and let my fingers work on her breasts and her sex. Listening to her moans and pants, I felt like I could orgasm without her even touching me. "Julia...do you feel how much you own me?" I moaned against the soft skin of her neck, her pulse beating wildly against my lips. So sweet and alive. "But you're mine. You own me, but you've always been mine."

"Ryan...oh," she cried out and she turned slightly so that we could kiss. Her mouth was frantic underneath mine as I sucked her tongue into my mouth. My hand closed around her breast and I squeezed gently, her pebble hard nipple and the wetness on my fingers of my other hand; beautiful evidence of what I could do to her. My heart swelled, bursting with love and pride that this magnificent creature belonged to me. Even if she couldn't remember our past, she was mine and I wanted her to know it.

I pushed two fingers inside of her and I felt her clench around me as I moved them in and out of her tight flesh.

"Uhhnnn, Ryan, don't stop..." she begged breathlessly as I searched for the ultra sensitive spot inside her that I knew drove her to distraction, while my other hand moved down to take over where the other left off. She started shaking and her legs trembled.

"Uh...Ryan, Oh God..." she sobbed into my mouth. Her body started to pulse and she arched into me. She couldn't help it; her body quaked involuntarily over and over as she came under my hands. I buried my mouth in the back of her neck and breathed her name over and over.

"That's it. Yes, Baby...Julia, I want you so much. Everything about you is so damn beautiful." I slowed the movements of my fingers, lightening the touch but not stopping, the spasms inside her lessening, but not subsiding completely. I kissed the tender skin on her neck again and moved below her ear. I could taste the faintest bit of salty perspiration on my tongue. I licked along the cord of her neck and then opened my lips and sucked, feeling the need to leave marks on her skin. It didn't matter if anyone else saw it. She'd know it was there, that I was marking her as mine. "I want...I want to mark you."

"Anything you want," she gasped out, her body still jerking with the aftershocks of her orgasm. I sucked on the skin at the back of her neck hard and then soft. I alternated like that for a minute or two and I raised my head to try to see in the darkness of the room. The flesh was purple in a small spot on the back of her neck.

"I'm sorry, honey, but you make me want things that no one else ever has."

"I want to touch you," she whispered. "Ryan, please."

I stood up and put her feet on the floor, and ran my hands down her arms. She turned and lifted up on tiptoe, her hands resting on my chest. I raised my hand to the side of her face, my thumb tilting her face to mine and my fingers curled around the back of her head, I bent to kiss her again. We were hungry. For me, it was the agony of almost losing her and the weeks of being near her without being able to be with her as I longed to do. I lessened the pressure of my mouth and tried to move away slightly, but her lips clung to mine, sucking my lower lip in between the two of hers. I kept my eyes closed as my breath hitched.

"Julia, let's lie down. You need to rest." I led her to the bed and threw back the covers. "Come on, I'll tuck you in."

She slid in between the cool sheets and grabbed my hand. "Please, don't leave."

I wanted every second with her, so I let her pull me down. My body was still aching, but I struggled to get it under control.

"I want to make you feel good, too," she whispered. "You're so incredible. You know just how to touch me."

I rolled onto my side toward her and propped my head up on my hand. "Yes," was all I said, my eyes searching her flushed face. Even in the dark, I could see the heightened color on her cheeks. I reached out and touched the tip of one still taut breast with a fingertip.

"You've had a lot of practice." It wasn't a question. "Touching me, I mean."

I watched the path my hand was running down her body and up again, sliding in the opening of the shirt and cupping her bare breast. "A little bit," I admitted softly, seriously, as my eyes flashed up to hers.

"Ryan, why wouldn't you tell me that we were *this kind* of close?"

I couldn't tell her the whole truth. I couldn't tell her that the loss of the baby was going to hurt like hell. I wanted to spare her the pain.

"I wanted you to remember me, to remember *us*...and I didn't want to scare you." My thumb brushed back and forth on her nipple and my body quickened again. "It just seemed important. It still does."

"I'm sorry. I'm trying. I want to remember."

"I know. I don't want to lose all the beautiful memories between us." My voice deepened. "It makes me sad, but don't be sorry, baby. It will come back in time."

I leaned my head against hers and nuzzled the side of her face. I wanted to distract her. Plus, I couldn't help myself anyway. I slid my hand down and resumed the slow movements I'd started on the piano bench. She was still wet, and her orgasm had made it even more pronounced. I watched her face as the feelings deep within her began to stir again as we lay there in silence, my fingers moving slowly, gently over and over.

Julia's eyes burned into mine. My eyes dropped to her pouty little mouth and I wanted to taste her. I brought my fingers up and sucked them into my mouth. She gasped and I groaned.

"Uhnngg...Julia, you're so sweet. You are the most delicious thing that I've ever tasted." My throat got tight and I tried to swallow the lump of emotion rising there. The love was overwhelming and I hardly knew how to save myself. "I want more. I want you to come in my mouth, Julia."

"Ryan, I..."

"Shhhh...don't talk. Just let me..." I moved and lifted her further up the bed and bent to kiss her mouth softly, licking at her top lip before I sucked it in between both of mine. "*Let me*," I whispered against her mouth. "I want to hear every breath you take, every moan...every little mewling sound that you make deep in your throat, Julia. It makes me so hard, I swear I'll burst."

I parted her legs with my knee and moved lower, looking into her eyes. I pushed the tails of the shirt up until she was naked from the waist down and then gently pushed her legs apart so I could gaze down on the treasure I was seeking. I could already smell her arousal. "Julia…Jesus! You turn me on so much." I bent to kiss her stomach below her navel and the muscles of her stomach tensed as I lay down between her legs and started kissing the inside of her thighs with a wet mouth. "Relax, baby. I already know how good you taste and I want it so damn bad. I want every single drop."

"Oh, God…" she gasped.

"Please try not to move, my love."

"I can't, Ryan. It's impossible," she breathed as she turned her head to one side.

Her hand wound in my hair and the other reached toward me on the top of the mattress. I took it and laced my fingers through hers. I laid my free hand on the flat of her stomach above her pubic bone and bent my head toward the delicious flesh I craved.

Automatically, her legs fell wider, allowing me better access and she involuntarily moved her hips so she rubbed against my mouth. It was extremely hot and made me harder than steel. I found my own hips moving against the edge of the bed in unison with hers as I suckled her sweetness, until I was moaning against her. Even though I'd told her not to move, it drove me insane. I was starving and she tasted so good. I told myself to go slow but I was so aroused by what was happening, I wasn't in complete control. Feeling her silken nub throb on my tongue, hearing her little pants as she got closer to the edge, and the friction of my cock against the bed, I knew I would come right along with her.

I moved lower so I could thrust my tongue into her and then laved up in long strokes. Her trembling and clenching around my tongue drove me over the edge. "Julia…come for me baby," I groaned against her sensitive flesh as I came hard myself. It had been so long and I was so hot for her that wave after wave of pleasure overwhelmed me. I shot off in a series of powerful spurts, all the while continuing to lick and suck on her. "Uhnnnn, Ugh…"

"Uh…Uh…Uh…Ryan," she moaned softly and her hand that was still holding mine tightened and her body arched violently as her orgasm overtook her. "Uhhhhhh…" she breathed. "Uhhhhh…"

I turned my head and kissed the inside of her thigh with my open mouth as her body still jerked with the aftershocks of her pleasure.

"You drive me insane. Julia, I love you. I love you more than anything in the whole world, do you hear me? I know I'm not supposed to tell you, but I can't fucking help myself after that."

She pulled on our entwined hands, silently asking me to move up toward her. The front of my sweats was soaked with my own cum. I wasn't embarrassed about it and crawled up over her on my hands and knees, careful not to press the mess into her. Her hands closed around the sides of my face as she looked into my eyes. Her eyes were dark with desire and an expression of languid satisfaction relaxed her features. "You're so gorgeous. I never want to look at anything else for the rest of my life," I said softly.

"Ryan…I can't believe you're real. You're so perfect." Her mouth reached for mine and I had no desire to deny her. My mouth closed over hers in a series of hungry kisses. Our mouths were perfect mirrors as we alternately sucked on each other's tongues, tilting our heads so we could delve deeper into each other's mouths. "I love you, too," she finally whispered as I placed one last kiss on her mouth. "I do."

I pulled back and stared into her eyes, brushing her hair back as my heart did somersaults inside my chest. *Did she remember?*

I rested my forehead against hers and closed my eyes, as we both struggled to get our breathing under control. "I've missed you so much. Being near you and not touching you has been living hell."

"I wish my ribs didn't hurt anymore. I want to feel you inside me," she moaned sensuously against my mouth.

"Oh baby…" *She would be my undoing.* "I do, too. There is nothing I want more." I moved to lie next to her and propped myself up on one arm to look down on her. Her hands moved to pull my shirt back down over her nakedness. "Are you cold?" I sat up enough to reach for the covers and pull them up over her.

She shook her head. "No, I just wish…" her sparkling eyes held mine captive as I lay back down beside her.

"What do you wish, honey?" I asked, reaching out to bring her hand to my mouth. "Tell me."

"That I could make you feel good, too."

"Baby, stop. The way you moved against my mouth was so hot."

"I couldn't help it. It felt so good." I could practically hear the blush in her voice.

I smiled gently, running a finger along the line of her jaw. "It told me that you craved my touch as much as I craved your taste. Oh God…" I breathed. "Julia, I came, okay? You didn't even have to touch me, and you made me come." Her eyes widened and her mouth dropped open. "That's what you do to me. It transcends anything I've ever experienced," I said softly, my voice thick with emotion, and the corners of my lips lifted slightly. "In fact, I need to change and clean up the mess." I bent to kiss her again. "Will you be okay while I do that?"

Her small hand came up to my jaw and she slid her fingers across it. She didn't speak, but only nodded.

"Okay. I'll be right back." I moved out of the bed and went into the bathroom to strip off the soiled sweatpants and use a warm washcloth to clean myself up. I went back into the bedroom, and to the dresser to find a new pair of sweats. After I put them on, I stopped as my hand hovered on the top drawer where her bracelet and her engagement ring were hiding in the back. I opened it and pulled the bracelet out, rubbing my thumb over the sparkling diamonds and our two entwined initials.

I had to get it back on her wrist after the lovemaking we'd just shared. I wanted her to know she was mine and, frankly, I wanted my possession of her out in the open. Moore would get the message, one way or the other. If Julia wearing the bracelet didn't work, then I'd take great pleasure in beating his arrogant face in. I turned back to the bed and she was lying on her side, her hands were holding the comforter up near her chest and her eyes were closed, her breathing deep and even. Fast asleep.

I knelt down and carefully replaced the bracelet on her left wrist. Back where it belonged. Satisfaction welled followed by intense love and possessiveness. I bent to kiss her forehead and brush her hair back. It had fallen from the knot at the top of her head during our love play on the bed.

Julia, you are so beautiful. And you are mine. I closed my eyes and breathed her in. *I love you.*

I slid under the covers and pulled her close, snuggling up to her warm little body. She curled into me, her legs tangling unconsciously with mine and her head came to rest on my chest.

"Ryan…" she breathed, and I was content.

For the first time in a month, I was going to get a good night's sleep.

~7~

Julia ~

SOMETHING WARM AND wonderful surrounded me as my eyes fluttered open and my hand moved over the arm wrapped securely around me from behind. The fine hair covering his skin was downy soft against my fingers. *Mmmm…Ryan.* The delicious memories of the night before flooded my consciousness. He was beautiful and amazing. And he loved me.

There was a gentle nuzzling at the side of my neck. His sweet breath washed hotly over my skin just before his lips found the sensitive place beneath my ear.

"Good morning," I said softly and tightened my hold on his arm.

"Mmmm…yes, it is." He moved to prop his head up on one arm and turn on his side, still leaving the arm I was holding onto around me, but his fingers moved up to touch my cheekbone and then slide softly along my brow. I looked up at him in wonder. His hair was wild and reflecting gold from the sunlight streaming in from the window and his blue eyes; intense. "How are you this morning?" He bent to place a soft kiss on my open mouth.

Immediately I responded, my mouth clinging to his in hungry ardor. His hand slid up to wrap around the back of my neck, thumb tracing the line of my jaw as I kissed him. He was careful not to crush my body with his. The kiss was so gentle. I wanted more, but it tugged at my heart how aware he was of my injuries and my needs. I slid my arms around his waist and up over the strong muscles of his back. I tried to pull him closer, aching to feel his hard muscled body sinking into mine. Finally, his tongue entered my mouth with a groan of surrender; each one giving and the other taking, and back again. It was perfection.

My hips surged toward his but Ryan resisted, softening the kiss and pulling away. Saying nothing, he nuzzled his nose against my face affectionately.

"Wonderful," I murmured, turning in to him. "How could I not be?" I had him beside me, holding me close to his body, his scent wafting around and his lips moving over my cheek and chin toward my mouth. "Thank you for last night," I whispered against his lips, hoping he would kiss me and never stop.

"Which part?" He pulled back and gazed at me. "Interrupting you with that jackass or for later, hmmm?" Emotions flickered in his eyes and when I wrinkled my nose, he smiled softly. I reached up to touch the side of his face with my left hand and rainbow reflections shot all over the room, falling across his features, the walls and the ceiling. I gasped.

"Uhhh…" My breath rushed out as my eyes flew from the diamond bracelet to meet his eyes. His hand immediately closed over mine and drew it to his mouth. He held it there, his lips moving softly over my skin and then the bracelet, his eyes never leaving mine. It was breathtaking. Our initials entwined like lovers, diamonds sparkling from the center and both sides, so delicate and amazing. My eyes welled with tears as my mind flashed to a dark place filled with candlelight, love and happiness. The feeling overwhelmed me. I closed my eyes, causing the single tears to slide from the corners of each of my eyes.

"Don't cry, my love," Ryan said as he kissed my right temple. "Julia, please don't cry."

I turned so he could fully enfold me in his arms. I ignored the pain shooting through my ribcage, buried my face in the curve of his neck and tightened my arms around him. "Oh Ryan…It's so beautiful. It's perfect. I've been missing it, haven't I?" I asked, my voice overflowing with emotion.

"Yes." He nodded ever so slightly, and then kissed the inside of my wrist again. "From almost the moment you woke up. I missed seeing it there, too." His words were soft and reverent, flowing like warm honey over my senses. That voice would be my undoing. "So much, I can't even tell you."

His hand was stroking my hair, down my arm and hip and back again, his touch so soft and reverent, like I was made of glass. I watched him through my tears. His features were soft, but he swallowed like his throat hurt and closed his eyes for a second or two.

"I *know*," I said in a whisper.

"Do you? Are you remembering anything?"

I swallowed the tightness in my throat as I searched for something in the back of my mind. I closed my eyes and the scene unfolded. "Yes. It was a place I don't recognize. It was dark, except for soft candlelight. I remember how I felt when you put it on my wrist." My voice cracked on the words and I looked at him. Finally, I was getting something that I could hold on to. "The love between us in that moment…so amazing."

"Yes. We went skiing in Colorado; just the two of us. It was our first Christmas as a couple and we wanted to be alone. It *was*…amazing." His hand cupped my face again, his thumb brushing away an errant tear along my cheekbone and his lips moved softly over mine like a feather caress.

I nodded silently. "That's when you gave me that beautiful poem, too."

His face split into a brilliant smile and he nodded. "Do you remember what you gave me?"

I tried but couldn't place anything. Ryan could see the struggle on my face. "Well, you've remembered something and that's enough for now. For the first time, I have real hope that you're coming back to me," he said softly, his tone low and velvet. My heart thrummed inside me.

"Ryan. I'm so sorry. This has to be hell for you." I played with the front of his t-shirt as his hands continued to stroke up and down my body.

He pulled in a deep sigh. I knew he wouldn't tell me how badly he'd suffered, so I searched his eyes imploringly, silently begging him for the truth. "I'm just thankful you're okay. Having you…alive…and whole, is the most important thing."

How could I have forgotten this incredible man? How could I forget the magnificence of a love like this? It filled me up to the point of bursting. I tilted my head so I could kiss his chin, covered in a full day's worth of beard by now. It wasn't prickly; it was soft and felt nice. He smelled divine. "You feel so good."

"So do you. I've missed you in so many ways." The words pulled from him as if he couldn't help it, his tone low and guttural. "Last night…was…"

"Mmmm…Yes," I said, smiling against his skin. He moved, pressing me closer. I moaned softly.

"Were you trying to make me jealous?" There was a hard edge to his tone. He wasn't mad at me, but it wasn't exactly the reaction I was looking for.

"No, I mean…I wasn't, but I'm glad it turned out this way. I was missing you and you did need a little motivation." I smiled at him. "It wasn't a *date*."

"Hmmph." He let out his breath. "Could've fooled me."

"Look what it got me. Here we are, all wrapped up together. All I wanted was time with you."

"It was hard staying away, but it was easier than being…close."

I pulled back, puzzled. "So why last night?"

He looked at me seriously. "You know *why*. Last night…I gave in to all I'd been fighting. I couldn't help myself and it was incredible. It feels so good to be able to tell you I love you out loud."

"I still don't understand why you had to fight *anything*. You should've just told me. You still should."

Ryan's hand stopped its gentle kneading of my flesh and he rolled onto his back away from me. The look on his face told me that the conversation was over. "I'd rather talk about what in the hell you were doing with that jerk-off," he said with false sharpness. He was teasing, but it was more an attempt to change the subject.

I couldn't help smiling. I loved jealous Ryan. It gave me all kinds of butterflies in the pit of my stomach. "My, you have so many colorful names for Spencer this morning," I teased. "I thought you said that you *weren't* mad." Now it was my turn to prop up on my elbow and tease. I winced and Ryan noticed.

"Julia, please stop doing things that hurt," he said shortly. He rolled off of the bed and bent to lift me into a sitting position near the edge.

"Well?" I asked, not letting him change the subject.

"I wasn't mad at you, but that prick crossed the line." He powered on his computer, I assumed because he wanted to check email, and shot a look over his shoulder.

"I was bored. I missed you. When he called…I wanted to talk about my trip to New York. He's the one person I can talk to about you. Jen and Aaron, even my parents, are doing what you ask and keeping their traps shut. Spence is the only one who can be impartial."

His face hardened, his mouth setting in a firm line. "Are you fucking kidding me? You could have talked to *me*," he muttered.

I got up and went to stand behind him, placing my hands on his shoulders. The muscles were tense and I squeezed slightly.

"You wouldn't tell me. You're avoiding it now, too."

"He knows the truth, but he didn't tell you either, right?"

"No," I said in defeat.

"We agreed that it would be best not to push you, but he's trying to drive a wedge between us. He wants you. I don't trust him anymore." He didn't move, didn't soften his posture, didn't turn towards me and take me in his arms like I wanted.

"Ryan, are we really arguing about someone who means nothing? He can't influence my feelings. Don't you know me better than that?"

It was like he didn't hear what I said. "You had to know how much you meant to me."

I shrugged. "To a degree. You were very loving, but I was afraid you were only being a good friend, feeling obligated to take care of me. I wanted *more*. Every time I ask anything specific, you either ignore or deny me."

Ryan turned and faced me. His eyes were flashing fire. "I *never* denied you. Not *once*! I fucking worship you." My heart squeezed inside my chest at the pain and love that crossed his face. I wanted to hold him, but he walked quickly over to his dresser, opened the top drawer and dug around in the back before slamming it shut. He was in front of me in two seconds. "You want to know what we are?" His eyes were blazing; Ryan pulled my left hand forward and slid a diamond engagement ring on the third finger. His voice softened on the next words. "We are everything, Julia. *Everything*."

"Oh my God," I breathed as I stared down at the beautiful ring. Tears flooded my eyes. Suddenly I was in his arms and he was burying his face in the curtain of hair at the side of my neck. "Ryan…I'm…" Between the emotions and the implications of the ring, I was speechless.

"I know you don't remember when I proposed, and if you don't want to wear it, I'll understand. I just…" he said as his arms tightened around me tenderly, "I want everyone to know you're mine. I need *you* to know it."

We held each other without speaking, his heart beating heavily next to mine. He was warm and safe. I felt very much loved and completely cherished. Finally, I found my voice. "I thought we established that we owned each other last night." My arms were around his neck and I moved both hands to thread though his hair and hold the back of his head. Love swallowed me whole and I held on for dear life.

"I guess we did," he said as his hold loosened and he tried to move back a little.

I couldn't help it, my arms tightened again. "No, don't let go." My eyes stung and my voice caught. "Don't let go. I'll never take it off."

"I've missed holding you like this." His arms were home, the hold he took of me was possessive and I wanted to be his more than anything; more than food or water or air. Nothing mattered more than Ryan. "Shhh, Julia," he soothed me as I wept into him. "I know this whole thing has been confusing. I've wished over and over that I could make everything better for you."

It was my turn to pull back so I could look into this face. "You *do*. Don't you see how wonderful you are? From the moment I saw your face, I knew this was *us*." I smiled through my tears. "Even though you're so stubborn."

He kissed my cheek and then my temple, all the while his arms still held me tight. "You're remembering on your own and I think it will continue. I'll tell you whatever I feel is safe, so can we just play it by ear?"

I should agree. After all, I now had a bracelet and engagement ring which was an amazing gift. If he wanted to take it slow, I could be happy with things for now. "Yes. Anything you want."

"Hmmmph," Ryan breathed. "Don't be saying that, babe." His hands slid down to cup my butt cheeks and he grinned as he gave them a gently squeeze. "What should we do today? I don't have to work until three."

He let me go and went into the bathroom. I could hear the water running in the shower and then he reappeared in the doorway. "Aaron will pester you to make breakfast, but I don't want you to bother with it. Let's go out."

I felt my lower lip extend in protest. "I've really missed you."

His eyes softened and darkened. I took in his body, lounging easily in the doorway, his arms raised up against the frame. The edge of his t-shirt was hitched up and I could see the fine trail of hair leading south and disappearing into his black sweats. I looked away, a flush in my cheeks. *I can't believe I'm feeling embarrassed looking at him after what he did to me last night.*

"Me, too." His eyes narrowed at the lust that he surely must have seen in my eyes. My girly parts were experiencing all sorts of throbs and tingles, leaving me shaken. Ryan had to know how he affected me; the look of lust on his face told me so. "I still have to work, but I'll try to spend less time at the library. Now that things are more…out in the open, maybe being with you won't be such torture." He smiled, teasing. He was so disarming I didn't stand a chance of resisting.

I ran a hand through my hair and moved toward the window to look outside. "I never wanted to torture you," I said softly.

"Didn't you?" he asked knowingly. "I don't buy it, Julia." His tone was amused so he wasn't angry. "You knew what you were doing when you went out with him."

I glanced at him and smiled. "Well, maybe I did hope that you wouldn't like it." I shrugged. "Just a little, though."

"Riiiggghhhht. Go get dressed, love. It's a gorgeous day, so let's get coffee."

Something about coffee and Sunday and cell phones passed through my head at his words. "Yeah. It's Sunday, right?"

"Yes, exactly." Ryan grinned and disappeared into the bathroom. I resisted the urge to follow, despite the open door. "And, what a beautiful Sunday, it is!" he called as I heard the shower door close behind him.

*****

Ryan was in the kitchen with Jenna and Aaron when I finished dressing. There were only two bathrooms, one in each of the bedrooms, which made it necessary to take turns. I'd dressed in jeans and a periwinkle cashmere sweater, and although I'd dried my hair, it was still slightly damp. I was anxious to spend as much time as possible alone with Ryan. He was leaning against the counter, talking to the others seated at the table, looking amazing in jeans and a blue plaid button-down left open over a white t-shirt. He was laughing with Aaron when his eyes caught my approach down the hall.

"Hey, Jules, you're looking fresh today," Aaron teased. Something in his eyes told me that Ryan shared some of our evening. I flushed.

"Um, thanks," I muttered uncertainly. "Did you guys have a nice time last night?" Ryan pushed away from the counter to take both of my hands in his.

"Yeah, you should have seen how Moore high-tailed it..." Aaron began, but Ryan cut him off.

"Aaron!"

Aaron rolled his eyes. "What, dude? You're kidding, right? After you stole her right out from under his nose, you should have seen his face." Aaron's deep laughter rolled from within his chest.

"Yeah! Damn, it was priceless!" Jenna added. "I thought his head was going to explode!"

Ryan was trying not to laugh until finally he couldn't help himself and joined in with Aaron and Jen. I smiled and nudged him in the arm. "You made your point. The poor guy probably won't talk to me ever again."

"If only I could be so lucky," Ryan said, sobering. My heart swelled as he squeezed my hands. The look on his face was possessive and I was thrilled and satisfied at the same time.

"You will be," I said seriously.

Aaron didn't miss the undercurrent and whistled. "I guess it's safe to say something *major* happened last night. Ryan doesn't have that pinched, miserable look on his face. Whatever you did, Julia, keep doing it."

I laughed softly. *It isn't what I did, it's what Ryan did.* I couldn't say it aloud so just nodded. "Planning on it."

"Aaron, leave them alone. You're embarrassing Julia," Jenna admonished. She and Aaron were dressed for the gym, no doubt taking advantage of a rare morning off together.

Ryan's arms slid around me and he brushed a soft kiss across my mouth. Suddenly, he was all that existed in my world. I kissed him back and he increased the pressure as our mouths played with each other.

"Julia," he breathed against my lips and then the side of my temple. "You taste so good. Are you ready to go? If we don't leave, we *won't*," he groaned, followed by loud grumbling coming from his stomach.

"That's what you get for not eating last night." I kissed his jaw, allowing one hand to slide across his abdomen. The skin on his face was smooth and smelled of musk and soap. His arms tightened in a gentle hug and I found myself wishing he wasn't so damn gentle. I wanted him to crush me to him, to feel his muscled frame pressing into my softer one.

"I had other things on my mind." His breath rushed hotly over my ear as he whispered the words then reluctantly released me, taking my hand in his. "Okay, we're out of here. Aaron, I'll see you at the hospital. Enjoy your day off, Jen."

"Yeah, it would be nice to have a whole damn day off with Aaron, but I'll take what I can get. You two have fun." I offered her a sympathetic look. I empathized because Ryan had been almost non-existent for the past two weeks. She winked at me quickly as we left.

I soaked in the beauty of the day. Ryan had opened the passenger door and I hopped in. The air smelled fresh and crisp, the scent of the lilacs that lined the street hung heavily in the air. The sky was a vibrant blue and the fluffy clouds floated all around.

I was grateful that Ryan's graduation was near. He worked so damned hard and that wouldn't change once he started residency. I wasn't sure what our arrangement was before the accident except that I lived in New York and he lived in Boston. I only hoped he would come to New York because I really wanted to find out about my job and start having a productive life again. My heart fell slightly and he noticed the look on my face.

"Hey, what's wrong?" he asked as he navigated through the quaint streets of the neighborhood.

"Nothing. Just…wondering about stuff."

"Baby, stop worrying, please?" He cocked an eyebrow; his cheeks had a rosy flush and his blue eyes, vibrant. The smile on his gorgeous mouth was relaxed, making my heart pound and my pulse increase erratically. I couldn't help but smile back. He was right, I shouldn't worry. Not today.

"Okay. But, that doesn't mean I won't pester you for information, Matthews."

"God forbid, that could *ever* happen!"

"Well, since you're so damn sure of me, I'd hate like hell to disappoint you," I returned dryly.

His grin widened and he shook his head. "Never."

The little coffee shop near the Harvard Campus was filled with aromas that assaulted us as we walked through the door and my stomach rumbled. Ryan had to be famished.

I listened to the sureness in his voice as he ordered me a large iced coffee, with sugar free vanilla syrup and a splash of cream. Inherently, I knew that was right. I loved the way he took charge and made sure I had everything I wanted.

He pulled out a chair for me and then set two bagel and egg sandwiches on the table along with his cappuccino before he took the seat to my left. Taking my hand, he kissed it, his lips grazing over the large diamond that was now in residence there, before picking up his food and taking a huge bite.

"So…coffee Sundays?" I questioned. Ryan nodded. "I remember cell phones in reference to coffee Sundays, so I guess we weren't always together."

"Nope, but we almost never missed this time together. Sometimes it had to be on the phone, but it was still our time to catch up and talk about our week. When I started working more hours it was harder. The last year has been rough."

"Ryan," I began. I took a sip of my coffee and then continued in a lowered tone. "Last night, I felt *so* close to you. Was this last year different than that?"

"No. We just didn't see each other as much as we wanted, sweetheart. My obligations here and your job were so demanding; we just couldn't get together as much as we wanted, but it didn't change things between us."

"I've been trying so hard to remember my job at the magazine and all I can get are a few names and faces."

"Yeah? Who?" He sat back in his chair and his eyes narrowed slightly.

"Andrea, Meredith and this guy named Mike Turner. Do you know them?"

He looked at me and tossed the last bite of his sandwich back on his plate. "Andrea is your red-headed assistant; perky personality and very bright. I like her a lot. Meredith's your boss; a little too viper for my tastes. She's ruthless, but she adores you." He stopped and picked up his coffee, not continuing on to Mike and I smiled. He was so jealous. I adored that about him. It made my inner vixen squeal in delight.

"And *Mike*?" I prodded gently before picking a piece of my sandwich off and popping it in my mouth.

"He's a photographer you worked with sometimes. He's a smarmy bastard, at best. Hmmph!"

I couldn't stop the bubble of laughter that burst out of my chest, almost causing me to choke on my food and sending a shot of pain through my ribs. It was still enough to make me cringe. "Smarmy," I repeated matter-of-factly, sending a smart-ass smirk in his direction.

"You forgot *bastard*." He joined in my laughter.

"Oh, sorry. How remiss of me." I bit my lip to stop the smirk. "So, I guess my job is pretty big if I have an assistant? I wish I could remember. Is there anything you can show me? The pictures of you helped so maybe there's something about my job?"

"I do have one thing I can show you. But, later. Let's go for a walk or something now. I'll give you a piggyback ride." His white teeth flashed and his eyes crinkled in a beautiful smile. "I'm feeling very fine today."

"And that offer is one I can't refuse, although I can walk, Ryan."

"Don't argue, Abbott." He pulled me up and out the door, both of us laughing happily.

*****

When we returned, Ryan showed me the photo that I'd given him the same Christmas he gave me the bracelet. I was stunned and it did help make connections to my job. The picture taken by Mike Turner while I worked at Vogue was sexy, but demure. I was mostly covered, but the expression on my face was…intense. Ryan lovingly ran his hand over the image and then hung it on the abandoned nail above his desk. I'd wondered what went there.

The day had been magical and now I missed him. Every second with him filled my heart to bursting. I almost felt silly, the giddiness reminiscent of a first high school crush. My face hurt, I couldn't stop smiling and it didn't go unnoticed by Jenna. She kept staring at me and laughing.

I was working in the kitchen cleaning up and getting ready to make dinner for Jenna and myself and a treat for the guys for later that night when they got back. "What?" I asked her, already knowing the answer.

"What happened last night? I see the jewelry is back."

"Yes. They're so beautiful. Exactly what I would have chosen. Did Ryan pick these out himself?"

Jen grunted as she planted herself on one of the stools. I grabbed two Cokes from the refrigerator and sat one down in front of her. "I'd love to say *no*…I mean, how perfect can that fucker be, anyway?" she giggled and popped the tab on her soda.

"Yes. He's amazing. Jen, he leaves me…just breathless."

"Well, I see nothing's changed," she scoffed and pursed her lips. "You're both so into each other it's ridiculous."

I smiled even wider and poured my Coke over ice. "That's my wish. That nothing will change. I can't remember everything yet, but I want us to be just like we were. For Ryan's sake."

"You will. He was so happy today. You guys must have done the nasty last night, hmmm?" She lifted her eyebrow at me and her lips twitched with a teasing smile.

"Not exactly." I blushed despite myself.

"Well something sure as shit happened. Spill already."

"He played piano for me. I sang to him…you know." I shrugged a little.

"He made love to you, Julia. Admit it. It's written all over you. Aaron and I have been hoping it would happen. Ryan's been so worried. He was wound tighter than a drum on the way to the hotel. I thought he was going to beat the living shit out of Dr. Moore."

My insides did somersaults. "We didn't make love like that. He was afraid to hurt me, but we did make out a little bit. Ryan…melts me."

"Yeah. It was obvious how hot you were for each other. Aaron tried to bet Spence five bucks that you'd dry hump in the cab on the way home. You should have seen his face! I was *dying*."

She giggled but I was laughing so hard my eyes watered. "He did not!" When she nodded, I continued taking out the mixer, a bowl and some of the ingredients for the cake I was making. "Aaron cracks me up! I feel sorry for Spence, though."

"Julia, he deserved what he got. You don't think he was just being a *good doctor*, do you? I wish I would have been there for Ryan's little talk. Aaron said it was…wow."

My eyes widened, anxious to hear the story. I almost felt guilty at the pleasure it gave me. "Really? What did he say?"

"Basically, to keep his hands off because you belonged to him, and he would tell you everything rather than risk losing you to, not sure what the term was exactly…a 'piss ant or son-of-bitch.'" She shrugged with a smile. "Something like that."

Ryan would tell me everything? What exactly was everything?

I leaned on the counter facing her. "He's possessive. Why does that make me so friggin' happy?"

"Because Caveman Ryan is hot."

I giggled and resumed my work. "Are you kidding? *Every* Ryan is hot. How in the hell could I resist him for all those years?"

"Beats the hell out of me. Ellie and I thought you were nuts." She shook her head with raised brows.

"You've got a great guy, too, Jen. Aaron is sweet and I can see how much he loves you."

"Yeah. I'm sort of surprised he hasn't asked me to marry him yet. We don't even talk about it." Her voice fell slightly and suddenly the beautiful ring on my finger felt heavy. I felt bad for her. Here I was, flashing a huge rock and I didn't even know how long I'd been engaged.

"I'm sure he will, soon. I'm not even sure how long Ryan and I…or how he proposed. It makes me sad that I've forgotten so many important moments, but I'm happy that he loves me. You should feel that way, too. You know Aaron loves you, right?"

"Yes. He'll probably get around to it. If he doesn't, I'll have to kick him in the ass."

"In what way?"

"You know…shake his cage a little. He's not the only damn man in Boston. Maybe he needs a wake-up call."

I eyed her skeptically. "Jen, really? You'd do that?"

"Just watch me," she said sternly. "I'll show him good."

My heart ached for her. For some reason, the sixth sense about Ryan left me confident that I wouldn't have to resort to playing games if we were in that situation. "Maybe you should just talk to him," I suggested gently.

"Aaron's motivated by actions and graduation is coming. Something's gotta give."

I was already mixing the batter of the chocolate cake and she stuck her finger in for a taste and she shook her head.

"What?"

"You and Ryan." She rolled her eyes, trying to lighten the mood. "Just unreal." She licked her fingers and left me in the kitchen alone. "I think I'm jealous," she said as she disappeared into her room.

Ryan~

It was after midnight and Aaron was still at the hospital. I left on time because I wanted to get back to Julia. *What a great day!* We talked, we laughed and we held onto each other for hours. Seeing her so relaxed and happy had been a balm to my sore heart and it didn't hurt that she was beginning to remember more.

Last night was incredibly sexy. I want more. My body throbbed at the thought.

I wanted her as much as ever and, if possible, I loved her even more. Nothing mattered but being with her. I needed to talk to her about my residency in New York, unsure what she was thinking. One thing I knew for sure, I was done being away from her. If Meredith asked her to go to Paris again, I'd do everything possible to convince her not to go. If I had to whisk her away and marry her on some deserted island, I'd do so without hesitation.

The apartment was dark, only a small light over the stove left on. The girls were both in bed and I glanced at the couch, hoping to God that Julia was in my bed; waiting. I smiled. It would even be better if she were naked, even if I was too tired to make love; I still wanted to feel her skin next to mine. The closeness was my contentment in the chaos of all that had happened. I scratched my stomach through my scrubs as I went into the kitchen. There was a note on the table and I smiled. *Julia. My beautiful Julia.*

I picked it up and flipped it open, holding it over the stove into the light.

-R
Thinking of you today. Dreaming of you now. Surprise in the fridge.
Yours,
-J

Sitting on the top shelf was a gorgeous Black Forest cake. Mmmm…my stomach grumbled and I opened the cupboard and took out a plate. I retrieved a fork and knife from the silverware drawer and pulled the cake and a bottle of water from the refrigerator. *God, she's so good to me*, I thought as I cut a thick slice of the cake and took it to the table.

It was insanely delicious. The perfect blend of chocolate, liquor and cream. Not too sweet, simply amazing. I was about halfway through with it, lost in my memories of Julia and the time we smashed cake all over each other before my move to Boston. I smiled to myself. They were such good memories, even though the separation had been imminent. We were on the verge of admitting our feelings, and even though those years as her friend required an iron will, I wouldn't change one minute of my time with her. *Other than the accident and the loss of our baby…*I set the fork down and ran a hand over the scruff on my jaw, wondering if I should shave before crawling into bed with her.

"Ahhhhhh! Watch out! Oh, my God! Stop!" Julia suddenly screamed from my bedroom, the sound piercing the silence like a knife. Panic seized my chest as I jumped and ran down the hall, bursting through the door. It was pitch black and I could barely make out her small form rolled into a ball in the middle of my bed. She was clutching at her middle and crying frantically.

I dropped to my knees beside the bed and enfolded her in my arms. “Julia, I’m here. I’m with you. You’re having a bad dream, love.”

“It hurts! It hurts…oh God, it hurts,” she sobbed.

Jen popped her head around the corner. “Is she okay?” she asked softly.

I shook my head and Jenna discretely left us.

My heart stopped. Julia was dreaming of the car crash. “Shh…my love. It’s over now. You’re okay and I’m with you. I’ll always be with you, Julia.”

Her arms wrapped around my neck and she sobbed into the curve of my shoulder. “Ryan…it hurts so much.” I held her for a long time until she stopped sobbing and released her long enough to strip out of my clothes and get into bed next to her.

She curled her warm body into me, her leg sliding between mine and her arm around my waist. I kissed the top of her head as she fell back into a deep sleep but I was worried sick and my mind was racing.

What would she remember in the morning…and what caused the damned nightmare? What has changed?

I racked my brain and then it hit me. In the last 24 hours I’d let myself love her, tell her things and show her how close we really were. I’d allowed myself to hope that she’d remember without much pain, but obviously, based on the nightmare, that was shot to hell.

We need to take it slower, even though that isn’t what she wants. My heart ached at the notion and my hands smoothed over the velvet skin on her arm. I closed my eyes against the pain rushing through me.

Ugh. Just when I felt like I was getting her back again...

I struggled back and forth with it. I needed to see if she remembered the nightmare, and I didn't want to hurt her more. What was I to do? Did I have a choice?

Distancing would confuse and hurt her and put me in hell as well. Whether Julia remembered the loss of the baby or I pulled back, she would suffer. Loving her and putting her first, I chose what I thought would be the lesser of two evils. It was going to kill me to do it, but, we had to take a step back. I wasn't strong enough to pull away completely, but I had to be careful with her. She was expecting that we'd let it happen now, and Jesus, I wanted it, too. There had to be a way to slow things down without pushing her away completely. How could I protect her from the loss of our baby? How could I protect us both?

I knew it wasn't possible and it was only a matter of time. *But, when?*

"Ryan...stay with me," she whispered without knowing it. I turned her more fully into my arms and placed a soft kiss on her sleeping mouth. I closed my eyes and tried to swallow the pain swelling in my throat. My eyes burned as what felt like two steel bands wrapped my chest, preventing my lungs from expanding.

"I love you, Julia." My heart was aching. "Don't forget that I love you. So much."

~8~

Julia ~

THE DISTANT RYAN was back and sadness hung over us worse than before. Now I knew what I'd been missing, and even though we talked and he was loving, we didn't spend time together. He didn't touch me as much and he'd only slept with me on Wednesday night. When I felt his warmth seep into me and his arms wrapped around me as he pulled me close in an exhausted sleep, I thought I was dreaming. I snuggled in closer and placed a soft kiss on his mouth but he didn't wake up.

Most nights, he didn't even come back to the apartment until after I was already in bed. I was taking the pain pills again. Not because I was in that much pain, but because it was the only way I could sleep. It had to stop…something had to give.

I remembered more about college, Aaron and Jen, and sometimes with Ryan, but still it wasn't enough. The biggest abyss was the space Ryan had just vacated. Those brief hours…*one day of really knowing*…left me wanting like never before.

After our coffee talk, more about my job came back. I called Meredith and asked if I still had a job.

"Pfffft. What do you think, Julia? Of course. What about Paris?" she asked, astonished at my uncertainty.

Paris. It flooded back and I had mixed emotions about that decision. Elation and despair all rolled up together. Leaving Ryan…had I seriously considered that? *Was I insane*? I gasped and sank to the couch when my legs started to shake, putting out a hand to keep from falling.

"Uh, I'm not sure, Meredith. Actually, I hadn't really thought about it." It was the truth. "Can I have a couple more weeks? I just need to figure things out." If Ryan was going to keep his distance, I could show him the meaning of the word. My heart constricted painfully and I closed my eyes. There was no way I would consider it, even the prospect of New York without him, hurt.

"Sure, doll, don't worry about it," Meredith insisted. "Andrea's doing a damn good job of holding things together. You might want to give her a call, and you'll need to give her a raise."

I laughed without much enthusiasm, still shaken up a bit. "Okay. I'll definitely do that. So big, my boss will chew me a new ass for going over budget." I tried to joke, but it fell flat.

"As long as you make it up somewhere else, I don't give a damn!" she retorted.

We talked a little more about the next few months' issues. It helped me organize the chaos of the jumbled up memories. Getting back to work would be just what I needed. I'd had enough of this life of leisure. It gave me too much time to think and wonder about the future.

There was nothing worse than missing him when he was so damn close. The week since the nightmare felt like forever. I almost rummaged through Ryan's room for clues to our past. I resisted, but only barely. Despite the way he was acting, I couldn't betray his trust. I sighed and threw my head against the back of the chair. I was positive there was nothing that he wouldn't want me to see; if the situation were normal, but now it would push my memory and he'd be upset. I trusted him and loved him with everything I had.

I wish that was enough. Breathing literally hurt as I leaned both of my elbows on his desk. I reluctantly got up and gathered my clothes for the day. The hours dragged, stretching in front of me endlessly. Not knowing if I'd even see Ryan made it worse and my heart dropped.

I finished getting dressed; pulling on dark jeans and a light pink pullover, then applied light make-up. It was Saturday and as I padded down the hall toward the kitchen, I heard Aaron saying goodbye to Jen. Ryan was already gone.

"Love ya, babe. Have a nice day off," Aaron said and kissed Jen lightly. He waved before opening the door. "Bye, Jules."

"See ya," I answered.

I threaded both hands through my long hair in frustration and flopped on the couch. I didn't turn on the television; I didn't look out the window. The room blurred and my throat ached. I felt helpless and I had no control of anything. Not my memory, not my relationship with Ryan…nothing.

Jenna handed me a cup of coffee. "Here, honey," she said and took a seat in one of the chairs to my right. "How do you feel?"

"Physically, I'm fine. I don't have much pain anymore. Mentally…frustrated as hell. Remembering part of the past is almost worse than starting over with nothing. It's confusing, trying to piece it together and still have huge gaps. It sucks."

She took a sip and nodded. "I notice Ryan is gone again. I thought you guys had turned a corner. He was so happy and I thought he'd be around more. What happened, Julia?"

I shrugged and looked down with a frown. "That's just it! *Nothing*! I had a stupid *dream* and he blames himself! I'm so tired of him taking responsibility for everything. He thinks getting close brought it on."

"He is brilliant in many ways, but his head is up his ass on this," Jen replied.

"Yes," I agreed. "Who's to say I wouldn't eventually remember the crash anyway? And, so *what*? It wouldn't be the end of the fucking world." My tone was full of defeat and frustration. "Maybe I should just *leave*," I said in disgust.

"What?" Jenna asked in surprise.

"I'm making Ryan miserable. It hurts that he's so unhappy. I miss him. I want him to stop over-thinking everything. Something could happen that helps me remember and that can't happen if he's avoiding me."

Jenna's expression was sympathetic, but she was frowning. "I know. It's screwed up, but I don't think leaving will help either of you. He'll lose it. It's not that bad, is it? He calls you, doesn't he?"

"Yeah, but he stays away until very late and leaves early. I hardly see him. My emotions are so screwed I hardly even know what I'm feeling anymore. I'm so…sad, I guess. Lonely."

"I'd ask Aaron to talk to him, but he already has. Ryan is stubborn as hell."

"He's so focused on making sure nothing shocks me that he is blind to what needs to happen. And if he won't let things be, there is nothing I can do but leave. Either he'll wake up or he'll get on with his life." I blinked as my eyes filled with tears. "Shit. All I do is cry." I wiped quickly at the tears. "Anyway, I've made an appointment with Spencer to try to sort this out."

Saying the words hurt. It was so hard vocalizing any attempt to be away from Ryan. Jenna's eyes widened in surprise, so I hurried to explain. "Uh, he's objective. Ryan and you…even Aaron. You're all too close to the situation."

"He isn't objective! Are you trying to make things worse?" Her eyes widened incredulously.

"I need help sorting through this. That's Spencer's job."

"Well, if you don't want to hurt Ryan, you have a damn funny way of showing it."

I paced around the room; before turning to face her. "I don't plan on telling him. He's working so much, he'll never know. Hurting him is the last thing I want to do."

"I don't know, Julia…" she added hesitantly. "You should talk to Ryan."

I sucked in a shaky breath and shook my head. "For what? He won't change his mind. If the episode in the bedroom and knowing I love him won't do it, what will?"

"He needs a swift kick in the ass, that's all." She tried to tease, but I was beyond it.

"Men run when they can't deal, but knowing it doesn't make it hurt any less." My lips lifted in a sad smile. "If I leave, maybe he'll be more motivated. I can't take more of grasping at a past I might never remember. I want to build a life with him."

Jenna covered my hand with hers. "I'm so sorry, but Ryan's not running very far and he'll never leave you. You know that, right?"

My eyes overflowed with tears again. I turned so I could brush them away. "Look, enough of my pathetic bullshit." I tried to change the subject. "Has Aaron gotten any closer to setting a date?"

She shrugged slightly. Disappointment and hurt flashed across her features. "After almost nine years, it should be a done deal."

"Maybe he's waiting until graduation," I offered gently. "Maybe he also needs a swift kick in the ass, hmmm?" I smiled despite the tears that still clung to my lashes. An idea formed behind Jen's blue eyes as a smile lit up her face.

"Let's go shopping! I hate sitting around feeling sorry for myself." She tossed her long blonde hair over her shoulders. "In fact, let's buy new clothes, new shoes, go to the salon, then we're going out tonight. Let them wonder what we're up to, huh?"

A big part of me didn't want to hurt Ryan anymore than he already was but going out with Jen sounded like fun. I found myself recalling times when Ellie, Jen and I would spend similar evenings together.

"Okay. It sounds great! Let's meet after my appointment. At the mall?"

"Nope. Downtown. The shops are more fun *and* more expensive. Feeling better just takes money, honey! We can go straight to the bar, afterward," she said mischievously, a new gleam in her eye. She was a woman on a mission and there would be no stopping her.

I laughed. "Aaron doesn't stand a chance!"

"You're perfectly capable of taking Ryan down if you want him, Jules. So *do it*," she said seriously. My heart and body tightened in anticipation.

"Okay. Yeah." The decision made, I checked my watch. I needed to go or I'd be late.

I put my empty coffee cup in the kitchen before heading out the door. "Okay, see you in a couple hours," I threw over my shoulder as I gathered my purse and slid my feet into my black leather boots. "I'll buzz you when I'm finished."

"Don't let him try anything, hon."

"Jen, please. This is purely professional. Besides, you know where my heart is and nothing will change that."

"Yeah, not even your lost memory," she said.

It was like an ironic epiphany suddenly rushed over me like a storm and I stopped. "Exactly. Tell *Ryan*."

"Well, tonight he's gonna get a clue," Jenna spouted with a grin. I couldn't help but laugh.

*****

"Julia, I was surprised you called. Is everything alright?" Spencer was pensive and distant, understandable considering the passionate display Ryan and I made at the Four Seasons.

"Yes," I said. I sat in one of the chairs in front of his desk for the last time. "I mean…not really. I don't know," I stammered and felt embarrassed at my lack of ability to even get out a coherent sentence. My face burned in a flush, and I pressed the back of my hand to my cheek.

His eyes narrowed and raked over my face. "What's this about?"

"I'm thinking about going back to New York. I remembered my job. I think I'm ready and I'm bored doing nothing. It's not my style."

"Forgive me, but…what does Ryan say about it? After last weekend, and," he motioned toward the diamond sparkling on my hand, "I thought you might have remembered. Have you?" His words were slow and measured.

"Not everything. I know that I love him and obviously that we were, *are* engaged. But, it's so much more than I could have ever imagined."

"Did you remember on your own or did he tell you about the engagement?"

"Ryan told me."

Spencer crossed his arms over his chest. "I see." The tightness in his tone was clear.

I shifted uncomfortably. “I’m not sure you do. Yes, he told me about the engagement, but the other stuff…I feel him within me. I can’t even explain it, but I *know* it. Even though I can’t get the whole picture yet, the love is so tangible that I can almost reach out and touch it. I don’t know how else to articulate it.”

He didn’t speak but continued to study me. I moved my diamond back and forth on my finger.

“What else has he told you?”

“I’ve been *begging* him to tell me everything. It wasn’t his fault. He’s been doing just as you asked, but I *need* to know. Ryan hasn’t said, ‘Hey, Julia. You’re crazy in love with me.’” I lowered my tone in mock imitation and flushed. “And forgive me, but I don’t see what this has to do with my going back to New York.”

“What is the real reason you’re thinking of leaving, Julia? The *truth*.”

I swallowed and looked away. “Uh, my being here is hurting Ryan. He’s struggling and won’t let us move forward. We had an amazing 24 hours and then everything changed again. While he is very caring and concerned, he’s not touching me or spending time with me and…I *need* to feel close to him. He needs it, too.”

“This is not what I expected. From what I saw of you two last weekend, I would have sworn he was going to take you out of there and tell you everything.”

“I wish he would have.”

Spencer sighed. “Julia, I want the best for you, and Ryan is doing that by letting you remember on your own. If you think you need to go to New York, then my advice is to do it. If you and Ryan are meant to be, it will work out.”

I felt like I was back in high school getting a lecture from my dad. “We *are* meant to be,” I insisted, my eyes burning into his, chin jutting out in defiance. "I can't live with anything less." My voice cracked on the last sentence. "I guess I'm hoping he'll realize he can't live without me."

"Julia, I'm here to help you work things out and no more. The other night…well, I see how much Ryan loves you. His actions certainly support that," he said quietly. "Has anything else happened?"

"Yes. I had a dream about the accident but that's really all, besides what I've already told you."

"And?"

"I barely woke up. I remember pain as I screamed Ryan's name. Truthfully, I handled it better than Ryan did. He held me afterward but since, he's distancing again…it hurts."

"Julia, he's a fourth year med student. He's extremely dedicated and so close to being finished. Don't take it personally."

"Seriously? Everything Ryan does is motivated by what's going on with me. He could work at the apartment but he goes to the library instead. All the time. I'm really missing him."

"I understand. When was the dream?"

"Sunday night."

"Ah, so right after the restaurant."

"The next night, yes. Please don't imply that being closer to Ryan caused it. And even if it did, I wouldn't change it."

"I'm only trying to determine what happened to see if we can make this easier for you. I figured something like this would push you into remembering."

It suddenly dawned on me. *Did you tell Ryan that being close to me could be the catalyst?* "I don't really care about making it easier, only *faster*. I don't want Ryan to hurt anymore."

He nodded, almost resigned. "Yes, I know it's been difficult for him and I see that you really do love him. He's a lucky man."

"No, I'm the lucky one." I studied his reactions. "Did you…talk to him about me?"

"Julia, I can't talk to him about what you and I discuss, specifically. That's professional privilege, but before you and I had our first session, he and I talked a little bit. About the accident and that you lost," he hesitated briefly, "uh, your memory, but that's all. Except for our conversation at the restaurant."

"Sorry about that. I should have considered it before I agreed to go to dinner. Ryan's very protective." Pleasure made blood rush into my cheeks.

Spencer laughed. "I'd call it *possessive* and it's perfectly understandable, but the dinner was innocent." He paused and searched my face. "If you could have anything you wanted, what would it be?"

While he meant well, it all seemed so pointless. I wanted validation of my feelings, validation of my decision to go back to New York, validation of resuming my life with Ryan. *Ugh! Isn't that the reason anyone goes to a psychiatrist? Fucking validation?*

"I just want my life back, even if I never remember completely. I want Ryan, to go back to my job and whatever our plans were. That is, if he'll tell me."

"Do you think you can ask?"

"I feel comfortable talking to him about anything. Whether he'll listen, is another story entirely."

His face was contemplative and relaxed. I couldn't help but consider what Ryan said about not trusting him, but today he'd only been supportive.

"He'll listen…eventually. He doesn't want to lose you, so he'll listen."

"Thank you. I hope so."

"No problem. It's been my pleasure, Julia. Truly."

My phone rang in my purse and I looked up apologetically.

"Hello?"

"Hey. What are you up to?" Ryan asked. His words sounded guarded, reluctant, like he wanted the answer but shouldn't be asking.

"I'm going shopping with Jenna. Are you at lunch?"

"Yeah. I just wanted to hear your voice."

"Well, you can hear it anytime you want," I murmured softly into the phone.

"Mmmm…" I could hear the want in his voice and my heart rejoiced.

"Listen. Why don't I pop over for a bit? How long do you have?" I asked.

"Only about 45 minutes. That sounds good though. If you can."

"I'll bring lunch."

"You don't have to…" he began. "We can just meet in the cafeteria."

"Hush, Ryan. Meet you in the courtyard, okay?"

"Okay," The smile came through in his voice. "I'll see you in a few. Bye."

"I'm on my way. Bye, honey."

I looked up at Spencer happily. "I have to go! Meeting Ryan for lunch." I popped up and rushed to the door without a second thought. "Thanks, again!"

*****

Ryan was waiting on a bench near the East edge of the court-yard, lots of roses and other flowers on the pathway. The hair falling casually across his forehead glowed golden in the sun-light. He shoved his fingers through it in his haphazard way and a smile flashed across his mouth. So gorgeous; scrubs, stethoscope and a pocket full of pens, he was a sight for sore eyes. Finally enfolding me in his arms, his mouth fell to my hair at my temple as he kissed me. I cursed the food in my arms that prevented me holding him back. The best I could do was stand up on tiptoe to press my open mouth to the base of his neck. His arms tightened slightly and he kissed the side of my cheek.

"I miss you," I said before I could stop myself.

"Miss you more," he said softly, released me and took the bags from my arms. "Did you bring enough for an army? Maybe I should see if Aaron is free." His blue eyes flashed to meet mine as we sat together on the bench.

"I'd just like it to be us, if that's alright."

He held my gaze, his features soft but he had dark shadows showing under his eyes. I handed him a can of Coke and then reached out to touch his cheek, my fingers brushing along his strong jaw. "You look tired."

"Yeah. A little bit."

"I wish you didn't have to work so hard." He handed me one of the chicken salad sandwiches and I started to unwrap it.

"After residency." Ryan quickly disposed of the wrapping on his sandwich and took a big bite. He looked a bit thinner and I worried he wasn't eating.

"I worry about you."

He smiled after he swallowed his food. "I'm fine. Just busy."

I picked at the crust on the sandwich sitting in my lap. I nodded once. "Okay."

"You look beautiful," he said in the velvet tone I loved. I couldn't stop the smile or the blush that spread out on my cheeks. "What are your plans today?"

"Shopping with Jenna."

He continued to eat and I managed a bite of my own.

"That will be good. Jen needs a day out too. Aaron works just about as much as I do."

"Hardly. Not even close," I insisted.

"Well, his specialty isn't as demanding."

The stilted silence between us hung like a storm as I struggled with what to say. Being so distant after our passionate evening was awkward. I swallowed one more bite of the sandwich and then wrapped the rest of it.

I took a deep breath and jumped in with both feet. "Ryan, I spoke to Meredith today," I began.

Immediately Ryan abandoned his lunch and his eyes connected with mine. "And?"

This was so hard! "And, I can go back to work whenever I want. I think it might be time."

He said nothing, but the muscle in his jaw began to work overtime.

"Well?" I pushed. "Don't you have anything to say?"

His tone was hard when he spoke. "Sounds like you've made up your mind, but if you're asking me what I think, then…*no*. I don't have time to discuss it right now."

Anger swelled at his easy dismissal. "Well, it's not about you. It's about me."

"Yes, I can see that it's *not about me*."

"What the hell is that supposed to mean?" I felt fragile and blinked rapidly to erase the tears as I busied myself with cleaning up the food. In seconds, everything was shoved back in the bag and I didn't give a damn if either one of us was finished or not.

"I have to get back to work. We can talk tonight," Ryan dismissed me again. I stood up straighter and against my will, my chin jutted out in defiance.

"No. We can't talk tonight. I have plans. Enjoy…whatever the hell it is you do with your time. Maybe I'll leave you a note taped to the bathroom mirror, or we can send up fucking smoke signals, since you don't seem to have any time to spend with me these days." I started laughing in strained hysteria.

He ignored the second part of my statement. "What plans?" he asked angrily and roughly took hold of my arm. I stilled and looked up at him through pain-filled eyes.

"I'm going out," I said flatly. Electricity passed between us where his hand held me…like always. Except this time it hurt. I was mad and I felt alone as hell.

"With whom?" he asked harshly, making no move to let me go.

"Does it matter? It sure as hell won't be *you*." My voice thickened in regret as I tried to pull my arm free and turn away.

"Julia, stop! Tell me. *Now*!" Ryan demanded as his hand tightened around my arm. People walking by started to take notice, sending glances and curious looks our way. I stopped struggling immediately. I didn't want it to appear he was holding me against my will. Ryan held me without touch, without words…no matter how angry I was. Panic filled his face and I huffed.

"Oh shit, Ryan! Jenna!! Just *Jen*…but you know, maybe we'll both find someone to pay a little attention to us. We could both use it. You and Aaron…you're both so damn blind." I yanked my arm free and started to walk away, only making five steps before both of his hands closed over my shoulders.

"I said *stop*!" he said through clenched teeth, eyes flashing fire.

"You're so jealous and it's completely irrational. When I came here today, I planned on telling you that I didn't want to go without you." I was breathing hard and losing the fragile hold on my emotions. "I'm standing here, and all I want is you with me.

And you're *pissed* because I'm going somewhere without you, when it's *your* choice!! It's *been* your choice, Ryan! Can't you see how insane that is?" I laughed nervously. "I mean, if it wasn't so fucked up, it'd be funny!"

I shook my head and glared until finally he let me go. His breathing elevated and one of his arms dropped to his side and he ran the other hand through his hair as he turned his back, but stood stone still.

I tried to steady my voice. "I can see you have better things to do, so have fun with that," I said softly and he turned quickly toward me again. I ignored him and walked back in the direction I'd come. The path, flowers and people, blurred in front of me as I picked up my pace.

"Julia!" Ryan yelled behind me. "Julia! Where are you going tonight? I don't have time for this shit right now! I have to get to work!" My heart thumped in my chest but I forced myself to keep walking. "Goddamn it! *Julia!*"

I pretended that I didn't hear him and threw the trash in a receptacle as I passed. Before I even reached the car, my phone vibrated in my purse. I opened the door and squeezed the steering wheel so hard it hurt. I tried not to look at the words on the screen.

Tell me where you're going to be. I'll be there.

*****

"Did you text Ryan back?" Jen asked anxiously. The music was loud, the lights low and flashing. The bass drums vibrated in my chest. Jenna had her hair piled up on her head and we both had on tight jeans and high heels. I splurged and bought some new Kenneth Cole's. Not quite Prada or Louboutin, but then if I were in New York, I'd have my nicely stocked closet.

"No." While I was still pissed, most of what I was feeling was hurt. This whole cat and mouse game with Ryan was getting old. He'd texted three more times, growing more and more upset.

Jen was bouncing to the music and sipping her second chocolate martini. I wrinkled my nose in distaste. *Gross.*

"Well, Ryan's got Aaron texting me, now. You didn't tell him how I felt, did you, Julia?"

I shook my head and motioned that I'd zipped my lip. "Never."

"Good. Let them cool their jets for a while."

We started giggling, my white wine adding to my relaxation. Jen's bright blue top was covered with sequins, but I'd chosen a tamer option. A low cut, white sleeveless top in jersey. It draped nicely in the scooped neckline leaving the top slopes of my breasts bare. I didn't wear a necklace, only some long drop diamond earrings and…I looked down at my left hand, still adorned with the delicate bracelet and engagement ring. They sparkled in the low candlelight. I put my right hand protectively over the bracelet. My hair was wilder than normal, as if I'd been caught in the wind, but Jenna nodded her approval when we finished at the salon. It did feel good to get dressed up and go out. The only thing that could make it better were if Ryan were here.

You're pathetic, Julia. Can't you get through a few hours without thinking of him? I cringed at my own weakness.

Goodlife was busier, livelier, darker and more fun now than it had been at lunch with Ryan. I started to sway to the beat and we started to sing.

"Between those rocks and that sappy look on your face, you're killing my buzz, Julia. No guys will ask us to dance."

"We're not here to pick up guys." I bit my lip and shook my head.

"No, but I want to dance." She shimmied her shoulders. "We can dance. They can look but not touch. Nothing wrong with that."

I laughed happily. "Ryan wouldn't agree."

"*Who*?" She widened her eyes and pursed her lips. "Who did you just mention?" she asked caustically.

"Okay. Point taken." Another message vibrated the phone in my pocket. Despite the dirty look from Jen, I pulled it out.

Julia, I'm done playing around. Tell me where you are, NOW!

I sighed. *Who was I kidding?* Ryan was clearly upset and I didn't want to hurt him.

"What has Aaron said? Has he called?"

Jenna took a big swallow of her drink. "Oh, yeah. He seems a tad put out."

"Ryan's pissed." I picked up my wine and almost choked as Jen grabbed my phone from me. I burst out laughing. "Oh my God!" I gasped. "Are you trying to get me in more trouble?"

"Hell, yeah!" She started typing and I tried to take it back but she held it out of my reach.

"No, Jen. Don't."

"Pfft. Lighten up, Jules."

We're at Goodlife. Julia looks hot. If I were you, I'd get your ass over here pronto. Jen.

She handed the phone back and I breathed a sigh of relief. It could have been worse.

"I'd say we have about thirty minutes to get drunker and find some victims to dance with. No way in hell are they walking in here to find us sitting alone. Uh uh." She picked up her glass again and clanked it against mine. "Cheers!" She tossed back her drink and waved the barmaid over for another round. Dancing sounded fun…but part of me was reluctant. What I really wanted was for Ryan to take hold of me for the rest of the night.

"Holy hell," Jenna groaned in disgust as she looked across the bar.

"What?"

"Ugh. Just that dipshit that's always chasing after your man." My head snapped in the direction Jenna was looking and my stomach clenched. "*Joy.*"

It had to be Liza. Strawberry blonde hair, pretty features, thin figure. "Oh." My mouth formed the word, but nothing came out.

"No shit. Well, we're safe enough until Ryan walks through that door."

"Why?"

"That girl is like a bitch in heat where he's concerned. She's made many pathetic attempts to get him in the sack. She's *sad.*" I visibly stiffened and Jen noticed. "Julia, don't worry. Ryan never touched her, but you need to be thick-skinned. That bitch is relentless. Can you handle it?"

"I think so, but that will depend on Ryan."

"Let's have some fun with it. He'll own you when he gets here, trust me."

"I hope he brings Aaron. This was supposed to be for you, too."

"Ryan will insist Aaron come along. He'd never leave me here alone when he hauls your little ass out."

"He won't *haul my ass out,*" I mocked.

"Remember, Caveman Ryan is hotter than hell, and have no doubt…he *will.* Either that or Liza will finally get an eyeful."

"Surely he's told her."

"That bitch is deaf and dumb. Aaron said she practically stalks him on campus," Jen said, sarcasm lacing her tone as her expression hardened.

I took another sip of my wine, thinking maybe I should switch to something stronger. Liza's gaze raked me from head to toe. I resisted the urge to get up and pirouette. I started to silently seethe. It was stupid. I didn't even know this woman; Ryan wasn't even here, but I hated her on sight.

"Why is she staring?" I asked Jenna loudly. I had to practically yell, the music was so loud.

"She knows who you are and there is that big rock on your hand, Julia." Jen mocked in false exasperation before she smiled happily.

"Oh, the same one that you wished I didn't wear tonight?" I teased.

"Yeah. Let's go dance!" A particularly rhythmic song was pumping through the sound system as she tugged me toward the dance floor.

"But…without guys?"

By the time we got on the floor, a new song started. Several men were checking us out as I cocked an eyebrow at Jenna. She was grinning and nodding, clearly aware. I had to admit, it was flattering and fun. Girls being girls, I let myself start to move to the music.

I was lost in the music, the alcohol haze dimming my common sense and thoughts of any consequences of my actions. The men at the far table whistled and sent cat calls our way. I just laughed. Jen flirted with them a little until suddenly Aaron appeared in between us and grabbed her by the arm. "Jenna! This shit is not happening!" he yelled, his face angry.

My eyes searched for a set of burning blue ones.

Ryan was standing at the table that Jen and I had vacated, clued in by the purses and blazers on the chairs. His face was hard as he stared at me.

“What the hell?” Jen said to Aaron behind me. “Did you miss me or something?” The noise in the club muted her words.

Jen and Aaron’s arguing dimmed when someone grabbed my hand. One of the men from the table on the end was standing in front of me.

“Want to dance? Looks like your friend is busy.”

“Uh…thank you, no…” I’d barely begun when a steel band wrapped around me from behind and my left wrist was grasped in an iron vice. “Oof…” I grunted as the air was knocked from my lungs. Ryan’s cologne engulfed me when I sucked in my next breath.

“See this, dickhead?” Ryan growled. He shoved the hand with my engagement ring up for the random man at the same time as he turned me back toward the table. “Are you fucking blind?” he spat out.

“Hardly. Dude, look at her. Any man would be stupid not to try.” Ryan’s face flushed and he looked at the shorter man sternly.

“Uh, no. Stupid would be if you don’t back the hell off *and fast*. This is over.”

The situation just struck me as funny and I burst out laughing. Ryan continued to walk to the table, my feet dangling off of the floor, finally setting me down.

“I’m glad you find this situation so fucking amusing,” he ground out. “What in the hell do you think you’re doing, Julia?”

I ran a finger down the front of his dark green, long sleeved t-shirt. He let it hang over the waistband of his jeans and I tugged at the hem. Looking up at him through half-lidded eyes, desire flooded through me; I wanted his arms around me. *Now.*

"Just dancing." My voice lowered and my hand slid under his shirt to the defined muscles of his bare abdomen and the trail of hair leading down toward the waistband. His muscles contracted under my fingers as he sucked in his breath. "Jen is right." Confusion flashed as his features softened slightly. "Caveman Ryan *is* hot. Soooo hot." The corners of my mouth lifted in a soft, teasing smile and he finally slid his arms around me.

"Quit it. Flattery won't work." His mouth twitched with the effort of keeping his smile at bay and his eyes twinkled. "At least, not yet."

"Mmmm…" I sighed into him, burying my nose into his neck and resting my forehead on the strong line of his jaw. "You feel good. You smell good. Bet you taste good, too," I murmured happily.

"Julia, are you drunk?" he asked as he pulled me in between his knees. He pushed my hair off of my face to cup the side of my cheek and then slid his hand further around the back of my neck. He looked intently into my eyes, his long fingers stroking my skin.

"Only a little," I said honestly. I couldn't look away from those blue depths. I was completely mesmerized. "I've missed you." I gravitated toward him, my nose brushed against his, his warm breath rushing over my face as he exhaled.

He nodded and swallowed. "I miss you like crazy, too." His hands were roaming over my back and hips, pulling me closer into his chest, his fingers kneading, probing. I couldn't resist, I let mine slide over his shoulders to the back of his head and into the thick hair. "Ugh, Julia. Why do you do this to me? I should be so mad right now, but I want nothing more than to kiss you senseless."

My fingers tugged on his hair, daring him to bring his mouth to mine. "I want more than that," I whispered against his mouth. "But, if kisses are all you'll give me, I'll take every single one."

He resisted the kisses I was dying for, his mouth hovering over mine. The music beat out a rhythm as his fingers continued to knead my flesh. My pulse quickened. "Do you enjoy tormenting me?"

"There's no need for it, Ryan. All of this stuff that has you in agony, you can have it. I'm right here in front of you…and I want you." My voice was filled with sex and I meant every word as I continued to nuzzle into him. "Why won't you do it?" The moment was so intimate it felt like we were the only two people that existed. I wanted to drown in him.

He groaned; the back of his fingers floated along the swelling flesh above the neckline of my top, his eyes following their path. "It's not that simple. It isn't just about what I *want*."

"Yes it is. Don't you know that?" His eyes rose from my breasts to my mouth and I closed my eyes. He was going to kiss me, finally. I waited, and then opened my eyes as he pulled away slightly and I moaned in protest. *Ugh!*

Ryan must have ordered drinks while I was still on the dance floor because the waitress walked over with four beers, another chocolate martini and a glass of white wine. He shifted me to one side, his arm still firmly clasped around my waist, and dug in his front pocket for his money clip.

"Hold this honey?" he asked. I took the money clip and he pulled thirty dollars out and handed it over before shoving it back into his jeans. He tugged on my arm gently and I fell to sit on his lap. I glanced back at the dance floor and Aaron and Jenna were making out with relish.

"Hey…wasn't Aaron supposed to propose to Jen when you moved to Boston? I remember a conversation we had…you said not to mention it because Aaron wanted it to be a surprise."

"I much preferred the conversation that just got interrupted," he grumbled and picked up one of the beers taking a long pull on it. I smiled and leaned down to place a wet kiss on the sensitive place beneath his ear. I lingered slightly and touched the tip of my tongue to his skin. Maybe the alcohol was making me bolder than usual, but I didn't care. He moaned and turned toward me, finally finding my mouth with his own. The kiss was soft, teasing and nowhere near long enough.

My fingers brushed his jaw when I spoke. "Yes, but Jen has been sad. She wants to get married."

"I agree he should marry her. She deserves it. She's put in her time."

I studied his face. "Is that why you proposed to me? Because I'd put in my time?"

His eyes settled and burned. "I proposed to you because my life began when I met you. I can't live without you," the words almost ripped from his chest and my heart swelled to bursting.

"Why are you trying to, then?"

"I'm not. I'm only trying to protect you and let you remember when you're ready."

I nodded. He was telling the truth and really thought he was doing the right thing.

"So does that mean you won't make love to me tonight?" I smiled sweetly.

His eyes didn't move from my face as I waited for the answer. "Julia, don't torture us both. It will happen when the time is right." My eyes stung and my throat tightened so much I had to look away. "I *love* you. You are the most beautiful, desirable woman I have *ever* laid eyes on. There can be no one else for me. Not in this or a hundred lifetimes." His thumb nudged my chin up. "Hey, look at me. You know you're it for me." His lips lifted in a small smile. "I mean, I chased all over town looking for you and I've got the worst case of blue balls I've ever had. You make me want you much. You tease the shit out of me."

I smiled despite myself.

"Don't think I don't know what you're doing. The little outfits, the little touches…why do you think I live at the hospital? You're killing me…I'm dying with wanting."

"Hey Ryan, who's your little friend?" a snarky voice broke into our Ryan and Julia bubble.

I didn't wait for him to introduce us, my eyes meeting Liza's without flinching. "I'm Julia. And you must be…*Lola*, right?" I widened my eyes and asked in mock innocence. Ryan's head fell forward, his shoulders shaking. He was laughing his ass off.

I was still on his lap and his arm tightened around me, communicating he wanted me to stay where I was.

"Guhh," she grunted. "*Liza*."

"Oh, sorry." I extended my right hand to shake hers, silently wishing that this one time I could be left handed. "You go to school with Ryan. He told me."

"Did he?" She pulled out a chair and pushed Jen's drink forward, replacing it with hers.

"He tells me everything. What are you drinking? It looks good."

"Amaretto sour. You should try it. And yes, I attend Harvard with Ryan. We've had a lot of classes together."

My inner bitch reared its head. “Yes, I know,” I answered sweetly. Ryan sat in silence looking between the two of us and doing his damnedest not to smile. “Baby, that looks really good. Will you get one for me?”

I stood so Ryan could go to the bar. “Ummmm, sure,” he answered uncertainly. The look on his face said he didn't think leaving me with this woman was a good idea, but he went to do my bidding anyway.

“So, are you the Sunday coffee girl?” the other woman asked. I let my eyes roam over her slowly. She was pretty, in a brash sort of way and her hair was wavy and frizzy. She had big tits, which most men would find attractive, and light blue eyes.

The Sunday coffee girl? Ah...she's the voice in the background. I remembered.

I smiled brightly, trying to hide my irritation. “Yep! That's me.”

“I was there the night they brought you in from your accident. It's good to see you're better. You are all better, right?”

Ryan came back carrying the drink and set it down in front of me before resuming his place next to me. He draped his arm over the back of my chair as I leaned forward on the table toward the other girl.

“Much better. How nice of you to ask. So, what classes did you have with Ryan?”

I spoke with Liza and Ryan checked out. She regaled his expertise in organic chemistry, pharmacy, gross anatomy and a laundry list of other subjects, making sure I understood how extensive her contact with him had been. It was amusing and slightly sad that she was trying to get into a pissing match with me.

My fingers toyed with the drink and finally I took a sip. Ugh! It was so cloyingly sweet it almost made me gag. I tried not to make a face, pulled the cherry out of the glass and started fiddling with it. Ryan's hand closed over my knee under the table in silent plea for me to end this charade.

"Believe me; I know how brilliant Ryan is." I pulled the fruit off the stem with my teeth and chewed.

Her eyes flashed in silent challenge. "So um…what is it that *you* do, Julia? I don't think Ryan has ever mentioned it."

Okay, honey, if that's how you want to play it.

"That's not true. I talk about Julia all the time," Ryan's irritation seeped through the words. I laced my hand through his under the table. His fingers were warm around mine and he squeezed gently.

"It's okay, honey. I knew what she meant." Oh, *did I.* I smiled at them both and then turned my attention toward Liza. "I'm Fashion Editor at Vogue Magazine. It's one of the Condé Nast publications. My office is in New York City."

"Really…" she murmured. It wasn't really a question. "What do you do exactly?"

"Liza, didn't you come with someone?" Ryan interrupted rudely and I almost laughed. "Shouldn't you go find them?"

"Thanks for your concern, Ryan, but I'm fine," she hissed at him. "I'm very interested in learning more about Julia."

"Well, I'm very interested in spending time *alone* with her," he muttered under his breath.

Jenna and Aaron returned and when Jen reached for her drink. She stood back and wrinkled her nose, her face twisting up as she nodded toward Liza from behind her chair. Aaron mouthed the words "What the fuck?" at Ryan, who simply screwed up his expression and shook his head.

I put the cherry stem in my mouth and sucked on it during the exchange, whirling it around my mouth and in between my teeth until I had it in a knot. I took it out and closed my hand over it.

"Mmm, well, I hire the talent; design the storyboards and the look of all the articles. Approve content, schedule photo shoots, scout clothing. I work with advertising to solicit appropriate sponsors for various features and for charity events." I rattled off everything nonchalantly.

I glanced in Ryan's direction, still holding his hand. "Don't forget the modeling…" he murmured his eyes flying to challenge Liza.

I shrugged. "Yeah, that."

Liza didn't move and my eyes moved to Ryan. I held up the perfect little knot I'd made in the stem with my tongue and then placed it in Ryan's hand. "Apparently, I'm multi-talented, hmm?" I raised my eyebrows suggestively and he laughed. Aaron broke out in a loud chuckle and Jenna smirked over her glass.

"Uh, listen Lizzy…Your ass is in my seat," Jen pointed out, waiting for the other girl to vacate.

"Liza, it was nice to finally meet you."

"Yes, it's a shame we didn't before. Didn't you ever come to Boston in all this time?"

Ryan looked annoyed by the questions. "All the time, but I never let her out of bed. We had better things to do than socialize." He dismissed her and pulled me up by our entwined hands. "Let's dance. If I don't get my arms around you in thirty seconds, I won't be responsible for my actions."

A soft song was playing. I was content to lose myself in his arms, feeling him close, heat flowing between us. "I'm sorry you had to go through that, sweetheart," he said seriously and brushed a soft kiss on my mouth. Instantly my face rose up to meet his. I wanted more…

I shook my head. "It's nothing. Thank you for making sure she knew about me."

"She hasn't listened, but now, maybe seeing how beautiful you are…and how much I love you, she'll finally disappear." His hands fisted in the back of my shirt, and I could feel his trimmed nails raking over my skin through the thin material. Goose bumps flooded the exposed skin of my arms. "You are all that exists for me, and as long as you know that, the rest of the world can go straight to hell," he groaned right before his tongue slid into my mouth. His words melted me, his touch burned me, and his mouth…devoured me. Still I wanted more and I opened my mouth and kissed him back until our breathing was erratic and he finally pulled back, brushing the back of his knuckles along my cheekbone as the song ended.

"Julia, you'll be the death of me."

"Take me home, Ryan." It sounded like I was begging. "Will you hold me tonight? I want to feel you."

"Oh, babe." His voice was thick as he rested his forehead against mine. "Yes. I never want to stop touching you."

Somehow, I had to convince this man to make love to me. Tonight, I would be happy with this small step. He was talking and he was touching…and the glorious kissing. I'd take what I could get and be grateful.

But soon…I was going to feel his hands on my naked flesh, his body embedded within mine, hear my name on his lips as he came inside me. Oh God. It *had* to happen or I would spontaneously combust.

~9~

Ryan~

"THE ONLY MEMORIES I ever get are when I'm with you," Julia implored, her hand running lightly from my forearm down to my hand and back again.

My God. It was getting impossible. I could barely keep my hands off of her, especially when she was all warm and giving. I could see the want in her eyes, but was terrified of what would happen if I gave in to what we both wanted. The last time had such consequences. *Those damn nightmares.*

I was still terrified of the repercussions. I'd even resorted to calling Spencer and he agreed, her mind could shut down even more, and we could lose all the progress we'd already made. Even though his ulterior motives were clear, logically, I believed he was right. She could withdraw and worse, hate me. I couldn't live with that.

The apartment was dark and we were lying on the couch all wrapped up in each other. By some miracle, I'd managed to keep from making love to her, but it was killing me. We talked a little, but mostly we just held each other. I leaned in and nuzzled the back of her neck, her silken hair that always smelled so wonderful, fell around my face. Kissing the skin at the side of her neck, my lips moved up near her ear.

"I know, baby. We're spending more time together now. You'll remember soon."

She arched into me, her head coming to rest on my shoulder and her little ass pressing into my groin as we spooned on the couch. My body quickened and I tightened my arms around her. I'd have to extricate myself from this situation or something was going to happen. Aaron and Jen were working and it was early evening on Sunday night. I had a shitload of work to do, but all I wanted was to hold her. Touching her more, it was getting ridiculous how much I never wanted to stop.

Julia reached for her iPod on the coffee table and I reluctantly released her, giving me the time I needed to get the throbbing under control.

"What are you doing?" I asked softly.

She unwound the headphones and then turned toward me. I lay back and her head came to rest on my arm, facing me, her leg nudging between my knees. I pulled her forward to keep her from falling off the edge.

"I want to share something with you. Will you listen with me?" Her dark eyes dug into mine and I nodded then captured her open mouth with my own. The kiss was gentle, soft and succulent. I inhaled as it ended and laced my fingers through her hair.

"Yes."

Sharing the ear buds, the soft strains started and her hand came up to my face. "Listen to the words, Ryan. To what they mean…"

She sang softly with the song. Words about faith and footprints on the past, honesty and inevitable roads leading out of the dark and back to one person, rocked me to the core. She was sending me a message. That all paths lead to each other and there was no other choice. We stared into each other's eyes, fingers stroking, bodies entwined. It was paradise. I never wanted to move for the rest of my life. My heart constricted at how amazing she was. She was the most beautiful person, the most beautiful soul, I had ever known.

"Julia…" I breathed.

"Shhh…listen,"

Thud. My heart dropped.

Stop looking back, Ryan, her eyes implored. Believe in us. Now.

My eyes blurred and her fingers on my jaw tightened before her moist breath rushed over my face and her open mouth settled softly on mine; coaxing my response. My heart ached from the poignancy of the moment; the song was perfect and I wanted nothing more than to give in to the want…to the mad love.

Always such mad, mad love. Nothing changed it. Not years apart, not the stress or other people, not the loss of our past. *I was touched in a place only Julia had ever been.*

By the end of the song, I had her beneath me, kissing her forcefully; Julia's glorious response deepening the kiss, our tongues mating and our mouths sucking on each other in a delicious dance of give and take. God, it was amazing and I felt like I'd die if I didn't have her. She clutched at the back of my head, her fingers tugging on my hair to bring my mouth closer as her body surged up into mine. I wanted kiss after kiss and to rip the clothes from her body right then and there. I grabbed the iPod and the earphones that had fallen between us and threw them aside, my hand itching to close around her full breast and feel her nipple harden under my fingers.

"Uhnnggg…" I groaned into the side of her neck as my arms drew her closer and tried to hold her still. We were both breathing hard, practically panting in unison. I closed my eyes and held on tight. "Julia, you know how much I love you, don't you?"

Her frantic, passionate movements stopped and she looked into my face.

"You're doing it again, aren't you?" she whispered brokenly. "Why?"

The pain in her eyes made it difficult to meet them and I pressed my forehead into the side of her face. "Because," I rasped out, "I have work to do and if we start this…" It was only partially true. Yes, I had work, but nothing was more important than touching her.

"Why are you doing this to us?" Her voice hardened and my heart broke, not meaning to add my misery to all she was dealing with.

I struggled to sit up and moved to the floor next to the couch, so I could look into her face. "We *will* deal with this, my love. The time is coming where we'll have no choice, but I have so much work and I will not be able to get my head in the game if we crack this open right now. You're all I think about as it is." Somehow I got the words out past the huge, swollen lump in my throat.

Her face fell but she nodded silently.

Fucking hell! I ripped myself away, softly cupping her chin and brushing my thumb across it before beginning the walk down the hall. Every step split me open further and I started to shake.

"Ryan…" she began but I kept going, throwing words over my shoulder.

"I *really* need to get to work, Julia. We'll talk later, I promise." My voice was trembling on each word and I prayed she couldn't see how upset I really was.

"Ugh!" she moaned in frustration, throwing herself back down to the cushions and hitting the back of the couch with a fisted hand. "Goddamn it!"

I left her on the couch and rushed into my room on the pretense of studying, but how in the hell I was going to concentrate was beyond me. The five weeks until graduation loomed in front of me like years. I fell onto my bed and put my hand over my eyes.

I was miserable and my heart was breaking all over again. Julia was here and right in front of me, yet I couldn't talk to her, touch her, and make love to her like I wanted, like my heart and body were screaming to do. I was drowning and nothing could save me. Except Julia.

For the first time since her accident, I let myself feel my own pain, pushing it down wasn't possible anymore. Frustration, sadness and want overwhelmed me like never before.

I'd lost my entire world and as hard as I tried to resist, I wanted to tell her the truth. *What good will telling her do if she can't remember the feelings behind all the time we'd spent together?* That part tortured me.

I was getting weaker with each passing day, needing her more and more. I *needed* her to remember us, to remember *me*. The loss was beyond anything I'd ever experienced. The only thing worse was the fear and helplessness I'd felt when she was fighting for her life or when I found out about the baby. I still carried that anguish around in my chest and as much as I wanted Julia's memory back, I knew what experiencing that loss would do to her.

All of those times when we left each other and said the words, "*Don't forget to remember me,*" flooded my aching head and heart.

Could it get any more fucking ironic?!

I felt myself breaking…crumbling, clutching and pulling on my shirt as if I could pull the pain out of my chest.

Julia was starting to see my pain and she gravitated toward me. She wanted to get us back to the place we were after the midnight session on the piano bench, but didn't know how. It hurt her too, which only compounded the guilt I felt. Each time she asked me to tell her, with those beautiful, imploring eyes…I wanted to, more and more. I yearned for her to know, but I needed her to *feel* and she couldn't do that if she didn't remember on her own. The memories would be hollow without the love behind them. It was killing me.

I sighed brokenly; the air shattering my lungs. I rolled onto my side as my throat thickened, eyes welling with tears. I fisted my hands in the covers and pushed my face into the pillow so she wouldn't hear in case the screams in my chest could not be contained. Tears rained down my face and the sobs I'd been holding in since Julia came home from the hospital, shook my shoulders violently. My heart was exploding, my lungs constricting. I was gasping for breath and there was not one damn thing that I could do about it. I let the sadness wash over me and just cried those painful, silent sobs that rock you so hard there is no sound except the deep rasps when you finally have to breathe. I felt more helpless than I'd ever been in my life as my body shook with pain.

Motherfucker!

I gasped as the sound of the sobs finally spilled into the room and was startled when a hand touched my shoulder. Turning my tear-drenched face around, I found Julia sitting silently next to me on the bed. I was so consumed with grief that I hadn't noticed her.

"Uhhhhnnn, Julia," I sniffed and quickly wiped at my eyes, trying to sit up against the headboard. My skin burned. I was embarrassed that she saw me in this weakened state. The last thing I wanted was to let her see my heartbreak or make her feel guilty. "I didn't...uh, know you were there."

Her eyes were full of tears and her chin was trembling. "I'm so sorry, Ryan. I hate that you're hurting like this...because of me."

I reached out and brushed a tear from her cheek as her hand came to rest softly on my chest.

"It's not you. It's the situation," I said ardently and shook my head. Only a small streak of light, streaming in through the barely open doorway, cast a soft glow over her tear-drenched features. I wanted to take away her sadness and see again the happiness so indicative of my Julia, shining there.

"I *am* the situation." She shifted to move closer to me. The heat radiated off her and I ached to reach out and draw her closer to my body. "I want this to go away, so tell me what you're hiding. Please. Just...*please*." Her voice throbbed thickly.

"I've told you so much already, honey." My voice was low and raspy. The remnants of the tears were still plainly audible. I swallowed and ran the back of my hand over each of my eyes.

She looked down and bit her lip. Those perfect lips that I longed to feel against mine. I couldn't tear my gaze away as she spoke and my heart started to thump in my chest.

"Not really. Why do you always pull away from me when we get to the juice, Ryan? I feel like if you'd just pretend that I remember, act like you normally would around me, then maybe everything would come back to me. I *feel* you. I know how deep this is."

I tensed at the track the conversation was taking, but I couldn't avoid it completely. I never could lie to her. "From what the others have told you and an occasional flash of memory, yes, but you don't *remember* it. *Knowing* it and *feeling* it are two completely different things," I argued softly. "Trying to force it would be unfair, Julia. And…we both deserve more than that."

Her face crumpled and she nodded, wiping at the tears raining softly down her face, and clinging to her lashes. "Is that what you really think or is it just the bullshit that Spencer fed you?" Her brow wrinkled and she looked down at her hands. "I just said I *feel* you! I've tried to tell you and show you, but you keep pulling away. *Please, stop.*" Her voice softened on the next words. "What about that beautiful night…and just now on the couch?"

I leaned up and kissed her temple before pushing off of the bed. I had to get away or I was going to give in to the pull. I wanted to gather her up and protect her, to love her and ease the pain, but Spencer's words kept rolling around my brain.

"I'm gonna shower. I'm meeting Tanner and some of the others to finish the final research paper for the surgery clinical." I brushed her chin with my fingers once more, went into the bathroom and shut the door. I clasped both of my hands behind my head, wanting to shout as I struggled with the constriction in my chest.

Oh my God. I can't do this anymore!

I turned on the shower and quickly stripped off my clothes, hoping the hot water could help clear my head. I stepped under the spray and leaned back against the tile wall of the shower stall, letting the water pelt my chest and run down my body. My throat still ached and my eyes burned with unshed tears. The steam began rising when I rubbed my face again and then turned to wet the back of my hair.

"So what? This is it, then? I ruin your life until you resent and *hate me*? Until you can't bear to look at me anymore? I don't want that, Ryan." Julia's voice was close, hard and demanding.

She'd startled me and I jumped, turning away from her. I didn't know which one of us I was protecting, but, in Julia's mind, we'd never been together like this, she wouldn't remember seeing me naked, even if it was common practice. "Julia, you've got to stop doing that. Get out of here," I almost groaned over my shoulder. "We'll talk later."

"Like hell we will," she choked out, her voice was urgent, broken. "Don't you think these months have changed anything? Do you think I'm indifferent to you? Can't you *tell*?"

"Yes, I know you trust me, and care for me…even that you want me, if that's what you mean." I gave up trying to hide my body from her view and grabbed the shampoo, squeezing some onto my palm and lathering up my hair. "But, is it just because these months are all you have to base anything on? You've had to rely on me and I don't delude myself. I can't afford…!"

My heart sank the second I said the words, the hurt on her face was killing me.

She gasped loud enough that I could hear it over the running water. "Really? Is it real or is it *fucking Memorex*?!!"

"Julia," I began but she cut me off angrily.

"Damn you for saying that," she said, her tone dead still, fists clenched at her sides and eyes liquid. "These feelings are *all I've got*! To me they are so real I can barely handle them. Don't you dare try to discount this into some doctor-patient bullshit. My heart remembers you, Ryan. Even if my mind can't!"

My heart was breaking. I wanted it to be true so bad I couldn't even stand it. I rinsed my hair in a hurry, suddenly aching to get the hell out of there. "Julia, we've got time. Just…stop worrying."

"I know you'll take care of me. I'm worried about *you*, Ryan. This hurts you, and I'm keeping you from having a *real* life. It's wrong and I'm scared that you'll end up hating me. I…I just couldn't bear that."

The truth swelled up inside me, threatening to burst free like water from a dam.

"You *are* my real life, Julia." The words were out before I could stop them. I turned to find her taking her clothes off as she looked at me. "You…always have been." I froze and my pulse quickened, "I could *never* hate you. It's…not possible," I stammered in resigned defeat as she moved toward me. It was over. I wouldn't be able to fight this. My heart was racing, my blood rushing, and my body on fire at the site before me.

"If that's true, then *take back* your life, Ryan. I'm *begging* you," she cried as she opened the shower door and stepped inside. My eyes devoured her naked form like a dying man in the desert. I hadn't looked upon her like this for four months. Since the night I'd proposed, since the weekend we'd conceived our child. My whole body started to shake with the undeniable emotion that I'd buried for the past three months.

Her hands came to rest on my chest and she kissed me just above my collarbone, her lips lingering on my skin and sending heat licking along my veins like fire. I stood frozen, wanting to crush her to me, but terrified of the consequences. "Take back what's yours…I know you want me, and I want you. So much," she whispered urgently against my skin and then nuzzled up toward my jaw, brushing her open mouth along it.

"Julia…I'm not made of stone. *Please…*" I begged; my hands coming up to lightly touch her waist. "Oh, my God."

My body was throbbing to the point of pain, springing to life the instant she started dropping her clothes. It had been so long since we'd made love and I was starving for her. Literally dying; my lungs struggled for air as I started to pant with the effort of it.

"Please…don't fight this, Ryan." Her voice took on the sultry tone that I had always found irresistible.

Julia stood on her tiptoes and pressed her body against mine, grinding my erection between us, her hands slid like silk up over my chest and around my neck. If she didn't remember, her subconscious was guiding her in her movements, each one so familiar. Her touch ignited every carnal urge I'd ever had, burning as her hands moved over me, until they finally fisted in my hair and pulled my head down toward her open mouth.

I could feel my resolve crumbling. I longed to taste her. I wanted to kiss her and never stop.

"Julia…" I whispered against her mouth as her tongue darted out to flick my upper lip. It was like she knew my weakness and I wouldn't be able to resist. A groan ripped from my chest as I finally let my mouth crush down on hers, tongue sliding into her mouth and entwining with hers. Dear God, she tasted so good and felt so amazing, soft and hot against me.

This was my Julia, the love of my life and she wanted to give me everything. It was more than I could take. Her mouth moving hotly under mine was driving me to distraction, and what I'd been dreaming about for months.

She whimpered at the onslaught, but opened her mouth further and met me kiss for kiss. I gathered her up and lifted her closer, pushing her against the shower wall. God, it was good. It was *us*, just as always. Our lips mirrored each other so perfectly, knowing what the other needed and willing to give it all. I was sucking intermittently with little licks and nudging her top lip with my lower one, before fully taking her mouth with mine and thrusting my tongue as deep into her mouth as I could. She pulled it in further, sucking on it and I ground my pelvis into hers, causing her to moan into my mouth. Desire engulfed me like never before. I wasn't sure how long we stood there, clinging to each other, our hands and mouths couldn't get enough.

I let myself be consumed as I kissed her, and my hands slid over her breasts, taking their weight and running my thumbs over the hardened tips. They weren't overly large, but still full, perfectly round and responsive. I knew just how to touch her, leaving her breathless and moaning. Her nipples hardened even more, as my knee slid between her legs and pressed into her moist heat. "Uhhnnnggg, Julia." I sucked in my breath as her nails raked down my back.

The blood pounded in my ears and my dick twitched thickly against her stomach. I was dying to bury myself deep within her, to feel her clenching around me and writhing in the incredible pleasure I knew that we would give each other. My hands moved lower over the round firm curves of her butt and I pulled her tighter against me, seeking the pressure and friction I needed. I was about to lift her and bring her legs around my waist when she spoke against my mouth.

"God Ryan, was it always like this between us?" she gasped out and I stilled instantly. "It's so amazing."

My heart ached at those words. She didn't remember what it was like having me touch her, or what it felt like to have me inside her, making love to her until neither one of us could take anymore. She didn't remember that I was the first one to take her, the *only* one.

I rested my forehead on hers as I struggled for control. I was shaking so badly I thought I'd fall to my knees. I braced myself against the wall of the shower behind her head.

And what if Moore is right? As much as I wanted to make love with her, as much as I needed her, I couldn't do it. Not yet.

My heart shattered into a million pieces as I worried how she would interpret my stopping.

This would hurt and it would hurt badly. For both of us.

I brushed her hair back and bent to kiss her softly on the lips. Julia responded and her hands pulled me back again, arching up to press her mouth harder into mine. It was killing me not to take her, to lose myself. I longed to pump every ounce of love I felt into her until she was left breathless and quivering around me.

"Julia, you have to know how much I want this, but…we…oh fuck, we *can't*. Not yet."

She pulled back from me as if I had burned her. I couldn't see her eyes, because she had them closed, but I knew the pain and rejection I would find in their green depths. My heart broke all over again when my suddenly empty arms were left to grasp at the space where she had been. "Honey, I…just think that we should…"

She pushed out of the shower with a bang, quickly gathering up her clothes and rushing into the bedroom. I grabbed a couple of towels and followed her. Her back was to me as she struggled to quickly pull on the clothes over her wet skin while I wrapped a towel around my waist. She pulled and pulled on the jeans as they stuck to her legs, her shoulders shaking with grief, the tears clearly visible on her face now. I could hear her crying and it put me in hell.

"Julia…" *How could I be so damn stupid?*

"Please." Her voice broke. "Don't…don't say anything. I'm so…humiliated. I have to get out of here. I c…can't be with you right now." She wouldn't look at me.

"Julia, don't. You shouldn't feel that way."

She finally turned to me as she threw her t-shirt back over her head. "Why!? Why shouldn't I feel that way, Ryan? Because

I just threw myself at you and you don't *want* me? Be…because you push me away and yet don't want me to go back to New York? You can't have it both ways! I can't do this anymore! You won't help me remember…and I want to remember you so damn bad!"

Frustration welled within me, pissed that she thought I didn't want her, hurt that she was hurting, angry at the entire situation. "You think I don't want you? You *see* what you do to me, Julia! I want you so much it puts me in physical pain! What I *don't want* is to hurt you! I'm so worried about what could happen. I…love you."

She raised her eyes to mine and I could see how much she was hurting, how angry she was.

"Yeah, sure. You love me so much, you ignore what I want, rather than let me touch you, hold you…feel you inside my body like I'm dying for! What I want is for you to tell me the truth, treat me like I imagine it should be like between us. Like I can tell it *was* between us, the way it is when you almost give in! *Tell me, Ryan*!" she practically screamed, both of her hands going up to grasp the sides of her head. "I want you to not be able to *help* yourself. I want you to want me like I want you…to love me so much you can't stop yourself from touching me." She sank down on the edge of the bed and cried like I'd never heard her before. Her heart was broken and I'd never felt more helpless. "Just now? That was us!" Silence hung between us like a storm until finally she screamed at me and I jumped inside my skin. "Wasn't it!!??" Her tone was hysterical and broken but softer as she put her hands over her face and sobbed, her little shoulders shaking uncontrollably.

Please, please you have to know how much I fucking love you!

I pulled on my clothes and sat down next to her, reaching out a hand to place it on her back. Julia flinched away while I struggled to find the words that would soothe her and not add to her pain. I sucked in a breath and opened my mouth but closed it again. Nothing I could say would change what had just gone down.

"You think I don't *feel* this, Ryan? Do you think it would hurt so damn much if I were fucking *oblivious*? I r-remember that I l-love you. Just b-because I don't remember everything we did together…doesn't mean I-I d-don't remember I l-love you," she cried brokenly. "D-don't you want that?"

"Oh, babe…" I began and tried to pull her close, wanting to comfort her.

Her sobs ripped at my soul. "Why won't you let me love you?"

I held her for a few minutes until she finally melted into me, as I pulled her onto my lap, and we both buried our faces in the curves of each other's neck. My throat was throbbing and my eyes were tearing. Her words had fallen around me like meteors crashing to earth, leaving mass destruction in their wake. My hand stroked her head, she sighed and finally the hiccoughing sobs lessened.

"Julia…I *love you* so much. You're my entire world. I feel like if you don't know that for certain, I just…I can't survive." She sat in my arms without speaking as I touched her, brushing her hair back and kissing her face, tasting her salty tears on my lips. Finally, she drew in a shaky breathe and pulled back to look into my face.

"All these months, I may not have remembered much, but I've figured some things out. I know you're the only man that's ever made love to me. *I know it.*"

"How?" I asked softly, a little bit afraid of the answer that was to come. My chest constricted at this small truth that she'd uncovered. It was monumental.

"*Because*. You're the only person that's shrouded in the darkness. I remember my parents; I remember my job and some of school. If I'd been with anyone else, if anyone had touched me like you have, I'd remember it. It's only ever been you, hasn't it?" Her hand brushed gently against my jaw, almost not touching.

My hand was trembling as I pushed her hair gently off of her face. The wet strands clung to her cheeks as my fingers slid across her delicate skin. Finally, I met her eyes. "Yes," I said softly, and she sighed into me. "It was like a miracle. Such a beautiful…gift."

"Will you tell me about it? *Please*? I know you want me like I was before, but what if I never remember? I want your pain to go away…to give you what I can, so tell me."

"Ugh, Julia." She was worrying about *me*. That was so typical of her. "I can't. Part of me wants to so damn bad."

Her eyes hardened and she pulled away from me once again to stand with her back to me, her hand plunking at the keys on my keyboard. "Just forget it. *You* won't come back to *me* either, don't you see that? I guess we're *both* irrevocably broken."

My heart fell sickeningly and I stood to place my hands on her shoulders. The instant I touched her, she shrugged me off.

"You'd better hurry. Tanner and *the gang* are waiting at the library. Tell Liza I said *hi*."

I dropped my hands in silence behind her, but she never moved. A hot flush spread out under the skin of my face and chest. I never felt so distant from her. My heart panicked, but I didn't know how to comfort her.

I packed up my books into my backpack and flung it over my shoulder and walked toward the door of my room.

I turned toward her again but she averted her face away.

"I do not think you're broken, Julia. I just want to give you time to heal and not do more harm. You mean everything to me."

Her face hardened and her chin jutted out as she looked at the floor. "Yeah, you've made that clear. I'll see you later," she effectively dismissed me.

I could barely make my feet move, but I turned and walked away. Hopefully, after she'd had some time to cool off, we'd be able to talk.

Maybe she was right, and she might not *ever* remember. But was I ready to lose her completely?

Not under any circumstances.

I wanted *any* type of life with her. Yes, it would be painful if she didn't remember, but not half as bad as the thought of a life without her.

I still wanted to make sure that telling Julia the past would be safe; and my dad would be straight with me. I took a deep breath as I got into my car, feeling slightly better after the decision was made.

I tossed my book bag into the passenger seat and started the car and threw it into gear, hoping distance between us for awhile would ease some of the pain. *Who the hell are you kidding, Matthews?*

I pulled out my phone and dialed Jenna first.

"Hey, shithead," she laughed into the phone as she answered.

"Julia and I just had a fight. Where are you? Aaron told me he wouldn't be home until midnight and I don't want her to be alone. Can you get there?"

"You know, Ryan, Julia isn't sick, she's physically fine and she's *not* crazy. She doesn't need us lurking."

"Jenna. Please. I'm…worried about her."

"What the hell did you fight about?"

"Uh…she wants to start over and to hell with her memory loss but I'm just…I'm terrified. She's not ready to remember the pregnancy, Jenna. If she could deal, she'd remember on her own. I can't risk it and she thinks I don't want her."

"Wow. Shit, okay. I'll be home in an hour after my shift ends."

"Will you call me? I'm going to the library for awhile but nothing is more important to me than Julia. If I need to come home, I'm there." I drew in a deep breath.

"Okay, I promise. It will work out, Ryan."

"Thanks. You're saving my life. *Again.*" I hung up and dialed my father.

Julia ~

"Aaron, can you come home? I need to talk to you."

There was a pregnant silence on the other end of the line…finally he spoke in a quiet tone. "Jules, what's this about?"

"Aaron, *please*. Will you just come home? I'd like to talk to both you and Jen. It's about Ryan." Even I could hear the desperation in my voice. My chest hurt and I knew what I had to do.

Jenna held out her hand for the phone, which I quickly handed over.

"Just come home," she said; her voice tense and her eyes trained on my face. "See you in a few minutes."

After Ryan left, I sat in the dark for what seemed like hours, until I got up and packed my things, as quickly as possible. I wanted to be gone before Ryan returned. Afterward, I went back and waited in silence for Jen and Aaron.

Aching silence.

Time stood still but dragged until Jen showed up and sat with her arm around me. It was like she knew what I was going through and she didn't try to pry.

"Is there anything you need?" Jenna asked softly.

I wrapped my arms around myself and shook my head. *Nothing you can give me.*

I needed to remember my *fucking life* and Ryan to let us happen. My soul was screaming for him. I didn't even know what I expected Aaron to say, but I needed *something*. Anything.

I went into the bathroom and leaned on the counter, staring into the mussed reflection in the mirror. I recognized my face. I remembered most of my life, so why couldn't I remember Ryan? I stared into my eyes and cursed the brain behind them.

I had fallen in love with him all over again and wanted to be closer to him still. It hurt desperately that he kept pulling back. Every time I felt he'd cave-in; he somehow found the strength to resist. I felt like my heart had been ripped from my body and someone had stomped on it. The agony on his beautiful face as he hurried out of the apartment had literally left me breathless, the pain was so intense. I was empty, like my heart was missing.

My red-rimmed eyes were a reminder of my evening; alone on the couch, crying for God knew what. Was it for my lost memory or Ryan's rejection? I couldn't tell anymore. I felt numb, hollow. My body and mind, exhausted.

I was tired of trying to figure shit out. I knew the feelings were new *and* reminiscent of our past but couldn't reconcile why he wouldn't embrace it. Ryan was good and kind, amazing in everything he did, but this went way beyond that.

We were *everything*. I knew it by the longing his mere presence brought forth and the few times when he had faltered in his resolve…the few delicious times when he had almost given in. In the shower or on the piano bench…I could see the love in his luminous blue eyes.

This is so fucked up.

Ryan needed me to remember more than I needed to remember for myself.

I put my hand up to cover my eyes as new tears dripped down my cheeks, the numbness dissolving into a torrent of sadness again. I thought that I didn't have any more tears left, but the well seemed endless. I finally got myself under control so I could be prepared to speak with Aaron and Jenna.

I went back into the living room, lost in my thoughts. The door burst open and Aaron strode in from outside while Jen emerged from their bedroom. They both came into the living room together. Aaron took the seat on my left and Jenna sat on the arm of the chair next to him.

Aaron nodded toward the bags on the floor next to the door.

"What's that about?" His usually smirking face was serious and worry flooded his features. "Julia?"

I glanced down at my hands, wringing in my lap. "I'm…I think I should…" I hesitantly met his eyes and then Jenna's. They'd been so good to me and I was grateful, but burdening their lives wasn't right. It wasn't fair to any of them. Especially Ryan.

"Julia, it'll be okay," Jen said.

I shook my head. "But, *it isn't*. Don't you see that?" My voice was shaking and my hands were, too. "Ryan is in so much pain." I didn't feel it necessary to share the details of the events of the evening. "I can't do this to him anymore. It's been nearly three months and, still, there are only glimpses of my past. It's time to resume my life in New York. Maybe it will help me remember and more importantly," I tried to swallow the rising lump in my throat, "Ryan can move on." I heard my voice crack. "He deserves to be happy."

Aaron shook his head. "This won't make him happy, Julia. I've tried to talk to Ryan about how asinine Moore's theories are, but he won't listen. You'll break him if you leave, Julia."

I stood and walked to the window. The lights from surrounding buildings outside blurred under my stare. I blinked and a single tear dripped from my lashes. I quickly reached up and brushed it away as I struggled for words.

"Spencer's on Ryan's side, but going back to New York might help me remember."

"Clearly you love him, Julia," Jenna said softly.

There was no point in denying it, and I couldn't even if I wanted to, but loving him wasn't enough.

"Yes. More than anything" I nodded and dipped my head, bringing both hands up to the sides of my face. "That's why I have to go. I see how it hurts him to have memories of us that I don't share anymore. It's like I died, but I'm here haunting him constantly. I won't hurt him like that anymore. I feel how he suffers and I can't stand it. I just can't, Aaron." My throat ached with tears, every syllable a struggle.

"Do you understand?" I almost whispered.

"Not really." Aaron rubbed the back of his neck. "Ryan will never get over this, Julia. Even if you went to the moon and he never saw you again, he'll always miss you. I saw it when…" His voice dropped off.

Once again the hesitation was revealing. Spencer did me a disservice when he told everyone who loved me that they couldn't talk to me. And now, tonight, Aaron was doing it again.

"You say that now, but as time passes he will. I'm holding him back. So I'm going back to my life." Aaron huffed and I shot him a questioning look. "What's the alternative, then? Will *you* tell me about my past?" I asked them both.

Aaron sighed and Jen's face was covered in sadness.

"*Will* you?" I asked again.

"This is Ryan's decision, Julia, not ours. He spoke to Dad and Spence and they both feel that it could do permanent damage..." Aaron began, but I interrupted him angrily.

"What the hell is *this,* Aaron? If it isn't permanent damage?! Not remembering Ryan is...from what I can tell, the biggest tragedy of my life," I said in defeat. "And his."

"Why can't you just build a new life together?"

"*Ask Ryan*! I want to, but he is afraid that he'll force me to remember whatever the hell it is he doesn't want me remembering." I laughed through my tears. "*Force me*, when I am *begging* him to tell me. The problem is; he doesn't want it to be like a story someone told me. He needs me to *feel* the memories, to have lived through them with him, and I...understand why he needs that. He *deserves* that."

"Julia," Jenna began, "have you told Ryan of your plans? He'll be..."

"*Fucking devastated*, that's what he'll be," Aaron said angrily. "Don't do this to him, Julia."

"Aaron, I *love* Ryan but he is suffering! He barely touches me now and it hurts too much to be around each other!" I was practically yelling, my body shaking and tears beginning to rain down my face. I went to the door and shoved my feet into my sneakers. "I just don't know what to do anymore. I keep hoping that something will happen, that one day I'll wake up and it will all come back to me, but it doesn't. Every day the hope in his eyes turns into disappointment when he realizes I still haven't remembered. It kills me and worse, it's killing *him*. I'm going insane with it!" I cried. "My heart loves him, my soul knows him, but my damn mind won't remember!" I cried; the sobs barely contained. My heart ripped apart inside my chest.

I rushed blindly to the door and picked up my bags. "I'll send for the rest of my stuff later."

"Julia, don't…" Jenna came toward me with Aaron close on her heels.

His expression had softened during my diatribe and he put his arm around me and pulled me close. One of the bags fell from my shoulder onto the floor as I melted into him and sobbed.

"I'm doing this for Ryan. Please take care of him for me. I love him so much."

"Then why go, Julia?" I moved out of his arms and looked into his face. I reached out to Jen. She took my hand and squeezed. "Ryan loves you more than I've ever seen."

"But it's not enough. He needs me to remember, and I can't give that to him right now. If, by some miracle it happens, then I'll come back. I promise. Thank you both for everything. I love you." I wiped at my tears, picked up my bags and left the apartment for the last time. I was leaving my heart behind with Ryan and it hurt like hell.

"Julia!" Aaron called after me, but I didn't turn back.

I rushed out the door, tears blinding me as I stumbled down the steps and onto the sidewalk. I stopped and gasped for breath between the sobs, my shoulders slumped. Struggling, I tried to wipe at my eyes.

Suddenly two strong arms enfolded me. "Where in the hell do you think you're going, Julia?" Ryan's voice was hard, but still smooth as silk. Still my Ryan.

Silent tears fell. "Let me go," I begged, torn between pushing away from him and letting myself melt into the safety of his arms. "You don't want me and I don't want to hurt you anymore."

I heard a sharp intake of breath. "Is that what you really believe? That I don't *want* you? I've never wanted anyone more, Julia." His voice softened. "I'm…*dying* with the wanting. I'm so consumed with it, I can't even think straight. I can't sleep. I don't want to eat…If you leave, you'll kill me."

"Then *why*?" I shook my head and looked up into his face as I felt his fingers flex on my shoulders.

"We've been over this. Spencer says…"

"*Fuck* Spencer, Ryan!" I screamed at him as I pushed out of his resistant arms. "I don't want to hear his name one more time in a conversation about us! And, fuck you, too! I don't know what else to do! I can't stand the pain I see your eyes! You won't let us be together like we need to be…" My voice weakened and cracked again. "So, I'm…*going*."

He looked away, the muscle working in his jaw as he struggled for words.

"I don't want you apart from me. Please…don't do this."

"All I want is to get closer to you, Ryan, but you keep pushing me away. Can't you see how ironic and ridiculous that is?" I almost laughed, but I was crying too hard.

"I'm sorry. I just…" he stammered and frustration bubbled up inside me, ready to burst free and scatter my body in pieces at his feet. I was lost. I swallowed hard and stared unflinchingly into his face. I could see the struggle going on behind his blue eyes and the torture on his beautiful features.

"Let this happen, Ryan! You say you want me and *I know* you love me. I can feel it, even if you never say it again. So *please*…Let it happen!" The words choked out. "Or, let me go."

He stared for a moment and then let go of my shoulders and stepped back. "I'm *scared*! I don't want to hurt you, and I…I don't want to hurt me. I'm…worried that you still won't remember me, even if I make you mine again, Julia. I'm not sure that's in either of our best interests. I'm trying to take care of you."

"Do you know how completely destroyed I am that I can't remember you, Ryan?" I asked softly. "I've never wanted anything as much as I want you." I lifted my hands in defeat but then let them fall back down to my sides.

He sat down on the steps and placed both hands on his head, fisting them in his hair. When he finally raised his eyes to mine, they were flooded with tears. "I imagine as devastated as I am, maybe worse, and I'm *sorry*."

"I can't do this without you. You are the only person in the world that can know how much this hurts because you're living it with me. Every fiber of my being is screaming for you and I don't give a damn if I *never* remember our past. I know that hurts you and I'm so sorry. It hurts me, too…but I love you *now*, Ryan! Don't you *get* that?" I said in broken defeat.

"How can you love me when you can't remember?"

"You are so Goddamn stubborn! I remember the last three months! I remember you taking care of me. The way you touch me…I can feel that you love me. Your voice soothing me and calling me back from *death*! Dancing, laughing, talking, cooking together, going for walks…being my best friend. When you kissed me in the shower, your hands on my body on the piano bench…" my voice dropped to almost a whisper, "When you tasted me and came with me. I want all of that and more, Ryan. I love you so much, it hurts."

I wiped the tears from my face, struggling to get more words out. "If that isn't enough for you, then…okay." I shrugged in defeat. "I can't make you believe it." My voice was trembling and I paused to try to get it under control, but I was failing miserably. "You seem to need the past more than I do…so, I have to go see if I can get it back, Ryan," I cried quietly now, heartbroken. “And if I can’t, at least you’ll be able to move on. It’s the b…best I can d…do for you right now.”

I covered my face with my hands as I struggled in devastation, until finally I turned around and went to get my bags. Before I went two steps, Ryan jumped up and whirled me around.

“Stop, Julia! You’re *not* leaving me!! I won’t let you go.” His breath was coming in heavy pants, his chest heaved with the effort and his eyes were glassy. Pain shot through my head with a memory. My hand rose to my left temple and I closed my eyes. We were in my bedroom, in New York…

“No.” Ryan was angry, his face tense, a flush rising up underneath his skin. His eyes flashed. “No, Julia. I’m almost done with med school! It’s time to start our life together. We’ve waited and struggled for too fucking long! I won’t let you go!”

As quickly as it started, the memory was gone, leaving me confused and grasping for more.

Had I been planning on leaving him? Were we breaking up?

I raised my troubled eyes to his. Ryan panicked and quickly placed both hands on the sides of my face, gently raising my chin so he could look into my eyes.

“Julia? Are you okay? What did you remember?” he asked urgently.

I was confused by my feelings, by trying to figure out the meaning behind these flashes. “Uh…I’m not sure. Ryan, we were arguing and you were yelling. You said that you wouldn’t let me go, that we’d waited too long to start our life together.” My face crumpled with more tears. “Was I leaving you?”

He pulled me into his embrace and kissed the side of my face and then my temple. “No! It wasn’t about us breaking up, my love. Oh, God, that was never a consideration, okay? There was no choice for us but to be together. Please believe that," he said; his velvet voice soft and soothing. "*No*, Julia."

The arms I'd wound around his waist tightened and I nodded in the crook of his neck. "Then what? Please tell me, Ryan," I begged. "Please?"

"I…I've hesitated because you're choosing not to remember and I'm afraid that being intimate will make it all come back too soon. You're obviously not ready and I can't do anything that might hurt you."

"Don't you want me to remember us?" My voice cracked on the last and he sucked in his breath.

"Yes, but not until you're completely ready. It isn't because I don't love you or want you. It's *because* I love you."

"I can't bear the thought of leaving you."

I felt his lips in my hair on the top of my head, moving as he spoke. "Then what the fuck are you doing with your bags packed and crying on the sidewalk in the middle of the night, for Christ's sake?" he murmured softly.

I was shaking, but being in his arms was all I needed in the world. "I don't want to hurt you anymore. I can't stand that you're in pain because of me, Ryan," I answered brokenly.

"Julia," he sighed and his arms tightened around me. "We're doing what we've always done; trying to take care of each other. Come on, sweetheart," Ryan nodded toward the house and then reluctantly released me. It was late April but I still felt a chill that the loss of his embrace caused, the cool breeze blowing my hair off of my face.

He bent to pick up my luggage and turned back toward the house. When he got up the steps, he opened the door and waited for me to precede him down the hall to the apartment.

Aaron and Jenna probably watched the entire scene from the window. "Would the two of you mind? Julia and I have some things to work out, and we need to be alone for a while. Aaron…can you get a room somewhere tonight? Please?" Ryan dropped the bags unceremoniously on the floor and then moved to my side.

"No problem, Ryan," Aaron said quietly as he left the room to gather his things.

They moved around the apartment, putting on their shoes and jackets. Ryan's gaze never wavered from mine.

My body was shaking but I wasn't sure if it was anticipation or fear. A palpable, tangible electricity filled the air…he was finally going to give in. The minute the door closed he took my hand to pull me roughly down the hall behind him to his room. Once there, the door slammed behind us and Ryan yanked me to him, but then his movements slowed notably. It was as if he were arguing with himself inside his head once again.

His hand moved up to cup my head and pull my face closer to his, the thumb brushing back and forth across my cheekbone reverently. His sweet breath rushed over my skin and I sucked it into my lungs like his essence was all I needed to survive.

"Are you sure?" he said huskily, breathlessly.

I nodded, using the motion to bring my open mouth nearer to his, nose nuzzling the side of his face, my mouth reaching, begging him to take it. I hovered on my tiptoes, reaching up to ghost over his mouth, my tongue shot out to lick his upper lip and he groaned, still resisting me. "You're all I want…all that exists for me, Ryan."

I reached up and grabbed his chin, trying to pull his mouth down to mine and his hands fisted in my hair and he groaned. "I've been fighting this so fucking hard. I've wanted nothing more than to touch you…to lose myself in you. To forget that you don't remember me."

I closed my eyes and waited, arching into him, my hands sliding up his chest and around his neck to hold the back of his head in a firm grasp, wanting him to feel how much I wanted him. He smelled so delicious and he felt so good pressed tightly up against me, but the months of wanting had taken their toll on both of us. His arms tightened and he pulled me closer still, his erection pressing into my stomach and immediately my body reacted. "It can happen just like that. If you'll let it, Ryan. We *need* this…*please,*" I whispered against his mouth.

My body was reacting to his nearness, his scent; the hard muscles of his body, so masculine against my feminine softness. The throbbing was familiar and instinctively I knew that only he could ease the torturous ache.

"Oh, Julia…" he moaned, the sound ripped from deep within his chest. "You win. I'm going to pour all the love I have into you, do you understand? You want to feel how much I love you? We're *both* going to drown in it. God…I want you," he whispered against my lips just before his mouth devoured mine.

Oh, God. My lips remembered his, my body molded to every hard contour of his and it was heaven as his mouth and tongue staked their claim on mine. My mouth opened and my hands fisted in his hair to pull his mouth closer, deepen into the kiss. He kissed me again and again, lifting me off of the floor and moving to the bed. Heat rushed through my lower body and a low ache began to pulse in the pit of my stomach. I sucked his tongue into my mouth as our mouths moved perfectly together, so hungry and passionate. My legs lifted and wrapped around his waist and he groaned as he lowered me to the bed.

Instantly, he was pressing into me, the bed sinking beneath me as I arched up into him, the pressure of his hardness against my softness driving me crazy with desire. "God, Ryan. I love you," I breathed as he broke the kiss to take a breath. "I love you."

"You are everything to me. My entire Goddamn life! I've missed you so much."

~10~

Julia~

RYAN'S STRONG ARMS were insistent and I clutched at the front of his shirt, pulling him closer as my mouth opened under his. *Always closer.*

"Uh, Ryan. God, finally." The words sounded foreign, like they were coming out of someone else's mouth. My voice was deep and needy as his fingers wound in my hair and our mouths were wild with each other. His hold tightened and he lifted me further up on the bed with one arm. "Finally…Babe, *don't stop*," I whispered against his mouth. "You'll break my heart if you stop."

His forehead rested on mine, his breathing ragged as he sucked in his breath. When he spoke, the warm moisture washed over my skin, my lips parted in anticipation. I couldn't resist reaching toward his mouth. He licked my top lip gently, nudging it in between both of his.

"Julia…I'm not going to stop. I…fucking *can't*." The hands at both sides of my face laced through my hair possessively. "But…I want to go slow…slow, honey."

"Ugh…no. No…I've waited for this forever, Ryan. God…*please*." His mouth took mine roughly, each opening to the other deeply. He groaned my name and plunged his tongue against mine as together they began a slow, sensual dance. Heat spread through me like fire licking along my veins as the throbbing intensity grew. His mouth lifted and came back for more, hotter and hungrier, like he was starving. He tasted heavenly and I never wanted him to stop.

He suddenly stilled, his fingers moving gently against my cheek and I slid my arms around his waist. "Baby…this is like your first time again. Everything has to be perfect."

Inwardly, I rejoiced at his tenderness yet moaned in frustration. He moved away slightly, but his hand slid down to mine and he pulled me with him. "I don't want to stop touching you," he explained as he dug in his desk drawer for a lighter and then placed my hand along his waist when he needed both of his to light the small candle he had on his nightstand and turned on the music. I moved forward and wrapped my arms around his middle, pressing my forehead into the strong muscles of his back. He turned in my arms, enfolding me with his, as his mouth came immediately back to mine.

The melody was soft, but I focused on Ryan and the way my body was reacting. I was lost as he kissed me over and over again, his hand moving to my breast, closing around it and squeezing gently. My heart was racing. Wetness pooled between my legs, my nipples strained against the fabric of my bra and shirt, the sensitive flesh aching…*beyond* aching. He'd only kissed me, yet I was helpless and wanton. Now I knew what he meant about physical pain. Only Ryan could ease this maddening quickening and I longed to do the same for him.

His erection was full and thick, straining against my hip, his pent-up frustration surging within him; the tension as his muscles coiled beneath the smooth skin of his shoulders as my hands pushed up the sleeves of his scrubs. "Take this off," I begged between kisses. "I want to see you…to feel you against me." I reached for the hem and pushed it higher. Ryan stopped and watched with passion-filled eyes. Beautiful and luminous, full of love and longing…I reveled that this perfect, amazing man could want me so much.

He raised his arms, pulling it over his head and flinging it aside. I stared at him in awe, he was sculpted and so beautiful to me. I felt his solid muscles working each time he'd held me, and finally, I could look upon him undaunted.

He swallowed, as his eyes fell to my mouth. His fingers began working on the buttons of my blouse, slowly exposing the black lace and creamy flesh as his lips left a hot path from my jaw down my neck to my collarbone.

"This is really going to happen," he breathed as he bent and ran a trail of hot, open-mouthed kisses to the curve of my shoulder. His fingers were soft, brushing over my skin and giving goose bumps as he pushed the blouse down my arms. "Dear God, babe. You're gorgeous. I missed touching you like this."

His fingers ghosted over the top swells of my breasts visible above the delicate edge of my bra. I closed my eyes and offered up my mouth, silently begging to end my torture, and my hand reached out to find the waistband of his pants. They were tied shut and I frantically worked the knot…he was still, except for his mouth running along my cheekbone and then back toward my mouth.

"I missed my mouth on yours, missed my hands on your body…missed being deep inside you." He was making love to me with his words even though he was barely touching me, and my body came alive. Every inch of skin burned for his touch, my lower body hot and pulsing, breathing was shallow and rapid. His hands tangled in my hair, gently tugging my face closer to his.

"Ryan, please." I flattened my hand against the large bulge in his pants…he groaned as my fingers closed around his hardness and started slowly stroking. He was so engorged that the head of his dick came out of his boxer briefs and to the top of the waistband. My hand found the silky smooth skin and I gasped at the bead of wetness I found there. My thumb moved the slick fluid around.

"Oh God, I can't take it, Julia. You have to stop. It's been so long…I don't want to come too soon. This is for you."

I shook my head. "No. I never want to stop. I want to see and feel how you want," I said urgently as I began to push his pants and underwear down his hips just slightly.

"Ugh…Julia you *can…*" His arms enfolded me then, lifting me until our mouths were on the same level and he turned me to lay me on the bed. The deep kisses resumed and I wrapped my legs around him, urging him on. I could feel him straining against me through my jeans, thrusting into me.

"Can I?" My hands clawed at his shoulders and my pelvis arched toward his, trying to assuage the ache, seeking the pressure I needed.

"You know you can. Look at what you do to me and we've barely even started. Just thinking about you gets me hard as steel." His voice was low and urgent, deep and rumbling…like hot silk settling all around me. He nuzzled against the side of my face and I clutched, pulling him closer but he moved out of my reach so that he could undo my jeans, not yet pulling them off. His fingers splayed out across the skin of my abdomen and moved up until both hands cupped the side of my breasts, his thumbs slowly teasing the taut peaks until I was writhing beneath him.

Eyes dark and passion glazed, he looked down upon me. "God, you're beautiful." The words tore from his throat in a low growl. "You leave me breathless. I'm…undone, Julia. There are no words to tell you how much I've missed you…how much I fucking love you."

Tears welled in my eyes, both of us mesmerized by the other as he stood over me and pulled my jeans from my body and then stroked his hands gently down my legs and then back up to start kneading the flesh of my thighs. "Then show me," I pleaded breathlessly.

Ryan stripped off the rest of his clothes and came back to lie next to me on the bed, his muscled thigh sliding between both of mine. I arched against him, gathering him to me and seeking his mouth once again. He didn't hesitate. His kisses were urgent and hungry, his hands insistent as they roamed my flesh. When the heat from my center made contact with his groin, he closed his eyes and gasped. "Uhhh…God." He hitched my leg up over his hip, then clasped my thigh and pulled my softness tighter against his steel hardness. I wound my fingers in his hair as he settled into the cradle of my body, rocking his hips into mine, creating that delicious friction we both craved. God, it felt so perfect.

"You feel so good, I want you, Ryan. Just *do it*." I didn't care if I was begging. This was the man I loved more than life and I wanted him more than anything. All that remained between us was the thin lace of my panties and bra. My hands raked the hard planes and smooth skin, gently kneading the solid muscles of his back.

"Uhnnnggg…Julia." My name ground out as he moved against my slippery wetness, driving me wild with desire. Ryan continued his onslaught, deeply kissing my mouth and then further down, his tongue leaving a wet trail in its wake. The coolness of the air, in contrast, left me shivering, but was quickly lost in our urgency. I moved with him, silently praying the panties to slip aside, so I would feel the heaven of Ryan pushing inside me.

His hand moved up to the top of my bra and pulled the lace down, baring the swollen flesh.

His hand wrapped around my breast just as his mouth closed around the nipple, his tongue circling and laving before sucking the sensitive flesh. I thought I would die. “Ryan, please…*please*. Now.”

“Please…*what*?” he said against my flesh, taking his time and moving to give the other breast equal attention. “What is it you want? Tell me and I’ll give it to.” His voice was full of sex and I fell apart, my body aching in anticipation. “Is it my mouth on you here?” he asked huskily as his fingers slid beneath my panties, to the place I wanted him most, touching the sensitive flesh. “My fingers…here?” He kissed me deeply again as he slid two fingers inside. I cried out into his mouth at the ecstasy of it as he raised his head to look into my face.

“Uhhh, Julia. I want to rip this shit off and bury myself inside you. I don’t want anything between us ever again. I need to know you’re mine,” he breathed. “Just you and me. Forever.”

“Yes. Yes…Ryan,” I panted into his mouth as, finally, his fingers closed around the lace and ripped it away. I could feel him pressing in slightly, arching up but his hand on my hip stilled me.

“Look at me, my love.” He moved the bulbous head of his cock up and down my folds, the pressure driving me crazy. I felt my body opening, aching for him to fill me. “Julia.” The head pushed inside and I gasped in pleasure. His hand moved to my face, brushing back the hair at my temples and his hips surged into mine, stretching and filling me until I thought I would rip open. His eyes closed.

“You feel so good,” he breathed against my mouth. He started to move slowly. “Julia, uhhhh…uhhhh. I’ve missed you, babe,” he moaned before his mouth closed over mine and soon our tongues and lips were imitating the movements of our hips, surging and sucking, I clutched and tugged at his hair as our movements became deeper. With long, slow strokes, he dug into me deeply and still it wasn't enough. We kissed and touched, moving together, worshiping each other, every touch growing more passionate as time stood still, our hearts and breathing getting faster with each passing minute. It felt amazing, exciting...desperate, brand new, yet familiar. My senses were on overdrive, I wanted him to feel every inch of me as my hands kneaded into his back, my heels pushing into the back of his thighs urging him on. I clenched around him in a rhythm of my own.

"Uh...that feels unbelievable...you're...so...incredible," he panted against my mouth. I sucked in his breath hungrily. I wanted every nuance of him inside me. My heart was so full of him I thought it would burst.

"Ryan, my God." My throat swelled and my eyes burned even as my body began to tremble and quake around his.

"Kiss me...I want your mouth. I want all of you," he moaned into me and took what he wanted. The more he needed, the more I gave. He was the most delicious thing I'd ever tasted, his mouth and tongue moving with mine in an intimate dance that only added to the wonder of the experience. I felt my body tighten more with each and every thrust. He was moving long and hard against me, deeper and deeper. It was more than I could take, yet somehow not enough. The velvet sounds coming from deep within his chest as he became more and more aroused were so erotic...he was so sensual and sexy, just beautiful in the way he worshiped my body with his.

We were both gasping and I reluctantly pulled my mouth from his to suck in a much needed breath. His hand brushed my hair back and his nose moved up my cheek, his panting breaths rushing over my skin in moist heat.

"That's right baby, I can feel you getting close. Julia, it's so beautiful the way you respond to me. . You're *mine*…"

His mouth came back to mine as he moved deeper and harder, building, building…I didn't want it to end, but he had me and I fell in an explosion of love and lust, quaking violently around him, my heart breaking at the strength of the love between us. "Uh, Uh…Ryan. I love you so much." He continued to thrust and I clenched and milked around him and seconds later he stiffened and moaned into my mouth as he came, both of us struggling to breathe.

Tears fell as I turned my face so that I could kiss his temple, my arms and legs wrapping tighter around him. After a minute, he rose up on his elbows and kissed me softly on the lips. His eyes were glowing as he bent to kiss the tears from my cheeks. "Don't cry, my love. I never want to be apart from you again. Do you feel how much I love you?" He nuzzled and kissed me gently, his body still embedded within mine.

"That was incredible." My voice cracked on the words. "The love, Ryan. It hurts so much, but it's so beautiful. I'm…overwhelmed. You're amazing."

"No, *we're* amazing. Every time, it's like this. It's a miracle every time we touch," he said softly. The emotion in his voice threatened to overflow. I held him close to me, stroking his hair and kissing his shoulder and neck. "If I died and went to heaven, it couldn't be better than this," he whispered brokenly.

I sobbed into him.

"Baby, don't cry. I can't bear to see your tears. Sweetie, please don't cry." He continued to brush my hair back over and over, nudging the side of my face and placing gentle kisses. "Are you sad?"

I shook my head. My throat was tight and my heart was pounding fast. "No. I'm just…sorry that I can't remember all those miracles. This must have been so hard on you. I don't ever want to see that pain in your eyes again. You're so wonderful. You deserve...*everything.* I want to give you everything."

He held me for a few moments until my tears were reduced to deep breaths and soft kisses. He finally moved to my side, withdrawing from my body. Instantly, I felt the loss. He pulled me close, arms going around me as he rubbed little circles on the skin of my back.

"I *have* everything," he said seriously. "Right here in my arms. You're safe and you love me. That's more than I have the right to ask for." His hand moved over my shoulder and up the side of my neck, his thumb brushing against my jaw. "You're all I'll ever want."

Ryan~

Her deep green eyes were luminous, lashes still wet with tears. She was beautiful and my heart stopped at the intensity of the last two hours. The fighting, the pain, the immeasurable ecstasy...the incredible love...all reiterated how much I needed her. I couldn't exist one minute without her. My brow furrowed as I looked at her. Her fingers running along my jaw stopped and moved to my mouth.

"Were you seriously going to leave?" I said against her fingertips and her eyes lifted to mine. I ran my hand across her bare back, needing to keep touching, her skin like silk sliding against me.

She pulled in a deep breath as she looked up at me. "Yes."

I'd never considered that she'd really leave me. It would have gutted me.

"It was killing me..." she paused, "I felt you needed to be free of...all this."

"If there is anything you should know for sure, it should be that I could never live without you," I said softly, the truth of my words was like a living thing.

"Why?" Julia raised her eyes to mine again and I met them without resolve; those beautiful eyes that held my life within them.

"Julia, come on. You're the absolute center of my universe, whether I like it or not." Her mouth opened, but no words exited as her eyes widened. I brushed the contours of her cheek and neck, over and over. "I'm in orbit around you, can't you see that? I can move around you, but never away," I said softly as my eyes seared into hers. "I'd be worried sick and miserable all of the time."

"You been so miserable *now*. I'm sorry." She moved closer, her forehead resting in the curve of my neck and I turned and pressed my mouth to her hair. The need to ease her pain tore at my heart as I searched for the right words.

"I *was* miserable because you lost *all* those memories...the time we spent together was so precious. You lost *us*. It makes me sad, a little." I blinked at the stinging in my eyes and cleared my throat as it tightened. I turned on my side and nuzzled against the side of her face, kissing her temple with my open mouth. "I'll get over it, honey. You don't need to worry. This helps a lot." I ran my hand down her arm and over her hip. "Did making love help?" She nodded against my chin and I held my breath.

"It evoked a lot of things, Ryan, but what I remembered was the love...some physical pain."

"Uh huh...that would have been our first time. I'm sorry that's the only part of it you remember. It was...the most incredible night of my entire life. Knowing no one else had touched you…it meant everything to me, Julia. I thought I loved you before, but that…wrecked me."

"This wasn't so bad." She smiled softly.

"Incredible, but it only leaves me wanting more." My finger touched the end of her nose and a smile spread across my face. She was glowing; so, so beautiful. Just stunning. My breath hitched.

"Even now…no one else has touched me, Ryan. I told you, I remember the love more than anything else. Even when I couldn't remember you, I was burning for you to touch me."

"I know, Julia. I can't…express what I'm feeling." I bent to kiss her, sucking her lower lip between mine. The kiss deepened and while soft and searching, it was hot, the saltiness of the remnant tears on my lips and tongue.

"Isn't that what has worried you? That I wouldn't feel the love behind the memories?"

"Yes." *And the loss of the baby.* My heart ached at the thought, trying to hide the pain in my eyes.

"Do you believe that I love you now? Can't you feel it when I touch you?" she whispered against my mouth when we broke the kiss, and I took her mouth again. Now that I'd started, I couldn't seem to stop. She needed to understand why I'd fought it so long.

"Yes. In time we'll have new memories and the pain over it will fade. I'm glad that making love didn't hurt you, sweetheart."

"It was perfect." She drew her index finger down my cheek and then to my lower lip. I bent and sucked the tip of it into my mouth; our eyes locked. My body stirred anew and I needed to prove to myself it was real.

"Ryan…can you please try to see things differently, just for a second? I got two *first times* with you," she murmured so softy, I had to strain to hear her. "To fall in love with you *twice*, and experience it all over again with you, so please don't be sad. I'm *happy*."

"Julia."

"Shh…I *am*. Tell me about us. We were best friends before we became lovers, is that right?"

I nodded and rolled her over, so that I could press into her, bending to kiss the curve of her neck. I spoke against her luscious skin. "Yeah, but I always loved you."

"Why did we wait then?" she asked breathlessly, one hand moving to tangle in my hair, the other drifting delicately down my back.

I let out my breath as she surged beneath me. If I moved just an inch or two, I could slide inside her again and I wanted it. My dick swelled until the skin felt it would split like a grape. "Hmmph. Because we were blind and stupid, I guess."

Julia stilled and stared up into my face.

"But…why?" she asked quietly and brushed her mouth on mine. I didn't want to talk, I just wanted to feel, but this was serious.

"Honey…I'm not sure how much I should tell you," I said hesitantly.

"Ugh!" she sighed in frustration and pushed away from me to sit up slightly. "Look, Ryan. Do you know what this is about?" she asked, exasperation lacing her voice.

This was not where I wanted this to go and my mouth set. "I have a pretty good idea, yeah," I said.

"So? Did it happen when we were *friends*?"

"No." I pulled her toward me again and propped my head up on my bent arm, looking down at her. I got her point. "Okay, I'll tell you some of it." I used my free hand to run down her arm and then took hers. Julia searched my face; a slight smile curved her pink lips up at the corners. "We were both afraid of changing the nature of our relationship. We spent every day together. If we got romantic and it didn't work out…" I shook my head. "Even though I wanted you and was so much in love, I couldn't risk it. We needed each other, and so we just…kept things the way they were."

"But…wasn't it hard? I mean, it's been killing me being this close to you without, you know, being *with* you."

"Julia," I sighed softly and pulled her tight against me. Her naked body was warm and soft against mine and I wanted her again. "Yes, it was agony. Being near you and not touching you drove me crazy with wanting you," I whispered and touched the tip of her nose with my fingertip. "It was all I could do not to murder the guys you dated."

"You were jealous." She smiled softly, her emerald eyes sparkling. I nodded. "Some things haven't changed."

"I've always thought of you as mine."

"When did we fess up?"

"When I got accepted to Harvard, there was no denying it anymore. The prospect of being apart hurt so much; I couldn't breathe when I got the acceptance letter. All I could think about was being away from you."

"I can imagine I felt the same way, hmmm?" She snuggled into me and placed a sucking, open-mouthed, kiss where my neck met my shoulder.

"Completely, yes. Only…You had some hare-brained idea that we should stay away from each other those last two months to get acclimated to separation. Hmmph. I was a moron for allowing it."

"Yes," she agreed and cocked an eyebrow at me. "How could you let me be so stupid, Matthews?"

"Don't you mean how could *we* be so stupid?" She looked so happy, her face and chest flushed from the aftermath of our lovemaking.

"Good question. I must have wised-up because I convinced you that you needed to move to New York. However, shortly afterward, you got a job offer that put you in L.A. for six months. We burned up the phone lines until finally we admitted our real feelings…we made love for the first time and then there was no choice but to do whatever was necessary to get closer to each other." My hand continued to move over her body, exploring every inch of her exposed skin with leisurely slowness. "Still, New York was too far." Her features were calm as she listened intently, running little patterns on my chest with her index finger. It seemed safe to continue. "As you may have guessed, I was planning on moving to New York for my residency after graduation so we could be together. *Finally*."

I stopped before I told her about the engagement or Paris. I bent to kiss her, letting my tongue enter her mouth and once again covered her body with my own. "Uhhh…It feels good to finally be able to talk to you about some of this," I said as the kiss ended.

"What about Paris?" she asked hesitantly.

"How do you know…?" I was nervous that it might lead to thoughts of the baby. I mentally stopped. Sometime I'd have to deal with her grief…and mine. Just not on this perfect night.

"Meredith asked if I wanted to go to Paris when we talked on the phone and then I remembered."

"*What* came back?" I asked anxiously.

She shrugged. "The offer to go to Paris; the job and my stupidity at even considering leaving you." Her eyes flashed and I touched her cheek again. "How do you put up with me?"

"Well," I smirked, "I'm hopelessly in love with you. You see, I have no choice."

"Yeah. You're *so* helpless, Matthews," she teased with a smirk. "Can't we still do that?"

Move to Paris? I needed clarification. "Do what?"

"Move in together." Relief consumed me. "You can still do your residency in New York, right?" Her hands were sliding over my butt muscles kneading and pulling me closer into her and I swelled against her even more. God, I loved her.

I sighed; my chest filling until I thought my lungs would burst. "If that's what you want. Nothing would make me happier, Julia."

"I want you. Always." She pressed her pelvis toward mine and I groaned. "See?" The corners of her mouth lifted but her deep green eyes were serious as she stared into mine.

"Obviously, the feeling's mutual." I took her hand and brought it to my erection. Her eyes widened and she hesitated just a second before her hand closed around it and her thumb rubbed over the head. "Mmm…that feels amazing."

"You're so sexy. The things you say, your voice, you're so beautiful, I just…"

"Mmmm. You're all of those things and more." I shifted her, moving her body beneath mine, her legs parted and the searing heat coming off of her burned me alive.

"This time…you've swept me completely off of my feet. Who could resist the most gorgeous man in the world, saying such tender things, *and* saving my life? And to top it all off…you tell me you're in love with me. I'm completely at your mercy."

Sadness tempered the ecstasy of the moment. "You didn't really get to experience it twice…baby," I said sadly, despite my intense state of arousal.

She looked up at me with intent eyes, trailing her fingers down my cheek. “No…But *you* did. So please, don’t be sad.”

My eyes widened as the verity of her words stunned me. *She was right.* Everything about being with her was a gift. *How could I have been so damn blind?*

“You’re incredible,” I said after a moment.

“Ryan…” I could see the concern in her eyes because of the show of emotions flashing over my face.

“Thank you, Julia.” I rested my head next to hers and breathed in her sweet scent as I closed my eyes. “Just…thank you.”

“For what?” Her fingers stroking the back of my head felt like heaven.

“For *forcing* this. For making me get my head out of my ass and for coming back to me. Because, you *are* back now, Julia. This is how we are. You’re still my baby. Maybe it will work to my benefit that you can’t remember everything. I might be able to get by with more,” I teased.

Her eyes sparkled with laughter, even as I tried to blink away the tears in my own.

“Don’t count on it,” she shot back.

I chuckled. Who was I kidding? She gave me everything I wanted…then and now.

Calm spread through me. I now had clarity from all the confusion. I knew what I wanted…what had to happen. My hand closed around the fingers of her left hand and I kissed the inside of her wrist and then the top of her hand. I held it there, brushing my lips over her skin. She looked satisfied and happy. I knew without a doubt that she was mine forever. Whether she remembered or not; I wanted nothing more than to be her husband and the father of her children. We’d talk, but now, I wanted to just *feel.*

"Let's make love again," I murmured against her mouth, my body pressing into her warm wetness and growing so hard the pulsing caused a painful ache. It was ridiculous how Julia made me want and want and want. Her hands were pressing on my shoulders and I looked down at her in confusion. "Do you want me to stop?"

"Never. I want to taste you. Will you let me?" she asked, as she continued to push me until I was lying back on the pillows. She bit her lip and moved above me. "I may not be very good at it, but I want to try."

My body tightened, engorging to the point of pain at her words, and my eyes fell to her mouth. That sweet mouth that could take me to heaven or hell.

"Oh, sweetheart," I gasped as her hands roamed over my chest and abdomen, her fingers grazing my nipples before stroking lower and closing around me. "Ugh…you're *amazing* at it," I moaned softly.

"It must be because I love you so much, then. You're so hot, Ryan. So gorgeous. I could look at you forever."

She squeezed and pulled and finally bent to take me in her mouth. So hot and wet…just exquisite. My head fell back against the pillows as I let her take me over, losing myself in the delicious sensations.

"Uh…" I grunted as her tongue circled and teased the head before she took me in deep and sucked hard. Over and over she tormented me with teasing licks and then long strokes up and down until I could barely stand it. My fingers threaded through her hair because I had to touch her, even as she brought me closer and closer to the edge of release. "Julia…Ahh…baby it's so good. Too good."

"Mmmm…Ryan," she breathed against me and then ran her tongue down my length. "I can taste you…It's familiar, I remember it, babe."

"Stop or you'll make me come too fast. It's too much." It only made her more determined to take me over the edge. The fingers of her left hand splayed out on the muscles of my chest as she pressed me back down and I was helpless to resist. "Uhhh…I love you, baby," I groaned out as her mouth and hands continued with their magic. My body coiled and throbbed and I knew it was over. I couldn't stop it even if I wanted to. "Oh, God…uh, I'm gonna come…" She didn't let up, taking me deep, her lips so hot and tight around me as I released hard into her mouth and throat. Her muscles contracted, her forehead resting on my stomach and I couldn't help thrusting deeper into her mouth as she took every drop. Physically and emotionally, I was overwhelmed. This was the woman I loved more than life, giving with such abandon. My legs trembled and when I finally relaxed after the orgasm subsided, I was breathing hard and my arms felt empty.

"Julia…come here." She released me and wiped her mouth with the back of her hand. I sat up and gathered her close until she was lying on top of me, her head resting on my chest and stomach. She continued to place kisses on my stomach and her hot breath rushed over my skin.

"Do you know how much I love you?" I asked thickly. Her arms tightened around me and she nodded before looking up into my face. Her eyes were filled with tears. "More than anything in the world." My own throat stuck on the words and my arms tightened around her. I loved the feeling of her breasts pressed into my chest, her legs entwined with mine. *It was real. It was perfect, and it was us*. "I *really* love you, Julia. You give me everything and you're all I want." My fingers brushed her hair away as I bent to kiss her forehead.

Her shoulders were shaking. She was crying, but not in sorrow.

"Ryan," she said thickly. "I can't imagine that I loved you any more before the accident, did I?"

"No. It's always been sort of surreal. It's…unbelievable."

Julia's hot breath washed over my skin and my hand ran through her hair to smooth the satin strands out on her back over and over to soothe her. The candle still flickered softly and the music played. I couldn't bring myself to get up in order to turn it off.

"Yeah. I *really* love you, too." We stayed like that, stroking and softly breathing in the aftermath of our lovemaking. No more words were needed as we slowly drifted to sleep. We'd already said it all.

*****

I woke to the smell of bacon and coffee, my arms searched the bed for Julia. I rolled onto my back and threw my arm over my eyes. *Of course she won't be here, she's making breakfast, dick-head;* I chastised myself and grinned like a fool. Last night had been incredible. Every time I touched her, heaven.

I grunted, crawled off the bed and pulled on my jeans. I didn't bother with underwear, I was too anxious to get to my girl.

At the stove, her back to me, Julia hummed softly as she cooked. I pulled out one of the stools at the counter bar and sat down. The scuffing of the chair on the floor startled her. She jumped and turned quickly. Her legs were bare and she had on one of my t-shirts, coming to mid-thigh. "Mmmm…You look good enough to eat," I murmured and leaned on the counter toward her.

"Maybe later," she teased.

"Promise?" I pulled at the crotch of my jeans which were getting uncomfortable at the reaction of my body. Jesus, we'd made love all night and, still, I wanted more.

"Long cruise, was it sailor?" She chuckled and cocked an eyebrow as she set a small plate of toast in front of me. I picked up a piece and took a huge bite.

"Yeah. Too long," I said seriously. "Let's not do that again."

Julia took the eggs from the skillet and placed them on two plates with the bacon, some chopped fruit and hash browns.

"Well, now that I see what I've been missing…I don't intend to be missing it." Her eyes were sparkling as she placed a plate in front of me and pulled the juice from the refrigerator. As I watched her every move, I decided I didn't want another minute without her. She plopped down next to me and picked up her fork. Without speaking, my hand found a place over my heart on my bare chest. I sucked in my breath and my heart exploded.

"Julia."

"Hmmm?" she said distractedly as she took her first bite. When I didn't answer, her eyes flew to mine. "Ryan, what is it?"

"Julia…will you marry me?"

"Yeah," she lifted her left hand in front of my face and waved it around. "See?" She smiled sweetly and leaned in to place a kiss on my mouth. My lips parted and my fingers flittered across her check.

"Yes, but I don't want to wait. I love you and we've been apart too long…waited too long," I said urgently.

Her eyes widened. "You're serious."

I nodded and took her left hand in mine. "Nothing would make me happier than if you'd agree. Please?"

"When?" Her expression showed her surprise.

I pulled her hand up, brushing my mouth over her skin softly. "It doesn't matter where or when exactly." I shrugged slightly. "Today, tomorrow, next week or next month, but not beyond graduation. If nothing else in my life is set, I'm sure I don't want one more moment without you as my wife." I stared into her stunned face, not flinching. I was dead serious. "I've loved you from the day we met and every day I love you more, if that's possible. I lived without you and I don't intend to anymore. I can't."

Her eyes welled as she gazed at me. It seemed all I did lately was make her cry. My heart squeezed painfully. I knew she loved me. It was there in her eyes and the tremulous smile lifted her luscious lips.

"Okay." The word was so soft I barely heard it, but her gentle hand reached out to stroke my face and two fat tears rolled down her cheeks. My heart leapt.

"Really?" I asked in amazement, joy filling me to the point of bursting. I didn't expect her to agree so easily.

"Of course. Is there really a choice?" she cried softly.

"Will you be disappointed if we don't have a big wedding? I know most women want that."

Julia was crying harder now and she shrugged. She put the back of her hand to her mouth as her shoulders shook gently. "I just want *you.*" As usual, she said the perfect thing. "I don't need all that stuff. Just you."

I pulled her off of her stool and into my arms, turning my face into her neck and breathing in her scent until I thought my lungs would burst.

"There is something that *I* need," I murmured into her hair as her arms wound around my neck and I shoulders. "I don't care about the fanfare and the people, but I want the bride I've been waiting for all this time. I need to know you belong to me." I pulled back to look into her face. Her eyes were luminous, a soft blush spreading over her perfect skin. "I want the dress and the veil, Julia."

She smiled through her tears. "I'll give you anything you want. I love you."

I reached out and drew her to me, cupping the back of her head with my hand as she turned her face into the curve of my neck. We were both clinging to each other like we'd never let go. "I love you more."

Breakfast was forgotten as my hands slid down over her body, gently lifting her until her legs wound around my waist. My mouth found hers in hungry desperation and she was equally insistent. Her hands wound to the back of my hair to pull my mouth even closer as our tongues entwined in passionate play. My body sprang to life and Julia ground her hips into mine. I tore my mouth from hers so I could see to carry her down the hall to my bedroom. "You're so sexy, and I want you. Again and again," I said huskily as I lay on the bed with her on top of me.

"That works for me, baby," she breathed against my mouth before we lost ourselves in the ecstasy of our love for each other.

~11~

Ryan~

"HEY, MAN. CAN we talk?" I found Aaron in the reference section of the library. At nine o'clock in the evening, the lights were muted and it was very quiet. I generally liked to spend this time here because there were fewer students. After the conversation with Julia, I needed to tell Aaron. We'd both been so busy; I hadn't talked to him in awhile. After what Julia said about Jen's intentions to leave if he didn't propose, I needed to find out his thinking.

Bent over a book, furiously making notes on a legal pad, Aaron looked up quickly and shoved back from the table. "Um, just give me a minute, we can go outside." I waited patiently while he finished what he was doing and packed his things in his backpack.

"Pharmacy final," he explained and I nodded. I'd taken it three semesters ago as a prerequisite for the anesthesia courses I needed for trauma.

"Dude, why didn't you just ask for my notes on that shit?" I smirked as his mouth settled into a thin line.

"Because I'm a huge-ass moron, I guess," he huffed. "So what's up? Haven't seen you much these past weeks but I chalked it up to finals and that you and Julia were finally getting busy…so I guess no more blue balls, eh, brother?" His dark eyes danced with laughter.

I ran a hand through my hair, returning his grin unabashedly. "Um, for sure. Things have been…amazing."

"Ryan, I have to ask…are you guys using protection? It's none of my business but you don't want to risk that now. Right?"

We were already at the car. I threw my books in the back and motioned for Aaron to do the same. "Yeah. I asked Dr. Brighton about it…before um, Julia and I ever got intimate after the accident. I thought it would remind her, but he just wrote a prescription and she didn't mention it." I told him over the top of the car as we both opened the doors. "The last time was an accident. Julia was taking antibiotics and we just weren't thinking."

We drove in silence for a few minutes. I was excited, yet calmness settled over me after Julia had agreed to marry me. More memories were surfacing and I found myself accepting of the things that she didn't remember yet. I knew, without a doubt, that she loved me deeply and it was enough. I pulled in a deep breath, filling my lungs to capacity.

"Ryan, you said you wanted to talk to me, so why aren't you talking?" Aaron finally broke into my thoughts.

"Julia and I are going to go ahead and get married." Aaron's face split into a grin and his hand came down on my shoulder twice.

"That's great! Did you set a date?"

"Um…yeah. The weekend of graduation."

He seemed somewhat stunned. "Wow. So soon? No big wedding?"

"As much as we've been through, that isn't important anymore. Our parents will be in town, so will Ellie and Harris. It just makes sense to do it then."

"Congratulations, bro'. Ex…cel…lent. So I guess this seals the deal about the residency in New York."

"Julia actually brought it up. I was so relieved." *Okay, so here I go. Just throw it out there, Ryan.* "What about you and Jenna? Are you ever planning on marrying her?"

"Yeah. I asked her that night."

"*What night*?" I asked in surprise.

"The night the girls took off without us."

"So…what's the story?"

"We started looking at rings, but no date yet." He shrugged and looked out the passenger window. Aaron never was one to spill his guts without prodding, which I found frustrating as hell.

I frowned and shook my head. I hadn't been able to wait until I could get a ring on Julia's finger and I'd been planning the day I could propose since the first time I made love to her. . Aaron was so blasé.

"Will you be my Best Man?"

He looked back at me and flashed a huge grin. "Dude. I'd beat your ass if you didn't ask me. I thought I may have lost that honor to that dickhead, Moore!"

I chuckled softly. Leave it to Aaron to make a joke out of a serious situation. "Should I smack you now or later?"

"Is Julia still seeing him?"

"Nope!" I popped the 'p' on the word in satisfaction. "He's history. The night she almost went back to New York she said he was supportive and I was doing the best thing for her…maybe he's not so bad." Aaron quirked an eyebrow at me mockingly and I had to smile. Who in the hell was I kidding? Moore definitely had the hots for Julia. "Anyway, that turned out for the best. If Julia hadn't threatened me with leaving, I might still have my head up my ass."

"Yes. You owe me two hundred and fifty bucks for the hotel you banished us to, by the way," Aaron laughed.

"What the hell?" I exclaimed. "Are you kidding me?"

"Hey, I just got engaged, dude. I didn't have a ring yet, so you know I put on the dog."

He was stroking his chin with his tongue in cheek, and we both burst out laughing. "Was the dog's dick dipped in gold?" I asked. Aaron threw me a sardonic glance. "I'm just sayin'…"

"Shut up," Aaron admonished. I laughed even harder. "No honeymoon?"

I shook my head. "That's the only thing that I regret, but Julia's already missed so much work and I have to be at St. Vincent's a week later. We really don't have time. After we get settled, I'll plan something big."

"Shit. With Jules gone, it'll be back to frozen pizza and McDonald's," he groaned in protest. He was teasing, but there was a shred of truth to it.

"You'll survive," I laughed softly, secretly thankful that Julia was going with me.

"Easy for you to say, dickhead. You'll eat like a king."

"She'll be busy with work. I don't expect her to slave away in the kitchen."

"Oh, only the bedroom?" he asked. I felt the corners of my mouth twitch, but kept my mouth shut. I wouldn't share that with anyone. When I didn't answer, he continued. "Anyway…Julia spoils you rotten. You won't have to expect anything."

"Hmmph," I expelled my breath. "She takes care of me pretty well, that's for sure."

Julia ~

The smells emanating from the kitchen were divine; fresh garlic sautéed in the pan with butter for the beginning of Alfredo sauce. A protesting Jenna grated a chunk of parmesan cheese while I chopped parsley and pulled the fresh fettuccini from the refrigerator.

"Fuck!" Jenna exclaimed as she accidentally scraped her knuckles on the grater. "No wonder I don't cook!"

I rushed to get a wet paper towel and examined the broken skin. Three of her fingers were bleeding slightly, but it wasn't too bad. "Are you okay?" I asked, glancing up at her face.

"Ugh, yes. I wish I could cook like you." She scowled. "Aaron likes to eat and I can't even grate some cheese!"

I smirked at her. "Anyone can cook, Jen. Can you read a cookbook?"

"Yeah. Sure." she moaned and plopped down on one of the stools. "I never see *you* reading the damn things."

I couldn't help chuckling. "Not anymore. I've been cooking since I was ten years old." I resumed with the cheese after I'd cleaned the grater. "What time did Aaron say he was coming home?"

Ryan mentioned he was picking up his brother but didn't think they'd be home before nine. It was almost that now but I couldn't finish the sauce until they arrived or it would scald.

"I'll send a text." She walked to the table and opened her purse. "Julia, after last night, I mean…is everything okay? What happened?"

I nodded and took a sip from my glass. I studied the wine as I swirled it around the sides. "Well, Ryan realizes that I might not ever remember everything, and I convinced him I love him as much as I ever did. I don't think he'll be pulling back anymore, but it still hurts him that I can't remember."

I poured some wine and took it over to where she was sitting before refilling my own. Jenna's beautiful face broke into a big grin and her pale skin flushed pink on her cheeks. "Good. Because the night we went out, Aaron was so worked up, he proposed!"

I rushed to put my arms around her. "Oh, Jen. I'm so happy for you! *Finally*!" Her arms closed tightly around my shoulders and she sighed loudly. Now I could tell her about Ryan's and my wedding plans.

"Yeah."

I moved back and picked up my wine. "*So*? What went down?" I prodded. The pleasure on her features filled me up with happiness.

"He was so pissed!" She lowered her voice and tried to imitate Aaron's low growl, *"What the fuck are you doing out here, shaking your ass in front of these assholes, Jen? You're practically my wife!"*

I laughed so hard I almost spewed my wine across the room. I could picture it. However, at the time, I was occupied with being hauled off the dance floor. I gasped for breath. "Oh, my God! That's not exactly a storybook proposal, but it is *so* Aaron! I love it! What did you say?"

"I crossed my arms and stared at him for a minute then said, *'To quote Beyonce', 'if you like it then you shoulda put a ring on it!'"*

"No you didn't! Jen! I wish I would have seen the look on his face!"

We fell into a fit of giggles when the door opened and the men walked in. They looked tired, but in good spirits.

Ryan's lips lifted in a crooked grin and my heart thumped in my chest. I couldn't tear my eyes away as he dropped his book bag on the living room chair before sitting on the couch to remove his shoes. "Something smells good, Julia. What are you making?"

"*We* are making fettuccini Alfredo, Caesar salad and garlic bread. Would you like some wine?" I moved to the back of the couch and placed my hands on his shoulders, then bent to kiss the skin on the side of his neck. "Mmm...Yummy," I whispered near his ear and his hand moved up to cover one of mine.

"Missed you today," he murmured with a promise in those deep blue eyes. "I want to kiss you," he said softly. I nodded as his eyes fell to my mouth. It was agony not to fall into his arms right then.

I looked at him regretfully when Aaron's voice intruded as he embraced Jenna in a tight bear hug.

"What's for dessert?"

"*Dessert*?" I teased. "What makes you think I made you dessert?" Reluctantly, I moved away from Ryan who held onto my fingers; he had no choice but to drop them.

"*Please*. You're you."

"Zabaglione and fresh berries. I've heard the doctors here prescribe a light finish." A bottle of Marsala waited on the counter until I would cook it with egg yolks and sugar, shortly after dinner.

I took the cream from the refrigerator and added it to the pot with the garlic and butter and then turned the heat on beneath the pasta pot.

Two strong arms circled my waist from behind and pulled me close as Ryan's head bent into the curve of my neck. His open mouth traced a series of kisses along my skin, sending shivers running through my entire body.

"Mmmm, God, you feel so good," he murmured softly. I turned my head so that he could capture my mouth with his. He tasted like mint and Ryan. I moaned as his lips moved in unison with mine. Always so perfect. He pressed into my backside and I could feel his arousal against me. "See, all I have to do is touch you and I'm wrecked."

I smiled. "Baby, I wish I could, but I have to watch dinner. You know this sauce is delicate, and we're trying to take care of our boys."

Ryan smiled and moved to the cupboard, pulling down a wine glass and filling it. Aaron and Jenna were in the other room, so they wouldn't hear our conversation. "Aaron proposed." He leaned back against the counter, close enough to feel the heat radiating off of him.

I flashed a smile. "I know. Jenna was just telling me. I didn't get a chance to tell her about us." He ran his index finger down my arm, left bare by the white, v-neck t-shirt I was wearing.

"I can't wait, Julia. Literally. I can. Not. Wait."

I reached up to cup his cheek, rough with a full day's growth of scruffy beard. His eyes burned into mine, unflinching, but his cheek pressed into my hand. "You make me very happy, Ryan. I love you, so much."

His eyes smiled and his hand grasped mine before he turned his face to place a wet, open-mouthed kiss on my palm. "Show me later."

"Ryan! Get your ass in here and play Guitar Hero!" Aaron called from the other room and I laughed.

"Go ahead. I'll finish this."

"I don't want to." His lips moved against my temple as he spoke.

"Ryan. *Go.*" His arms tightened in protest as he kissed my cheek and lower toward my mouth. I couldn't let him continue if I wanted to keep my wits about me. I turned my head away so his lips landed on my cheek again. He groaned aloud. "If you don't want scorched cheese sauce, you'll go."

"God forbid. Okay, I'm *going.* But, it's under duress."

My heart swelled as I watched him leave the kitchen. I was overflowing with love for him. It was in his eyes and every touch of his hand. He loved me, too. *Could things be any more perfect?*

Ryan~

It was dark. I glanced toward the nightstand where the clock shone bright red in the darkness. 3:17 am. I was lying across Julia, my head resting on her now fully-healed chest, right arm around her hips. I closed my eyes and breathed in her scent, feeling her steady breathing beneath me, her warmth all around me. I was as content as I'd ever been.

At dinner we talked with Aaron and Jen about our plans for the wedding. I enjoyed the pleasure that blushed Julia's cheeks and the smile dancing on her mouth as Jenna went on and on about dresses, and flowers. Julia's eyes would meet mine on occasion as she bit that luscious lower lip. Maybe I was wrong to deny her a big wedding. She deserved all the things girls dream about and there was no denying that I wanted to see her dressed as a bride. My bride.

I ran some butterfly kisses along the concave planes below her navel. Her skin was like velvet beneath my mouth. She was the sexiest thing I'd ever seen, always so warm and giving. The strength of my love for her never ceased to amaze me and, over time, only seemed to intensify. The fact that she loved me in return was the greatest gift of my life.

Her hand started to massage my scalp and tug softly on the strands between her fingers. I lifted my head slightly and nuzzled underneath her right breast and then placed a gentle kiss on the soft swell.

"Can't sleep? I thought I wore you out before." Her voice was whisper soft, but wrapped me up tight.

"Mmmm…*Never*." I moved up so I could pull the nipple of her breast into my mouth and suckle gently. She sighed heavily and arched her back slightly, bringing her flesh even deeper into my mouth. I increased the pressure and she moaned. "Do you know how much I love you, Julia? Every day it's more," I sighed against her, letting my breath rush over the nipple still wet from my play. "You're probably sick of hearing it."

"I'll never get tired of hearing it. I love your words, your mouth…"

My hand closed around her thigh and pulled it over my hip as I moved so I could look for her reaction. I pressed my now raging erection into her. She smiled. "Your hands, and mmmm…" Her hips surged against mine in delicious want. We moved slowly, my hands exploring her curves, her hands kneaded the muscles of my back and ass as she pulled me closer. My mouth and body were hungry, but I wanted to talk to her about the wedding.

"I want to talk for a minute. If we start making love, there will be no more words." Her eyes opened, yet hooded with desire. *God, she is stunning.*

I brushed her hair back as her full lips parted. She wanted me as much as I wanted her, a gift of immense passion and overwhelming love. My heart actually ached with it.

"What about?" Her hand came up to grasp my jaw as her mouth asked for mine. Her lips moved and she licked my upper lip with the tip of her tongue and then sucked my lower lip in between hers and nipped at it with her teeth. I tried to resist, but gave in with a groan and rolled on top of her as my mouth took hers hungrily, my tongue plunging deep into her mouth as she opened and kissed me back deeply. *Oh God…*I pressed my hips forward seeking her heat. She was as ready for me as I was for her and I slid inside her without even trying. She moaned into my mouth and she drew her knees up so I would sink even deeper into her body. Soon, we were lost in the passionate dance, frantically clutching and kissing, we couldn't get close enough as we rolled around on the bed. Minutes ticked by, the rhythm tangible, passion palpable.

"Julia, I could make love to you forever. I never want this to end." Her hands clutched in my hair at both sides, her liquid eyes filled with a mixture of love and desire. I nuzzled her nose with mine, our breath mingling, as I pushed into her again and again.

"Uhnnngg…Ryan, never stop," she whispered breathlessly and I could feel her insides quivering and clasping around me. I slid my hands beneath her to grasp onto her shoulders so I could increase the pressure of my pelvic bone on hers as I felt my own climax build. I turned my forehead into the side of her face as we worshiped each other.

"Oh yes, Julia…I want to feel you baby, come on." My hand moved between us and I softly massaged her swollen nub and felt her involuntarily squeeze around my cock. Damn, she was hot.

I felt every touch of her hand and every tremor of her body around mine. Every breath, every little mewling sound she made deep in her throat drove me insane with desire. Her breathing was labored, and she panted in time with my thrusts. It was so fantastically sexy and sent me over the edge after three more strokes. I stilled as I came hard, spilling deep into her body. Her legs wrapped around me and her heels dug into my ass, pressing me deeper as her hands twined in my hair and we kissed again as our bodies tensed and twitched.

"I'll never comprehend how incredible this is." My body still embedded within hers, I lifted my head and my fingers traced the line of her face.

"This isn't possible, Ryan. Oh, God…"

I rolled to my side and slid out of her body, pulling her until she was nestled on my chest, head under my chin as my arms tightened around her. "It's possible, Julia. I swear." Emotions welled and I felt my throat tighten. "You own me so bad," I said, expelling a shaky breath.

Her arm that was across my middle tightened and she lifted her head to kiss my chest, her mouth hovering and then opening to press hot, sucking kisses. "What did you want to talk about?" Her features were soft, satiated…full of love as her chin rested on one of her hands. My hands threaded through her hair as I stroked it down and over her back.

"Well, I'm wondering if I'm being selfish asking you to forgo a big wedding." She started to speak, but I placed a finger to her lips. "If we get married now, we won't get a honeymoon and I want to give you all of that." I searched her face, looking for her true feelings as I continued to stroke her hair.

"Weren't you listening? You are all I want," she said softly. When I didn't respond she continued. "Ryan…could any honeymoon be better than this? Every moment we're together is perfect and I just want more of these moments. I want to get married as planned. I've already told everyone and they're so happy. Harris's band is coming to play for us. Ellie is already working with designers on the dresses. I just wonder if we should run off to the courthouse and not bother with the dress. Is it silly when there will be so few people with us?"

"No. If you're not doing the dress, then I won't do the wedding like this. I told you, Julia. I *need* that. Please."

Her eyes glossed over and her arms wound around me, two hot tears fell on my skin as she lay on my chest. "How are you so perfect?"

I smiled into the darkness. There was a small stream of moonlight shining in through the window and casting a soft blue glow across her bare skin. I was distracted by the slope of her breasts and the curve and swell of her waist and hips.

"Mmmm." My hand ran down her body to rest on her hip. "I don't want the courthouse. Maybe we could get a ballroom at the Four Seasons, get married and have a small reception all in the same space. I'm thinking around 75 people. What do you think?"

"I think it sounds wonderful."

"Good. Because our moms are already working on it with Ellie and Jen."

Her head snapped back and her eyes widened. "Is this a conspiracy?" She climbed up to straddle my lap. Julia clutched the sheet around her, holding it together at her breasts and I shifted beneath her until I was sitting up against the headboard.

I tugged on the sheet until she let it fall, revealing the glorious treasures underneath. "Yes," I whispered. "I conspire to make love to you, everyday for the rest of my life." I leaned up and slid my arms around her back and hips, pulling her closer as I rained kisses over her chest and over her shoulders. Finally, our mouths married in another series of soft, yet passionate kisses.

My hands lightly traced the soft curves, roaming over the side swells of her breasts, thumbs circling both nipples over and over. Her eyes glistened, almost glowing in the darkness and her hips surged into mine. I could feel her heat against my hardness. I wanted it.

I let the back of one of my hands brush over her taut stomach, the place where my child used to be and I swallowed the pain, knowing that, more than anything, I wanted to see her swell with the evidence of our incredible love. I drew in a breath and kissed along her chin and spoke against her skin.

"Julia…have you thought about…*children*." My heart stopped as I waited for her answer, continuing to kiss her softly. Would this make her remember? She needed the opportunity to remember before we were married, in case she was angry and didn't want to be with me. I waited without speaking as she drew in a breath.

"Of course, I've thought about it." Her hand went up to my face, her fingers feathering across my chin and jaw. I watched her reaction carefully, but I didn't find any recognition. "I love you…so, yes, I want your children. If…you do. I think you'll be just an amazing father. You're so full of love." Her voice trembled on the words and my heart exploded inside my chest.

I sat up suddenly and gathered her close, burying my face in her hair. "Oh, sweetheart. Of course I do. Nothing in the world could make me happier. I want to give you everything. I love you so much."

Once again…she left me breathless.

Julia ~

Ryan pushed the food around his plate without eating. His beautiful brow was furrowed and his mouth set. I knew what was bothering him. I was going back to New York for the final two weeks before his graduation, to get back to work and give him the space he needed to concentrate on finals. I took a deep breath. Ryan heard me, his bright eyes flashing angrily.

"What?" he asked sharply.

I reached forward so that I could take his big hand in mine. "Babe…it's only two weeks and…" I began, but he interrupted me.

"Yes, I *know*," he retorted shortly. "I was there when we discussed it. Remember?"

Moody ass was rearing his ugly head. I bit my lip to hide a smile. It made my heart fill that he was upset that I was leaving, but at the same time, I was concerned how it would affect him. He'd already been through so much.

"Ryan," I said quietly, urging him to look at me once again. He sucked in a ragged breath.

"Look, I need to get to the hospital." He was already dressed in scrubs and ready to leave. Jenna was taking me to the train station later that morning. This would be the last time we'd see each other until I came back for the graduation and the wedding. *The wedding. It was really happening.*

I got up and lifted the arm he had resting on the table so I could climb on his lap. He stiffened and turned his head away as I wrapped one arm around his shoulders and pressed my forehead to his cheek. He smelled so wonderful, the scent of his cologne so heady. I pushed my fingers up his chest, around his neck and into the thick hair at his nape. I gave it a little tug and drew back to look into his eyes.

"I am well aware of your objections, but this is the absolute last time we'll be separated. I need to get back to work so when you're there, I can concentrate more on us. This is a new beginning."

"I like our old one," Ryan snapped sourly. His lower lip jutted out like a petulant child. I tugged on his hair again. Usually that brought a reaction but, when he still didn't move, I bent my face closer. My breath fanned out over his face and his eyes finally moved to mine before closing slowly.

I smiled and pulled that lower lip between both of mine and sucked lightly. I could feel him softening, as my mouth coaxed his to come out and play. "Come on. You know you can't resist," I teased. Finally one arm slid across my thighs and the other moved up my back as he turned into the kiss, finally opening his mouth hungrily over mine.

Truthfully, I was torn as well. I did need to get back to work, but I didn't want to leave him. I didn't want to miss the last times I'd find him hunched over his computer studying, when I could rub his shoulders and bring him coffee or food. It was a big chapter that was closing and even though the future was bright, my heart couldn't help but feel a little loss. I'd been remembering more of the past, but there were still a lot of holes. Like the time just before the accident. I still struggled with it, but was trying to concentrate on the present. Now that Ryan was with me, my life was pretty much perfect.

He threaded his hands through my hair as his mouth lifted breathlessly from mine and he groaned in protest. "Ugh…I'll miss you. I don't want you to go."

"You know I need to go." His arms tightened and pulled me into a tight hug, as he buried his face in my neck and shook his head.

"All I know is that I need you with me." When he pulled away, his features had softened and he looked deeply into my eyes. His fingers traced my cheekbone, jaw, and temple in soft butterfly touches.

"I will be, soon. We're getting married, remember?" He smiled; despite himself and he was so gorgeous. "I have to get the dress fitted. Doctor's orders. He won't marry me without it, remember?" Many different emotions flooded his features and I wanted to comfort him. "Just don't let *Lola* chase you too much in a last ditch effort to land you before you're off the market," I challenged, crooking an eyebrow and grinning. "You didn't invite her to the wedding did you?"

He burst out laughing. "Hell, no! She's one of the things I will not miss about Boston."

"Mmmm," I murmured. It was only 6:30 am and Ryan had to be at the hospital in half an hour. "Does Aaron work today?" I asked.

"Yeah. Later I think."

My mind raced with an idea. "Ryan…Jen wants to get married soon, too. Should we invite them to have a double wedding with us?"

Ryan's eyes narrowed slightly. He hesitated only briefly. "No."

I was surprised at the shortness of his reply. "Why? Your parents will be with us already and Aaron and Jen do everything with us. Ellie and Harris will be here. They could stand up with us. It just seems logical."

"They don't do everything with us. Not *this*."

"But…"

"I said *no*," he said adamantly and shook his head once. "I don't want to share this. It belongs to us, Julia. For one damn day the world is going to revolve around you and me. *Please*."

My heart tightened at his tender words. I nodded. "Okay." I placed a soft kiss on his mouth. "Like the world doesn't revolve around you *every* damn day," I teased.

The lopsided grin I adored split out on his face. "If that were entirely true, you'd keep your sexy ass in Boston until we could go to New York together."

I was silent in his arms, both of us stroking the other. My arms around his shoulders allowed for my hand to thread through his hair and Ryan had one arm around my waist and the other rubbing the top of my thigh.

"Julia, it's just…I've shared you with your job, with distance, with time…I'm so *done*. I won't give anything else up."

Thud. My heart stopped in my chest. The words that fell from his lips never ceased to amaze me.

"I love you so much," I whispered against his mouth as his lips brushed over mine in another series of kisses. "Only two more weeks and forever starts."

"Oh, honey, it started eight years ago in Psych 101."

~12~

Julia ~

THIS PAST WEEK was a whirlwind. Andrea was happy to have me back, although I was unsure what our roles would be. She'd been doing my job quite well for the past four months. I glanced at her from where I was sitting behind my desk. She was efficiently continuing on with details for the August issue and my heart dropped; glad to be back, yet seeing how smooth the machine was running. I wondered if Ryan had been right and I should have stayed in Boston until the wedding.

Thinking about it filled me with excitement, yet I was calm. I couldn't reconcile it. Elyse and my mother were arranging everything via internet and phone with Jenna acting as the liaison in Boston, while Ellie wrangled the dress designers in L.A. While some brides might want to be more involved, I was grateful for the help. We decided on shades of a silvery moss green for Ellie and Jenna; Ellie's a lighter hue and then a silvery white for my dress. My dress I hadn't seen, but described to Ellie and I trusted her to make it happen. She had access to some of the top designers in the world and it would be made to order. Extremely expensive, but she insisted it was her wedding gift. I felt a surge of melancholy at her tangible absence in my day-to-day life.

I spoke briefly with Ryan every night by phone. He was finishing finals, and the last week before graduation would be spent packing up his apartment. I was filled with pride at all he'd accomplished,

Gabriel and Elyse, along with Jenna's parents had already arrived. Somehow, the wedding guest list had swelled to around one hundred people and it was all falling into place. Mike Turner called from Los Angeles and offered to fly in for the wedding photos. I was truly touched by the gesture.

The pages before me blurred as I struggled to write the vows that I would say to Ryan next Saturday evening. My throat ached as I poured over how to put into words exactly what he meant to me. *Impossible.*

When we talked about it the night before, he'd been so tender, and I missed him immensely. There were no doubts, not one, that marrying Ryan was the only choice. He wasn't really perfect in the true sense of the word…everyone has flaws, but he was perfect *to me*. Incredibly so.

My eyes finally overflowed as I pulled myself back toward the headboard and rolled to my side, bringing the notebook with me, to rest on the pillow next to mine. Ryan's pillow. My hand ran over it lightly. Surely, my heart would explode as I gazed at the wall to where his poem hung next to one of my portraits of him. As if he could read my mind, my phone rang as it rested on the comforter next to me. I answered and pressed it to my ear.

"Hello?" I murmured softly.

"Hey, how's my beautiful girl?"

"Missing you. *Bad*."

"Oh, babe. Me, too. I can't stand it."

I closed my eyes, picturing him sitting in the near darkness on the bed with his legs stretched out in front of him.

"Are your parents there yet?"

"Yeah. They got in around four o'clock and are so excited to see you."

"I can't wait to see them, too. Elyse said she may take the train down on Wednesday and ride back with Ellie and me on Thursday morning. It would be really nice to spend extra time getting to know her again." I wiped at my leaky eyes with a tissue. My emotions were fragile. "I *really* miss you. How did we manage this before?"

"It's harder this time, even for me." The ache in his voice echoed mine. "Julia…Are you crying? You're not having second thoughts, are you?"

"Oh, Ryan. No." My heart stopped at the thought. "I'm working on my vows. It overwhelms me a little."

"Yes. I wasn't sure how to put it all in thirty seconds worth of words."

I loved that velvet voice as he spoke my thoughts aloud. I never heard quite that tone when he spoke to anyone else. It was one he used on the phone when he missed me, or when he made such sweet, tender love to me. The rustling in the background told me he was rolling over as he let out a deep sigh. "Nothing can do it justice anyway. I can't find the words to tell you."

I smiled despite the tears. "Should we write them together?"

"Honey…I'm tempted, but no. Is that okay? I want you to hear them for the first time during the ceremony. Am I a sap?"

"I still don't understand where you came from. Too wonderful to be real."

"I can't wait to see you in your dress. I've been dreaming of it forever. There is nothing in the world I want more than to marry you, my love."

The tears rolled unabashed down my face, the emotion so overwhelming it threatened to choke off my breath. I couldn't speak.

"Julia?"

"Y…yes. I'm here."

"Baby, are you okay? I wish I was touching you right now."

"I'm okay. I'm fine, just anxious." I cleared my throat and sat up, hoping I could stop crying, wiping at my tears with my free hand. "How does it feel to be finished with school, Dr. Matthews?"

He chuckled softly. "Great, actually, but I still have to take my boards and graduate before I'm official, sweet."

"Mmmm…Well, lots of things are becoming official these days."

"Yes. How is work? Is Meredith being easy on you?"

"I'm energized to be back at it; but Andrea is so efficient, I'm wondering if they really need me." I couldn't hide my disappointment.

"You'll be back into it soon enough, but I don't want you overdoing it."

"*Please*. I'm perfectly fine. Stop being so overprotective."

"You love that about me." The laughter in his voice was unmistakable.

"One of many things." I giggled into the phone. "Ryan, Mike offered to take the pictures and I thought it was very sweet of him. What do you think about that?"

His laughter died and the silence was deafening. "Ryan?"

"Uh…I guess. If that's what you want."

"He's very good and, he'd be able to get the prints turned around quickly. He said he'd fly here on Friday to get some shots of me in the dress. It's by some famous designer that Ellie lined up and an original, so we may be using the photos in the mag at some point. *Please*?"

"No naked pictures in sheets, unless I'm naked with you, understand?" he teased.

I laughed again. "Hey…you love that picture, so stop complaining already."

"I do love it. I'm looking at it right now."

Thud.

"What about the lingerie? Do you want…?"

"Uh…" he began hesitantly.

"Just for you, not the mag."

"Was that Turner's idea?" he said rather shortly.

"Never mind. It was a stupid idea. I just remembered how happy you were before and I thought…it would make a nice wedding present."

"You remembered it *all*?" His voice was full of questions.

"That Christmas. Every beautiful detail."

"Okay. I would like the pictures, if I'm honest. But, if he touches you, I'll beat the shit out of him, so tell him going in."

I smirked. "Don't worry. Ellie will be there. She's coming in tomorrow."

"Aaron and Tanner are arranging this big bachelor party and Jen wants a girl's night out with anyone who's in town, including our moms. Will you be up for that?"

"I don't know. I won't be there until early Thursday. There's so much to do, so maybe, but I'll have to play it by ear. Harris will be there with his band, so please include them, okay?"

"I'm not a schmuck, babe. I talked to him already."

"Okay, I should have known."

"Julia…In one week, we'll be *married* by this time." His excitement made my heart do flip-flops. I actually had goose bumps wash over my arms.

"I know. It's a dream."

"I love that you think so, too. I miss you."

"Miss you more. Sweetie, I want to keep talking, but I need to finish the vows. They have to be as perfect as the man I'm writing them for, right?"

"Are you gonna start crying again?"

"Probably, yeah."

"Mmmm. I'm sure I'll cry like a baby when I hear them, too."

"You think?"

"I'm sure they'll be...*aamaaazing.* More than I could hope for."

I sighed into the phone. "Ryan, when you say things like that I just...miss you so much."

"Well, if you'd have done as your man asked, I'd be making love to you right now. I'm not letting you out of my sight after this. Ever."

"Promise?"

"Mmmm, yes. You know the next time I make love to you, you'll be my wife."

My heart thumped loudly as tears overflowed.

"My *wife*," he whispered again. "Always mine. You didn't forget to remember me, did you?"

My breath hitched on his words. "Never. I'm glad you wouldn't agree to the double wedding. You were right. My focus is totally on you. Even if we were the only two there, it couldn't mean more to me."

"Julia. No one else will exist in that moment. I love you like crazy."

"I know," I said, smiling softly. Whether I was worthy or not, I knew that he loved me and I was ready for a lifetime more to come. "Just us."

*****

"Ellie!" I squealed when she finally arrived. "Oh, my God! What did you bring?" I asked after we hugged tightly. Her eyes danced as she flitted inside and instructed the cab driver to deposit her bags in the middle of my living room, with three huge white boxes.

She handed him a fifty and then turned toward me. "Well? I had to give you choices, but I'm pretty positive which one you'll choose. Ryan is *dead*, I'm telling you! You'll kill him when he sees you." We were giddy and giggling, hugging and jumping up and down. "*Finally,* the boy is going to make an honest woman of you."

When we drew back, we were both crying. She wiped an errant tear away quickly and rushed toward the boxes and began opening them. She proceeded to pull one after another of the white dress bags out and hang them up in my closet, bringing them one by one into my bedroom and carefully opened them. I felt like a kid at Christmas, grateful to have such a good friend.

"Ellie…thank you." I grabbed her hand and stopped her in the middle of her task. She looked up with a tremulous smile.

"Julia, give me a break. Of course, there's nowhere I'd rather be. I love you."

"I love you, too. Everyone is so…I just…I mean," I stumbled around the words as I sank down on the bed, her fingers parting the wrappings on the first dress, revealing a soft, shimmery white silk. "I'm so blessed. All of you are so amazing. Ryan and I are so thankful."

"I need a drink! All this blubbering will do me in. Do you have a bottle of wine?"

I nodded and wiped my eyes, trying to laugh. "Yes. I'll get it."

"No red, Julia, okay? We don't need any accidents."

"Sure. White it is. I'll be right back." I jumped up and ran into the other room, gathering two glasses, a corkscrew and a bottle of Pinot Grigio from the refrigerator.

The first dress was completely unwrapped when I walked back to the bedroom. Very simple and elegant with very little embellishment, the dress relied completely on the lines and fabric for effect. It was a big dress with a full ball gown skirt.

"So? Do you want to try it on?" I nodded and Ellie proceeded to produce a bevy of foundation lingerie and she quickly had me suited up. The fabric was a fine raw silk, with a deep v-neckline and a large array of handmade silk roses at the left side of the waist. The layers of petticoats were heavy and too much for my small frame.

Ellie was shaking her head as she read my mind. "Nope. Too much dress for you, Jules."

My hands smoothed over the delicate fabric, feeling its richness. I nodded in slight regret. "Yes. But, it's so beautiful."

The next one was a trumpet style that hugged my curves all the way down before flaring out at the knees. I didn't like the way I looked in it. "I feel fat. I'm sorry, Ellie. All this shirring…I guess."

She deftly undid the buttons and the zipper. "No worries, but you're far from fat, Julia." A bright smile split her face, her grey eyes lit up as she brought out the last dress for me to see.

My mouth fell open as the wrappings fell away.

"Oh…Ellie!" I said softly, my hand reaching out to touch the delicate sequined lace, my heart thumping so loudly that Ellie must've heard.

"Exactly," she said smugly. "I knew it. This is it and you haven't even tried it on yet. Like I said, Ryan's a goner."

*****

The week passed and we were finally on our way back to Boston. My parents were flying in the same day. Harris and his bandmates had trekked across the country in the new bus their record company had provided and were set to play at our reception. Elyse had helped Jenna finalize the details for the ceremony and Ryan and Gabe picked out the tuxedos. Ellie cranked up the stereo and we sang at the top or our lungs during the drive. We had an absolute blast, just like old times.

I didn't bring much with me, save the chosen dress and veil, some lingerie for the wedding night and three changes of clothes for the rehearsal, graduation and traveling back to New York.

When we pulled into Ryan and Aaron's neighborhood, anxiousness overwhelmed me. The culmination of the last eight years; the friendship, the love…the pain suffered through separation and all Ryan had gone through during my recovery made my heart squeeze inside my chest. My parents came rushing out of the front door to enfold me in their arms. My mother was crying and my dad lifted me off my feet and twirled me around.

"Oh, I missed you guys! I'm so glad to see you!" I gasped, glancing over Dad's shoulder to see Ryan leaning up against the porch railing, watching intently, a big smile on his face. "Just a second!" I kissed them both and then bolted toward Ryan who started moving toward me the minute I left my father's arms.

"Oh, baby." His strong arms enfolded me as I jumped into his arms, my legs wrapping around his waist. "I missed you every second. Only 53 more hours, Julia," he said so softly, only I could hear, the spicy scent of his soap mingled with the smell of his skin. His blue eyes were brilliant and shining with happiness. He was gorgeous!

"Get your mouth on mine, this instant," I said happily. He laughed and then complied with relish, his mouth closing over mine in a deep, open-mouthed kiss. I moaned into his mouth.

"Mmmm…You taste so good." His arms tightened around me and his hand pressed into the back of my head as I felt his lips on my temple and closed my eyes. "I love you."

Aaron emerged behind us, groaning in exaggeration. "Will you look at what I've had to put up with? Sickening," he laughed. The others joined in as he went toward my car and gathered Ellie up in a big bear hug. "Little bit! You're here!"

She laughed loudly. "Aaron! Where's Jen?"

"Working. She's got the rest of the weekend off, and is very anxious to see you. Where's Harris?"

"Getting in later this evening. He won't miss the bachelor party, I promise!!" Ellie said.

The rest of the afternoon went by in a blur and soon it was time for the boys to leave. Elyse and Gabriel arrived an hour before and the girls decided to go get manicures and pedicures early the next morning in lieu of going out. It was so long since we'd all been together, and I just wanted to talk to them. Meredith and Andrea were coming into town tomorrow and Mike was taking my portraits before the rehearsal. The next day was the wedding and Ryan and Aaron's Harvard graduation on Sunday afternoon.

We sat around and gabbed about the men, laughed, and got a little tipsy on champagne cocktails. Ellie and Jen fell asleep in Aaron's bedroom as I sat quietly with Mom and Elyse for a few minutes, talking about the wedding and graduation, the past, and the beautiful man that would become my husband. My thoughts must have been reflected on my face, because Elyse reached out and took my hand. I was lying on the couch and she was in the chair next to it. I glanced at her through teary eyes. "Thank you, Elyse. Truly. Ryan is so amazing, and it's due to you and Gabriel. You're all so remarkable. I'm so lucky to join your family."

She got up and knelt in front of me, our arms wrapped around each other and we both cried. Mom wiped away a tear and looked away for a second. "We think you're pretty amazing yourself. You make Ryan so happy."

"I think now is the time, don't you?" Mom asked Elyse, coming over to place one hand on her shoulder and another on the back of my head.

Elyse pulled back and I looked up into two pair of tear-filled eyes. "Yes." She smiled softly and nodded.

"I do, too." My mother sat next to me, and Elyse went to her purse on the table, returning with a white handkerchief in her hand.

"Julia, we've got some business to discuss," she said matter-of-factly. "Gabriel and I love you and Ryan is our pride and joy. I wore these at my wedding when Gabriel's mother gave them to me. They were hers, and we want you to have them. They are something old, but not borrowed." She carefully opened the handkerchief and lying inside were a dozen or so hairpins, each with a sparkling diamond on the end. "I wore them scattered in my hair under my veil. I'd love it if you'd do the same. I told Ryan that I'd give them to the girl he chose to marry, and here we are." She laughed lightly as she placed them in my hands.

"They're just stunning," I said in awe as I looked at them. I was speechless at the unselfish gesture. Each one must have been at least a carat, totally priceless, mounted in the white gold pins.

"Ryan called the day he met you, Julia. I could tell by the tone in his voice that these would be yours one day. I love you as if you were my own daughter, and as a mother, I couldn't ask for anyone better for my son."

I was crying like a baby, and both of the other women were, too. "He…touches me, in ways that no one else ever could. I love him more than anything in the world."

She nodded. "I know. I trust that, Julia."

My mother wrapped her arm around my shoulders and I leaned my head into the curve of her neck and rested my head against hers. "My baby."

"Mom." I choked out.

"You'll always be my baby. I wouldn't trust anyone but Ryan with you."

Elyse took a tissue and wiped at her eyes. "What a bunch we are."

"Do you have something blue and borrowed?" Mom asked gently. "The dress is new, so…"

"Um…Ellie gave me the gloves that go with the dress and they're embroidered with our names and wedding date on the inside of the cuffs. The embroidery is pale blue. Does that count?"

"Yes. Now, what about something borrowed?"

"Mom, you know I don't believe in all this superstitious stuff."

"Humor me. I have a handkerchief that I was going to carry, but I'll give it to you to use."

"Okay, if you want it back full of snot. I expect to be a huge mess!" We all three burst out laughing, just as the door opened and Ryan entered looking very handsome in black jeans and a white button down, sleeves rolled up to his elbows. He set his keys on the table in the hall and walked in slowly. I looked at the clock.

"Hey. You're back early. Where are the guys?" He looked good enough to eat, his hair a little longer than usual and tousled, like he'd run his hands through it a hundred times.

"Hmmph." He let his breath out and came to stand in front of us. "Enjoying my bachelor party. I wanted to be here. But…I don't want to interrupt." He glanced at our mothers and then down into my eyes. He seemed pensive, his brilliant mind racing. The blue eyes were intent and did not move from my face.

Elyse and Mom understood and both rose at the same time. "When your father comes back with Paul and the boys, let him know that Marin and I went on to the hotel." She hugged Ryan as my mother hugged me.

"Thank you, both. Tonight was wonderful. I love you."

"Oh, Julia. My pleasure," Elyse touched my face and then started toward the door.

"Julia, what time tomorrow? Ten?" My mom asked as she waited to give me one last hug.

"Uh…" I tore my gaze away from Ryan to look at my mother. "Yeah. I'll swing by the hotel and pick you up."

When they left, Ryan sat down in the big chair and put his feet up on one of the boxes that were strewn around the room, ready for the moving truck on Monday. I walked up behind him, went down on my haunches and wordlessly slid my arms around his neck from behind. Instantly, he grabbed my hand and pulled it to his mouth, rubbing his lips lightly back and forth over the top of my knuckles thoughtfully. I turned my face toward him and placed an open-mouthed kiss on the tender skin below his ear. "Uhhhh," he sucked in his breath. "Come here."

As I stood to do his bidding, he never let go of my hand, gently tugging on it until I sat on his lap. I curled into him, my head coming to rest in the curve of his shoulder, my forehead resting on the side of his face as he pulled me close and wrapped his arms around me.

I nuzzled into him and my hand inched up his chest to the opening of his shirt. I opened one, then two, of the buttons and slid my hand inside. His skin was warm to the touch and the light smattering of hair there tickled my fingers.

His lips found my temple and then my cheek, waiting for me to speak or turn my mouth up for his kiss.

"What's wrong?"

"Not a thing. I just wanted to be here more than there. I missed you. I haven't seen you in two weeks and I wanted you in my arms."

"Ryan," I whispered. "I missed you, too." Finally his mouth found mine, opening hotly; his tongue plunging hungrily into my mouth. We clung to each other, both clearly aroused and wanting. I raked my hands down his chest as his fingers found the skin beneath the hem of my shirt and started moving in slow circles. I could feel him getting hard beneath me as he pulled his mouth from mine in a groan, only to return and place a few soft, sucking kisses back on my lips.

"I want you. *So much*." The words practically ripped from him, but his tone was soft and breathless.

"Yes," I whispered breathlessly, no hesitation.

"I can't believe I'm saying this, but not tonight, Julia. Not tomorrow night. Not until I'm peeling that wedding dress off of your luscious little body."

"Uhh…why?"

"Because," he whispered against my mouth. "I want it to be perfect and any little thing I can do to make it that way, I will." His hands were roaming my body softly, arousing in his touches, in his hardness beneath me, in the way his breath was coming in hot panting rushes over my skin.

"Will you at least sleep with me, then? I can't bear to let go of you."

"Just try and stop me."

Ryan~

Chairs were lined up on a wooden parquet floor that would later become the platform for Harris's band and dancing, but now was adorned with sparkling lace bows and candles. The large, ethereal flower arrangements on all of the white linen covered tables were breathtaking in their simplicity. My heart pounded furiously as I watched our friends file in and take their seats. The girls had certainly outdone themselves. My mother and father stood near as I looked into the room from the doorway. There was a beautiful white cake towering on a table along one side of the room and a bar would be set up in the back after the ceremony when Julia and I would take a minute to ourselves.

"It's perfect," I murmured softly, glancing at my watch for the twentieth time in as many minutes. My mother placed her hand over mine.

"Breathe, Ryan," my father cautioned, but with an indulgent grin on his face.

"Are you nervous?" Mom asked gently. "You look so handsome."

I was wearing a modern version of the traditional tuxedo with a fitted white linen shirt and a long black tie instead of a bow tie. "That suit is so gorgeous on you." Her voice cracked on the words.

"Mom. Stop. I'll be a blubbering idiot in a few minutes, so can we not cry right now?" I begged. She hugged me close.

"Yes," she said with a sympathetic glance.

I looked at her anxiously. "Have you seen her? How is she doing?"

My dad put a calming hand on my shoulder. "She's breathtaking, son. I don't think I've ever seen a more beautiful bride." I smiled when my mother elbowed him in the ribs. "Oh, except for your mother."

She grabbed his chin and planted a quick kiss on his mouth. "You'd better say that." When she let him go, she turned back to me. "Ryan. Julia is so gorgeous." She bit her lip as her eyes filled with tears. "You'll be heartbroken, she's so beautiful."

Thud. My heart pounded and then stopped, my emotions threatening to overwhelm me. I nodded as their faces blurred before my eyes. I blinked in rapid succession to keep from losing it, and put a hand over my eyes to brush an errant tear away. "I can't believe this day is finally here."

Aaron moved toward us to offer his arm to my mother. "Time to get seated Mom. Dad?"

"All right. Looks like this is it. I couldn't be more proud of you, Ryan," my father told me as he turned to leave. "I know this marriage will last."

I took a ragged breath as I watched Aaron escort my parents down the makeshift aisle. Little votives flickered at every place-setting and larger candles on pedestals lined up on both sides of the altar. Everything was glistening softly. I wasn't sure who was responsible for all of this, but I couldn't have pictured anything more perfect. There was a large round floral arrangement in the same style as the ones on the tables hanging from the high ceiling, over the altar and a white runner along the floor that was strewn with red and white rose petals. The petals were also all over the tabletops and classical music was being played by a string quartet seated at the front of the room.

I was nervous as hell, which I didn't understand considering this was what I'd been dreaming of for almost eight years. I wanted to pull at the front of my shirt to ease the tightness in my chest.

"Are you okay, bro'? You're looking as green as Jen's dress," Aaron said caustically after he'd delivered my mother to her seat.

"I'm good," I said as I ran a hand over the back of my neck. "Except I can't…feel my hands. Do you have Julia's rings?"

I'd had two more thin bands, each encrusted with diamonds, connected on either side of her engagement ring when she left it with me before she went to New York. *"This is the last time this comes off," she'd said and kissed my hand after my fingers had closed around the diamond ring.*

Paul and Marin approached as I waited outside the double doors. Marin was dabbing at her eyes with a handkerchief. I tried to concentrate on what she was wearing, but ten minutes from now I wouldn't be able to remember. Only that it was a very light shade of green and made of silk.

"Hello, darling," she said as I wrapped my arms around her. "You look so handsome. Julia is a lucky girl." Her arms tightened for a second before she stepped back and I offered my hand to Paul.

"Thank you both so much for just…for having her." *Damn throat. How am I going to get through the vows if I can't get through this?* "I'm sorry. I need you both to know that Julia is my entire life. There is nothing that I wouldn't do for her."

"We know that, son. We couldn't be more proud to have you in the family. Our little girl loves you a lot." Paul placed one hand on my shoulder and squeezed. "Come on, Marin; let's get you to your seat."

I took another huge breath as I watched Paul take her to the front row on the left, and then return back up the aisle. "Here we go, Ryan. Are you ready?" he asked with a smile.

I returned the smile and nodded. "Yes. Thank you, Paul."

"Just don't cry on Julia's dress. She'll kill you," he teased me lightly. If he was trying to put me at ease, it worked a little bit.

Harris and Aaron stood next to me as Paul retreated down the hallway. My heart was pounding so hard I could hear the thrumming behind my ears.

"Let's go, Ryan," Harris said quietly. "This is it."

"Yeah," I said more to myself than to either of them. The minister was already at the front of the aisle waiting, and once we took our places, the music changed to 'Canon in D' by Pachelbel. It had always been one of Julia's favorites, and was the processional song for all of the girls.

First, Jenna stepped into the opening. She looked beautiful, her hair swept up with a few loose tendrils falling around her face. She carried a bouquet of red roses and her dress was a medium shade of moss green. It was strapless and fitted with lace trim on the top that was sprinkled with sequins.

Ellie was next. By this time, I felt like my skin was literally falling off of my body. My palms were sweating and I was sure my heart would leap from my chest. Her gown was a lighter shade of the same color and with some sort of fluttery fabric on the skirt. Ellie smiled as she took her place next to Jenna. I took one last calming breath and looked at my feet for a split second trying to steady myself for what I was about to see.

When I looked up, Julia was standing in the doorway with Paul and my lungs stopped working.

Holy mother of God. She literally took my breath away. My mother was right. Heartbreakingly beautiful…unbelievably stunning. It was like my heart was made of glass and it had just shattered in a million shards inside my chest. My hand went to the front of my suit in a silent plea for breath to fill my lungs.

My eyes widened as I looked at her, trying to comprehend the magnitude of the vision before me as I tried to memorize every line. This was a sight that would be with me for the rest of my life. Her white dress dipped in a low scoop on her chest, leaving the top swell of her breasts bare and the neckline continued up to the slope of her shoulders. It was barely sitting on the top of them, accenting the graceful curve of her neck and collarbones. It was fitted until just below her breasts where it fell from an empire waistline straight to the floor. The design was simple but the lace dress glistened softly from top to bottom. She wore white gloves that went to about two inches below her elbows, but otherwise, her arms were bare. Her skin was radiant and with a soft blush to her cheeks, and her mouth a soft shade of pink. Her hair was piled up in soft curls atop her head and adorned with my grandmother's diamond pins and two or three white camellias nestled in the chestnut strands. She held a bouquet of more camellias and some other small white flowers. Her veil was one layer and edged in the same shimmering lace of her gown, cascading down her back to the floor to drag behind her and the blusher over her face fell just above the flowers in her hand. Completely mesmerized, I couldn't tear my eyes away.

As she came closer, I watched her face. Her large green eyes were liquid and her lower lip, trembling. My heart swelled and my throat constricted painfully. I swallowed hard, my fingers aching for hers, as Julia waited on the other side of her father.

"Dearly beloved…" the minister began, his words muted as my eyes locked with hers. She was so beautiful, I wasn't even aware of anything else. I wanted to touch the porcelain skin on her face and shoulders, feel the heat of it under my fingers, and to kiss her full mouth. All I could think about was how much I loved her and that she belonged to me.

"Who gives this woman to this man?"

"I do," Paul said and then he bent to kiss Julia's cheek through her blusher. When she turned to hug him, I could see the back of her dress, the scoop neckline echoing the front, but dipping lower, almost to her waist. She looked every bit the bride. Perfect in every way.

Paul placed her hand in mine and finally, my world felt complete. I used my free hand to cover hers, holding it between both of mine.

"Julia and Ryan have made it through so much and have loved each other more because of, and in spite of, all of their obstacles. They have asked that they be allowed to pledge their love with vows that they have written for each other as we all bear witness as they declare their love for one another under the eyes of God. Please join both hands."

Ellie moved forward and took Julia's bouquet and soon both of my thumbs were rubbing over the tops of her gloved hands, my eyes never leaving hers.

"Ryan, you may begin."

This was it, time to tell her how much she meant to me. I knew it wasn't possible to put the magnitude of my feelings into words, but I was going to give it my best effort. I tried to swallow the emotion, but my eyes were already starting to sting and my throat ached with the effort. I drew in my breath and prepared myself to completely lose it. When I spoke, my voice shook, but the love in her eyes was so reassuring.

"My beautiful Julia. You are…the most stunning thing I have *ever seen.*" I watched her reaction to every word, and when her lower lip began to tremble, I had to stop for a few seconds as my own emotions welled up.

"I can't comprehend what I've done to deserve someone as wonderful, giving and amazing as you. The fact that you have chosen to spend your life with me confounds and humbles me like I've never been." The first tear slipped from my eyes as two fat drops finally spilled on to Julia's cheeks and tumbled down her face. I cleared my throat for control.

"From the moment I laid eyes on you, I've known that your gorgeous face...is the last thing I want to see this side of heaven." She closed her eyes as more tears squeezed out. I felt myself breaking yet I pressed on through the tears and the crack in my voice. "You were meant for me and I've loved you since before either of us was even born. Everything about you calls to me and I want to protect you and give you everything in my power to give you. I would lay down my life with just a word from you."

Her fingers squeezed around mine as she gasped, trying so hard not to sob out loud. I could see her struggling, her throat constricted and her chin visibly trembled. "You make me want to be a better man, to be more than I am...for you and you alone. This *mad, mad* love that we share is...a truly immeasurable a gift...the most precious miracle of my life."

I had to stop then and fight for control. I glanced down at our entwined hands and I rubbed my thumbs over her fingers again and again. This was much harder than I'd ever imagined. Not the words, but holding in the emotions that they stemmed from, was impossible. "I promise to be your husband and everything you need me to be, to take care of you and to love you with all my heart, to worship you with my body. With everything I am, I love you and I am yours, now and forever. I want your time, I want your love and I want your children...I want *you,* always. To tell you that I will love you forever can never be enough." The tears were rolling down my face as her luminous eyes burned into mine. I watched the tears spill from her eyes as

I said the last part of my vows, "Forever *will never be long enough to love you*, Julia."

The room was so quiet you could have heard a pin drop, save for the soft snuffling, as many of our guests cried with us.

"Now, Julia," the minister said softly, "whenever you're ready, my dear."

My heart thrummed inside my body. I realized that my entire life was just a pathway to this one moment. Here, standing in front of me, in this beautiful and loving package, was the entire rest of my life. My heart was so full it ached as I tried to prepare myself for her words.

"Ryan. Every day…you *amaze* me." Her voice was shaking, her hands trembling in mine and tears flowing freely down her face. She sucked in a shaky breath, pausing to breathe, but her eyes never left mine. "The way you always put my needs ahead of your own, leaves me in awe and inspires in me the need to give you *everything*. Everything you do tells me how much," her voice broke on a sob, "you love me and I'm overwhelmed by how much I love you in return. I sometimes can't believe that *a love like this* even exists."

I wanted to gather her in my arms and never let go of her for the rest of my life. I felt like my heart was going to explode and kill me on the spot. "If this intensity isn't a dream, I am certain that we are the only two people to ever love this much." She closed her eyes and I rubbed my fingers over hers in silent communication. "I love you so much it consumes me; fills me up so completely that I am left shaking, wanting and breathless…just *undone*. Every time you look at me or whenever you touch me, there is nothing I want more in this life…than to be with you, to be your wife, to have your children, to be certain that you are mine. I *feel* you within me and it is the greatest gift I will ever receive. You are truly…" her voice broke again, the tears in each and every word, "truly a *miracle* to me; the love of my life, my very heart and soul…now and always. Without you, I am only half of myself…with you, I am whole. I will love you and I am yours, *will only be yours*, forever."

I was a mess and I didn't care. I was completely and utterly lost in her words and her eyes. The emotions running between us were palpable and I was certain the hundred or so people in the room could feel what flowed between us.

Even the minister was affected. "Uhggg…" he cleared his throat. "Ryan, do you take Julia to be your wife, to have and to hold, for all the days of your life?"

"I do." Finally, words easy to say. She smiled through her tears and my face split into a wide smile in return.

"And Julia, do you take Ryan to be your husband, to have and to hold, for all the days of your life?"

"Yes, I do." She nodded; the smile still firmly in place on her beautiful, tear-stained face. Her eyes were clear and sparkling, the tears still coming, clinging to her dark lashes.

"Julia and Ryan will now give the symbol of their unity and pledge. The rings, please."

We let go of each other's hands briefly as Ellie and Aaron produced the rings. Julia removed her left glove and handed it to Ellie at the same time as she took the ring. I took her left hand in mine as I slid her rings back onto her finger. My hands were shaking so much I was surprised I didn't drop them. Her long, graceful fingers were freshly manicured, as beautiful as the rest of her, and her bracelet glittered on her wrist. "With this ring, I thee wed."

I could hear her intake of breath as I said the words. My eyes darted up to meet hers and I brought her hand up to my mouth to kiss it.

She repeated the process and slid the platinum band with one large diamond bezel set in the center onto my hand. "With this ring, I thee wed." Her little fingers closed warmly over mine and I waited for the words that would allow me to pull her into my arms.

"I now pronounce you husband and wife. Ryan, you may kiss your bride."

I inhaled deeply as I looked at Julia while gently lifting her veil. After all we'd been through and all it took to get to this place, I wasn't about to rush any part of it. I touched her face, brushing away the tears, which only made her cry harder. I wasn't sure how it even happened, but she was in my arms, her feet dangling off of the floor as we held each other tight. We were laughing and crying together as I turned my face into her neck and breathed in the scent of her perfume, her skin and her tears.

"Julia, I love you. I love you so much." I held her as tight as I could. "So much, I can't breathe."

"Ryan," she sobbed into me. "Oh, God, I love you, too."

Then our mouths were moving with and on each other's and there was no one in the room but us. This was no chaste kiss, but more of a desperate and hungry plea. I held her tight and kissed her as the room erupted in applause and cheers. "Ladies and gentlemen, may I present, Ryan and Julia Matthews!"

I didn't want to let go, but I reluctantly set her on her feet and took her hand in mine as Ellie handed back her bouquet and we walked back down the aisle and ran straight to the elevators. The staff had to get ready for the reception so we had a few minutes before we needed to be back for pictures. Time we wanted alone.

I wiped my thumb under both of my eyes before I took her into my arms again. "You are so beautiful. Utterly breathtaking.

I can't tell you how I felt when I saw you…knowing you were mine. I'm so happy right now!"

She laughed through her tears. "The vows…Ryan, they were so incredible. I wanted to sob my eyes out. Those words were so beautiful, they physically hurt. I love you so much."

"Julia, yours too, sweetheart. Just amazing."

"We've got it bad."

"Yes. I wouldn't have it any other way, Mrs. Matthews." It wasn't the first time I'd called her that, but now it was real.

Julia ~

We spent a few minutes, clinging and kissing. Long, reverent moments of silence, lost in each other, in our love…realizing that we were married. Ryan balked gently when I asked him if I should take off my veil before going back downstairs.

"Not yet. Please?" His blue eyes were burning, beseeching mine as he ghosted his hand over the side of my head where the edge of the veil glistened next to my hair. "You're so stunning and you're mine. *My bride*. Let me have you like this for a few hours."

I reached up to touch his face and could already feel the slight stubble starting. I closed my eyes and raised my face up so I could press my lips to his. I let my tongue flick out and lick the top lip, and his mouth instantly parted, his breath rushing out over my face and his full lips nudged and coaxed mine. I pulled away after a minute or two because if we didn't go down soon, we'd be missing our own reception.

"There is something incredibly sexy about a man that can grow hair this fast." I smiled against the hard line of his jaw and then dragged my nose along the slight sandpaper surface. "So much testosterone. Mmm…It makes my girlie parts get very excited," I teased and he burst out laughing.

"Ah, Julia. I love your girlie parts," Ryan chuckled and buried his face in the curve of my neck. "*Love* them."

Happiness welled like a tidal wave and I kissed the side of his face. "We have to go down now. Ellie probably has her panties in a bunch by now."

"Mmmm…Only one set of panties I'm interested in."

I cocked my head as a brilliant smile spread over his face. I cleared my throat and reluctantly climbed off his lap. His hand ran down my arm to enfold my hand. I'd removed my gloves and laid them on my suitcase. "Let's do this. Lots of people down there want to get a look at your gorgeous ass. Meredith was practically drooling last I looked. You're so handsome," I said in all seriousness. "Really Ryan. Just beautiful."

"Hush or I'll have to take you this instant." He started walking backwards and pulling me with him toward the door. I lifted the bottom of the veil and draped it over my arm as we left the room. He held my left hand in his and his right arm wrapped around my waist as we went downstairs and back into the ballroom, where Mike was waiting with everyone else in the wedding party. He hugged me tightly when he was done with the photos.

"Julia, Ryan is one lucky bastard," he said softly and smiled slightly. "You're gorgeous."

"Thanks. It means a lot that you're here."

Ryan extended his hand. "Thank you, Mike. We really appreciate it. I'm looking forward to my present." His lips twitched in a smile.

Mike grinned and nodded. "You *should* be. Indeed."

Surrounded by our parents and best friends, the evening passed in a flash. Dinner was delicious, the music wonderful and the hand in mine was constant. Aaron and both of our fathers made heartfelt toasts and Ryan's hand tightened around mine when Ellie stood up with tears in her eyes and raised her glass.

"Julia is one of my best friends. I love her like a sister. When she met Ryan, she blossomed. She became freer, happier, more loving. He brings out the best in her, and he adores her. All of us close to them knew years before they would admit to even themselves, that one day we would be standing in a place just like this, as they vowed their love. And what a love it is. Sophocles said 'One word frees us from all the weight and pain of life: That word...is love.' Ryan and Julia...my beautiful, wonderful friends...you must surely be the freest souls to ever exist, because the love you have between you is like nothing I've ever seen. May God bless you, always. I love you both. To Ryan and Julia Matthews!"

Harris stood next to her and motioned to some of the musicians. Two of the violinists from the quartet took their places next to the piano and the rest of Harris' band cleared away as he adjusted the microphone.

"Ryan has requested this song be played for Julia tonight, and I was only too happy to oblige. He is quite a gifted musician himself, but wanted to share this dance with his bride. This is another perfect choice, my friend."

When Harris' hand struck the keys in the first chords, Ryan stood and took my hand, leading me to the dance floor. As the song played, he held me and softly touched my face; brushing my hair back and then resting his head on mine as he gathered me close. Harris' melodic voice filled the room and the lyrics were amazing and perfect...promises of forever, through joy and tears, best friends and undying love. It wasn't long before tears were falling softly once more.

Ryan leaned down and kissed me gently. "I love you, Julia. Thank you for marrying me. It's the happiest day of my life."

My arms tightened around him and I buried my face in the front of his shirt as my shoulders began to shake. I wasn't sure if my heart was breaking or exploding, but the force of it shook me to the core. It hurt; a mixture of pleasure and pain. The strings and the soft notes of the piano, so beautiful, lifted up to the heavens.

As the music faded, the room was silent and I looked up at my husband and Ryan's face was damp with tears, just like mine. The blue depths reflected the same mixture of love and confused pain, hunger and desire that surely must be in my own.

"Don't cry, my love," he whispered in my ear as his mouth traced over my face and then settled on my mouth again, his nose nuzzled against mine as he lifted his head, finally sensing the silence, many sets of tear-filled eyes trained on us. Elyse's hand was over her mouth as she leaned her head on Gabriel's shoulder and my mother was openly crying. Aaron's arms enfolded Jenna from behind and Ellie had joined Harris at the piano.

My throat ached with the strength of my emotions, preventing me from saying a word.

Ryan pulled me to his side, wrapping his arm tightly around me.

"Um…Julia and I are grateful for all the love and support you have shown by sharing this special evening with us. I know it's early, but if you all don't mind, we really need to be alone now." The room erupted in cheers and applause. "Please stay and enjoy yourself. For those of you staying for the graduation, we'll see you at brunch tomorrow morning. If you'll excuse us…"

Ryan bent and lifted me bridal-style and carried me out of the room, the happy cheers and catcalls following. His arms tightened around me as I laid my head on his shoulder and I whispered his name. "Ryan, the song was perfect. Thank you for choosing it." It felt like a prayer as I closed my eyes. "I love you more than anything."

He didn't speak, just kissed my forehead, leaving his mouth resting against my skin. As he carried me through the hotel, through the lobby, and to the elevators, I could hear the din audibly lessen. Everyone that saw us stopped and stared. Ryan's chest expanded underneath me and I snuggled closer, winding my hand in his hair.

Ellie had good intentions, buying me a negligee, but it wouldn't make it out of the suitcase. I'd save it for our first night back in New York.

When Ryan pushed the door open and carried me inside, the room was full of candlelight, soft music and white rose petals everywhere. There was a magnum of champagne on ice sitting next to the couch in the sitting room of the suite, but he wordlessly walked past it into the bedroom. The bed linens were down and more rose petals were scattered over them.

The arm underneath my knees loosened and his hands moved to the back of my head to finally lift out the comb that held the veil to my head. I was mesmerized by him as he slowly removed the diamond pins. My hair started to tumble down my back and the flowers fluttered to the floor. Then his mouth was on mine, so soft and searching, his hands threading in my hair. My hands came to rest lightly on his waist. It was clear that he wanted to go slow and I let him lead.

Ryan's mouth never left mine while his hands lightly traced over the skin of my exposed back and shoulders, igniting a trail of fire wherever he grazed the skin. My mouth opened and searched for his, seeking more pressure and my hands fisted in his shirt, tugging it free of his pants. I felt my dress loosen and finally open, Ryan's hands lightly pushed it from my shoulders and it fell in a pool at my feet, leaving me standing before him in just the bridal lingerie…a white lace bustier, bikini and thigh-high stockings. I stepped out of my shoes as his glowing eyes traveled from head to toe. His breath caught as he moved to take me in his arms again.

My hands worked their way up his shirt, undoing the buttons and then moved to his belt. He stood before me helpless, until finally I could take no more. "Ryan…touch me. I want your skin on mine."

"Uhgg…Julia. You don't know what you do to me. You're so beautiful. Just looking at you…hurts."

The clothing fell away in pieces, our hands gentle and reverent as we explored each other. The passion grew as the seconds passed until eventually he lowered me to the bed and followed me down, his knee coming to rest between mine, his hands teasing my body to life, and his eyes burning into mine.

"Ryan…God, I love you…"

Minutes or hours passed, I wasn't sure, but we continued to touch and kiss. I moaned as his mouth found my breasts and he suckled each nipple into his mouth, careful not to rush. His hands on my body were gentle, his fingers parting the flesh between my legs to begin the teasing torture that he was brilliant at. He could play me like an instrument and he knew it.

He sighed at the warm wetness he found there and kissed his way down my body, his forehead resting on the skin below my navel and lower, until my legs fell open and he started feasting on my heated flesh like he was starving. Suddenly, his patience was gone, but only for a moment. His tongue and lips lightened when he felt me start to arch, silently denying me, letting the orgasm barely begin before he moved up to kiss me deeply, letting me taste myself on his mouth.

It was so intimate as he wound his fingers through mine and pulled me up so we were facing each other. My thighs hugged Ryan's hips as he pulled mine closer until I was straddling his lap, our bodies rubbing and rocking together.

"Uhhh, oh, Julia. I've never wanted anything as much as you."

I couldn't get close enough, touch him enough and eventually I was writhing and clawing…pulling him closer and arching…silently begging for his possession of me. We were both panting when our bodies finally came together and we kissed madly, passionately, professing our love in heated whispers. The position so close, so intimate, I could feel him so deep inside me, filling and stretching as one hand guided the movement of my hips and the other wound into my hair to arch my neck back so he could trail his tongue along my skin, placing a series of open-mouthed sucking kisses as our bodies moved together. My arms wrapped around his shoulders as he lifted me and lowered me onto my back, still embedded within me, his brilliant eyes damp with tears.

The moment was so powerful, it left me desperate and needy. "Ryan, uhhh…oh, my God. I love you," I whispered.

Emotions overflowed as he moved inside me, lifting one of my knees and hitching it over his arm so that he could sink deeper into my body. Between the long passionate kisses, our tongues mating, our mouths mirroring and savoring in their exchange, Ryan began to speak in a whisper, reciting his vows all over again. "I promise to be your husband and everything you need me to be, to take care of you and to love you with my heart, to worship you with my body. With everything I am, I love you and I am yours, now and forever. I want your time, I want your love and I want your children…I want you, always."

My heart swelled; the experience so amazing that soon I was sobbing softly, even as he brought my body closer and closer to ecstasy. Ryan was shaking and crying with me, holding onto me for dear life and, as we quaked together in climax, still entwined in the aftermath of our glorious lovemaking…he finished his words in a husky breathless tone, his lips moving against mine in the start of another kiss. “Forever will never be long enough to love you…never long enough for *this*.”

I wrapped him up in my body, my arms and legs enfolding him as I cried into his shoulder. His body still embedded in mine and still moving softly, he kissed the side of my face. “Dear God. Every time I touch you, I love you more. I’ve never loved you more than I do in this moment.”

I was shaking and clinging, my body racked with pleasurable spasms. “Ryan. I can’t believe how much I love you. I can’t believe there could ever be more, but there *always is*. Don’t ever let me go.”

“Julia. I can’t. If I do, I’ll die. This is one of those moments you remember the rest of your life, in every single detail. Remember how much I love you. Don’t ever forget to remember how much I love you.”

~13~

Ryan~

"JULIA. BABE." I shook her shoulder gently. "Wake-up," I said softly as I pulled her naked body against mine. She moaned in protest to the sun streaming into the window.

"Sleep. Need sleep." She turned to me and buried her face into the curve of my shoulder. I could hear the smile in her voice. "My husband kept me up all night."

I grinned and tightened my hold. "Mmmm…I like the sound of that." She stretched in my arms, like a satisfied cat, the movement pressing her pliant body more firmly into mine. She was warm, and willing, soft and loving…mine. I didn't realize that I'd said the word aloud but I must have.

"Yes," her voice hissed softly before she nibbled on my lower lip slowly. "Yes, Ryan!"

I smiled against her mouth. Right here, in this bed, was my entire life and if I never left it again, I would be happy as hell. My face hurt from the smile I couldn't contain.

"I love you, Mrs. Matthews." She sobered and lifted her right hand to gently brush the hair from my forehead. Her slightest touch caused me to ignite. I gazed in wonder as her little pink tongue darted out to wet her luscious lips. "Julia…" I bent to brush her mouth with mine. "Don't tempt me, babe. We're late for brunch and we only have two hours until I have to be on campus." It occurred to me that it was the last time that I would go there. It must have shown on my face because Julia instantly picked up on it. She knew me so well.

"Hey," she said gently, the back of her fingers brushed along the line of my jaw. "Are you sad, sweetie?" Her soft green eyes filled with sympathy.

"Uh…sure, some; especially Dr. Brighton. He's been a great professor, a valuable advisor and good friend." I was contemplative but pulled her closer, until every bit of exposed skin was somehow touching. "But, I'm *so* happy, Julia. We're starting our life together. I have everything as long as I have you."

Her lower lip shot out in an adorable pout, but it wasn't a sad one. I watched the emotions cross her features, and pulled her into a tight hug while her arms clasped around my waist. "I love you, *Doctor* Matthews," Julia said softly with a series of kisses along the line of my jaw. "Scruffy boy," she teased.

I rubbed my chin along her cheek and she squealed loudly, following by a fit of giggles when I continued. "Ugh…do you want me to look like a lobster at your graduation?" Julia protested. "That hurts!" Her hand reached around and pinched my ass as hard as she could, her face wrinkling with the effort. I laughed happily.

"So did that!" I protested with a grunt.

Over her shoulder, a ray of sun landed on the bridal gown now hanging over the back of the bathroom door causing a rainbow of prisms to dance around the room. So beautiful. What an amazing picture she made wearing it, the memory alone stole my breath.

I rolled onto my back, taking her with me. She sat up, straddling my hips, looking glorious as she looked down at me. Her hair was a wild mess, but, her face glowed with happiness and her naked body…*perfect.* I sighed softly as I ran my hands and my eyes over her, down her sides, softly cupping her breasts and then gliding down to her hips. I bit my lip as my body responded beneath her.

Julia cocked her head to one side. "We don't have time, my love," she murmured and reached out to touch my face. "The others are already waiting." Her eyes softened, full of love and my heart swelled.

I nodded. "I know." My thumbs rubbed back and forth over her hip bones. I couldn't help myself, I pulled them forward and surged mine in return. "I always want you, Julia. It doesn't matter if I've just had you minutes before or if there is somewhere else I need to be. Right now, I'd blow off brunch with my family,and even my own graduation, just to spend the time alone with you," I said seriously.

She smiled and bent forward to kiss my lips softly. Her tongue came out to lick along my upper lip and I raised my head so I could kiss her back more fully. She tasted so good and felt amazing. My hands tightened on her again as I pressed my arousal into her soft flesh, slowly grinding against her. I could feel the heat, the wetness starting between her legs. It was like magic between us.

The kiss grew more passionate, but she turned her head to the side, leaving my mouth wanting, so I let it roam over the side of her face, until it came to rest on her temple.

"Ryan. I want you, too, but we have to go. Your parents and *I* have waited four damn years to see your ass up on that platform, getting your degree and that crimson collar. You're *going*." She smiled wickedly then grasped around my erection. "*This*, can wait until later." She laughed when my eyes widened and then jumped off of the bed and ran into the bathroom. Within seconds I heard the shower running.

"Ugh!" I groaned and lifted my head to look at the throbbing appendage, still hard as steel. I sat straight up and bounded off the bed, briskly walking into the bathroom. Julia was already in the shower, humming some nondescript song. The room filled with steam, the mirrors full of condensation; the air thick and heavy.

I was in the shower with her in a flash, my arms enfolding her at the same time she jumped in surprise.

"Ryan, you scared me!" she said.

I slid my hands down her body, slick with soap, her skin like silk beneath my fingertips, roaming over the luscious curves of her butt, to the back of her thighs. Her lids fell and her mouth opened as I bent slightly to lift her and bring her legs around my waist. There was nothing I wanted more than to make love to my wife.

"I'm soooo hungry; and, not for brunch. Baby…Don't say no," I whispered against her mouth.

Without speaking, her fingers slid into my hair and pulled my mouth to hers in a deep kiss, our tongues reaching out to circle and lave each other. It was all the answer I needed. I pushed her up against the shower wall and slid into her body. "Uhhhh…" I groaned against the curve of her neck as my hips surged into hers over and over. "I love you."

Her fingers tightened and started tugging on my wet hair, her mouth reaching up for mine again in obvious want as her body clenched in rhythm around mine. I pulled out almost all the way and pushed back in hard as we kissed hotly. Last night had been gentle and slow where now it was needy and desperate, fast and hard.

I had her in my arms, her heat around me, her mouth demanding beneath mine, and I loved every second of it. Giving and taking what we wanted and needed from each other. "Oh, Ryan…" she moaned into my mouth. I felt her body responding to mine in our beautiful mating dance, the answering tightness building deep inside, getting ready to explode. “Uh, baby, don’t stop…” she breathed as her hips rocked in unison to mine. “Don’t stop.”

“Oh, God…Juuullliiiiiaaaaaa.” The air rushed from my lungs as my body tensed and her fingers dug into my scalp and shoulder blade. I could feel her tumble over the edge, her body shaking and clenching tightly around my cock as she sucked every last drop from me as I shot off deep inside her.

We were both left panting, my arms still wrapped tightly around her and she turned her face to kiss the curve of my neck. I could feel her breath on me, despite the steam and heat from the shower. Her hand pushed the wet hair back off the side of my face and we both looked into each other’s eyes.

“I love you,” we said in unison. I was smiling like a stupid schoolboy and I didn’t care. Her lips pulled back when she laughed softly at the expression on my face.

“Yes,” she nodded, “we are definitely missing brunch.”

I laughed in agreement. Time was ticking away, yet I felt no desire or urgency to disengage or to remove my arms from around my delicious little wife. “Definitely, but, I don’t care.” I placed a soft kiss on her mouth and nuzzled her nose with mine.

A loud pounding resonated through the rooms and I let Julia slide down my body and reached around to shut off the water.

“Crap. Whoever it is must be breaking down the damn door,” Julia muttered and grabbed for the towels. She threw one at me and hurried into the other room rapidly wrapping one around herself, hair dripping as she went.

“Hey! Julia, Ryan!! Dad sent me to get your asses out of bed!” Aaron’s voice boomed in the hallway outside the suite. “Enough marital humping already!” He was laughing his ass off, knowing full well his voice carried through the hallway to the other rooms.

Julia and I gaped at each other.

"I think you need to answer the door, hon," Julia said flatly as she grabbed some underwear from the suitcase and ran back into the bathroom. I went to the door amidst more pounding.

"I'm coming, Aaron! Jesus!" I called. When I swung the door open he was leaning on the doorjam.

His eyes widened as they raked over my half naked and wet body. "For Christ's sake, Ryan! You miss your wedding brunch and you're still in a fucking towel?" Aaron was all dressed up in a dark grey suit, white collared shirt and red and grey striped tie. "Or is it; in a towel, *still fucking*?" he asked with a smirk.

"Did someone die? You never wear a suit," I teased flatly, turning back into the room.

"Shut up. You know it's under duress," Aaron admonished. "Get your pathetic ass dressed, would ya? We have to go. Dad said he'd take Julia with him and Mom."

"She might go with her parents, not sure."

"Well, see? If you'd show up when you're supposed to, you'd know Ellie and Harris are going with Paul and Marin, and Jen and Julia with Mom and Dad. I'm here to get your sorry self, so move it," he said dryly. "You have fifteen minutes, Ryan." He sat on the couch and grabbed the remote.

I went to the bathroom door. "Just a second, Aaron." I cracked the door open to poke my head in the door. Julia was combing her wet hair and dressed in a matching blush lace string bikini panty and bra. It was almost the same tone as her skin and emphasized her womanly curves. My eyes roamed over her form in the mirror. "Baby, Aaron is here and hustling me out, so is it okay if I come in and shave?"

She rolled her eyes at me. "What do you think?" She smiled and threw the comb back onto the vanity before reaching for a bottle of lotion and propping a leg up on the toilet as she worked it into the skin of her calves and thigh.

"I wish I had time to do that for you." I lathered up my face with shaving cream and ran the razor under the running water as she switched to the other leg.

"Just get a move on, Matthews."

"We're going ahead and Dad and Mom will take you and Jen."

"Okay. Is Aaron here?"

I nodded between strokes of the razor. "Watching TV."

Julia stepped behind me and wrapped her arms around my waist, one of them sliding up over my abs and to my chest. Her fingers splayed out and she placed a wet open-mouthed kiss on my back between my shoulder blades. "I'm *very* proud of you."

"Couldn't have done it without you and your pushy little ass."

She laughed and moved toward the bathroom door. I glanced at her, my eyes falling on the firm round curves. "Mmmm, and what a luscious ass it is."

I was soon pulling a fully dressed Julia into my arms for one last kiss before I walked out with Aaron, passing a flustered Ellie on the way. She would help Julia pack up the gown and the rest of our things. We had one night left in Boston; then on to New York and the rest of our lives. Happiness flowed until I thought would burst. Aaron put his arm around the top of my shoulders. "Let's do this and blow this Popsicle stand, brother. Fucking A…*we did it*!"

Julia ~

I dabbed at happy tears. Elyse squeezed my hand as we watched Ryan and Aaron claim their degrees. The officiate called Ryan's name followed by '*graduating Summa Cum Laude*', placed the red collar over his gown and handed him the leather-bound degree. I leaned forward and watched Gabriel sitting on the other side of Elyse, a look of love and pride on his handsome face.

Even Jenna, never one to really show any flowery emotion, was crying. My parents were on my right and my father's hand came out to close around mine. Everyone that mattered most in the world was here. Ellie and Harris were sitting directly behind us. I watched as Ryan walked to the right side of the platform, he waited while they called his brother up to get his degree and then they shook hands and hugged before exiting and returning to their seats. Two boyhood dreams now realized. My heart thudded, realizing being away from Aaron might cause Ryan some stress, but this was a day to celebrate.

The afternoon was warm and I was thankful that I'd worn the short yellow dress made of cool linen, sleeveless and about 4 inches above my knees. Most of my things were either in New York or packed up already but Ellie made sure I had something appropriate for the graduation and a pair of jean shorts and t-shirt for tomorrow's drive.

I was excited to start my life with Ryan. He turned to meet my eyes before he sat down, puckering his full lips in a little silent kiss and winking with a devilish gleam in his eyes. Butterflies buzzed around my insides and my lips split in a huge smile. Blushing, I couldn't do a damn thing about it. Even in this gargantuan moment, he was thinking about me. So handsome, his eyes sparkled and flashing a full smile, the dimples in his cheeks were enough to make my knees go weak.

Elyse nudged me with her shoulder. "Ryan looks so happy," she whispered as the ceremony continued.

I squeezed her hand. "Is it just me or is he the most beautiful thing you've ever seen?"

"Oh, Julia. I love you," Elyse's voice thickened on the words. "I just love how much you love my son."

"I can't help it, Elyse. He's worked so hard. They both have. They'll want to party hard tonight!"

Elyse chuckled and nodded. "Gabe's exact words, but I don't think Ryan's mood is only due to graduation. We missed you at brunch," she teased knowingly. I had the grace to flush. I would gladly spend every moment in Ryan's arms. Nevertheless, the heat infusing underneath the skin of my chest and face gave me away.

"Your son is very…um…persuasive." I offered a cheeky grin and a slight shrug.

Her smile widened and she laughed again with a nod. "A gift he acquired from his father. There's no use but to give in, when he makes up his mind."

Elyse looked stunning in a light mauve brocade jacket over a solid dress in the same shade. Her hair was up in a smooth chignon and her make-up impeccable; always so perfectly groomed. Gabriel was distinguished and polished, with the same blue eyes that I loved on his son. Both of them were so beautiful, it was no wonder Ryan turned out to be so gorgeous.

My parents were beaming. This was the most relaxed I'd seen them with each other since before their divorce. I didn't think my father would ever get over his bitterness, but after my accident, the abyss between them seemed to close. All was right in my world, even if those few months of my memory were still missing

The sweet spring air, ripe with the scent of lilacs and freshly cut grass filled my lungs. The sky was brilliant blue, dotted with billowing white clouds and the temperature was perfect. I glanced toward where Ryan and Aaron were sitting. Aaron shoved his index finger under the edge of his mortar board to scratch his temple, sweat beading and dripping down the side of his face. Ryan shifted and dropped his head. The bored look on his face told me he was anxious for the proceedings to end.

There were many rows of black and red robes of graduates and faculty in front of us. The graduation was on one of the larger lawns of the medical school grounds, with beautiful limestone buildings on three sides. Manicured and extremely elegant.

After nearly two hours, the graduating class was finally announced and we were all filing out. My heels sank into the lawn slightly which made walking awkward. Jenna was laughing when I made my way to her side to embrace her. She hugged me back warmly.

"Ugh, finally, right?"

"Yes. Are you speaking of the graduation or the years of school?"

"Both. This was a long ass day. I need a drink!" Jen laughed. "Who's with me?" she asked. Everyone murmured their agreement. *First we have to get our men,* I thought as we turned to walk toward the reception area where Ryan and Aaron would be speaking to the faculty and saying goodbye to friends.

Suddenly, slim arms wrapped around both Jenna and I from behind. "Hey, chickies…wait up!" Ellie's voice was breathless with excitement. "Let's get into some trouble tonight. Who knows when we'll be able to see each other next?" She was looking down and both Jenna and I wrapped an arm about her waist.

"Yes, I'm in the mood to raise a little hell," Jen chuckled. "Where should we go, Julia?"

"Well, the folks might like the Four Seasons, but maybe later we can take the boys to that hole in the wall bar they always go to? What do you think? Ellie?"

"Yes, that sounds like a plan," Jenna agreed.

"Sure!" Ellie was only too happy with anything we picked out. "This is your town, so lead on."

As we approached the men, they were laughing and talking with Tanner and one of their professors. Liza tried to get Ryan's attention. I stiffened involuntarily and slowed my steps as she touched his arm and he turned. His smile faded slightly, but he spoke and shook her hand. She ignored his proffered hand and put her arms around his neck. He looked uncomfortable, but hugged her back loosely.

"*Uh uh!* No that bitch did not do that!" Jenna's voice hardened.

"It's okay, Jen. This is the last time he'll see her."

"Who is she?" Ellie wanted to know.

"Ryan's stalker. I wouldn't be surprised if she chases him down to New York." My heart fell. I'd never even considered that.

"That's *her*?" Ellie's eyes widened, disapproval plain on her delicate features. "Pfft. No contest, Jules."

"Yeah. *If she only had a brain*," Jenna scoffed in a sing-song voice. We all burst out laughing.

"Jen!" I gasped. "She is graduating from Harvard today."

"So what? Thanks to your husband and others who saved her ass countless times."

"Well, I don't like her shoes. I'll bet the dress under that gown is equally offensive," Ellie sniffed haughtily, looking down her nose at the other girl.

"Julia's way too civilized about that hag. I would have scratched her eyes out months ago if she'd pulled that shit with Aaron," Jen said as she pulled on Ellie's arm. Her voice dropped a couple of octaves so the parents wouldn't hear her. "I can't *believe* the nerve of that twit!"

We were still giggling and Ryan and Aaron heard us. They smiled, Ryan moving to disengage from Liza's grip. He moved forward and reached for me, arm slipping around my waist to draw me to his side. "Liza, you remember Julia? My *wife*?"

Shock crossed the other girl's face before she quickly masked it. "Really, when did you get married?" She glanced down at Ryan's left hand and her mouth thinned. I almost laughed at her surprise.

"Last night," Ryan stated without hesitation. He leaned in to whisper in my ear. "And what a night it was." He kissed my cheekbone and then my temple.

I smiled brightly up into Ryan's dazzling face. His hair was wild from his hands running through it, his teeth flashing brightly and cobalt eyes bright. He was gorgeous and I could see it in his expression…he was mine and I didn't need to worry about Liza.

I turned, offered her my hand in greeting.

"It's nice to see you again." I could afford to be gracious, considering that Ryan was my husband and I was held tightly to his side. She took my hand limply and shook it, her face falling slightly. "Congratulations."

"Thank you. You, too."

"Will you be staying in Boston?" I asked, wanting to know her plans. We were interrupted when Jen moved toward Aaron.

"Yes, we're all proud of our brilliant boys," Jenna interjected. Aaron hugged her before turning toward his mother.

Gabriel hugged both of his sons soundly, patting them hard on their backs, his eyes glistening with unshed tears. Liza moved away silently as the family closed around us, her eyes falling on Ryan's face. I could see the sadness there. A small part of me empathized, knowing how my heart would break if he didn't want *me*.

Ryan's eyes caught mine and he reached out to take my hand in his, his thumb rubbing over the top of my fingers, lightly caressing my skin and circling the diamond on my ring finger. He lifted my hand to place a soft kiss on the inside of my wrist. "What?" he questioned, his eyes intent on my own.

"Just very proud of my husband," I said and then stood on tiptoe to place a kiss on his smooth jaw. "Mmmm…and *very* happy. I'm feeling very lucky right now." I glanced in the direction of Liza's retreating back. If Ryan noticed, he didn't acknowledge it.

His lips lifted slightly at the corners as he watched my face before placing a soft, wet kiss on my mouth, oblivious to the few hundred people surrounding us. "As if I had a choice, baby. You're burned in me forever. *Remember*?" He looked at me hopefully.

My mind flashed back to a time in a coffee shop when I'd said those very words, after he convinced me to try to find a job in New York City. My free hand wrapped around his bicep and I leaned my head against his strong shoulder.

"As a matter of fact, I do."

Ryan~

My mother, Marin, and the rest of the women had all gathered at one end of the table chattering away. Dinner had been delicious, filled with congratulations, praise and lots of laughter. My father's hand came to rest on my shoulder and squeezed. He and my mother were leaving early the next morning, as were Paul and Marin. We were dropping off Harris and Ellie at the airport on our way out of town, leaving my car in Boston with a plan to come back the following weekend by train to pick it up. I was leaving all of the furniture with Aaron and Jen, only concerned with my keyboard and some clothes.

Julia's gaze fell on me, electricity running over my skin like a whisper that reached all the way to my bones. She smiled softly, knowingly. Her exhaustion was clear, yet she was still so lovely. My heartbeat quickened. Even though we had the rest of our lives to be alone, I found myself wanting nothing more. The last few days had passed in a blur and emotions flowed between us like thunderous waves, leaving us both spent.

Ellie ordered two more bottles of wine and I walked down to where my bride was sitting between Jenna and Marin. Her dark hair was falling in soft chestnut curls around her face and down her back; her features were soft and full of love, content. My heart expanded and tightened at the same time as I ran a finger along the curve of her cheek and then under her chin.

I pulled her up and took her place, settling her back down onto my lap.

"Ryan," Mom frowned in disapproval. I didn't care. I shrugged and ran a hand down Julia's hip to rest on her thigh.

"It's okay, Mom. Lighten up."

"Okay," she agreed with a nod. "I guess you and Aaron have earned some special privileges tonight. Are you glad it's over?"

I sighed as Julia's fingers brushed up and down on my stomach. "Yes. I still have to take my boards, but I'm anxious to start my residency."

Marin's face lit up with a smile. "We're all so proud. Aaron, make sure to invite us to the wedding," she called down, getting my brother's attention.

"Of course," Jenna answered with enthusiasm. Aaron scooted her chair closer to his so she could lean into him.

The waitress came back with the wine, offering Ellie a sample, then went about filling the glasses around the table.

Ellie stood and took her glass in her hand, her voice cracking slightly. "I miss you guys a lot now that we are all scattered to the wind, but I'll always love you. You're the family I never had, so let's promise to make time to see each other."

Harris joined her as I glanced at Julia. Her lower lip was trembling with emotion. My arms tightened and she leaned her head against mine, closing her eyes.

"We'll get together soon," I said, mostly for Julia, but loud enough for all to hear. My hand smoothed the hair at the back of her head, stroking it down her back over and over until she went to hug Ellie.

Soon all of the women were tearing up. "I'll miss you, Ellie. I'll miss all of you." When she turned out of Ellie's embrace, Julia's hand moved to my shoulder which I quickly covered with my own.

"Let's all plan on Christmas in Chicago. Paul, Marin, you, too. We have enough room and nothing makes Elyse happier than having a full house for Christmas," Gabriel said jovially.

"That sounds great, Dad. I'll volunteer my chef wife to kitchen duties, and myself to eating with abandon," I said, trying to lighten the mood. The conversation continued around us but both Julia and I had fallen silent. I squeezed her hand gently and her fingers threaded through mine. "Are you tired, my love?"

I knew the answer. All of the preparations, the wedding, making love all night, it was all finally catching up to us. We were both wiped out. I kissed her hand as she nodded.

"Yes, but you should stay with your family. The girls talked about going to that bar," she said with a small smile, but her words were weary.

I shook my head. "It's not happening, babe. We have a long day tomorrow." I started to get up from the table as I spoke. "I just want to snuggle up with my girl."

"Ryan! You're not bailing are you, bro'?" Aaron said as he saw my movement. "We're going out! Harris and Ellie are up for it!"

I patted Julia's left hand between both of my own. "Uh…" I began.

My father looked at me in understanding. "Aaron, let them go. They're tired. It's been a busy weekend."

"I'll make breakfast for everyone," Julia said and instantly Aaron perked up.

"Blueberry muffins?" Aaron asked, with an over-sized grin.

"Sure," she said, while she bent to kiss his cheek. "I'm proud of you, you know?"

"Stop," he teased with a grin. "You're making me blush!"

After we said goodnight, I took Julia's hand and led her out of the restaurant. I didn't have my car, so I had the valet hail a cab. We both had imbibed several glasses of wine during the course of the evening, and it was better that neither was driving and when Julia curled into me and leaned her head on my shoulder, her heavy lids closing almost before the car pulled away from the curb, it only got better. I gave the driver the address in a quiet voice and leaned my head back on the seat, my arm stretched across her legs and her arm wrapped around it.

She sighed softly and I wasn't sure if she was asleep or not. "I love you," her soft words answered my thoughts.

I turned my head and pressed my lips to her forehead. "I love you more." She smelled so sweet. The perfume she'd worn ever since I'd given it to her on her birthday eight years earlier, coconut from her shampoo, wine and the scent of her skin.

Ambrosia. I inhaled deeply, relishing and memorizing the moment.

I carried her over the threshold, and pushed the door shut with my foot.

"Hey. I can walk, baby," she said sleepily.

"Hush. This is tradition, right? I'll take any excuse to have you in my arms, you know that." I didn't bother with the lights, the moonlight filtering through the windows allowing me to see. Julia's breath came in even huffs against my neck, so soft and warm. Surely, she was on the verge of deep sleep.

I released her knees, but kept my arm around her back, and her head lolled into my neck as I pulled down the covers on the bed. This would be the last night I would hold her in this bed, in this apartment, where we had found each other again.

I sighed in regret. Even though we had so much to look forward to, there was a part of me that didn't want to let go of these last few months. As painful as they'd been, they were so full of our love. After I'd accepted that she truly loved me despite the holes in her memory, we had some of our most precious times together and so many new memories to cherish and build on.

I undressed her gently; lifting her and placing her in the bed. Her tired eyes opened slightly and she looked up at me, her hand reaching for me. "Come…" she requested in a sleepy whisper.

"I will. Let's get you out of these pretty scraps of lace." I unhooked the clasp on her bra and gently pulled it from her shoulders and let it fall to the floor near her dress. Soon the skimpy panties followed and I felt a rush of desire as I looked at her. *So perfect.* I wanted to kiss her all over, but settled for a gentle kiss on her tummy and then one slightly longer one on her open mouth. Instantly, she responded, despite her sleepy state. Her hand curled around my neck into the hair at my nape, a move that completely aroused me. I touched her cheek as my mouth pulled reluctantly from hers. “Sleep, honey.”

I stood as she moaned and rolled to her side while I quickly divested myself of my clothing. I glanced around the room in the soft glow of moonlight from the window. Everything was packed. The closet now empty, the picture of Julia gone from above the desk, the laptop already loaded into the trunk of her car. All that remained was the keyboard. My eyes fell on it and then on the bench as my mind touched on the first night I’d touched her after the accident. My breath rushed out. Utterly amazing, just like every moment that I touched her before or since. The source of my musings called to me.

“Ryan, come…I miss you,” she murmured in her sleep.

I went to the bed and slid in next to her. Instantly, our bodies entwined, her head resting in the crook of my neck and her arm dropping low on my waist as I gathered her close.

“I’ll make lemon,” she whispered, so softly that I could barely hear the words.

“Hmmm?” I said and placed a kiss on the top of her head.

“Lemon. I’ll make lemon, too. I promise.”

I smiled in the darkness. “I know, honey. Go to sleep, precious girl. I love you.”

Julia ~

Ryan shoved a muffin in his mouth and then stopped at my dazed expression. “What?” he mumbled. He could barely get the word out with his mouth so full.

“*What*?” I asked incredulously. “Are you kidding me?”

He grinned and quickly chewed and swallowed the offending culprit. “We’re almost there, babe. It’s been ages since we’ve eaten. I'm starving." He reached out and tugged my hand to pull me closer so he could lean down and kiss me hard. "Besides, these are so good."

We were just getting into Manhattan and still had probably 40 minutes in the car before we arrived at *our* apartment. Ryan was driving and I'd been able to watch him for most of the trip. I couldn't help but giggle as his hand rooted around in the bag for another muffin. I pulled it from him and reached in myself and handed it to him. "Try not to inhale it, hmmm?"

Ryan nodded as he took it. This time he took a big bite, and then held it out to me. "Want some? My wife is an amazing cook. You won't be sorry," he added cheekily.

He was dressed casually in ripped jeans and a white t-shirt. I couldn't tear my eyes off of him. When I didn't answer, he threw me a quick look. "Julia?"

"No, thank you," I said softly and then let my hand reach out and wrap around his right thigh, my fingers drawing patterns on the denim and poking through one of the holes to scratch the skin underneath, the light covering of hair was soft to the touch. "You are so damn sexy," I almost growled at him. My body reacted just watching him munch away happily on the muffin. He finished it and grabbed the water bottle resting in the console and drained it before returning it to its original place.

"Julia," he murmured as his hand covered mine, pressing it more firmly into his leg and caressing my fingers in the process. "I'm glad we're almost home."

"I'm sorry that I fell asleep last night. Not very bride-like of me."

"Honey, we were both exhausted. We have time and uh…" he hesitated, "well, do I get my present tonight?"

I smirked, wondering if he was referring to the photographs or to making love.

"Mmm…present? Was there something specific you wanted?" I was feeling frisky and my hand worked its way further up his thigh. When my hand reached my destination between his legs and I pressed into him, I could already feel his body hardening beneath my fingers. "Yum…I want to go down on you tonight. I'll give you a massage, too, baby."

Ryan's mouth fell open in surprise and his breath rushed out, his hips involuntarily lifted and pressed into my hand. A low groan emanated from his throat. "Julia, don't make me have an accident."

I felt the heat pooling between my legs as my fingers curled around his length under his jeans. He was fully erect now, the large bulge straining against the confines of the zipper. I eased it down slowly, watching his face. He swallowed and closed his eyes for a split second.

"Julia. Later, sweetheart." He turned his face toward me. "I would *love* to let you continue, but there is something very precious in this car that I don't want damaged." His reached toward me and his fingers brushed down the line of my face. "Okay?"

My heart thrummed in my chest as my hand stilled in his lap. I was so full of love and lust for this man that it was impossible to comprehend. "Okay," I said reluctantly. "I just…I want to make you feel good." Even I could hear the ache in my voice.

"You're not making this easy on me," he groaned. "We have all night, baby."

I didn't answer, just put my hand into the one he had offered and let it rest on my lap as our fingers threaded together. His hands were so big, with fine, long fingers of a piano player, a surgeon…and a *very* gifted lover. I closed my eyes letting myself drown in the sensations racing through my traitorous body.

"What are you thinking about? My present?" he asked softly.

I raised an eyebrow. "Uh…I didn't think that was the track you'd be on tonight but, yes. I thought you might have forgotten."

"When do I get to see it?" The anxious look on his face was like a little boy at Christmas. I couldn't help but roll my eyes at his flushed expression. His excitement was contagious.

Ryan was in for a surprise. A big one. I dropped my head and bit my lip so he wouldn't see the smile I tried to hide. "Mike had the photos delivered. They should be at the front desk, but we have to unload the car first, Ryan. The keyboard…"

"Ah…already the slave-driver wife. I love it," he laughed.

I chuckled as his fingers closed more tightly around mine and pulled my hand up for a kiss. Ryan parked in the space reserved for me. I'd have to arrange for another one so Ryan's car could join mine. "I can't wait! You were so beautiful. I'll never forget a single moment of that day, Julia." His tone turned serious.

"Me, either. We really *are* married, right?" I teased.

He nodded as he shut the car off and turned, his hand coming up to slide over my jaw and cheekbone then to the back of my head in a loving caress. I took a deep breath as his open mouth closed hotly over mine. He tasted so good and we kissed over and over again, our mouths moving and tasting, until I finally pulled away and rested my forehead on his cheek.

"Welcome home," I whispered and brushed my mouth along his strong jaw. His beard was scruffy, a full day had passed since he'd shaved and I rubbed my nose through it. "Let's go."

Ryan loaded me up with my overnight bag and three pillows before reaching into the backseat to pull out the keyboard. "Let's leave the rest until tomorrow."

"Yes. You won't need clothes tonight, baby." I punched the up button on the elevator.

"Or any night, I hope."

We were both laughing when we finally got to the apartment and I put the key in the door and pushed it open. *Is it possible to be this happy?* I thought I would burst with it.

"Julia, wait." My head shot up in question. "Stay here."

Ryan went in and set the keyboard on the couch cushions, then came back and took the bag and pillows from me before throwing them inside the door. He whisked me up in his arms again and I squealed in surprise.

"Babe. What are you doing?"

"I'm carrying my bride over the threshold."

"Again? You did it at the hotel and at your apartment in Boston already."

"Yes and I'm going to do it in every new place we live, forever. Get used to it."

"You're crazy!" I dipped my head and bit into the muscle between his shoulder and his neck. Not enough to hurt, but definitely enough for him to feel. Within seconds, his mouth was on mine in a slow kiss and then, just as suddenly, he set me on my feet and was rushing toward the door. "Where are you going?" I called.

"To get the pictures! I'll be right back. Love you!"

I stood there stunned, staring at the open door, now devoid of him. I gathered up the bag and the pillows from where he had unceremoniously dumped them and carried them into the bedroom. I found the bridal trousseau that Ellie provided, two pieces; one bridal white, long and elegant, the other black as night, sheer and short.

I hesitated a second and then stripped off my clothes and ran into the bathroom and started the shower. I piled my hair in a haphazard bun at the top of my head, and jumped under the water to rinse off, quickly soaping my body. Within five minutes I was standing in front of the mirror, dressed in the gorgeous black chemise. Sheer over the torso with lace over the breasts and a matching lace thong, the sides slit up to my hips. I pulled some of the hair out of the bun, creating messy tendrils and quickly put some lip gloss on my lips.

"Julia! I'm not waiting to open this! I can't stand it," Ryan called from the other side of the door. I wanted to see his reaction, but remain out of sight, so I opened the door and watched his reflection in the mirror.

He was silent, barely moving, as he looked at the photos. He was holding the one of me in my gown and veil on the steps of one of the buildings on the Medical School campus. I didn't even know the name of the hall, but Mike suggested it, in true fashion photog form. It was a brilliant idea and I knew Ryan would love it. I'd only seen emailed prints when Mike sent the digital proofs so wasn't sure how he'd cropped them.

Ryan was frozen, mesmerized by what he saw. He moved to another, which I assumed was a close up of my face with my bouquet and he gasped. "Julia…" he breathed and reached out to touch the photograph in front of him. "Holy fuck!" He sat down on the bed and my heart fluttered when he got to the sexy pictures in the lingerie. Mike was a pro at setting the stage and from Ryan's reaction, he'd hit the mark. "If these weren't so damn amazing, I'd beat the piss out of that little bastard," he said softly, almost to himself.

I decided it was time to show him the live version and turned into the open doorway. "I can't wait to see the ones of both of us together and of my handsome groom."

"Julia, these are…" he stopped when he looked up and saw me standing there. "Just…*gorgeous*." His eyes were filling with tears. It never ceased to amaze me how sensitive and loving he was. "I'm…" he put his hand over his heart, "overwhelmed. You are so fucking beautiful. And, look at you right here in front of me." I moved toward him and put my hand to his face. "Incredible. I'm so…in love with you."

"Ryan," His name tumbled from my mouth like a prayer as I moved closer to him, ever so slowly. "I love you and I'm yours. You're welcome to look at me for the rest of your life." I stood in front of him waiting as his eyes roamed over me, the outfit leaving little to the imagination. Finally, he reached for me, his hands hovering over me, barely touching but lighting me on fire, his eyes blazing.

"Like I said, not long enough." His mouth found the nerve at the base of my neck and opened hotly over my skin, sucking and nipping as he dragged his lips over me. I closed my eyes as his fingers began to work their magic on my body. "I want more than forever. I want to devour you; to dissolve right into you. My one and *only* love."

I gave myself over to Ryan and he gave himself over to me…anything and everything. Over and over again, we got lost in each other and it was heaven. For the rest of our lives it would be heaven.

~14~

Julia ~

I ROLLED OVER on the couch and stared out at the twinkling lights of Manhattan. The apartment was dark, the full moon was shining brightly through the windows, its light falling in angles over the furniture and floors. Our music played on the iPod and I sucked in a huge sigh as it filled the room. Missing Ryan was a constant ache. We worked like dogs and on the odd night he arrived home on time, inevitably, I'd be stuck at the office. *Newton's Law.* A irony of it stung like fire and I blinked angrily in protest of the tears that tried to form in my eyes.

We'd been married three months. Ryan easily passed his boards but the hours that residents put in were ridiculous. There were times I didn't set eyes on my husband for 36 hours. His keyboard sat next to my art table, everything cramped in the small room. We'd looked for an apartment in Lower Manhattan closer to St. Vincent's, but the rent was so outrageous, we couldn't justify it. Ryan insisted we save our money for a nice house once his residency was finished. I hated that the subway meant another two hours apart every damn day.

I reminded myself to concentrate on the time we were together. It was wonderful and amazing, but never seemed like enough. My phone buzzed and I reached for it on the coffee table. It was my mother.

"Hi, Mom."

"Hey, how's my baby girl?" she said happily. "Sorry for calling so late. I forgot about the time difference until just this minute."

"It's fine. I'm just waiting up for Ryan." My voice was flat. "What are you doing?" In the time since my wedding, my parents were in touch and I secretly hoped that they would get back together.

"Oh, not much. Just cleaning up the house. Your dad's coming for a visit."

"Holy shit! Really?" I sat up in my excitement and smiled happily. "I was hoping but…when did you decide this?"

"Just, I don't know, Julia." She sounded flustered. "We've just been talking more and I realize how much I miss him."

I leaned back on the couch and propped my feet up on the coffee table. "I'm glad you're finally talking. This is good. I'm happy for you. I never felt that Daddy ever got over you."

"I know. He told me. I feel silly, like I'm back in college or something. It's stupid." She chuckled nervously.

"No, it isn't. I think it's great."

"The wedding pictures! Oh, my God, they are gorgeous! Everyone looks so beautiful. That photographer is just wonderful!"

I flushed with pleasure. "Yes, he's great. One of the best I've worked with. We have a shoot tomorrow for the September issue, in fact. Meredith has me working on a project for *The New Yorker*, too. It's a feature on an AIDS benefit that's being held at the Met in November. I'm exhausted."

"Why isn't Ryan home?"

"Still working, but dinner is cold and I'm sitting here in the dark. Business as usual." My fingers tugged at the hem of my shirt as I shrugged. "I just…miss the shit out of him."

"I know, honey. I'm sure he misses you, too. How is it though…I mean, otherwise?" Her tone filled with laughter.

I flushed at the pictures her words conjured and almost giggled. "Mom. You're not asking me about the *sex*, are you?" I teased. "Because if so, it's open season and I might have to interrogate you after this weekend with Dad."

"Julia Anne," she admonished sternly, her tone turned teasing. "Not *just* sex. Everything! How is life? Talk to me."

It was nice chatting with my mother in a happy, lighthearted way. "Just about perfect, Mom. We can't keep our hands off of each other, if you want the truth."

"That's how it should be. I'm very happy for you, darling. I was wondering if he'd be able to live up to those lofty vows he wrote. He set the bar quite high and so did you."

"We've gone exploring and found a new Sunday coffee place. Even if he's working, I call like when we were apart. We spend a lot of time at home, cooking together and just…well, *not keeping our hands off of each other*." I drew in a deep breath as my heart swelled and I smiled when Ryan's key turned in the lock.

"Uh, Mom, Ryan's here. Can I call you tomorrow or later in the week?" I turned and watched my weary husband wander in, wearing navy blue scrubs, his hair was a mess. He pulled the stethoscope from around his neck and tossed it with his keys on the coffee table in front of me, smirking despite his tiredness.

"Sure, baby. Tell Ryan I love him."

"What am I? Chopped liver?" It totally jazzed me that my mother loved Ryan so much, but I couldn't resist a little teasing. *What wasn't to love, anyway?*

Ryan motioned for me to wrap up my call and I grinned up at him.

"You know I love you. Talk to you later."

"Take care, Mom. Love you." Before I even had the phone back on the table, Ryan's arms were lifting me fully into his arms. He supported my weight under my bottom as I wound my arms around his shoulders and neck while my legs wrapped around his waist.

"Hey, you," he said softly as his mouth settled on mine. One of my hands moved over his cheek and into his hair, raking it back as I did, the soft strands sliding between my fingers as we kissed each other hungrily. Ryan sat down on the couch leaving me to straddle his slim hips as we clutched at each other, both moaning softly through heavy breathing.

"God, I missed you," he breathed as his mouth blazed a trail down my neck and his hand pulled the neckline of my t-shirt aside to make way for his exploration. I was trembling, his touch and his mouth setting my body on fire and I pressed my hips into his. His arms tightened around me and he groaned in answer. "I love you."

"I love you, too. The nights when you're away last forever." As caught up as I was in our love play, I worried about him. His hours and routine were so demanding and sometimes he didn't take time to eat properly. "Are you hungry? I have roasted chicken and vegetables."

"Later." He buried his face in my neck and wound his hand around my long hair, gently pulling my head to one side as he tasted my skin and rocked his hips into mine.

"Mmmm, hmmm." Words were scarce as his mouth found mine again, our tongues laving each other again. We were both starving and it showed in the desperate kisses and frantic dry-humping, heat pooling in response to the friction between our bodies.

Ryan stood and carried me down the hall to our bedroom. I was denied his mouth so I licked and sucked on the sensitive skin below his ear, which I knew, drove him wild. "Truth or dare?" he asked as he kicked the door shut behind us. The light was extinguished by the closed door, the curtains blocking out the moon and city lights.

"Mmmm…dare," I whispered against his mouth as his strong arms lowered me to the bed in one smooth movement.

"I dare you to not touch me, until I make you come. You can't touch me at all." His hot breath rushed over my face as he spoke.

"Ryan, no. I miss you too much," I moaned longingly as he threw his shirt over his head. He was so beautiful and I wanted to run my hands over his muscled shoulders and abs, to feel his biceps and back flexing beneath my hands as he made love to me. "Anything but that. *Please*."

"Do this for me, and I'll do anything you ask." His lips were moving down my body as he slowly peeled off my clothes. His eyes were intent on mine, burning as he threw my clothes aside piece by piece. "Anything…" he whispered as I arched up as his tongue circled a nipple and his hand parted the flesh between my legs. "Oh my God, Julia, you're always so ready for me. You're so beautiful."

"Uhhh…" My breath left my lungs in response to his expert touch. My body was wound so tight already, he had my flesh humming with the briefest of touches. He was on his knees at the edge of the bed and he wrapped his arms around my thighs and pulled me toward him and instantly he was moaning into me. The sounds he made as his tongue and lips worked their magic were low and guttural, his fingers splayed out on the flat plane of my stomach. I was completely and utterly helpless to fight the building ache.

"Ryan…I want to touch you, baby."

He ignored me and alternated between strong swipes of his flat tongue and light suction. "Fuck, Julia, you taste so good. I thought about this all day."

That velvet voice was muffled against my flesh and in seconds he had me undone, writhing against his mouth and moaning his name over and over again as I fell apart. Ryan didn't let up until I was completely still, his arms locking around my thighs, refusing to let me pull away. He kissed me softly once more and then the inside of my thigh, over my stomach and up the side and peaks of my breast until he found my mouth, my taste still lingering on his lips, so intimate and perfect. "See how delicious you are?" he said softly between the slow, deep kisses we were sharing. Jesus, it was amazing.

"Uhh…you're so mean," I complained breathlessly. He chuckled ever so softly as I pulled him back for another kiss. "You make me take and not give…when I *want to give*," I said softly as his mouth hovered and teased at mine, until he sucked my lower lip in between both of his. "So take, Ryan. Anything and everything…until there is nothing left."

"I want your love, Julia…and all that goes with it. I want your humor and intellect, your beauty, and kindness…your magnificent soul and your words. Without you, there's nothing." He looked at me seriously, his hand stroking down the side of my face and his nose nuzzled into me. My heart swelled though it was already so full of him.

"Ugh, I'm trying to seduce you, and you're making love to me with words." My voice was thickening, my throat tightening. "After you've just made me feel so good, baby, I want to do the same for you."

"You *do*." His blue eyes were lidded, so sensual and deep. I pushed him back on the pillows and climbed on top of his lap, straddling him and his hands roamed over my body, gently brushing the swells and curves. I positioned myself over him, not waiting for him to take control as I pushed until he was sheathed deep within me. "Uhhh," he gasped and closed his eyes. "I want your touch, Julia…I want your body surrounding mine, alive under my hands and mouth. I want every one of your orgasms for the rest of your life to come from me; every panting breath, every little moan, every shudder and each delicious kiss." He punctuated his words with his body, his hands gripping my hips as I rode him and his body met mine. My head fell back as he filled me and the tight throbbing began to build again. "I want you to belong to only me. *Say it*," he demanded, his thumb going to my clitoris as he bit his lip, his brow furrowed and his eyes closing as pleasure flowed through him. The ecstasy on his face consumed me.

"I belong to you. Ryan…Oh God, I love you so much. You own me."

"As *you* own *me*, my love…" He sat up and wrapped his arms around me, his feverish mouth taking mine in a series of deep, sensual kisses as we moved together, our tongues warring and worshiping, just like our bodies. The experience so amazing, I found myself sucking and clutching at him, pulling him further into my body, my hands fisting in his hair as our mouths slanted across the other's insatiable hunger. Silence surrounded us, except for the music of our breathing and the sound of our kisses as we made mad love to each other, the sounds getting more pronounced as we climaxed together. We clung together, slowly caressing, our mouths still tasting and licking until Ryan nuzzled the side of my cheek with his nose and exhaled, his breath washing over my skin as I collapsed in his strong arms.

Every time he touched me, he left me breathless and in pieces all around him. "Oh, baby…" he groaned into my neck as he continued to hold me close. "You. Are. Everything. Everything, Julia."

Ryan~

"Hey, Doctor! You're looking refreshed, did you get a good night's sleep?" one of the nurses asked. I was in my own little world, smiling and reliving the night before. The day had become something of a blur. A broken arm, a heart attack, a stab wound, and despite all of it, I was smiling. I chastised myself, but all I could think about was my gorgeous wife.

Time crawled and I ran a hand through my hair impatiently. Still an hour before my shift ended and I was anxious as I glanced at the nurse. She was probably my age, or a couple years older. Thin with long blonde hair that she usually wore in a ponytail and pretty. I wouldn't call her beautiful. I smirked internally. No one could compare to Julia.

"Something like that, Jane. Didn't I ask you to call me Ryan? I'm not used to the doctor thing."

"Well, *get* used to it. You're a very good one," she said warmly as I handed back the chart I'd been making notes on.

I smiled slightly. "Thanks."

The three months since I'd been at St. Vincent had flown by. The workload was tremendous and the hours so extreme I felt like I lived there, but I loved helping people and there was a serious need for trauma surgeons in New York. The traffic in the ER was non-stop. If it weren't for how much I missed Julia, I'd love everything about it. *Except the lack of sleep.* Newly married, I wanted to spend much more time with my wife.

My wife. I couldn't keep the smile at bay. Sleep was the sacrifice for those precious moments together but the exhaustion was worth it. Lately, I was really dragging. Julia saw it and insisted I spend more time sleeping and less time making love. I was feeling the loss of the intimacy; of our bodies and of the hours we spent talking. Tonight, though, I was scheduled to get out on time and was looking forward to several hours alone with her.

Half an hour later, as I was chatting with Jane and another doctor, a young woman rushed into the ER screaming, her arms holding a small child. The child's face was bright red and turning purple. Clearly, her airway was blocked.

Immediately, I sprang into action, as did Jane and another nurse. "Ma'am, can you tell me what happened?" I asked quickly as I took the little girl from her mother's arms and rushed her into one of the rooms to lay her on the gurney.

The young woman was crying hysterically and could hardly speak. "Jane, have Nancy get the vitals, but first we need to bag her. *Now*!" She nodded and ran to the cabinets on the side of the room to get what we needed. "I'm sorry to put you through this right now, but we need the information," I spoke to the mother as I examined her little girl. The baby's tongue was swollen but there was nothing lodged in her throat. I was certain it was a severe allergic reaction.

"Your baby appears to be suffering from anaphylaxis, an allergic reaction to something. Do you know of any allergies? Food, nuts, shellfish?" Even as I said it, I realized this girl was too young to even eat anything like that, barely one year old. My hands ran over her arms and legs searching for an insect bite and I found one on the underside of her left wrist. "Bee sting. Were you outside?" I leaned down, placing my ear over the baby's mouth and nose. No breath.

The woman was sobbing very hard. "Yes. We were on a picnic in the park. She was playing by the swings when I noticed her fall. Then she was wheezing and coughing."

My mind raced as I took the bag from Jane and tilted the baby's neck back so I could put the tube down her throat. "Jane, suppress her tongue please. What's her name?"

"Mallory," she cried. "Is she going to be alright? Please help her!"

The next few minutes ticked by in a flash, yet everything seemed to move in slow motion. Another nurse took the screaming mother from the room as we worked. I administered Epinephrine and started CPR as Jane continued to squeeze the bag in an even two breath rhythm, in between my compressions of her chest with my two fingers.

"Come on, breathe!" *Breathe, Goddamn it! Please.* I was a machine as I worked over her. Again and again I pushed her chest in the 30 push pattern between the two breaths Jane was squeezing into her. "Come on baby…come *on*!" *Dear God...please*, I silently begged.

The little girl's face was purple and her body was still, her little eyes blank. Tirelessly I worked over her until finally I felt a gentle hand on my arm. "Ryan."

My mind was counting off, twenty eight, twenty nine, thirty as I pressed her chest, trying to start her heart. I waited for Jane to continue her work.

"Jane, squeeze the bag," I said frantically. "*Jane*!" I looked up and her eyes were sad, welling with tears. She shook her head slightly. "I *said*, squeeze the fucking bag, Jane!"

I pushed her hands aside and squeezed it myself and then went back to compressing her chest. One, two, three, four…Jane's hand was on my arm again, only this time with more force.

"Ryan. It's over. You did the best you could, but she got here too late. We didn't have enough time for the Epi to work." I felt like I was hearing her words through millions of gallons of water and I was drowning in it. I kept working. "*Dr*. Matthews!"

My hands stilled as I looked down on this little life…now lost. My body started shaking. Something as simple as ten more minutes. *Ten more minutes!* My mind screamed at me. *Just ten more fucking minutes was all I needed to save her.*

I felt my body slump and I leaned on my hands on the edge of the gurney. Jane stood by silently, but moved her hand to my shoulder, gently rubbing back and forth, trying to comfort me. Nothing could.

"Do you want me to go speak to the mother?" she asked softly.

I shook my head numbly. "I need to do it." I could barely get the words past the lump in my throat. I turned back to the little girl and ran my hand over her little head, still warm to the touch, her dark hair like silk through my fingers. A tear slipped out and then another. I angrily brushed them away. "Maybe I'm not cut out for this job," I mumbled. "I can't handle this shit."

Jane and Nancy were waiting, and Nancy spoke. She was older than I, maybe mid-fifties, eyes full of tears. "No. You care so much. That's why you are *perfect* for this job. You are a wonderful doctor."

Jane nodded and stepped forward. "Ryan…no one could have done more."

I inhaled deeply, the pain in my chest protesting. I didn't feel like I deserved to be comforted. I walked into the waiting room where the little girl's mother was sitting. She stood quickly at my approach, her face worried and full of tear tracks. I didn't even know her name and I was going to have to tell her that her baby was dead.

My throat closed and I tried desperately to clear it. "Uhhggghhh…I'm Doctor Matthews." I stopped and wrung my hands in front of me. "I'm very sorry, ma'am. We did everything we could, but…" I didn't get the words out before she crumpled in front of me screaming.

"Nooooooooo!" she sobbed. I felt like I was dying as I caught the woman in my arms and she clung to my chest, her legs giving out on her. "Oh, God! No!" she sobbed, the sound tearing at my heart, her tears soaking through my shirt. Only one other time in my life had I felt like this, and it was also in an Emergency Room when I'd just found out Julia had lost our own baby. I felt sick and disoriented. I didn't know what I should do or what I needed, except that I wanted to be with Julia.

"I'm so sorry," I said as I blinked back the tears that stung my eyes. "I'm so very sorry. Is there anyone we can call for you?" I asked the young woman gently and then helped her sit down.

She stared ahead numbly and then looked at the well-used tissue in her hand. "My husband, Bill. Can I see her?" She looked me in the eyes. She had the same dark hair as the little girl on the table in the other room.

I nodded as Jane came forward and put her arm around the mother and guided her into the other room. I stood there in the waiting room, watching them go. I swallowed hard. This was almost the worst night of my life. *Almost.*

*****

I was an hour later than Julia expected, but she was used to it. I felt the hole in my chest the entire way home, but I was numb as I put the key in the lock. The smells coming from the apartment told me that Julia was baking something delicious and when the door opened, music was playing and she was singing in the kitchen.

"Hey!" she called happily, working on something on the stove. I let my eyes roam over her small form. Baggy, beat up jeans sat low on her hips, a small white t-shirt and bare feet, topped off by the messy knot of hair she'd tied atop her head, leaving the long line of her graceful neck, bare. She glanced over her shoulder and her smile faded immediately at my expression.

"Sorry I'm late," I murmured.

She turned off the stove and walked over as I threw my keys on the table, her brow furrowing. She knew me so well.

"Ryan, are you okay?" She reached out to grab both of my forearms and I let my hands rest on her waist.

I closed my eyes and breathed in her perfume, willing her essence to take away the happenings of the past two hours. I pulled her tightly to me and buried my face in her hair. "I am now," I whispered and her hands stroked through the hair at the back of my head.

"Baby…what happened?"

"It was…I had a bad day." She pulled back slightly to look up into my face; her green eyes were wide and worried. I searched her face, her soft skin was flushed pink and her lower lip was hidden by her top teeth.

"Do you want dinner or a drink? Do you want to talk about it?"

"It smells good, sweetheart, but I'm not in the mood to eat right now. A drink sounds good, though."

"Okay. Do you want to shower while I get it? Beer?"

"I'll change, yes. And scotch, okay?" I didn't drink scotch often at home, but she didn't question me, only reached up to run her hand over the stubble on my chin and then kiss my mouth softly. She was so sweet and her touch eased the ache, just like I knew it would.

"Yes."

I kissed her briefly, before walking down the hall and peeling off my scrubs. I wanted all evidence of the hospital gone and jumped in the shower to rinse off. I felt antiseptic and sterile and

I needed to feel like myself. I quickly combed my hair, pulling on old jeans and a ratty old T-shirt from Stanford, took a deep breath and then went into the living room.

Julia was waiting on the couch with my glass of scotch sitting next to her wine on the coffee table, the music switched to a softer venue; songs that she felt would comfort me.

I sat next to her and reached for my drink, slamming the entire contents in one gulp. Julia waited patiently, her hand scratching soft patterns on my back, until I leaned back and turned toward her and put my hands on her bent knees to pull her closer, leaning my forehead against hers.

"I needed this. You are my solace in the madness."

"Madness?" Her voice was gently questioning. "Baby, what happened today?" Her hand covered one of mine.

"Oh, Julia. It was so horrible. I lost a patient." The stinging started in the back of my eyes again and my voice cracked.

She sighed and wrapped her arms around me and both of her hands wound in my hair. "Oh, Ryan. I'm so sorry, honey."

I started crying then. The gentleness in her touch and voice somehow gave me permission to let the emotions loose. I couldn't hide from her and I didn't want to. Her arms tightened around me and I gathered her in a close embrace as I buried my face in her shoulder.

"A little girl. She had a bee sting," I told her miserably, starting to sob. "It was just a *bee sting,* but the mother didn't get her to the hospital in time. *Fucking New York traffic* and she didn't know to call an ambulance and get some paramedics on the scene. They were having a picnic in Battery Park. A *picnic*, Julia. One minute you're having a picnic and the next, your child is dead."

Her fingers pushed my hair back and she kissed the side of my face over and over again. "I'm sure you did everything humanly possible, my love." The trembling voice told me she was crying with me, her big heart feeling every twinge of my pain. "Oh, Ryan, I wish I could take this away. I *know* you did everything you could."

My shoulders were shaking and her voice was cracking. I broke down even further. "She was just a baby, barely a year old. We worked so hard and still we lost her. Julia, *we lost that little baby*!" In my grief, I'd forgotten myself, but the instant the words were out, my heart stopped and suddenly Julia stilled in my arms.

How could I be so Goddamned careless?

I pulled back frantically, my hands on her forearms as I searched her face for recognition. She was still as stone while she looked at me, her eyes filled again and her lips lifted in a smile.

A smile? I couldn't believe my eyes and my heart felt like it would fly from my chest.

"Oh, Ryan! We're going to have a baby!" My heart jumped up in my throat. If this day could have gotten any worse, it just did. She cupped both sides of my face and her face sobered at the pain in my eyes. My heart split apart, like steel knives, cutting and ripping my flesh as they fell.

In about three seconds she would realize there was no baby and there wasn't a damn thing I could do to stop it. She took my hand and moved it to her flat stomach and I was in literal hell. I knew what was coming. Finally, we had to deal with it.

"Julia…" I began, but she moved back, looking down at her stomach and then back to my face. It was finally dawning on her that she should be eight months pregnant by now.

I couldn't breathe it hurt so bad, my heart thundering around inside my chest was killing me. I struggled for the words, for any type of sanity that would help me cope with my own pain at finally facing the loss, and show me some small way to comfort her as her world fell apart.

"Babe..." I reached for her as her face crumpled, the silent sobs racking her body as her hands came up to cover her face. "Oh, Julia..." my voice cracked on the words and my eyes began to blur.

"Uhhh...oh, no! I lost it, didn't I?" She looked at me in stunned disbelief, the pain clearly written on her face. Julia started to shake her head. "I lost it in the accident! Oh, God, Ryan," she cried into me as I gathered her shaking body close to my own. She wasn't making any sound but her body was wracked with violent sobs until. after what felt like a lifetime, she gasped loudly for breath. Tears rolled down my face and I closed my eyes in agony. "I *wanted* that baby. So much. It was *you*...You and me. God, Ryan! Noooooo!"

I could do nothing but hold her, my hand stroking her long hair, both of us clinging to the other in our shared sorrow. I searched my heart for any words that would console her, but there were none, even though I would have given my life to find them. My heart ached; the love I felt pouring into her.

"We'll have more babies, Julia. Oh, God, as many as you want, I promise," I whispered it over and over as I kissed her face and stroked her hair. "I wanted the baby, too. More than anything. I was so happy for the two seconds I had to process it before Jenna told me that you'd miscarried. Part of me died that night. The only thing that saved me was that I still had you."

Her arms tightened and more sobs burst from her chest to fill the room around us. "I'm sorry. I'm so sorry!" she cried brokenly, her tears completely soaking through my shirt on my shoulder, her fingers clawing at the material. These tears were as precious as diamonds because they were hers. "You must have been in hell all those months, Ryan. I'm sorry I left you alone with all of this."

I pulled her onto my lap while I settled back into the cushions so I could rub her back. I kissed her hair over and over again as she cried and cried. "Hush. You have nothing to be sorry for. It was an accident, my love. It was an accident."

"I was so happy when the test was positive." She looked up at me with her dark green pools so full of grief; my heart broke all over again. "El…Ellie…Sh…she figured it out," she was gasping for breath through the words, her fingers fisted in the front of my shirt. "I was c…coming to tell you. I couldn't tell you on the phone. I wanted to see your face when I told you that you were going be a daddy."

Oh, God, it hurt to hear her say those words.

"I know, sweetheart." My throat ached and I tried to swallow it down. Her pain, my pain, all of it was sucking the air from my lungs, the tight bands around my chest refusing to let my chest expand.

"I wasn't going to Paris. I couldn't…take that away from you. I wouldn't," she sobbed again. "You'll be such an amazing father, Ryan. I wanted to give that to you."

"Oh, honey. You *will*." I brushed my fingers against her cheek, brushing away the tears. "And it will be the most beautiful experience and the most beautiful baby ever born, I promise."

"It won't be *that* baby," she sobbed. "I want that baby, Ryan."

I sucked in my breath, and stilled. *Fucking hell, how can I comfort her?* I wasn't sure how much time passed, but the sun set and it was darker in the apartment. Neither one of us bothered to turn on a light as we lay on the couch together.

Then the question I'd been dreading for months finally fell from her lips. "Why didn't you tell me?"

Thud. My heart pounded and I considered how to answer, emotions threatening to choke me. I needed to see her face, so I eased back slightly.

"Julia, look at me."

She moved back a little more and I wiped at her tears before I took both of her hands in mine. I looked at our entwined fingers as I struggled to speak past the pain. Finally, I tore my gaze back up to hers.

"I'm sorry you're so sad. I'm…sorry I did this to you," she said and then sniffed as another sob shook her shoulders. All I wanted was to take away her suffering. We were like one person and it had always been that way, each of us feeling the other's emotions as if they were our own. It was a beautiful, amazing…*painful* miracle. My thumbs rubbed over the tops of her hands and I shook my head.

"You didn't do anything to me, sweetheart. This is something we're going through together. It happened to both of us."

"Why didn't you tell me, then?"

"Julia…you were so fragile and I was focusing on getting you better. That's all I could think about because I knew I wouldn't survive without you. There were lots of reasons. I was so scared."

"Of what? I mean, after you knew I was better? Why not tell me then?"

I didn't take my eyes from hers. "I was afraid of *this.* I knew you'd be heartbroken and I wanted to protect you in any way I could. There was also the risk it would be so traumatic to you that you'd block everything out forever, and I *needed* you to remember me, my love. To be able to *hope* you would." The tears welled and spilled down my cheeks, first one and then another. "It was selfish, but I couldn't bear losing the memories, how we met; the love between us…especially this *mad, mad love*." Her face, so full of sorrow, softened, the love glowing there to comfort me. I had to touch her, and reached forward and cupped the back of her head with my right hand as her fingers began to stroke my jaw.

"Oh, Ryan. I never really forgot you. I always *felt you*. Like a moth to a flame, you had me helpless. As you always have."

"But I had no way of knowing. I couldn't bear losing so much of us. I was…tormented. Please don't be mad at me."

She shook her head. "I'm not. How could I be? I understand your feelings." She was calmer now, but tears were still flowing softly. Her hands tightened around mine. "I *do* love you, Ryan, and I don't deserve you."

"I'm not worthy of *you*. You're so perfect." Julia leaned forward and kissed me softly, her mouth opening and coaxing a response from me. I wasn't finished with my explanation, so I reluctantly pulled my mouth from hers as I stroked her cheek with my thumb.

"There's more." This was the hardest part to admit, but I wouldn't hide anything from her ever again and I knew we'd survive anything. The love between us was stronger than either one of us on our own and I needed to trust that.

"Okay," she said softly and waited. "Tell me. Whatever it is, it'll be okay."

"As much as I wanted you to remember me, I wasn't sure if I wanted you to remember losing the baby." I'd said the words aloud for the first time and they hurt like hell. *We lost our baby.* Maybe we couldn't feel it or touch it like the poor woman in the ER today, but that didn't make it any less real or the pain any less intense.

"That's why you wouldn't make love to me." She knew it was true without asking. "You thought being close would bring it back?"

I nodded. "It killed me. I wanted to reassure myself that we were still us in the most profound way possible, but I couldn't risk hurting you."

Julia looked sad and confused. "At least if I had known, I could have offered you some sort of comfort, Ryan. It wasn't fair to you," her voice cracked and new tears fell. "I'm…so sorry that I wasn't there for you."

I shook my head. "But you *were,* baby. I got to look at you and touch you every day and that was the one thing that kept me sane. I was terrified that if I told you about us and the baby, it would've been more like a book you read and not something you lived through…" My own voice trembled as I struggled to speak. My throat was so tight and the tears thickened my voice. "I *needed it to be real*, Julia. I couldn't bear it if you knew and still didn't remember or…"

"What, honey? Just say it, Ryan," she begged.

"I didn't want to suffer this without you." I wiped at my tears with the back of my hand before I continued. "I felt selfish, needing you with me to mourn this loss, but I just…I couldn't bear facing it without you. There was only one thing that could have been worse…if I'd lost you, too."

We both were crying and touching, wiping each other's tears away until finally we melted together, both of us lost in our grief.

"Ryan, you can never lose me," Julia said softly. "Just remember how much I love you, that's all you need to do. Even if I would have died…"

My arms wound around her and tightened to stop her, "Jesus, don't even say that, Julia," I begged. "*Please*."

She shook her head and pressed on. "I'd still love you, even then. *Always and forever*."

I lay back and pulled her on top of me. I was exhausted and I wanted to feel her against every inch of me. She snuggled in and I held her as we both quieted. I was getting tired, the long day and all of the emotions left me spent. Julia's breathing evened out as I ran my hand up and down her back, rubbing little circles as I went. I took a deep breath and knew we'd get through this and anything else life threw at us.

"I can live through anything as long as I have you," she whispered and my heart felt like it would explode.

"You'll always have me, Julia. And you know what you said about it not being *that* baby when we finally have one?"

She stiffened slightly in my arms as she answered. "Yes."

"I don't believe that." My words hung in the air as she digested them.

"What?"

"Well, I believe the baby is destined to be with us. It just wasn't his time to be born yet," I said softly, and then kissed her forehead. "He's up in Heaven waiting, Julia. That little soul belongs with us, and he *will* be, okay?"

She turned her face into my neck and our arms tightened around each other. I never wanted to let her go. "Just like you and I are meant to be together," she stated quietly.

I smiled into the darkness and stroked my fingers up and down the bare skin of her arm. "Yes. Always. I can't put into words how much I love you and how much I want you to have my child. You've got all of your memories now, so I know you won't forget," I teased gently.

"No. I won't *forget to remember you*…ever again. I promise."

"Mmmmmm," I chuckled softly, content despite the heart-ache of the evening. My chest expanded in a deep sigh as I expelled some of the stress.

"Ryan?" she said softly, her breath rushing in a hot wave over the skin of my neck and shivers raced down my spine.

"What, love?" I said sleepily.

"Thank you." She placed a soft, open-mouthed kiss on the edge of my jaw and I turned into her body so I could twine my legs with hers and look into her sparkling eyes.

"For what?" I reached out and ran a finger down the side of her beautiful, perfect face.

"For the story about the baby waiting in Heaven. It's a beautiful thought."

"I believe it. We'll have a beautiful baby girl with your green eyes and golden brown hair or a little boy with blue eyes and dark hair. It will be incredible and I can't wait." I kissed her lips very softly, brushing mine across hers again, before pulling that luscious lower lip into my mouth and sucking gently.

I wanted to worship this woman. Somehow the day from hell was ending in peace and contentment. The touch of her hand and a soft word was all I needed to erase it all.

"When do you think the baby wants to be born?" she asked, her hand running down my chest to the waistband of my jeans and up again.

I flashed a smile at her because I couldn't help myself and then flipped her underneath me so fast that she gasped in surprise and laughed softly. After all of the tears, it was like music to my aching heart.

"Soon. *Very* soon." I kissed her gently but it soon deepened into more, our need for each other was always undeniable. Her mouth opened to mine and my tongue plunged deep inside, hungrily moving with hers. She tasted so good, and I needed her, wanted her without question. I nuzzled into her cheek with my nose. "But, that's up to you," I said between breathless kisses. "Just say the word and we can start trying. I love you so much."

"No, it's up to *us.* Everything is always us, because I love you *just as much*."

More beautiful words were never spoken and I knew…it was the truth.

And now…
The beginning of the unforgettable final installment of The Remembrance Trilogy;
A Love Like This…

~1~

Julia ~

I WAITED OUTSIDE the ER for my husband, Ryan, to come out at the end of his shift. He was halfway through his first year of residency at St. Vincent's in Lower Manhattan. Later in the evening, we'd be flying up to Boston where his brother, Aaron, and one of our best friends, Jenna, were finally getting married. I was so happy for Jenna. She'd been waiting almost nine years for Aaron to marry her, but the responsibilities of college and then medical school had been his priority. She had supported his efforts without complaining and finally, after a little gentle nudging, Aaron had proposed.

Ryan and Aaron fulfilled their childhood dream of attending Harvard Med together, but afterward, Ryan chose to do his residency in New York City so that we could finally be together. We'd gotten married on a spur of the moment decision at the same time that he and Aaron were graduating last June. Every minute since then had been heaven. At least, the moments we actually spent together.

I tapped my hand nervously on the steering wheel of my Mazda as I looked around the parking lot, a mixture of impatience and uneasiness filled me. The ER was always busy with all kinds of cases, and Ryan regaled me with details on several occasions. Most were just what you'd expect, but there were a lot of gangs in New York and Ryan was constantly dealing with shootings, beatings and stabbings. I shuddered as the fear I tried to push back resurfaced. It wasn't as if the many hours he spent away from me weren't bad enough without worrying about these types of people hanging out at the hospital while their 'homies' were treated for the latest fight or drive by.

Take tonight. There were several rough looking young men hovering outside of the entrance, smoking, spouting trash-talk and generally harassing anyone who tried to go into or out of the hospital. No distinctive racial group, they were a mixture of white, black, Asian and Hispanic descent, but collectively, they were a scary looking bunch. Two or three of them looked particularly agitated during the conversation. I couldn't make out their words, but I could tell from their expressions that they were arguing. One tough looking thug, who was clearly the leader, shoved another one of them with enough force to send him sprawling on the pavement.

"Do that again and I'll kill you, man! I'll fucking kill you!"

I flushed and shrank down in the seat a little further, hoping they wouldn't notice me while I waited for Ryan. My heart constricted in worry that he would have to walk through them on his way to where the car was parked across the lot.

An old man entering the hospital glanced in the group's direction and was rewarded with a bitter threat, which was loud enough so I could hear clearly. "What are you looking at, motherfucker?! Stay out of our business or I'll cut you!" I jumped when he pulled out a switchblade and waved it at the old man.

I swallowed and made sure the doors to the car were locked. The gentleman put up both hands in front of him in a silent plea to be left alone as he hurried inside the double doors. It was no wonder Ryan didn't like me waiting out here alone. I hardly ever came down here at his insistence… at least not at night. My job at Vogue was on the Upper East Side and our new apartment was in Midtown Manhattan and rarely did Ryan allow me to visit him at work.

I glanced at my watch. Ryan would be out any minute and we'd go straight to the airport. It was ten minutes past four and I was grateful for the daylight that remained. It was cold and I had to keep the car running, leaving the defroster on to keep the windows from fogging up.

As I waited, I let my mind drift. Jenna had planned a big affair and was holding her reception at the same hotel where Ryan and I were married. Our wedding was smaller and more intimate than the one Jenna had planned, but it was a perfect reflection of our relationship. Very close and tight; so, so intimate.

Gah! My heart thudded within my chest at the memory of the vows and the incredible night of lovemaking that followed. It didn't matter how much time passed, I was more and more in love with my beautiful husband every day. He was my entire world and I was looking forward to the time alone with him in

Boston. His work schedule had been so frantic that our time together was precious, and there were days when we wouldn't see each other at all beyond a kiss as we passed each other coming and going. I missed him like I hadn't seen him in years.

I grabbed my purse from the passenger seat as the phone rang and reached in to retrieve it.

"Yes, Jen!" I smiled as I answered. She was so anxious.

"When will you be here?"

"Soon. We will be there. Relax."

"I'm relaxed. Aaron, on the other hand, is a basket case. You'd think he was being led to the gallows," she mocked with a chuckle. "I think he's more excited to see you and Ryan than he is to marry me!"

"Nah. He's probably just yanking your chain. You know Aaron."

"I'm so happy, Julia! The dresses came today. Ellie has outdone herself again."

I looked cautiously at the group of men, now beginning to take notice of me sitting in my car and I bristled in my seat. I was frightened but I couldn't let it come through in my voice. "I can't wait to see them. Jenna, were you able to get the suite for us?"

"Yes. It's a good thing that the Four Season's has more than one honeymoon suite or you would have been shit out of luck!"

Excitement raced through me as I remembered Ryan's reaction to spending the weekend in the same suite where we'd spent our wedding night. I smiled a secret smile in retrospection, but then one of the unruly young men was making his way toward me, leaning down to look into the front window of the car. I turned my back and faced the opposite direction, hoping he'd leave me alone.

I looked anxiously at the door and wondered if I should pull closer. One of the smaller men was nudging the leader and pointing in my direction. I bristled in my seat.

"Thank you. I can't wait to see you! Will you be at the hotel tonight?" I ignored the men and concentrated on my call with Jenna but my pulse quickened and I shuddered.

"Yes. Gabe and Elyse are already here and my parents are arriving around the same time as you and Ryan."

"Ellie and Harris?"

"They're here already and Marin and Paul arrive on Saturday morning."

"Yes, Dad is busy with a case and can't be away too long, but I'm happy that they will be there. I never expected to have us all together this soon." This was going to be the first time I'd seen my parents together since their reunion at Ryan's and my wedding.

Ryan finally appeared behind the glass of the hospital entrance and was soon walking toward me across the parking lot. My heart stilled as he glanced in the direction of the men and nodded to them. It seemed to calm them slightly and they dropped back letting him pass without incident. I breathed a sigh of relief and realized how scared I really was when my pounding heart reminded me.

"No shit. I'm excited to see everyone!" Jenna said breathlessly.

"You deserve this, finally. Ryan is almost to the car, so I'll call you when we land. Love you."

"You, too! Bye!"

Ryan opened the passenger side door and slid into the black leather seat and I quickly relocked the doors. He looked tired but he leaned in toward me after he was in the car and cupped the side of my face with his hand.

"What's the matter? Did those guys bother you?" he asked, intently searching my face.

I shook my head.

"No, but they are scary looking. Do they always hang out here?"

"No. Don't worry. We get some rough people here, but other times they're just idiots. Tonight, someone got pushed off of a roof while they were sparring, just playing around. They don't understand how dangerous that kind of injury can be. The kid had a ruptured spleen and went to emergency surgery. If we didn't get it out, he would have died of internal bleeding. Stupid fuckers."

His scent enveloped me and I longed to melt into his arms and feel safe, to know he was safe. I searched his face for reassurance, but my heart constricted despite myself.

"Ryan, they look like a gang."

"There are gangs in New York and every city, baby. I'm just glad you work uptown."

My eyes searched his. The blue depths were intent despite the fatigue that lurked there.

"It's adorable how you worry so much, but there is no reason for it. I'm okay except I'm missing my wife so much it hurts," he said in his most velvet voice and I pressed my face into his warm hand.

I smiled, taking in the dark circles beneath his deep blue eyes. "Ryan, you're so tired. I'm sorry." I was more at ease now that he was here beside me, but the men were still watching us from a few yards away. Ryan didn't seem to notice, his focus was completely on me.

"I'm okay." His thumb brushed over my bottom lip and pulled it down slightly and his gaze dropped to my mouth. "Give me some of that," he smiled softly before his other hand closed around my forearm and he pulled me toward him and his mouth settled on mine in a gentle kiss.

I couldn't help it, my mouth opened and my own hands reached out to clutch at the front of his dark blue button down between the opening of his black leather jacket. He'd changed out of his scrubs for the flight and he was looking good enough to eat. He responded by increasing the pressure of both his mouth on mine and the hand holding my head. His thumb brushed back and forth along my jaw as his tongue plundered my mouth. We kissed deeply for a minute before his mouth lifted and then returned to tease my lips in a series of sucking kisses.

"Jesus, you taste so good. Why does it feel like I never fucking see you?" he said and kissed me one more time.

"Maybe because you never fucking see me," I quipped in return and he groaned, his mouth reaching for mine again, but I rested my forehead against his, denying him the kiss he was seeking.

"Baby, I could kiss you forever, but we're going to miss our plane. Besides, those goons are still eyeing us, and they scare me." I reached up and brushed my fingers along his jaw and then up to push the hair back off of his brow. "We should go." I moved more fully into my seat and put the car in gear.

"Don't be scared. I won't let anything hurt you, sweetheart."

"The only thing that hurts me lately is the lack of time with you."

His mouth twisted and he frowned, pulling the seatbelt down and buckling it.

"Um hmm, and here I thought getting married and moving in together was going to make things easier," he said apologetically. His hand reached out and his warm fingers closed around mine, lifting my hand to his mouth to brush his lips across the inside of my wrist. His touch always set my body on fire and my heart thudded in my chest.

"Mmm... well, I'm thankful for the time we do have together. This weekend will be hectic, but at least we'll be together for 72 hours. I want to make sure that you get some rest tonight."

"Well, I want to make sure I get some lovin' from my gorgeous wife," he said with a devilish grin. "Lots and lots of lovin'." He turned in his seat and looked at me seriously as I navigated my way through the city.

"Ryan, what is it?"

"I know this weekend is about Aaron and Jenna, but I want some time for just us, if we can manage it. I really miss your words and just being with you. Alone."

I knew what he meant. He was my best friend in the world and we were closer than any couple I'd ever seen. Lately, we hardly saw each other and when we did, we were so desperate for the physical connection we devoured each other. Rarely did we have time to go out and do anything together, instead we opted to closet ourselves away from the world and soak up as much love as we could in the short time we had. His eyes were sad and I desperately wanted to see him smile.

"Oh? I remember now, it's my words you can't live without. Not my body, right?" I cocked my head and raised my eyebrow. It worked.

Ryan laughed and squeezed my hand. I knew by his response that he remembered the conversation that I was referring to. "That's right. I'll be completely miserable making love all night if I can't talk to you first."

"Yeah, right. Okay, then, I'll make sure to throw out the new lingerie I bought for this weekend when we get to the hotel."

Ryan sobered, his thumb rubbing back and forth over the hand that he held. "I love you, Julia," he said seriously. "I do want to talk to you. I want to find out what's going on… but I'll love that you think about me that way. You always know just what I need."

"Because you mean everything to me. Even if I can't see you so much, I wouldn't trade one second of my life with you. I love you." I threw a glance and a small bittersweet smile at him before returning my focus back on the traffic.

Since my accident, there were times when he'd get deep and brooding, withdrawing into himself when he remembered the way he suffered when I almost died nine months before. I was sometimes amazed by how much it still affected him. I'd learned to recognize it by the look in his deep blue eyes and the silence in which he'd cloaked himself. The pain that flitted across his perfect features from time to time ripped at my heart and I wanted to make it vanish forever. As much as we loved each other, we no longer took any of our time together for granted, having seen how precarious life could be and how much we needed each other.

My throat tightened as I tried to speak. As usual, he could read me like a book. My emotions and my thoughts all laid bare to him.

"I never want to go through something like that again." The pain in his voice was still so prevalent whenever he spoke of it and I wondered if he realized that had I not been in that accident, we'd have a month old baby by now. Despite the happiness we shared, despite my memory being fully restored, he still held that pain so close to him. We both still suffered, but Ryan had endured so much more during the time when I didn't remember the past, the baby, or what he called our mad, mad love. It still got to me; I'd been so freaking oblivious to his suffering.

My heart thumped loudly in my chest remembering the night it all came rushing back when he had poured out his pain as I had poured out mine. Every precious moment brought us closer. It seemed impossible that anyone could love this much.

"Babe, I know. I love you so much." My voice trembled and my eyes welled slightly. I fought back the tears forming as we drove in silence, our hands laced together. I could feel his eyes boring into my profile so I turned my face toward him. "I have a surprise for you later," I said softly and his eyes met mine and the corner of his mouth lifted in the crooked smile that always took my breath away.

"In addition to the lingerie?" he asked. When I nodded, he smiled even bigger. "I have one for you as well."

"Really? Tell me what it is," I said anxiously, the mood suddenly lighter.

"Not a chance," Ryan said shortly but with a wide grin. "If I have to suffer, so do you."

"Mmmm."

"Julia, do we have to meet up with the others tonight? I don't want to. Not tonight."

"Ryan." I shook my head at him in exasperation. "Yes. Your parents are here and we're meeting them with Aaron and Jenna in the bar for drinks. We don't have to stay long, but we do have to go for a bit. Aren't you anxious to see them? It's been six months and you're the best man."

"I suppose I should be, but I just want to get you alone and wrap myself around you all night. I don't give a damn if it's selfish."

"We can get some wine. It will help you relax so you can sleep tonight. When we go back to the room, I'll run you a bath and give you a massage. We'll just visit with them for a little while. We'll have plenty of time to be alone."

"Okay," he said begrudgingly, his lower lip extending in a slight pout. My heart leapt at the adorable gesture, and the obvious emotions behind it. His desire to be alone together only echoed my need to have his arms around me. "But I disagree. There is never enough time to be alone with you. I feel like I haven't touched you in forever."

"You're touching me now."

"You know what I mean, Julia. I want to make love to you. I need to lose myself inside you." I drew in a deep breath as his voice reverberated in several waves of electricity. Yes, I knew what he meant. I craved his touch like air. "I want you. Every second." The tone of his voice lowered huskily.

"It's only been four days," I said in an attempt to offer comfort. The fact that I was aware of how long it had been since we'd last been together was not lost on him and his hand tightened around mine.

His schedule was so erratic that we rarely were home together at the same time and when we were, he was beat. I 'd had to insist that he sleep.

"Four days too long."

*****

Ryan~

I watched Julia from a few feet away at the far end of our group. My parents had reserved four tables along one side of the room near the band. She was laughing with Ellie and Jen, their faces full of animation and their eyes full of light that was visible even in the dimly lit room. Thank God we were able to check in and take a quick shower before we'd been required to come down to socialize.

I cringed and inwardly chastised myself. For Christ's sake! It was my only brother's wedding. Even if we weren't related by blood, we were bound by life, love and experience. The least I could do was come to life long enough to celebrate.

The girls' tinkling laughter filtered down from the end table where they huddled. Jenna's younger sister, Anna, her parents and two other couples along with my family, and Ellie and Harris, rounded out the party.

I squinted in the direction of the people I didn't recognize, trying to place them. While they were vaguely familiar, I couldn't put names with the faces, and tonight, I was too tired to try. I should have paid more attention when we first arrived. I rubbed a hand over my face from my temples down over my chin and scratched at the twenty-four hours worth of beard growth. I hadn't taken the time to shave after my shower and I was sorry now. I had no desire to chafe Julia's perfect alabaster skin, but there was no way I wouldn't be kissing all over her curves later. My fingers played along my jaw as I judged how harsh it would feel against her smooth flesh.

My mother's hand traced over the muscles of my back and brought me out of my personal thoughts and back into the room around me. She was sitting on my right and my dad was on the other side of Aaron. The two men were in deep conversation, a concentrated frown on my brother's face and one of wry amusement on my father's.

"Are you alright, Ryan? You look so tired." Mom's voice floated around me. I turned toward her slightly and covered her hand with my own, trying to reassure the worry out of her voice and her expression.

"Sure, Mom. The hours are hellacious, but I'm fine. It's nothing that a few hours of sleep won't cure." I lifted the corners of my mouth in the start of a crooked smile.

"Yes. I remember when your father went through his residency. There were times when I barely saw him," Mom continued.

I groaned softly in protest. "Don't remind me." My eyes snapped back to the gorgeous picture of my own bride, giggling with her friends. Her voice sent little tingles through me and found me wishing all to hell that we'd have been smart enough to tell them that we couldn't get in until the morning and snuck off to some small hotel where we could be alone all night.

A good portion of porcelain skin on Julia's shoulders and back was open to view by the neckline of her deep pinkish purple sweater. It did have long sleeves, but it was meant to be provocative and it was. She must have felt my gaze because her soft green eyes landed on mine followed by a half smile lifting her soft lips. It was an innocent gesture and full of love, but damn if my body didn't tighten immediately in response. Those pouty little lips, the lower one jutting out slightly before being captured by her top teeth combined with those deep green pools would be my undoing. I was so fucking hungry for her I could barely restrain myself from hauling her up to the room. My eyes narrowed and I smirked at her. She was well aware of the effect she had on me. She knew it well, and milked it for every last drop. I loved that shit.

"Julia looks beautiful. Married life agrees with her," Mom observed, her hand still moving lightly over my shirt.

"Mmmm. Uh, yes." I pulled myself out of my daze to answer her directly and turned my head in her direction. "With both of us. We're very happy except we do wish we had more time together. Has Dad been very busy? Why don't you guys take a trip or something? Shit, if it were up to me, I'd be whisking Julia off to some remote part of the world at least once a month."

"I thought this was a trip, and once a month is a bit excessive. Even for you, darling."

Harris came back from the bar with three more bottles of wine and handed one to me with a corkscrew, followed by a waiter with a bucket to chill the one bottle of white.

"The money this place charges and I have to open the damn wine?" I grinned at him as I grabbed the bottle and sat up in my chair, letting Mom's hand fall from my back. The waiter glanced my way apologetically and stood patiently beside the table until he could take the bottle, wrap it in a white linen napkin and placed it inside the chiller.

"I didn't want to wait," Harris said shortly, his tone stilted as he threw a hard glance in the direction of the women. My gaze shot to Aaron's, who widened his eyes and shook his head just enough to communicate that I shouldn't go there.

The music coming from the band was a cover mixture of various things and there were people dancing and the lights were low. The atmosphere was much the same as it had been the night when I'd found that asshole, Moore here with my Julia. That night had started out badly, but where it ended couldn't have been better.

I still thought about that night all the time. The kissing on the dance floor that finally connected Julia and I after months of denying the love and the lovemaking afterward had been so fucking profound, the earth had moved. Jesus, the thought of it still rocked me to the core. Fuck, it had been hotter than hell. We didn't even have sex, in the traditional sense, but it had been one of the most intimate nights of our lives. Every time we touched I was left amazed at the intensity.

Harris poured another round of wine after I'd finished opening the bottles and then flopped back down on the other side of my mother. He seemed out of sorts so I took it as an opportunity to speak to Aaron.

"Aaron. Why aren't you on the dance floor with your bride? Get your ass out there and show me how it's done." I nodded my head in the direction of the girls. Jenna was talking to the group and using her hands in a flamboyant way to express her words. Julia threw her head back and let out a peal of laughter at whatever Jenna was saying. He nodded and walked to Jenna and grabbed her hand, pulling her with him to the middle of the dance floor. Jenna was radiantly happy, her cheeks glowing and a brilliant smile dancing on her lips.

The music pulsed and my eyes moved away from the couple on the dance floor to the woman walking toward our table. When Julia reached us, she leaned down and kissed my father on his cheek and moved around me to lean down to hug my mother. "I've missed you two."

"You look beautiful, sweetheart. How are you?" Gabriel asked.

"I'm fine, but Ryan is tired." Her hand found its way to the top of my head and her fingers threaded through the hair at my forehead, pushing it back. The sensation of her touch felt wonderful and my lids dropped over my eyes right before she leaned in to kiss my temple. Her perfume only added to the miracle of Julia and I reached for her free hand.

"Yes. He's been putting up a good front, but a mother knows these things."

"You're having a good time, so I can go up and you can stay with the girls, babe."

Her face twisted sardonically, clearly showing me how absurd she thought that idea was. "Don't be crazy. Of course I'll come up with you. It's late." Julia's eyes lifted from mine to glance between my parents and then to Harris who was still brooding and staring in Ellie's direction without saying anything. "Do you mind if I steal my boy away?" she asked gently.

I rubbed her hand lightly with my thumb and leaned into Harris while Julia said goodnight to my parents. "Hey, man, what's up? You okay?"

"Huh?" he looked up at me while I stood from my chair, still holding my wife's hand.

"Oh, sure. I'm a little preoccupied, that's all. How have you been, Ryan?"

"Really good. Every second is occupied so it feels like the time since Julia and I have been in New York City has literally flown. How is the band doing? Julia mentioned you got a record deal a few months back, right?"

"Yes. We've just started promoting it and hopefully we'll have a tour in a couple of months."

"That's great, man. I'm looking forward to hearing all about it."

"Sounds good. We'll talk more tomorrow. Have a good night, dude."

Julia pulled her hand from mine and turned to hug Harris goodbye. "Bye, Harris. See you tomorrow." Her arms tightened around his neck and he hugged her back lightly. "Love you."

My hand slid automatically around her back and pulled her close to my side as we walked through the hotel and rode up the elevator. I drew in a deep breath.

"What's going on with Ellie and Harris?" I knew that she'd know. Ellie would have told her everything and, if I knew my wife, it was bugging her.

"They're struggling a little. He's asked her to marry him multiple times and she won't say yes," she said softly. Her hand reached around my waist and she leaned her head on my shoulder.

"What? That's crazy. Isn't it? I thought she loved him." I felt her head nod against me and I turned my head to place a kiss on her forehead as we walked together.

"She does. But they've distanced some due to his traveling with the band and the demands of her job. They'll work it out. You have enough to worry about," she said softly as we made our way through the hotel room door.

Finally alone. I reached out and grabbed her arm, pulling her roughly back into my arms while my eager mouth sought hers. "Julia… Come here."

I gathered her close to my chest and her arms slid up over my chest and around my neck as we kissed hungrily and I turned her toward the bed. It hadn't escaped my notice that this was the same suite we stayed in on the night we were married. I was aware of it earlier as we showered and rushed out, but now I let my mind wrap around it. Did she arrange this? My perfect girl.

We kissed for a few minutes, each of us caressing and grasping, feasting on the other's mouth like we were starving for each other. "God, you taste so good," I murmured as Julia turned her mouth away from mine to gasp for breath. I slid my hand up her back to twine in the hair at her nape. "This suite…" I murmured as my arm tightened around her waist to lift her onto the bed and follow her down, never letting go of her.

Julia nodded against my neck, her mouth kissing along the skin. "Yes," she answered breathlessly. "We have it all weekend."

I settled down on top of her, and she welcomed me into the cradle of her body, arching up to meet me. I pressed my erection into her softness and pushed my hips against hers in a slow rhythm. “Mmmm… Julia.” I pushed up her sweater with eager hands and started to kiss her again but she pulled back slightly, her hands threading through the hair at both of my temples.

“Ryan, you need to rest, my love. I’ll give you a back rub to relax you, but you need to sleep.”

I growled in protest. “I need you. I want you. Right now.”

She smiled and continued to stroke my hair. “Baby, we have all weekend.” Her luscious mouth reached up for mine and she sucked the top lip between both of hers. “All weekend…”

My hand continued its quest upward underneath the soft cashmere toward the swelling flesh I wanted. My hand cupped around it gently and the hardened nipple brushed my palm. Her breath rushed out, causing even more blood to rush into my dick. I wanted her, badly.

“Julia… I’m so hard it hurts. Please.” My free hand found her hip and I held her in place as I ground my hips into hers. “God, I’ve missed you.”

“I’ll take care of you, but I want you to relax. Lie back.”

I sighed against the skin of her throat as I pulled the neck-line of her sweater down. “Take this damn thing off,” I commanded.

She lifted her arms for me and I pushed it up and over her head, exposing the delicate black lace bra she wore underneath. I let my gaze roam over her, the sheer lace leaving her nipples and the swells of creamy flesh visible underneath.

“You’re so beautiful. Julia…”

I kissed her hungrily again, my tongue thrusting into her mouth, demanding a response. Her mouth opened and her hands in my hair pulled me closer as she gave in, moaning softly into my mouth. Those sweet little sounds she made as I loved her drove me fucking insane.

We rolled around on the bed dry humping and kissing until we were both panting and when she reached down between us and rubbed me through my slacks, I thought I'd explode. "Ryan. Please lie back, baby."

I slowed my frantic movements and rolled over onto my back, pulling me with her. I couldn't bear to lose contact. "Okay, I'm on my back, now make love with me," I said against her mouth, licking her top lip and then kissing her softly beneath the curtain of her hair.

The room was dark and Julia moved up to turn on the lamp by the bed. "What the hell? Julia, are you stopping?" I groaned and used my hands around the back of her waist to pull her back.

She laughed softly. "No. I'm not stopping. You'll have your way, but I want mine, too."

"Don't you want to fuck your husband, Mrs. Matthews?" I smiled between kisses.

"Mmm… Constantly. He's sooo hot."

"Is he?" I teased.

"Yes, irresistible."

She sat up, straddling my hips and went to work on the buttons of my shirt. She was smiling down at me, a devilish look on her gorgeous face and I couldn't take my eyes off of her, roaming over the graceful curve of her neck and her collarbones, down her full breasts covered in the provocative black lace and down over her bare stomach.

Soon she was working on my belt buckle and I was working on the button and zipper of her black pants. Before I could get the job done she was pulling my pants and boxer briefs down my legs, bending to kiss my stomach and run her tongue up my length as she moved down my body. I sucked in my breath.

She pulled off my socks and then moved off the bed to shed her pants, revealing a matching black lace string bikini. "Wow. Julia… That's amazing."

"I wanted to give you a massage tonight, but since you are determined to make love, who am I to deny you?"

She settled back on my lap and my hands roamed over her slender form as we started to kiss and move against each other. I could feel her heat against my groin and her hands on my body. It was too much to withstand. Soon I was pushing aside the lace and finding her entrance with my fingers.

"Oh, honey…" The breath rushed from my lungs as I parted the moist flesh and began a slow pulse against the swollen nub. I knew just how to touch her and I was anxious. Her mouth hovered over mine until finally she bit down on my lower lip. Oh, God.

"Uh… Uh…," she was panting, pulling at my shoulders and pressing her pelvis into my hand and lap.

"Ryan, baby... Don't wait." Her knees curled around my hips. The want in her voice was my undoing. I pushed myself inside her, moaning as I was sheathed in the delicious heat.

"I love you. Uh, babe. I missed you."

After that, words were lost as we drowned in our love together. We were frantic. Our hands moved over each other's bodies in the desperate need to get closer to each other, our mouths slanting over each other and tongues hungrily warring together. I felt my body tighten too soon and tried to slow down but she was insistent, her hips rocking into mine in a relentless rhythm. She knew she'd have me.

I pulled my mouth away and slid my hands to both sides of her face, my thumbs running along her jaw as I looked into her eyes. She was beautiful. Breathtaking. That luscious mouth was wet and open and her heavy breathing was like music…

Exquisite evidence of the effect I had on her. Her green eyes languid and the lids dropped and her head fell back.

"Julia. Slow down baby. I'll come. I don't want to come yet. Stop. Stop!"

"No. I want you to let go," she whispered breathlessly. "Give it to me. I want it all." Her head lifted and she bent toward me to take my mouth with hers and her body kept moving on mine. I could feel every curve of my erection rubbing in and out, back and forth and the pressure brought me to the point where I didn't want to stop it anymore. She felt so good and it had been too long.

I pulled the lace of her bra aside and gently squeezed, rolling her nipple between my fingers as my tongue plunged into her mouth. Julia started sucking on it at the same moment her body clenched in cadence around my body. She was coming and I could feel every tremor of it. It sent me over the edge and exploded inside her with a groan, my body quaking and jerking against hers as my arms tightened around her.

As our bodies came down we kept kissing. Her fingers curled into the muscles on my shoulders and she moved her mouth along the side of my face in a series of kisses from my temple to my jaw. She pulled back slightly, still straddling my lap and I pulled her hips into mine tightly, still deeply imbedded inside her body.

I struggled to get control of my breathing and rested my forehead against hers, running my hands up and down her back in a light caress. I finally unclasped the bra and slid it from her body. I wanted to keep touching her. To never stop. I buried my face in her neck, kissing the slight sheen of sweat from her skin and running my tongue along her collarbone to end with an open mouth kiss on the sweet skin of her neck. "My God. I love you, Julia."

Her fingers fisted into my hair and she pulled back to look into my face. She smiled softly. “I know.”

I would never get used to the effect she had on me and my throat tightened and I brushed her hair off her face.

“Thank you for getting this suite. Thank you for being mine.”

The smile went away and she nodded slowly. “You’re all I want.”

I swallowed and lifted the corner of my mouth. It was my turn to smile in the wonder of it. “Sweetheart, your pill cycle is up at the end of the week, isn’t it?”

She nuzzled into the side of my face with her nose. “Yes. Don’t worry. No period this weekend.”

I chuckled softly. “That’s good. I mean… wouldn’t stop me. I miss you too much.”

“Me, too.”

“Julia. Look at me.” I pulled her hand to my mouth and kissed the inside of her wrist as her eyes met mine. I could see the love behind the green depths and it never ceased to amaze me. “I think it’s time.”

She didn’t ask for me to elaborate. She knew. “Are you sure? You’re working so much and I’m not sure if I want to go through that without you around.”

“You always could read my mind.”

“No.” I shook my head with a smile. “I can read your heart.”

***A Love Like This* is expected to be released in Fall 2012**

CPSIA information can be obtained at www.ICGtesting.com
Printed in the USA
BVOW011911060912

299659BV00001B/98/P

Ryan Matthews has everything he ever wanted. Close to graduation from Harvard Medical School and on the verge of marrying his gorgeous and accomplished girlfriend, Julia Abbott, his dreams are about to come true and all of their sacrifice is finally at its end.

When tragedy strikes, their relationship is hurled into turmoil that leaves Ryan devastated. His sorrow drives him to keep his distance yet leaves him aching; consumed with desire and love he refuses to let manifest.

Julia is inexplicably drawn to Ryan and longs to build a future with him, but his agony over the loss of the heart-stopping memories she no longer shares with him, leaves him unable to trust that she could truly love him without their brilliant past.

When love so unforgettable has been forgotten, can Ryan find enough faith to believe that Julia's heart will remember, even when her mind can't?

The second book of The Remembrance Trilogy follows Ryan and Julia's quest to rebuild their stunning past. An incredibly beautiful and heart-breaking romance, full of passion, intensity and truly immeasurable love that will leave you spellbound, breathless and longing for more...

"This series is Ah-mazing with a capital 'A'! ...Intimacy that leaps off the page! Ryan and Julia are among my favorite and most unforgettable fictional couples!" ~ *BookishTemptations.com*

"This was absolutely a stunningly, beautiful book...It's complex and intriguing...yet it's real...both heartbreaking and beautiful. I literally feel each and every emotion that both Ryan and Julia felt. It tore my heart in two more than once! The passion...is amazing." ~ *ReviewsByMolly.com*

"This is a beautiful, captivating, and deeply moving love story that grabs you by the heart from the very start." ~ *RomanceInReview.com*

"So beautiful and precious. It's just absolutely amazing. This has been the best book I've ever read and I will compare every book I read to it. Forever. The characters were so brilliantly written I couldn't help but fall in love with them and as I turned the last page, a little tiny piece of my heart broke." ~ *ReadingaLittleBitofEverything.blogspot.com*

"This story was, in a word, beautiful." ~ *RavingBookAddict.blogspot.com*